T0146619

The Argentia Dasani Adventures

The Shadow Gate Trilogy
Lady Dasani's Debt
The Gathering
The Dragonfire Destiny

The Reaches of Vengeance Duology
The Crown of the Revenant King
The Guildmaster's Gauntlet

The Tokens of Power Trilogy
Mouradian
Sylyth[*]
Aefrit[*]

---

[*] Forthcoming

An Argentia Dasani Adventure

Mouradian

C. Justin Romano

MOURADIAN
AN ARGENTIA DASANI ADVENTURE

iUniverse books may be ordered through booksellers or by contacting:

iUniverse
1663 Liberty Drive
Bloomington, IN 47403
www.iuniverse.com
1-800-Authors (1-800-288-4677)

ISBN: 978-1-5320-6578-1 (sc)
ISBN: 978-1-5320-6580-4 (hc)
ISBN: 978-1-5320-6579-8 (e)

Library of Congress Control Number: 2019900470

Print information available on the last page.

iUniverse rev. date: 02/15/2019

For Aslan Romano,
who also loves dragons…

Acknowledgements

As always, foremost to my family for their infinite patience and unwavering support. To the team at iUniverse for their editorial input and expert assistance in preparing the manuscript. To Zach Turner for once again dispelling the myth that you can't judge a book by its cover. And to everyone who's read Argentia's previous adventures, with apologies for the lengthy hiatus and hopes that the return will prove the wait worthwhile…

Prologue

Kill Beltoran of Argo…

With the swipe of a katana, it was done. The wizard's headless body remained upright, as if unaware that death had come. Then the blood geyser started: crimson blasting from the stump of his neck, chasing the arc of Beltoran's head through the air. His knees buckled. His robed form crumpled to the floor. His head landed on a nearby table, toppling glassware and scattering alchemical apparati. It rolled onto its side, eyes staring like accusatory stones.

All too easy, the huntress thought. She had come in the guise of a friend, and that had been sufficient to get her past the house's formidable wards. Once inside, the foolish spell-tosser's magic had been no match for the surprise of her attack or the speed of her blade.

"Magus?"

A servant. The huntress spun, but this time she was too slow. The door opened. "Is all well, Magus? I heard—"

The huntress didn't wait. Snapping her blade away—she'd been ordered to kill the wizard, not his slaves—she bolted for the window, bracing her forearms across her face as she crashed through the glass and out into the cold night.

She fell two stories. Landed awkwardly. Something gave in her ankle: a flare of pain all the way up her leg that sent her tumbling hard on the frozen ground. Grimacing, she struggled to her feet and fled, trying her best to run.

In the death room above her, the servant was screaming into an oculyr.

M

The chase was on.

Beltoran's servant had used the crystal ball to contact Argo's Watch, but it was just bad luck that put the pursuit after the huntress so quickly. The garrison's desk sergeant had relayed the message to all patrols in the vicinity. A unit heading for their shift at Argo's sea dock happened to be less than a block from the wizard's property and spotted the huntress limping out of the gate.

Had she been uninjured, she would have outran them like a doe flying from hounds, but she knew from the first this was not a race she could win. As the four Watchmen closed the distance, the huntress veered across the manicured lawn of a park and into a copse of white ash. Winter moonlight dropped cold spears through the canopy. The white trees were ghostly. The shadows between them were very dark. The huntress might have crouched in any of those, waiting to strike or to slip away once the Watch passed by.

Instead she went up.

Clambering into the lower branches of an ash, she watched the two Watchmen waving their moonstones about below her. Safely above the illumination of the magical stones, she enjoyed her pursuers' curses and the frustrated plumes of their frosty breath. When they eventually gave up, she would climb down and head off. Her ankle hurt like hell; she really couldn't expect to go on much longer without tending it, but she would go on long enough to—

The branch she was standing on broke and she fell.

It was a shorter drop than the one from the wizard's window, but it took her by surprise and she landed awkwardly again, coming down hard on one knee. Pale light blazed upon her as the Watchmen spun around.

It took them a moment to realize what had happened, where she'd come from. Time enough for her to lurch to her feet. Injured as she was, she couldn't run. She would have to fight her way out of it.

A Watchman grabbed for her. She snapped an elbow into his chin, fast and hard as a punch. Caught his arm and slung him into the other Watchman. The pair went down in a tangle of limbs. She stumbled past them, hobbling through the dappled darkness and out the far side of the grove.

Where the other two Watchmen were waiting.

"Hey! Stop!" one of them ordered.

The huntress reached for her katana.

Something slammed like a battering ram into her side. Drove her into endless blackness.

M

Augustus Falkyn shivered, drawing his cloak more closely about his blue magi robes. The night wind off the White Sea was chill and damp with the promise of a nasty season ahead. "I can't believe how cold it is," he grumped. "Even my feet are cold."

Kest Eregrin glanced down at the halfling's bare feet, their tops covered with curly hair that was as thick and wooly as a mountain sheep's coat, and shook his head. "You didn't complain in Nord," he remarked. "It was much colder there."

"But in Nord you didn't drag me out of my warm bed in the middle of the night," Augustus said, trying his best to make his cherubic features frown.

"I was sleeping, too," Kest reminded him. He'd been listening to Augustus' almost constant complaints since they'd met at the garrison and he wasn't in the best of moods himself. With two deaths on the books already, the prospect of getting back to bed tonight looked dim. "Don't blame me. Blame whoever killed Beltoran."

"I do," Augustus huffed. He could see Beltoran's home beyond the fence. The wizarding community was small. Beltoran had been recognized in it as a talented magus. It wasn't easy to kill a talented magus, but someone had done so, and then been killed by the Watch while trying to escape.

Neat and tidy... Except Augustus was sure it wouldn't be neat and tidy at all once they started poking at it. Sensing Kest had heard enough from him, he kept that thought silent as they crossed the hoary grass of Edgewater Park.

Outside a copse of white ash, six Watchmen were waiting beside a cloak-covered corpse. They looked as miserable and cold as Augustus felt, but came to attention quickly when the wizard and the captain approached.

"Well, what have we got?" Kest asked once the obligatory salutes had been made. Kest was a tall Nhapian with close-cropped black hair, the nut-brown skin typical of the Easterling people, and glasses over quick black eyes. His promotion to captain had been recently made, and he was still adjusting to having men under his command.

"A woman, Captain," one of the lieutenants answered.

Kest and Augustus exchanged a glance. "Just as long as it's not another cat-woman," Kest muttered. They'd had some trouble with a pair of rather feline twins several months ago: trouble that had landed them in a chase across half of Acrevast and cost four of their friends their lives.

"Sir?"

"Nothing, Lieutenant. Go on."

"Sir, we were heading to the docks for shift change when we got the call about the attack at the wizard's place. We saw this woman fleeing the property. We ordered her to stop. She didn't. We pursued and cornered her here. She attacked so Travian shot her."

Kest nodded. "Any idea what this is about? Is she Black Fang?" he asked. The Fang were the lowliest of Argo's thieves. Not even a true guild, its members would take any job, from robbing old women in the Market Square to cutting throats in back alleys.

"Not that we could tell, Captain. She wasn't carrying their sigul if she is."

"Not likely, then." The Fang were constantly trying to prove their relevance among the guilds of Argo's Undercity. They never did anything without leaving their mark. "Well, let's have a look. Then I want to talk to—"

The words died in Kest's mouth as he bent and drew aside the cloak covering the body.

"Aeton's bolts." Augustus gasped. He knew what he was seeing, but he didn't believe it. "Kest—what happened? How could— Why would she—"

"I don't know." Kest shook his head. "I don't know."

With a trembling hand, he reached out and gently pulled the cloak back over the body of Argentia Dasani.

Part 1

Body Count

1

Kill Promitius of Valon....

The command echoed in her mind as she stood in darkness across the street from the wizard's manse. She had no difficulty with the command itself. It was the fence that was the problem.

Nigh twenty feet tall, it ringed the Promitius' home with an impregnable array of iron spears and great gargoyles mounted on stone posts. Winged granite nightmares, the gargoyles looked like statues. In truth they were misshapen magical sentinels waiting to swoop down and snare intruders. She knew this because...

Because I know....

She didn't know how she knew, or why. Had she encountered such things before? It seemed she had, but the memories were vague things, like the clinging webwork of a dream that shreds upon waking.

And why was not important. Not really. It was enough that she knew the gargoyles for what they were: a problem that might hinder her from obeying the command to kill the magus. There was no way around or through or under the fence. There was no way over it. *Not unless I can fly....*

M

"Good of you to come, old friend," Promitius said, squinting as the flash of aether strobed the chamber and Ralak the Red materialized out of the magical gate.

"I am here," Ralak said.

"You sound less than pleased to have accepted my invitation. Perhaps you believe I have summoned you for some trifle?"

"Promitius of Valon does not trifle," the Archamagus of Teranor replied. He was shorter than his host, and more slender, dressed in vermillion robes and leaning on the silver Staff of Dimrythain, symbol of his authority over all the crowndom's magi. Black hair was swept back from his brow, falling neatly to his shoulders, and a short black beard descended sharply from his jaw. He fixed his dark eyes on Promitius like a hawk studying a rabbit in a far-below field. "That is precisely why I was loathe to come."

"Well, we shall speak of it in more civilized environs, I think." The russet-robed wizard, whose tonsured head gave him more of the appearance of a monk than a magus, gestured and the door of the conjuring chamber opened. The duo proceeded down a corridor hung with tapestries into a brightly lit dining chamber. Ralak took the seat proffered at a polished mahogany table. Wine poured itself from a floating decanter into a crystal goblet. Promitius took his own seat and his own drink. "Superb," he said, closing his eyes for a moment to savor the wine. "The grapes are from the Palaber vineyards in Rominji. Aged in oak for—"

"Promitius...."

"Of course, of course. Always straight to the point with you, isn't it, Ralak? Very well, then. I fear I have lost something of great value."

"What?"

"A medallion of summoning."

Ralak's goblet was halfway to his lips. He set it aside with the wine untasted and leaned forward. "How long?"

Promitius hesitated. "I have only now discovered it missing, but it has been gone four months and six days."

"A curiously precise determination."

"That is the time since I dismissed the wretch who stole the medallion from my care."

"Explain," Ralak said.

"Pandaros Krite—my former apprentice. He had promise, but he was rash, headstrong, and greedy for power. I hoped that might change, that he might learn patience and respect for the discipline of our art if he was well instructed. For five years he served me and I taught him, until...."

"Until?" Ralak pressed.

"We had a falling out over a failed casting. Something I had been working on for months. Pandaros was too hasty in his combining of ingredients at the critical moment. I lost my temper and dismissed him as hopeless. He took what few spell scrolls he had mastered—and my medallion."

"A summoning medallion is no conjuror's toy," Ralak snapped. "In the wrong hands—"

"Spare me the lecture, Archamagus," Promitius said, his eyes flashing. "I am steeped as long in the ways of wizarding as you or any other magus. I know the risks of such a token."

"Then how could you let it be stolen?" Ralak demanded.

Promitius sighed, calming. "Pandaros was greedy, but I never thought him deceitful. He knew the medallion was very valuable to me. He must have taken it for spite when he left. I did not think on it until today, when I went to use it and found only the empty box. I was foolish, Ralak. Blind and foolish."

"Does this Krite know the extent of the medallion's powers?"

Promitius spread his hands. "I cannot—" He frowned, his brow furrowing. He looked up sharply. An instant later, shrieking filled the air.

"What is it?" Ralak asked.

"My gargoyles," Promitius said, rising swiftly. "Intruders."

2

The stone monster bore the huntress aloft.

A screeching goat-eagle thing with horns and talons and huge wings, it had attacked her as soon as she began scaling the post beneath its perch. The instant the monster sprang to life, the huntress dropped to the ground. The gargoyle dove after her. She leaped high, landing on its back and locking an arm across its stony throat.

The gargoyle bucked and cried in fury, mounting skyward, lifting the huntress over the fence. She released her hold and tumbled off its rough back. The moment her boots hit the lawn between the wizard's fence and his house she was running.

Two more gargoyles launched themselves from stone pedestals flanking the front door. The third monster was right behind her, its swiping claws almost catching her long red braid. She spared no glance back. Ran harder, right at the two onrushing gargoyles. At the last instant she dove, skidding on the frosty grass, not quite quick enough to escape a stinging hail of shards as the three flying guardians crashed destructively into each other.

On her feet again, she saw that not all the gargoyles had been obliterated in the collision. One stumbled and staggered towards her, its wings broken, one arm a shattered stump, half its goatish face sheared off. She whirled away from it—her weapons were no use against stone—and sprinted the last distance to the doors.

M

Ralak followed Promitius from the dining chamber down the stairs and into the foyer. The perimeter glyphs brayed. "What intruders?" Ralak asked even as he reached into the aether, opening his mind to the world beyond the walls of the house to catch a sense of the attackers. "Who would dare strike at you?" *One only, and almost to the doors....*

Promitius laughed, a touch of paranoia in his brown eyes. "We have not all been so blessed as you and your late brother, Ralak the Red, to boast the title of Archamagus and the strength of the Crown to support our work. I have made my fortune as I had to. Not all my dealings were with men of honor."

He extended a hand and his staff flew to his call. It flared with angry blue aetherlight as he caught it. "I do not know what enemies come against me this night, but I know they shall end as all the rest!"

He pointed and the doors to the manor flew open, crashing against the walls. The bright foyer light fell upon an onrushing figure being chased by a crippled gargoyle. "Halt if you would live, wretch. Promitius the Brown commands it!"

Ralak, a pace behind Promitius, saw the figure freeze for an instant. The shock of recognition stunned the Archamagus.

The figure unfroze. Snapped a dagger from her belt and flung it at Promitius.

"No!" Ralak shouted as silver-blue aether forked like lightning from Promitius' staff, catching the woman before she could dodge, flinging her down. The gargoyle fell upon her. Blunt fingers vised over her face.

"No!" Ralak shouted again. He shoved past the slumping Promitius. The Staff of Dimrythain blazed forth magic, blasting the gargoyle into dust—an instant too late.

Before the magic struck it, the gargoyle broke the woman's neck with a single vicious twist.

Ralak stumbled as he went toward her, unable to believe what he had seen. A thousand questions cometed across his mind, but none of them changed the reality that Argentia Dasani now lay dead before him, a single rill of blood, red as her hair, dribbling from her lips to stain the stones.

"Rash fool!" Ralak cried, wheeling on Promitius.

The other wizard was on his knees in the doorway. A dark stain was spreading around the dagger jutting from his shoulder. "I am hurt," he gasped.

"Fool!" Ralak repeated. "What have you done?"

3

Ikabod had dreaded this moment all his long life. The butler had prayed it might pass him by, that death would claim him first. That was how it should be: the old died, the young buried them and lived on. It resonated with his sense of propriety and order.

Instead—this.

It was too cruel that it should happen at all, but especially that it should happen now, not even a year after Argentia had defied impossible odds and rescued him from Togril Vloth's ice pyramid in Nord. Neither the guildmaster's gauntlet of lethal servants nor even the collapse of his crystal palace into the frozen wastes of the world had been able to stop or stay her.

But her luck had finally run out.

"My friend?"

Kest Eregrin's voice drew Ikabod from his grim reverie. The Watch Captain had been among those who had survived to tell the tale of the siege of Vloth's Frost Palace. *Better you had died there a thousand times and Argentia still lived!* Ikabod thought bitterly. But what had happened was not Kest's fault, even though it had been the men of Argo's Watch that had ended Argentia's life. It was unfair to cast blame upon him.

The butler ran a hand over his thinning gray hair. "Forgive my distraction. This is…difficult."

"No," Kest said. "It's difficult for us. I can't imagine what it must be like for you, and I can't tell you how sorry I am. She seemed indestructible."

The butler looked away. Kest sighed. The uncomfortable silence that falls only between men who wish to say more but do not know how dropped over the small office in the Watch garrison. Augustus plucked at an eyebrow, a habit when he was nervous or upset.

Ikabod, who knew well what the officers of the Watch required of him, finally summoned the dignity to put an end to the awkwardness. "Well, Captain. I imagine there are certain formalities that require my attention?"

Kest nodded gratefully. "I'm afraid there are." He gestured at a sheaf of papers on his desk. "If you can just complete these attestations?"

"Of course, Captain." Ikabod took the proffered quill and moved it deliberately to the paper. His right eye was covered by a patch, courtesy of Togril Vloth's feline enforcers, and reading and writing were exercises done more carefully now than when he had learned them so many winters ago. As he handled the hateful sheets he felt suddenly nauseous. The papers gave reality to a thing that had seemed unreal.

All through this dark night and dawn, from the moment the Watch had come pounding on the door and even after he had seen Argentia's body upon the table and laid his hands upon her cold, lifeless flesh, part of Ikabod had stubbornly persisted that this was all a hideous dream. That Argentia was not even in Argo, but wandering far away and safe.

The nib upon the paper scratched that hope to death.

Dead like her....

At that, Ikabod almost broke. He dropped the quill and jerked up from the table, his long, narrow face contorting as he fought to hold his composure. Kest rose quickly and placed a hand on Ikabod's shoulder. They were almost of a height, and similar in build, though the Captain had the lean muscularity of thirty winters, and the butler the brittle boniness of seventy. "Easy, easy," Kest said.

With remarkable effort born of years in service to a singular duty, Ikabod recovered his self-control. "Thank you, Captain." He straightened the lapels of his gray livery. "If there is nothing else?"

"Nothing else," Kest said. "I know this is no consolation, but the Argentia we knew was as brave and true as any in Teranor. I don't know what she was mixed up in or why she murdered Beltoran, but I promise you, we will find out. If some treachery forced her hand, we'll bring it to justice."

Augustus nodded. "You can count on us."

Ikabod just shook his head. "It doesn't matter now."

7

4

Despite being aware that there was much work to be done, for perhaps the first time in his life Ikabod could not do it. He knew there were funeral arrangements to be made, Argentia's few friends to notify, the testament to see to, but those things, urgent though they were, seemed beyond him.

The ride up the white-gravel carriageway to the manor atop the hill had been the longest of his long life. The original Dasani manse had stood in this same spot until it was destroyed in an explosion crafted by Argentia's enemies. She had seen it rebuilt exactly as it had been, but had spent barely three months in her new home before leaving again. Ikabod had never tried to talk her into staying. That was not his place, and staying was not in her nature.

It is now, his overwrought mind corrected. Now she would stay forever, interred beside her parents' monuments in the rear of the yard behind the manor.

Ikabod looked at the magisterial lion-headed fountain in the center of the turnabout. At the gabled roofs and gray stone and frosted-glass windowed façade of the great house. He could not imagine living out whatever remained of his days here. It was not being alone that worried him—he had been alone far more oft than not these past twenty years—but being in this house without a purpose.

Time enough to settle that later, he told himself as he dismounted slowly from the driving board. Today, at least, he had his last duties to Lady Dasani to perform. He meant to begin them after a short rest. It was nearly noon, and he had been up almost all night.

As he prepared his meager lunch, more out of habit than any true desire to eat, he noticed a bottle of the clear liquor that Argentia had favored standing on the counter. He decided on a small drink to settle his nerves and honor his mistress.

Midnight found him in the same chair he had taken at noon. The only thing that had changed was the level of liquor in the bottle on the table beside him. Mostly full when he sat down, it now stood a swallow or two from empty. Though Ikabod did not drink habitually, he did not think he would find a better day to be drunk if he lived another seven decades.

Perhaps it had helped for a while, but now most of the dulling effects of the liquor had worn off, leaving only a bitter taste in his mouth and a bitter scree on his mind. *She's gone, and this is how you honor her memory?*

He grabbed the bottle and hurled it into the fireplace. It exploded against the stone, making the fire he had no recollection of starting blaze up brighter for an instant.

"Why?" he moaned, clenching his fist in frustration and banging it upon the table. Once. Twice. Thrice. Harder each time: like the knocking in the night that had heralded this disaster.

How he wished he had never opened the door. That he had left the Kest and Augustus and their hideous news to rot there outside the manor.

Pulled by the weight of despair, a tear trickled from Ikabod's single eye. He missed the other more today than he had on any other day since losing it. Wanted it for its tears. *Oh, my Lady—*

A flash of light sundered the chamber before him.

5

Ikabod flung an arm up, shrinking back in the chair. His heart was hammering, his pulse ramming in his neck, deafening in his ears, but he was so frightened he barely felt it.

"You!" Ikabod gasped, recognizing the figure materializing out of the aether. This was not the first time Ralak the Red had appeared to him in such a dramatic fashion.

"You told me once the old do not sleep well," the Archamagus said wryly. "I am sorry to see it is true."

"These are sorry days," Ikabod managed, calming enough to come to his feet. He was unsteady.

Ralak moved to help him. "Sorrier than you can imagine, my friend. But sit." He assisted the butler back into the chair. "I bear grim tidings, and you would do best to hear what I must speak while seated."

Ikabod turned a curious, bloodshot eye on the wizard. "Why have you come, Archamagus?"

Ralak bowed his head. "Argentia is dead."

"I know," Ikabod said.

Of all the many responses Ikabod could have made, this was the last the Archamagus expected. "They say ill news travels on swift wings," he murmured. "How did you learn?"

"Last night, from the Watch," Ikabod said. "I identified her body at the morgue this morning."

"You identified her body at what morgue?" Ralak asked carefully, uncertain whether the shock of his news had wrested the butler from his senses.

"Argo's," Ikabod replied, fixing an equally perplexed look on the Archamagus. "Where else?"

"Lady Dasani died in Valon, at the home of Promitius the Brown," Ralak said. "I tried to stop it. I failed. Her body remains there still."

"I beg your pardon," Ikabod said heatedly. After all that had happened today, it was too much for even one of his self-possession to be trifled with like this by anyone, the Archamagus of Teranor included. "Argentia was killed by the Watch in Edgewater Park. They say she murdered a wizard."

"Murdered a wizard? Perhaps it would be best if you showed me the body," Ralak said, frowning deeply.

"I think I should know my own mistress—alive or dead," Ikabod retorted.

"Show me the body," Ralak repeated.

6

Solsta Ly'Ancoeur, Crown of Teranor, strode briskly down the corridor, stripping off her riding gloves as she headed back to her chambers in the west wing of Castle Aventar. The heels of her white boots clicked against the stone; her long, red wool skirt switched back and forth; her evergreen cloak snapped at the air. Solsta always went wherever she was going as quickly as possible, but when she went this quickly, she was angry.

"What do you mean?" Her tone was as clipped as her steps. "How can there be *two* bodies?"

Walking abreast of the Crown, Ralak said mildly, "If her Majesty would prefer to discuss this at her better leisure...."

Solsta glanced at the Archamagus and slowed her pace—not much, but perceptibly. "I'm sorry, Ralak," she said. "It's been a long day. First Argentia, then the expeditionary force I sent into Grimnoir met with resistance—I don't think we'll ever clear that wood of monsters. And there are reports of goblinoids massing north of the Gap Outpost, but the Nordens seem little inclined to offer aid against them. And this afternoon the Peerage was being stubborn about my plan to levy property tariffs to pay for the repair of roads and bridges."

"I understand, Majesty. As I said—"

"No." Solsta shook her head. The corridor's lightstones caught the blaze of white in her chestnut tresses: the Mark of her rule. "My problems are no excuse to be short with you. You must be exhausted as well."

In the span of the last day, the Archamagus had teleported from Aventar to Valon to meet with Promitius, back again to Aventar to alert the Crown to Lady Dasani's death, then to Argo to make that same announcement to Ikabod. Confusion had ensued, and he was forced to make another trip to Valon to take charge of the body there before finally coming home to Castle Aventar a few minutes earlier.

Each of those journeys had covered many leagues in mere moments thanks to Ralak's ability to walk the aether, but the gift of teleportation was not without its price. So many aetherwalks in so short a span taxed even Ralak's powers and stamina. "A brandy would be welcome," he admitted.

"Of course," Solsta said. "I think I will join you. Afterwards you may tell me once again that my youth is showing in my concern for the safety of my realm and my frustration with these imbecile noblemen, and then explain this mystery of yours."

"I have never criticized the youthfulness of your rule, Majesty," Ralak said. "Nor the zeal with which you govern. I merely once stated that if you continue at this rate you will wear yourself to death trying to accomplish decades of work in a single winter. I would not wish you to have the shortest reign in Teranor's history."

"But think how much would have been done in that time," Solsta countered, her big, dark eyes flashing brightly.

Ralak shook his head. Solsta laughed victoriously. The pair rounded the corner leading to her chambers. Two Sentinels, armored in gold, came to attention, snapped off salutes, and opened the doors.

"Majesty. Archamagus." Herwedge, the Crown's portly butler, nodded formally when Solsta and Ralak entered the sitting room. "Was your ride enjoyable, Majesty?"

"I've had better," the Crown replied honestly, handing him her gloves and cloak. "Too much on my mind." She had gone riding expressly to try to forget some of those things, at least for a few minutes, but the hour's excursion had done minimal good. *I'll try a long bath later....*

"Pity, Majesty," Herwedge said. "Will you take tea?"

"Brandy, rather. For the Archamagus as well, please," Solsta said, flinging herself into a deep chair upholstered in white leather. She was extremely petite—unbooted she was not quite five feet tall—and strikingly beautiful. Her creamy skin accentuated her dark hair and eyes. A small scar on her right cheek, memento of an assassin's dagger, was the sole blemish in her complexion. Her nose was shapely (she thought it a touch too large), her lips capable of making exquisite pouts. She was elf-slim and small-breasted (this ranked ahead of her nose in her list of personal peeves) but her hips rounded nicely, and beneath her skirt were excellent legs. Rubies sparked in her ears and at her throat, but no rings graced her fingers. She fiddled with the gold buttons of her plaid vest as she waited for the drinks to be poured.

"Mirk is here!" Mirkholmes the meerkat scampered out of Solsta's bedchamber.

"Hello!" Solsta caught the little animal in her arms and kissed his fuzzy face. His amber eyes gleamed joyfully. Just looking at Mirk never failed to cheer Solsta up. "And how was *your* day?"

"Mirk was bored," the meerkat said, his round ears flattening. He slipped from Solsta's embrace and began walking along the arm of the chair.

"Well, tomorrow you can accompany me to my audiences with the Lord Paladin, the Golden Serpents, and the ambassadors from Sultan Skarn."

"You are also sitting for the artist tomorrow, Majesty," Herwedge added as he returned with the brandy.

"Of course, the artist." Solsta was less than thrilled with the prospect of posing for a portrait for the Hall of Crowns, but—like so many other things in her life—it was an inescapable duty of the throne.

"Mirk will just stay here and be bored," the meerkat decided. Solsta burst out laughing and fed Mirk a bit of maple scone as she sipped her brandy.

"Now," she said to Ralak when the Archamagus had sampled his own drink. "What is this 'two bodies' nonsense all about?"

"As I said, Majesty: a mystery. The body in Argo was undoubtedly Lady Dasani."

"Then what you saw in Valon...."

"Was Argentia as well."

7

"How can this be?" Solsta exclaimed, setting her brandy aside so quickly it sloshed onto the table. "How can Argentia be dead in Argo *and* Valon?"

"Majesty, I do not know," Ralak replied. "There are creatures called maleons that can assume the shape of men in perfect likeness, but they resume their true form upon death. Both these presumed Argentias kept her form."

"What other possibilities are there?"

"That one is Argentia and the other not. Or that neither is Argentia at all," Ralak replied, stroking his beard.

"How?" Solsta was becoming agitated. Four years earlier, before the assassination of her parents propelled Solsta into the throne, Argentia had led a small group to rescue Solsta from a vampyr. Later, she had risked her life time and again to bring an end to the threat of the demon horde and the Wheels of Avis-fe.

Far beyond her debt to her for those brave acts, however, Solsta had come to look on Argentia as an older sister. She could accept her death— she'd seen more death in her twenty-one years than most saw in five times so long—but this uncertainty was intolerable. It defied reason. "How can there be two bodies?" she repeated. "And what if neither is Argentia? Then where is she, and what happened to her?"

"I do not know," Ralak said again.

"What can we do?"

"Promitius is bringing the body from Valon, and Ikabod the one from Argo. When they arrive, I will examine them. Perhaps they will yield some clues to the truth, whatever truth it may be."

"How long?"

"Five weeks, perhaps six, depending on the snows. Corpses cannot be taken through the aether, so we are at the mercy of the road."

"Nothing can be done before then?"

"Nothing that I know, Majesty," Ralak said. He had some dark suspicions, but unless they materialized in the form of further evidence, he had no intention of burdening the Crown with them. *She has enough on her mind already....*

Solsta shook her head, feeling impatient and useless and thwarted, though she understood they were doing all that could be done. "Are you—"

There was a sudden commotion outside the door to Solsta's chambers. Shouts were heard, and deep barking, and scuffling sounds.

"What is that?" Solsta asked as the barking grew more agitated.

Ralak drained his brandy. "It would appear there is a dog loose in the castle."

8

He had journeyed far and hard.

He had tried to save The Woman, but the wooden barrier had repelled him time and again. When it finally yielded with a crash that left splinters in his silver-black fur and bloodied his muzzle and he had slammed out of the chamber where he had been sleeping before he caught wind of the danger, he was only in time to see The Woman and The Other for an instant.

Then came a flash of brilliant light, so painfully bright it made him howl and cringe, and The Woman and The Other were gone. He nosed around the chamber's wet floor. It was hopeless. Everything was overwhelmed by the cupric stench of blood and the raw-meat reek of death: two smells that were acutely familiar from his rearing in The Cold Place, before he had followed The Woman into this new life.

What to do?

Find her.

But her scent ended where the light had been. Possibly he could find it again if he could get free of this place. He padded into another chamber. There was another wooden barrier. Two leaps against it told him this one would not fall no matter how hard he attacked it.

Frustrated, he began to bark—deep, throaty woofs—until he heard human noises and banging on the wooden barrier. He barked the louder. Heard more noises. The barrier opened and there were men and women smelling of anger and confusion.

He ignored their raised voices and raced past them, bounding down the steps and out of the wood-brick-glass confinement into the cool freedom that was the night—even night in this place of heavy, unnatural scents of masonry and too many men.

He wandered for a time, hunting the streets and alleys for signs of The Woman or The Other. He found vague traces from earlier in the night, but they led back to the place he had left, and he knew they were not what he sought.

Still, he had to find The Woman.

He did not understand where this impulse came from, only that from the moment of their meeting in The Cold Place he had known with the unerring certainty of instinct that she was for him and he for her: kindred spirits.

So he had followed her, loyal without truly understanding what loyalty was. She had accepted him, and they grew in the bond that exists alone between canines and humans, until they shared a kind of empathy by which he knew that The Woman—wherever she was—was in a great deal of trouble.

Find her.

It drove him, this impulse. Made him remember a place they had stayed many moons ago: another human dwelling. Not by the water, like this one, where the air was laced with salt and the flying things cried in the skies, but inland: a place of steel and stone where they had spent warm weeks resting before journeying on. The Woman had felt safe there, and he knew she had been among others of her kind that she cared deeply for, and who cared for her as well.

Instinct told him help was there, in that other place. That was where he would go.

So began the journey far and hard.

From the human dwelling he went across the wild upheaves of the Heaths, where the ground was broken and harsh and mostly lifeless, and mountain cats and goblinoids hunted beneath the cold moon. There were squalls of snow as well, but those were nothing to him, who had been born and raised in a place where there was always ice and snow cloaking the ground and the wind cut like a blade.

He went as fast as he could, but the terrain and the lack of food and water slowed him. When he grew desperate, he ate the snow, often suffering a noseful of rocky earth when he burrowed too deep. It helped a little, but he longed for a solid meal: a coney, a deer, a fox, even a marmot or some tunneling rat. Anything with flesh.

After a fortnight and more of this, he sensed the change in topography. The ground smoothed into fields as the Heaths yielded to the fringes of what the humans called the Plains of Aeyros. And here—joy!—he found streams that were not wholly frozen and hunted up a quail from the withered gorse of lands gone sere with the season. The bird was scrawny and feathery, but he feasted with the careless eye of the ravenous.

A few days on, he found the Toll Road and by that strange combination of memory and instinct that was his compass, turned north. The going became easier: this way was wide and flat and well worn. The forage became easier too, for he was traveling a route frequented by men and horses—their scents were pounded into the very earth—and their camps frequently had orts enough to satisfy his shrunken stomach.

Small human settlements began to appear along the road. He visited these, raiding the garbage behind noisy buildings for food, once even sleeping beneath piled trash on a particularly bitter night. In some of these villages, human children took note of him and tried to make him fetch sticks and balls. He understood what they wanted, but he had no time for such games. In others, grown men and women chased him with sticks and shouts, spurning him as if he were some wolf—which in part he was, and how could their sadly deprived senses be expected to discern the difference?

He fled the attacks easily enough, not caring to turn and fight any more than he had cared to stop and play. Only The Woman mattered.

Almost another fortnight north and he came to a place of trees. Here shadows and darkness lay low on the land even while the sun rode high, and the cold was not a natural cold. There was much malice in the forest; he heard its whispers and its movements in the dark. He made his way slowly from dawn to dusk, keeping always to the narrow path, fighting past the overgrown briars that clutched from the verges and the low branches that stabbed like spears, hungry for blood. At night he hid, and the dark things in Grimnoir Wood that capered and cavorted beneath the bony moon passed him by.

Three grueling days brought him forth, nearly exhausted by the ordeal. Still, he continued on, day after day across farmlands that lay as dead as the Heaths.

A week after escaping Grimnoir Wood, he came at last to his destination.

After his solitary trek in the empty wilds of Teranor, the human dwelling whelmed him with its sights and scents and sounds. Food waited to be found in nearly every narrow alley or byway. Humans were all about, and there were many dogs, some with their masters, others wandering the streets, inviting him in their language to stay and feast and rest and play and mate.

All these temptations he resisted. With the last of his devoted strength he tracked his way through the concentric stone rings to the huge dwelling beyond the water. There, by great metal barriers, stood men in steel. Though this was where he needed to be to help The Woman, he understood from their threatening scents that they would not admit him willingly.

So he waited. With nightfall, a group carrying small fires for light and warmth came to the men in steel. The metal barriers were opened. He seized this smiling Fortune and darted inside.

The shouts and the pursuit came as he ran through warm, well lit, well known spaces, over wood and stone and grass-soft carpet, tracking the scent of The One he intuited could help The Woman. At a great wooden barrier held against him by more men in steel he was forced to fight, for they would not let him pass. He would not yield—snapping and growling, barking and lunging—until, finally, the barrier opened and The One he had sought appeared and spoke in her commanding voice, and the men in steel stood down, and the journey far and hard reached its end.

9

Silence followed Shadow's tale.

Solsta had gone with Ralak to learn the source of the commotion at her door and it had taken only a moment for them to recognize Shadow. The Crown had ordered the knights to stand aside, and Shadow came obediently to her when she called, wagging his lupine tail. Solsta knelt, making the big dog appear almost larger than she was, and ran her hands across his head. "Shadow," she said in amazement.

"He has come a rough road," Ralak said, noting how much leaner the dog appeared than the last time he'd seen him, and how abused his coat was. Its ebony fur, threaded with shimmering silver, had lost most of its luster and was filthy and knotted with burrs and twigs.

"But from where? And where is Argentia?" Solsta asked. "Something must have happened to her. Can you see his thoughts?"

"No, Majesty. With men I will not deny some skill in that art, but an animal's mind is closed to me."

"But he must know *something*." Solsta bent her head close to Shadow's. "Do you know what happened to Argentia?"

Shadow barked once—possibly in affirmation—and sat panting before the Crown.

Suddenly Solsta rose, an inspired light in her eyes. "Mirk, come here," she called.

When the meerkat scampered up, the Crown, playing on a hunch, asked Mirk to speak with Shadow. It was not as easy for the meerkat as she might have imagined, but the canny little animal turned the trick, and related Shadow's tale.

"Can this be?" Solsta asked when Mirk had concluded his narrative.

"Such loyalty is not unheard of in animals," Ralak said.

"That wasn't what I meant. This abduction… If Argentia has been taken prisoner, can this explain the two bodies? And can we find her? We must find her. Can Shadow tell us more details?" Solsta said. "Mirk, can you ask him?"

"Mirk is thirsty and tired of talking," the meerkat groused.

"Mirk…."

"Very well, cruel mistress," Mirk huffed. Solsta gasped. "Mirk is only joking," the meerkat added quickly.

"I hope so."

"Only joking," the meerkat assured her. "Perhaps when Mirk is finished talking, *nice* mistress will give Mirk some wine." His amber eyes gleamed.

"Oh— Be serious, please!" Solsta swatted playfully at the meerkat.

"Mirk *is* serious." But the meerkat turned his attention back to Shadow. A few minutes later he delivered as much clarification as he could.

The city was a port, and not as large as Duralyn. They had not been there long, having hunted goblins in the wildlands prior to their arrival, and they had been with other humans. The one who had taken Argentia was not one of these. Shadow was not sure what she was: her scent was human but not human.

"What does that mean?" Solsta wondered.

Ralak shook his head. Mirk scratched his fuzzy chin. None could say.

"It's not very much to go on," Solsta said, stroking Shadow's strong neck.

"No," Ralak agreed. "But enough to have given me an idea."

10

Ralak's chambers in the top of Aventar's eastern tower were cluttered with every imaginable sort of arcana.

Mostly there were spellbooks: standing on shelves that had warped beneath their weight; stacked on tables; on a desk; on the floor. There were also scrolls, their parchment yellowed with age, rolled in piles or jammed between tomes. Urns, lamps, and boxes, most all of them magical, added to the overflowing collection of curiosities. Tables and cabinets were devoted entirely to glassware for mixing potions and powders. A work in progress bubbled through a complex array of tubes and vials, attended by a pair of sinister-looking but harmless imps. Several skulls—ostensibly paperweights, though one, Solsta noticed, had its cap removed and was holding a collection of quills—leered at the visitors in the glow of many lightstones.

"What is this idea of yours?" the Crown asked.

"It is— Do not touch that!" Ralak said sternly.

Mirk yelped in surprise and quickly pulled his slim paws from the curved side of an ancient bronze lamp. "Mirk was just looking," he complained.

"Had you opened that it would have released magic that turned you into a thing unspeakable," the Archamagus warned gravely.

Mirk's amber eyes narrowed. "Into worm?" he asked.

"Or something worse," Ralak agreed.

"Mirk did not like lamp to begin with," the meerkat decided. He climbed up into Solsta's arms and let her hold him. He had pilfered his share of spells and magic from this tower, but something warned him that he would be better to save such escapades for another night.

"Go on, Ralak," Solsta said.

With a final, forbidding glare at the meerkat, the Archamagus resumed. "As I was saying, Shadow reached Duralyn by some instinct, but he would have followed Argentia by her scent, had he been able. When you were taken prisoner by the vampyr, Majesty, my brother Relsthab fashioned a silver collar to enhance Mirk's senses, allowing him to track you across many leagues."

"And you could do the same for Shadow?" Hope lit Solsta's dusky eyes.

"Possibly. But such a casting would take time, and the search even longer," Ralak said. "I believe there is a faster way."

"What way?"

"Argentia's token—" He stopped, struck by another thought.

"What?" Solsta pressed.

"I wonder if I saw it on either of the bodies." Ralak shook his head. If his plan was on the mark, he would know soon enough. "The dragon's tooth is a thing of powerful enchantment. Like all such tokens, it gives a unique signature in the aether. If I can find that signature—"

"You could find Argentia?" Solsta completed.

"Precisely."

"Can you find it?" Solsta asked.

"I believe so, Majesty. It will be difficult and it will take time, but not nearly as much time as forging a collar and sending a pursuit to some unknown corner of Acrevast."

"Then, Archamagus, I suggest you get started."

11

Ralak prepared to cast his spell.

He had rested for a time, slipping into a wizard's trance: a state not so very different from the sleep of elves, wherein the body was restored but the mind capable of functioning. Now, as midnight drew nigh, he was ready to begin his search.

Despite the apparent disarray of the chamber, Ralak always knew exactly where every item he might need was stored. He extended his hand. A book bound in red leather flew off a shelf into his waiting grasp. Flipping to the page containing the dweomer of detection he would use to find Argentia's token, Ralak walked straight through an illusory set of shelves and into the narrow stairwell leading up into the very apex of the tower.

Unlike the room beneath it, Ralak's conjuring chamber was pristine. It had to be. The shades and minor demons summoned in such places were very dangerous entities. If they could get free of their confinement or attack the magus who summoned them by finding a defect in the pentagram, they would do so gleefully. As one never knew what a fiend might find useful as a weapon, the rule among magi was to present them nothing that could be turned to their ends.

"Illumen," Ralak commanded, bringing aethereal light to the dark, empty chamber. He knelt in the center of his precisely etched pentagram. He was not summoning, but a magus scouring the aether for an extended period of time was bound to attract the attention of the beings that dwelt in the magic, not all of which would be friendly.

After checking the diamond-dusted markings to make certain there were no imperfections, Ralak scanned the dweomer and began to recite. At the first words, he felt the power thrum through him like a great intake of breath, as charging and tantalizing this time as it had been the very first time he ever cast a spell. It was a feeling of unfathomable possibility, a connection to the infinite and eternal. Each time he drew upon the aether Ralak thought it little wonder that so many magi went mad with the sheer power of their art. *Like Promitius' boy....* He reminded himself that the theft of the medallion from the Valonian magus remained to be dealt with, and then turned his focus fully to the casting at hand.

With a circular sweep of his palm, he opened the fabric of reality, exposing a hole into the aether: a depthless black struck through with blue and silver lightning, forever malleable yet essentially unchanging. A font of life and power that few could touch, and fewer still could manipulate.

Ralak the Red was one of these few.

From the safety of his pentagram he sent forth his mind into the aether, probing. He conjured an image of Argentia's dragon's tooth token and searched for a matching spark amid the millions of sparks of the aether.

Searched, and searched, and searched....

12

The painter was a surprise.

He was young. He was handsome. He was witty.

He made Solsta laugh. He made Solsta flush.

It had been a long time since that had happened for the Crown: three years since the loss of her husband to an assassin's dagger and the loss of Artelo Sterling, her first and true love, to the arms of a shepherdess. Still, she told herself that she had fit the sittings for the portrait into her schedule only out of a desire to be done with it. As for her initial resolve that the entire project be postponed—well, she had simply changed her mind.

The gown she had selected for the portrait was the same she had worn for her coronation. A shimmer of sleeveless, backless silver tailored perfectly to her trim figure, it fell to her favored mid-calf length over black stockings and above black heels. Silver satin gloves ran past her elbows, and a black velvet cape lay across her shoulders. Her hair was drawn up and piled in loose curls atop her head. The Mark shone whitely in the coif above her bangs.

She was luminous.

This was the second sitting. Each lasted some two hours. She would have spared more, but in good conscience she could not—nor was she entirely displeased to have the process drag out over several days, though the sitting itself became tedious, even with Ittorio's banter and compliments on her beauty (somehow from an artist these seemed more honest) to keep her smiling.

She studied the painter as he studied her. Ittorio was not very tall or very muscular, though his forearms, visible beneath the turned cuffs of his shirt, were sinewy. His features were almost effete: the turn of his lips; the softness of his eyes, green as Jengikutoan jade beneath fine brows and full lashes; the wave of his brown hair, worn long and loose.

Sensuous, Solsta thought, finally placing a word to describe him.

Just as she did, a flash of light exploded in the sitting room.

Solsta gasped in surprise. Behind his easel, Ittorio Tyntoryn jerked violently, his brush slashing across the canvas. He clapped a hand to his face. "Aeton's bolts! Ruined...."

"My apologies, all," said Ralak as the afterglare of his magical entrance faded.

"Ralak! How many times must I tell you to use the doors?" Solsta shouted, rising from her seat.

"Likely as many as your father told my brother," the Archamagus replied slyly.

The Crown shook her head in despair. "The portrait?" she asked Ittorio.

"No!" Ittorio quickly grabbed the canvas and turned it down, hiding the work. "Majesty, it is ruined, trust me."

Solsta, who had been curious to see the painting as it progressed, frowned. Then she smiled flirtatiously. "Pity. We shall simply have to begin again."

Ittorio smiled as well. "Would that the ruin of all my works might provoke so pleasurable a torment. Shall we begin now, Majesty?"

Solsta shook her head, looking from the artist to the Archamagus. The wizard's interruption could only have been for a reason of great import. "Ralak?"

"I have found her, Majesty."

13

Waiting.

This had been the sum of Shrike's existence. Since the murder of her parents when she was a child, all the years of training and practicing and proving herself by stalking and killing until she was an immaculate, flawless instrument of death were in truth just years spent waiting for revenge.

Tonight, that waiting would finally end.

Crouched upon the dark rooftop, Shrike made herself utterly still as she studied the quarry. Not her quarry, but his. Gideon-gil: the infamous elven assassin whose black blades numbered among their victims Shrike's parents, thus setting in motion the vengeance that had driven and defined Shrike's life.

She forced such thoughts aside. There must only be the stillness now. Anything else risked alerting the cunning Gideon-gil to her presence—a thing that would surely turn revenge into disaster.

So Shrike was still as she studied the quarry: a stupid-looking, lazy-looking thief who was neither stupid nor lazy. He had risen swiftly to power in Telarban. Too swiftly and to too much power for the liking of the guildmaster Togril Vloth, who had hired Gideon-gil to make an end of this enemy.

Shrike had spent days and nights staking out the location that the wizard had provided, wondering all the while if Gideon-gil was watching as well. If he was, she neither saw nor sensed him, though with Gideon-gil, as she was acutely aware, that meant nothing.

Yet she trusted in her own skills and stealth, for some of the innate gifts that made Gideon-gil so lethal were in her blood as well, and she did not make mistakes. Certainly the thief's guards, stationed on the balcony and the roof across the street, had no idea they were being observed.

Nor will he....

She had anticipated how the elf would come. It would be only a matter of seconds before the guards were dead and he was inside, and then only more seconds before the thief was dead.

Those were the seconds in which Shrike would act.

She glanced at the bow beside her, its arrow nocked and ready, its barbed tip enchanted to pierce brick or stone, the thin rope attached to it anchored to the roof. She had considered taking Gideon-gil with the bow, but even with her mastery of the weapon there was too much left to chance, and this was one kill she could not—

It was happening!

The guard on the roof across the street was suddenly gone. A moment later, like a shadow given life, Gideon-gil materialized on the wall above the thief's balcony. He had come across the roof, killing the guard that patrolled there. So perfect was his concealment that even Shrike's remarkable eyes had not noticed him until he folded himself over the edge and began his head-first descent towards the two unsuspecting guards on the balcony.

Shrike exhaled slowly, steadying herself, not watching the black-clad elf as he dropped like a spider toward his prey, but the spot on the wall where she would place the arrow. The line would create a tightrope bridging the two buildings. She would be across in moments, poised to strike when Gideon-gil emerged.

She reached for the bow. *Now...*

A voice behind her shouted: "Hey—"

14

"You're sure she's in Telarban?" Amethyst Pyth asked.

The guildmistress of the Golden Serpent—once Duralyn's most prominent thieves' guild and now the throne's personal network of well-placed informants and agents—was seated opposite Solsta and Ralak in one of Aventar's smaller dining rooms. A vital, strong woman, Amethyst was voluptuous in her habits, appetites, and appearance (which, it was rumored, had received some magical enhancements). Without her high-heeled boots to cheat for her, she stood only a little taller than the Crown, but any resemblance to Solsta ended there.

Amethyst was brazen-haired, round-cheeked, and dimple-chinned; heavily curved in breasts and hips; muscular and solid through her limbs. Dozens of gold bracelets, many of them enchanted, decorated her wrists, and an obscenely large rectangular diamond sparkled on one long-nailed finger. She was not precisely beautiful, but she exuded an almost primal sexuality and it was a rare man who could resist her charms when she set her green eyes upon him.

They're almost the color of Ittorio's, Solsta realized as she watched the guildmistress lean back in her seat and stretch, making her ruby-red angora sweater cling even more tightly to her ample bosom as she awaited Ralak's reply.

"I am sure," the Archamagus said.

"I wonder if Vloth's behind all this, whatever it is," Amethyst mused. The Telarbanian guildmaster and Argentia were long-standing enemies. The last round of their battling had gone to Argentia, but none of them truly believed Vloth would abide by the terms under which Argentia had spared his life.

"When we find her, we'll know," Solsta said.

M

A short while later, Ralak and Amethyst aetherwalked from Duralyn to Telarban, where they met Bendrake Ironclaw. A dark-skinned Sudenlander, Bendrake was the Golden Serpent's agent in the city on Crescent Lake. He was accompanied by three of his men. "Mistress Pyth. Welcome back," Bendrake said.

"Thank you." Pyth rubbed a hand across her face, trying to find her equilibrium after the instantaneous disintegration and reconstruction of her body by the magic of the teleport. "Ugh, that always makes me feel like vomiting. I don't know how you magi do it," she muttered.

"An acquired skill," Ralak replied.

"You haven't seen Lady Dasani?" Amethyst asked Bendrake.

Bendrake shook his head. He had assisted Argentia on her last trip to Telarban, when she had come to infiltrate Togril Vloth's guild. He remembered the red-haired huntress very well. "No, Guildmistress. If she's here, my men don't know where."

"She is here," Ralak said. He closed his eyes, folding his hands together. When he opened his eyes again, they glimmered for an instant like an owl's in torchlight. "Follow me."

They went out into the city. Telarban was as dark and dingy as Duralyn was bright and beautiful. A hub of inland commerce, it was rife with corruption, boasting several of the realm's most cutthroat thieves' guilds.

The night wind off Crescent Lake was bitter. Amethyst wrapped a fur close about her, and even Bendrake, tall and strong and battered as a well-used blade, bent against the cutting breeze.

Ralak stopped before a gray building three stories tall, with dark windows and barred doors. It looked like a warehouse of some sort, but for all Amethyst knew it might have been a guildhouse in disguise. In Telarban, things were not always what they appeared. "Argentia's in there?" she asked.

"No. On the roof," Ralak said.

"The roof?"

"Trust me."

"Maybe she's not a prisoner after all," Bendrake said. Based on what Amethyst had told him, he had brought three of his best men in anticipation of having to free Argentia from some type of imprisonment.

"Let us assume nothing." Ralak was as confused and troubled as the rest by this turn of events. Shadow's account and the presence of the strange twin Argentias pointed to the huntress being in danger, but the aethereal signal of the dragon's tooth token was clearly coming from this roof. *Perhaps Ironclaw is right and she's escaped on her own....*

"Check the others sides for a ladder," Amethyst said to Bendrake's men. "If you don't find one, we'll use the grapnels."

"Not necessary," Ralak said. "Take hold of my staff. Don't look down."

They did as the Archamagus bid them. Ralak's staff began to glow and they rose off the ground. Higher and higher the magic of the Archamagus took them, one of Bendrake's men chanting a prayer for protection the entire time, Amethyst now absolutely certain she was going to vomit, until they touched down on the roof.

"There," Ralak said quietly. He pointed across the roof, where a crouched figure was barely visible in the shadows.

They started forward. Amethyst hailed the figure. "Hey—"

15

Shrike whipped around as the unexpected call shattered the night. Her hand flew to her belt, her speed blinding as she fired a pair of daggers at her attackers, felling two of them, scattering the rest.

This can't be happening.... She had been betrayed. The wizard had delivered the elf, as promised, but sent killers of his own to dispatch Shrike while she was busy at her revenge.

Against all reason, Shrike spun back for the bow. Gideon-gil was gone from the balcony—so were the guards—but there was still time for her to get across. *There has to be time....*

Before she could grab her weapon, the roof blazed up with aethereal light. Caught in the sudden illumination, Shrike wheeled back to face her foes, wondering for an instant if the Island Wizard himself had come to see her dead.

Then the bolts of aether seared the air, and a crossbow clicked and fired.

M

Amethyst saw the woman's arm dip, coil, and snap forward. She dove down without ever seeing the weapons flying past her. Heard the thud of them striking flesh and the thump of flesh striking the roof: two of their party down like swatted flies.

Could've been me....

That thought almost kept her on the ground, frozen in fear, but she couldn't let her Serpents face death and danger while she cowered. She rolled to her feet just as the tip of Ralak's staff blazed like a star, flooding the rooftop with light and freezing the woman on the far side in mid-spin.

It was not Argentia Dasani.

Their adversary was a petite, slender woman clad in fitted black leather. Her olive-toned face was ovular, almost elven in its thin brows, sharp cheekbones, and slim, straight nose, though there was an insolence to lips, and above the left corner of her mouth was a small beauty mark that no elf would bear. Her eyes were hidden behind strange ebony-lensed glasses. Her inky black hair was swept off her high brow and dangled in a ponytail that reached to her narrow waist. Argentia's dragon's tooth token hung about her neck.

Amethyst gathered all that at a glance. Then her eyes widened as Ralak loosed forks of blue fire from his potent staff and the black-clad woman dodged them all, twisting and bending her body, supple as a dancer, faster than anything Pyth had ever seen.

Bendrake fired his crossbow. Amethyst watched as the woman dodged that shot too. Then a familiar little weapon was in the woman's black-gloved hand and aethereal crescents stabbed through the air: steely streaks in the battle-light.

Ralak stepped in front of the guildmistress and swept his glowing staff across his body, conjuring an aethereal shield that bounced the missiles harmlessly aside. "*M'anere!*" he thundered

The woman staggered, whelmed by the magical force in Ralak's voice. She stumbled close to the edge of the roof, teetered for an instant, and toppled off.

M

Falling, Shrike shot a hand out and snared a window ledge one floor below the roof. She hung there for a moment, shaking off the effects of the spell that had knocked her momentarily off balance. It should have frozen her in place, but her elvish blood resisted such magic.

She could hear her enemies running across the roof above. With eerie dexterity, Shrike holstered the handbow, fished a silver disc from a pack slung low on her back, and dropped it to the street below.

She raised her head. Saw the woman and the red-robed magus peering down. "Tell the wizard he dies for this treachery," she spat as she let go of the ledge.

M

"No!" Ralak shouted.

The woman fell, dropping feet-first precisely onto the strange disc. There was a blinding flash. When the glare faded the disc remained, but the woman had vanished.

16

From the shadows of the thief's balcony, Gideon-gil watched the people on the roof across the street. The woman who had been stalking this place—stalking him—for the past days was not among them, though she had been on that roof when he made his attack.

His elven vision unimpaired by the dark, he recognized the Archamagus and the guildmistress of the Golden Serpent, both known from earlier encounters. Something was clearly afoot; something of importance if the Crown had loosed her pet wizard from Duralyn to deal with it.

Where is the woman? She was somehow the key to this, Gideon-gil sensed. He did not know who she was, but there was something strangely familiar about her movements, and she was good at her craft. Very good—though had the Archamagus and his friends not intervened, she would have learned to her cost that Gideon-gil was that much her better.

He had seen the battle-lights while about his swift and deadly work in the thief's chamber. By the time he emerged, whatever fighting there had been was ended. Was it possible the woman was dead on the roof?

Back up the wall he went, the tiny spikes affixed to his boots and the fingertips of his gloves allowing him to climb with the fleetness of an insect. The roof of this building looked down upon the roof across the street. There were indeed bodies, but the woman's was not among them.

Interesting....

The elf watched the Archamagus extend a glowing hand over the wall, levitating what appeared to be a metallic disc off the street. Gideon-gil debated following the group to learn what they were about. Decided not to. Their business in Telarban did not appear to have anything to do with him, and as he intended to be gone from this squalid place as soon as he collected his payment, it was even less of a concern.

But the woman.... Might she be the challenge he had been seeking for so long?

The assassin smiled at that possibility. Eager though he was to face a true test of his abilities, he would be patient, as he was always patient. She had come once; she would come again.

When she did, she would join the dead ranks of all who had ever crossed Gideon-gil's black blades.

17

Solsta paced her chambers.

It was a habit when she was deep in thought or deep in frustration. Right now, she was in the throes of both.

Mirkholmes, familiar with Solsta's moods, stayed well afield and practiced fencing with a letter-opener Ralak had given him. The tool, a replica of the demon-slaying sword Scourge, served the meerkat nicely as a weapon. Herwedge, also skilled at reading the Crown's emotional weather, cleared the remains of breakfast from the table and quietly withdrew.

Shadow—cleaned, healed, rested, well-fed, and looking much healthier for it—lay by the foot of a couch and watched Solsta with his gray eyes. Always her own harshest critic, Solsta felt reproach in the wolf-dog's gaze. She had dispatched Ralak and Amethyst to Telarban, and they had returned in the dark before dawn not with Argentia, but with many new mysteries.

The black-clad woman wearing Argentia's token had escaped using a magical trick the like of which even Ralak had never seen before. The Archamagus was already back in his chambers, trying to pinpoint the token once more, that they might capture the mysterious woman and get some answers.

Solsta was waiting, and not doing it well. She was even more worried for Argentia than before. *It's the token....* Solsta knew how much that simple adornment meant to Argentia, who had once refused to ransom it to a dragon. *She'd die before parting willingly with it....*

Yet the woman in black had it about her neck.

"What does it mean?" Solsta asked aloud, vexed. Mirk stopped jabbing at his reflection in the vanity mirror. He stood with his whiskers quivering for a moment before resuming his fencing. Shadow continued to watch Solsta with his placid, confident eyes.

And Solsta continued to pace.

M

Where is she?

Ralak's brow furrowed as he searched the streaking depths of the aether. He had been having difficulty concentrating on this casting, and the magical signature of the dragon's tooth token remained elusive.

His distraction was understandable. He had expended a great deal of his power over the past days. He needed rest in order to recover from those exertions. Even more than that, however, what kept dragging his mind away from the task at hand was the disc.

He had never seen anything like it, though its purpose was clear enough. The disc was a portable aethergate. It appeared to be made of glass, like a circle cut from a mirror. It would not break—Ralak had tried everything from striking it with his staff to dropping it from a tower window—and it would not work. The magic expended itself after a single use, preventing any unwanted parties from following where it led.

At present, Ralak was almost more concerned with where the disc had come from than where it went. Aethergate chambers, which permitted mortals to travel as did the magi, were few in number and carefully maintained by magi or clerics. With this disc, the possibility of aethereal travel was greatly expanded. Of course, there still had to be a fixed arrival point, but to be able to teleport from any place the disc was to that point opened the door for much mischief, as they had seen upon the roof.

Such trivializations of magic were things the Council of Magi, knowing well that the aether was far more dangerous than most realized, had long stood against. *There was one who flouted those restrictions,* Ralak mused. *The Great Maker—and his mark is upon the disc. I would know it anywhere....*

Ralak had found the symbol—an M inscribed in a circle—on the back of the disc. He recalled the words of the woman in black in the instant before she fell: Tell the wizard he dies for this treachery.

But that is impossible....

With an effort, Ralak wrenched his mind from the mystery of the disc back to the problem of the woman in black. Wherever she had escaped to, she had to be found. *I fear Argentia's life depends upon it....*

The Archamagus bent his will to the aether again, seeking the telltale glimmer of the dragon's tooth token.

18

The throne hall of Aventar was the single chamber in her castle that Solsta hated.

It had been designed to awe, and in that capacity it was exceedingly effective. Its twin doors, massive golden slabs, opened onto a long, rectangular space whose vaulted ceiling rose over domineering, buttressed arches. The sides of the hall were tiered. There the nobles of the Peerage took their seats in boxes marked with the crests of their families, the more powerful and prestigious houses having the higher seats. A purple carpet ran down the center of the hall. Any who had business with the Crown had to walk that length to its end, where a flight of black marble steps, each one stationed by a pair of Sentinel knights, rose to the throne of Aventar.

Solsta knew the arrangement of the chamber was as much for her defense as it was to display the might of the Crown. Still, she had seen too many men tremble their way down that purple carpet to prostrate themselves at the base of the steps, and she thought it a hideously unfair representation of her rule to look down upon the people she served.

If Solsta disdained the pomp and circumstance of the throne hall, however, the nobles assuredly did not. Ralak and several other close counselors had warned her against bucking tradition by changing the venue of her councils. While willful, Solsta was also savvy beyond her years. She knew she could accomplish much more with the support of the Peerage than without it, so in the matter of the throne hall she abided— though when the choice was hers she took her meetings in other chambers.

This morning, the choice had not been hers. The ambassadors from Sormoria had come to give their farewell and promise of continued good will between the realms, particularly in support of Solsta's efforts to rid piracy from all the waters of Acrevast: a topic particularly near to the heart of Sormoria's Sultan.

The delegates finally departed and Solsta, who had suffered through the ceremony with all her grace though her mind was far from pirates and realm-relations, dismissed the Peerage shortly afterwards. She had just risen from her throne to return to her chambers when Ralak appeared at the foot of the steps amid his customary flash of light.

Solsta took one look at his troubled face as he mounted the steps and resumed her seat with a sigh.

"I cannot find the token, Majesty," Ralak said without preamble. "There is no sign of it in the aether."

"How can that be? You found it before."

"Either the woman destroyed the token, or she has entered a place where magical detection cannot reach her." After a moment he added, "I doubt she has the means to destroy that token." Then he fell silent, stroking his short beard.

"What's wrong?" Solsta asked. "Tell me, Ralak. What is it you know?"

"Nothing that I know, Majesty. Much that I suspect."

"What is it?"

Ralak paused again, and then shook his head. "No. Let it be for now, Majesty. What I suspect is almost madness. I will not speak of such things unless I am certain. When the bodies have arrived and I have examined them, then—whether I am right or wrong—I will tell you all my mind on this matter."

Solsta trusted Ralak completely. Hard as it was to restrain her curiosity, she would let him hold his mysterious silence. "As you will. Until then, you are certain there's nothing else we can do?"

"Nothing but wait, Majesty."

"I was afraid you'd say that."

19

Kill Maneryl of Harrowgate....

She came for the magus in the throes of a storm. The tower wall was slick as she climbed handhold by handhold, mounting towards the single yellow light of the topmost chamber, a beacon against the storm-dark.

She reached the perch outside the window. It was a narrow stone ledge, slippery beneath the fresh soles of her boots. Within, the magus was bent over a cluttered desk on the far side of the chamber, all unaware that death had come for him.

Frigid rain slashed at her. She paid it no mind as she extracted a runestone from her pouch. Waiting for the lightning, she used the larger glare to conceal the small flash as she touched the runestone to the casement, stripping the warding glyphs of their power. A blow from the heel of her hand sent the window flying open.

As the magus looked up, perhaps thinking that the storm had forced the casement, she unsheathed a dagger, drew back her arm to throw—

The raven flew up into her face. Dark wings filled her vision, beating around her head like an explosion of night. The black beak stabbed at her eyes.

She flinched from the unexpected assault and fell from the window before she even realized her boots had lost their precarious purchase. Her scream was swept away by the storm, as was the splashing impact when she struck the rain-soaked ground nearly a hundred feet below.

Likely she was already dead before Maneryl, his familiar now perched on his shoulder, leaned out the window high above, stretched a hand toward the roiling heavens, and cried *"Eloin-han!"*

If she was still lingering in life, the lightning bolt the magus dragged from the storm made certain of her end, blasting her with a column of blue-white fire that vaporized the red-haired huntress and most of the puddles around her into a scar upon the stones of the wizard's courtyard.

M

Kill Donparlion of Fars Gate....

She watched the wizard shuffle away from the apothecary. He was a fat thing, and weak, struggling with the parcels and sacks he'd purchased in the shop.

She let him pass by without striking. It was not a question of disobeying the command, merely a precaution. It was early evening and there was still enough activity in Teranor's northernmost port to make her concerned about being seen.

When Donparlion was safely past, she retreated down the alley and raced along a parallel street. She had already scouted another location for her attack: closer to the wizard's home, safer from prying eyes and potential intervention.

She took up her position well ahead of the wizard. Observed his approach. His head was down, more mindful of the awkward packages than anything going on around him. He was practically begging to be killed.

She glanced in both directions. Twilight had deepened, drawing shadows across the cobbled street. There were a few people in sight, but no Watchmen and no one near enough to cause her trouble. She slipped back into the gloom between two buildings.

When the wizard appeared in the mouth of the alley, she sprang forward, seized him, and spun him past her. Donparlion tumbled down into the trash, spilling most of his packages. He flailed over onto his back. "Wait, wait!" he cried, his round, pink face going waxy with fear, his eyes wide beneath lank blonde hair. "Don't do this!"

She fell upon him like a mountain cat upon a crippled boar. Stabbed a dagger into his ample gut. Donparlion squealed. She freed the dagger for a second strike but pain and terror gave the wizard wild strength. He shoved her off him and sat up, his breath coming in short, terrified gasps as he fumbled in his pocket.

The huntress tumbled heels-over-head, coming smoothly to her feet. She registered the thing in the wizard's fat hand was no weapon, just a glass bottle. Attacked. She had to be swift now: she should have gone for the throat immediately, instead of taking the sure strike at his girth. *I won't make that mistake—*

The contents of the bottle hit her in the face.

She recoiled, swiping at her face with her free hand. At first she thought he'd meant to blind her, but she could still see. She wiped the dripping liquid from her face. Smiled coldly at Donparlion. Raised the dagger again.

And the burning started.

Bolts of fire sank into her skull. She dropped her weapon, clutching her face as its flesh sloughed off and ran like mucous down her gloved hands, the basilopard acid eating its relentless way through skin and muscle and bone, turning her beauty into bubbling chum.

She fell forward, trying to scream without tongue or teeth. By the time Donparlion had gained his feet—slow work given his size and the ruinous pain in his stomach—the acid had devoured most of her head. He listened to her red hair sizzling atop the deflated dome of her skull as he pressed a glowing hand to the hole in his robes, using the aether to temporarily stop the bleeding where she had gored him.

Still moving slowly, he gathered his packages from the alley, wondering all the while who she was and why she had attacked him. He had no answers. He would seek a cleric's attention and file a complaint with the Watch. Fars Gate was not as safe as it used to be.

M

Kill Ravagant of Shriv's Port....

She followed the wizard at a discreet distance. He was wary, his weaselish head darting this way and that as he traversed the docks, his hood up, his cloak drawn close to conceal his robes from the lading crews that worked through the night so the wagons could roll and the ships could sail with the sun. His business here was best done unobserved.

Wary too was the man Ravagant was meeting. A thief of some power and prominence in the seedy city at the mouth of the Mir River, he had need of tools only a magus could deliver to rid himself of a potential rival.

The wizard and the thief met in the shadows behind a tall stack of wooden skids at the end of the dock farthest from where most of the work was taking place. There were dozens of such stacks around them: a small forest of square, limbless trees. The thief had come in a rowboat and would depart the same way, never having been seen on the docks at all.

"My price?" Ravagant said.

"Five hundred, as agreed. Now give me the sticks."

As the bag and purse exchanged hands, there was a flash of steel from above and a shape leaped from atop the stack of wood.

The thief did not pause to think where the attacker had come from or who her target was. He dropped the bag the wizard had given him. Pulled a handbow from its holster on his hip. Tracked. Fired.

The shape jerked in mid-air. The steel went flying. The body fell upon Ravagant, knocking the wizard sprawling. He quickly scrambled to his feet.

The shape did not rise.

The thief loaded a second bolt. Fired a shot into the back of the red-haired head, just to be certain.

"What?" Ravagant was aghast. "Who could have known? How? Who is this?"

"Someone who meant one of us a great deal of harm," the thief said, looking around. He did not think the altercation had been noticed, but he was taking no chances. "Help me with the body."

"Help yourself," Ravagant said. Clapping his hands together, he vanished in a flash of aether.

"Bastard." Hustling in case the sudden glare attracted attention, the thief maneuvered the woman's body to the edge of the dock and pushed it over. It hit with a splash that echoed too loudly for the thief's liking and sank out of sight in the dark water of the harbor.

Still hurrying, he grabbed the bag the wizard had given him and was about to climb down to his boat when he spotted a familiar pouch on the ground: the five hundred gold crowns he had paid for the explosive sticks. The wizard had dropped it during the attack. The thief claimed it again. *Call it a fee for saving your life, you miserable weasel…* He was fairly certain the wizard had been the target, but he was not about to linger to find out for sure.

Smiling at this turn of Fortune, the thief climbed down into his little boat and rowed away.

M

Kill Tonoto of Exetus....

She had breached the wizard's home with ease. Found him in a prayer chamber, kneeling on a stone block between two blazing braziers. Before him was an idol of some strange goddess with six arms and three heads. Thin sticks of incense in a copper urn sweetened the air. Otherwise, the wooden chamber, like much of the wizard's house that she had seen, was devoid of decoration.

She stood in the doorway, her hand on her dagger. The wizard was deep in his meditation, but she would not risk going closer. There was no need. One throw and it was over.

She drew the dagger. Exhaled a slow breath, focusing on the center of the wizard's back.

The dagger tumbled through the air: a perfect throw.

It struck the wizard's katana and clattered harmlessly aside.

"If you would kill me, let it be with honor," Tonoto said. He had risen, turned, drawn his weapon, and struck the dagger away with incredible—perhaps magical—speed. Now the Nhapian wizard faced the red-haired huntress as if he was not at all surprised to see her. His dark hair, nut-brown skin, almond eyes, and the style of his garb—a short robe over flowing silk pants—were strangely familiar to her, but she could not place from where or why.

Doesn't matter....

She drew her own katana. Sprinted forward, attacking with a blistering five-blow combination. The strikes came high and low, left and right.

Tonoto parried them all. Forced her back with a single, measured thrust at her chin. She leaped in again with another combination. Only the wizard's arms moved, blocking expertly.

It went on thus for several minutes. Then Tonoto disengaged, took a step backwards, raised his blade high, hilt to the huntress, and shook his head. "You cannot win," he said. "You fight with a master's skill, but without a master's imagination."

As he spoke this last word, Tonoto snapped his hands forward, releasing his katana. It flipped once and impaled the huntress cleanly between her breasts.

To her credit, she came forward still, but the light was fast-fading in her eyes, and her legs failed her, pitching her into darkness at the feet of the wizard.

Tonoto turned from her body and knelt once more on his stone block, praying Sh'vya would forgive the desecration of Her shrine.

M

Four nights. Four cities. Four attacks.

Each by a red-haired swordswoman. Each ending in her death.

One thing was clear nonetheless: the magi of Teranor were under siege.

20

"Dead, dead, dead. He-heee...."

As the words and manic laughter echoed across Castle Aventar's dungeons, Ralak the Red crossed the bare stone floor and faced a small, seedy-looking man through a barrier of bars. There were not many prisoners in Aventar's cells—Duralyn's common dungeons held its common criminals—but those that were in the Crown's custody were there for good reason.

This particular prisoner had been crowing ever since the sheet covering one of the bodies Ralak had ordered brought to the dungeon had slipped aside long enough for him to recognize the huntress who had captured him four winters ago. "She's dead!" he exulted. "Red-haired fiend! She stole it from me and she has paid now. Oh yes, she has paid!"

"Al'Atin Erkani!" Ralak said sharply. "I grow weary of your jabbering. Utter one more syllable and I will wither your tongue with magefire." As he spoke, his voice took on a strong and terrible weight and his eyes lit with a baleful glimmer. Erkani shrank from the bars and cowered in the corner, whimpering.

Satisfied, the Archamagus returned to the chamber where he had been laboring. Upon a table of ancient oak lay three bodies: one from Argo, one from Valon, one from Exetus. For all the art of his magic could tell, they were identical in every respect save the marks laid on them in death—but it was the mark laid on them in life that filled Ralak's heart with dread.

Ralak stared at the bodies again: three of six that he knew of. The others had been destroyed in their attacks on the magi. *There may be more of them. I can wait no longer. We must decide a course....*

Wiping his brow, he went to another table and waved a hand over an oculyr. "Majesty," he said when the smoke in the crystal ball had cleared. "If you and the others would join me in the dungeons?"

M

"Are you certain you're up to this?" Solsta asked Ikabod.

"I will face whatever truth the Archamagus has to tell, Majesty." The butler had arrived on the prior evening, bringing with him the last of the three bodies. He looked much more haggard than when Solsta had last seen him. From his desolate tone of voice, Solsta understood that, despite the mystery surrounding Argentia's apparent death, all Ikabod expected was to be informed of which of the bodies was truly that of his mistress.

It broke her heart. *But that may well be what we learn*, she reminded herself. If so, she would see the huntress given a royal funeral and would use all her considerable power to make certain whoever had killed Argentia was brought to justice.

She would also offer Castle Aventar for Ikabod to make his new home as her honored guest. She did not know if he would accept, though she hoped he would. Even more, she hoped such an offer would not even be necessary.

Time to find out.... "Ralak is ready for us," she said, and led the procession of Ikabod, Amethyst, Mirk, and Shadow down to the dungeons.

They met the treble spectacle of death in silence.

Finally Amethyst pronounced the thought that was on all their minds: "I just don't believe it."

"Which is Argentia?" Solsta asked. "How can you even begin to tell?"

"You cannot, Majesty," Ralak said. "For all are Argentia, and none."

Solsta stamped her foot in annoyance. "Explain, and no riddles."

"They are simulcra, Majesty. Things of magic. They were made to be perfect likenesses of Argentia, and they are. So much so that even those who know her best could not tell the deception."

He looked meaningfully at Ikabod. The butler nodded. In the shade of its hair, the turn of its lips, the faded scars from battles unnumbered, the dragonfly tattoo, and every other detail, each of the bodies was a perfect image of Argentia. "Then how can you be certain, Archamagus?" he asked.

"They reek of the shadowaether used to create them," Ralak replied.

"Of that you will simply have to take my word. But also because of this." He rolled one of the bodies onto its side. "I will wager your mistress bore no such mark as that."

There, below the curve of the simulcra's left hip, branded in glaring red upon the pale flesh of its thigh, was an *M* inscribed in a circle.

"Not that I knew of," Ikabod said.

"What significance would that symbol have to Argentia?" Amethyst asked.

"It has great significance, but not to Argentia," Ralak said. "Look on this." He lifted the silver disc taken from Telarban and showed them the back.

"The same mark!" the guildmistress exclaimed.

"What does it mean?" Solsta asked. "Whose mark is that?"

The Archamagus sighed. "This is the sigul of Mouradian. I have not seen it in more than fifty winters. I thought I would never see it again."

"Why not? Who is this Mouradian?"

"A wizard, Majesty. One believed dead since shortly after my brother Relsthab was made Archamagus…."

M

In the dungeon chamber, they listened as Ralak unfolded the tale of the Great Maker, the drowned island, and the Forbidden art of simulation.

Oh Argentia, Solsta thought when the telling was ended. *What has befallen you?*

Part II

Argentia and the Island Wizard

21

Eleven weeks earlier....

M

The Salty Dog was Argentia Dasani's kind of place.

It was a sailor's tavern (in her experience, most of the best taverns were), full of smoke and bustle and the smells of greasy food and malty drink; warm against the chill night beyond the doors; and loud: with music from the minstrels on a wooden platform in the far corner, with the clatter of utensils on dishware and the clink of glasses and mugs, with conversation and argument and calls for more drink to harried serving girls and a bartend who was pressed to meet demand. The noise was not a tidal thing. There was no ebb and flow, just a river of din that drowned out thought.

That was fine with Argentia. She wasn't there to think.

After rescuing Ikabod from Togril Vloth's Frost Palace in Nord, Argentia had returned to Argo with detours in Duralyn and Telarban along the way. She had stayed for three months: long enough to oversee the finishing touches on her new estate, move in, and rest from a road that had taken her to the reaches of Acrevast.

But the peregrine in her soul came calling before the summer's end, and soon enough she was packing a bag and leaving her home behind yet again. Her aimless path eventually brought her and Shadow to Harrowgate, where she had hired on with a group of mercenaries called the Harvester's Gryphons.

It was like old times. A fortnight of hard riding and fighting in dangerous caves, with two score goblins killed before their raiding parties could threaten any villages or travelers. A job well done, and just the thing Argentia had been yearning for when she left Argo.

But the Harvester's Gryphons? Really? What a stupid name for a company... Argentia snickered to herself as she knocked back the last of her drink. Her head was full of a pleasant, warm fuzziness.

"What's so funny?" Vartan Raventyr asked, taking her hand from across the table.

Drawn out of her reverie, Argentia looked at the leader of the mercenaries blankly for a moment before she realized she must have snickered aloud. *Bad idea....* The Gryphons—eight men who were actually among the more competent she'd worked with—took their name very seriously.

That made her laugh again. "What?" Vartan pressed.

Argentia composed herself as best she could. "Nothing," she said, hopping down from her tall chair (Did it seem even taller now? Quite possibly it did, a little, and she found that funny, too, but managed not to laugh). "Dance with me."

Nothing had passed between Argentia and Vartan, but the potential had been there from the first, and it had only built over the past fortnight. Vartan was tall, well built, and handsome enough, with an open smile, tanned cheeks, dark eyes, and a mop of unruly brown hair.

Tonight or never, Argentia thought as they danced, their bodies teasing together, slipping apart, moving with rhythmic grace to the beat of the music, the room whirling with them, whirling around them. She was leaving Harrowgate in the morning, heading back to Argo. She would collect Ikabod and ride north to celebrate Yule with the Crown and her other friends in Duralyn—although it currently looked as if noon might be a more realistic time of departure than morning.

From the floor they went back to the table for another round, and then to the throwing board, where what began as a friendly contest among five of the Gryphons and Argentia whittled down to a final competition between the huntress and Vartan. A single throw with an extra share of the take for the goblin job on the line.

"Let's up the stakes," Vartan said. "Winner gets the loser's whole share."

"That's the best bet you can come up with?" Argentia said, arching a brow. The gathered Gryphons—all eight now—and other patrons of the Dog who had become onlookers to the sport laughed.

"Hey, I'm a gentleman," Vartan protested to more and louder laughter.

"Even a gentleman could come up with something better than that."

"Fine. Full bounty and the loser has to do whatever the winner wants for the rest of the night."

"That's better. First throw's yours."

"Fair enough." Vartan took aim. Threw. Cursed as soon as the dagger left his hand. It stuck outside the black center of the cork circle by less than an inch.

"Not bad," Argentia said. She drew her own dagger.

"Sure you're not too drunk?" Vartan asked as Argentia's arm coiled.

Argentia stopped. "I'd have to be stoned on Stromness stout to lose to that throw." With one fluid move she turned and fired her dagger dead center in the black spot.

"Shit," Vartan said, shaking his head. "Do you ever lose?"

Argentia grinned triumphantly. "Nope."

22

It was closer to dawn than midnight when Argentia and the Gryphons came staggering into the Mast and Nest, singing raucously and feeling the lateness of the hour no more than they had the frigid bite of the wind as they walked from the Salty Dog to the wharf-front inn.

They made their farewells, knowing it was doubtful they would all meet again. The Gryphons split up, some headed for their own chambers, some back out to find another tavern or brothel or other sport. Vartan made a show of escorting Argentia to her suite, and to much cheering and ribald laughter, followed her and Shadow up the stairs.

"Time to pay loser's dues," Argentia said when they'd reached her door.

"Would if I knew what I was paying," Vartan replied.

"Here's a hint," Argentia leaned up and kissed him. Vartan pressed her to the wall as she wrapped her arms around his neck, the kiss quickening. *Definitely not leaving until afternoon,* Argentia thought.

Shadow barked.

"All right, all right." Argentia managed to get the door open without fully leaving Vartan's embrace. "Go on." She swatted playfully at the dog. Shadow barked again and loped towards the bedchamber. "No!" Argentia ducked out of Vartan's arms and gave valiant chase but Shadow easily beat her to the bed, where he sprawled with a look of supreme satisfaction in his gray eyes. "Really?" Argentia leaned on the doorframe, shaking her head in mock exasperation. "You'll pay for that," she promised, laughing. Closing the bedchamber door, she turned back to Vartan. "Now, where were we?"

Vartan shoved the door to the suite shut. Argentia met him in the middle of the sitting room.

Neither of them noticed that the door had not locked, so when the trouble came later, it had only to walk in.

Their mouths were together, tongues exploring, their hands everywhere on one another as they swayed, barely keeping balanced. Argentia's heart was pounding. It had been a long time since she'd taken a lover. Tonight drink and desire made her almost desperately hungry for this.

Cloaks fell away. Weapons' belts clattered off and were kicked aside. Clothing followed frantically. Argentia heard something rip, though whether it was part of her outfit or Vartan's she neither knew nor cared.

They stumbled towards the sitting room's couch, but they were on the wrong side and Argentia ended up bent over its back, Vartan behind her, spreading her legs with his knees, stroking her full, firm breasts, his face shoved into the tangled fire of her hair. He groaned something against her neck.

"What?" she gasped. She was ready, so ready.

"Why'd we wait?"

"Don't wait, don't wait." She reached behind, guiding him into her, bringing almost instant and delicious relief. *Oh, yes....*

M

Eventually they made their way to the right side of the couch, and some time later from there to the bath chamber. The frenetic lust of a fortnight had been slaked, but it lingered not far off even as they enjoyed more leisurely ministrations.

"Ummm," Argentia sighed. She lounged in a steaming bath, while Vartan knelt beside the copper tub, rubbing soapy lather in her hair, massaging her scalp with his strong fingers. "That's so nice. You could have just done this all night."

"Please tell me you're joking."

Argentia smirked. "Well, maybe, but don't stop."

He didn't, until finally Argentia twisted around, rising up on her knees, her body slick with suds. "I think you'd better get in this tub."

A minute later, she was riding atop Vartan, eyes closed, back arched. She didn't hear the water sloshing wildly over the sides of the tub, or Shadow's barking, or anything but their mingled moans.

Until the strike of steel against flesh.

23

As her mind registered that impossibly out-of-place but utterly unmistakable sound, something scalding sprayed Argentia's face and breasts. Her eyes opened to the horror of Vartan's headless body jerking spasmodically beneath her, his arms slapping feebly against the tub, blood fanning from his neck, painting the white walls crimson.

Screaming, Argentia twisted violently, falling sideways in the tub, going under for an instant, coming up through the bloody suds, choking and gasping.

Steel touched her throat.

Argentia froze.

"Get up."

The voice was as emotionless as the blade against Argentia's vulnerable flesh. She obeyed, rising slowly, hands spread to her sides, water sluicing down her body, soapsuds pouring from her hair to burn her eyes.

The steel rose with her, its tip never wavering.

The cold air struck Argentia like a slap, bringing sudden clarity. She assessed the battlefield.

Her enemy was an elfishly slim woman, black-clad, black-haired, with strange ebony glasses hiding her eyes and a katana extending from her gloved hand to Argentia's throat. *Mine. My belts, my handbow....* Then came the mounting dismay as she realized it was her own weapon that had killed Vartan. "Who—"

The katana moved a fraction, drawing a nick of blood that turned quickly pink as it ran down the wet slope of Argentia's breast. "Out of the tub," the woman said.

Argentia stepped forward. Something bumped her leg: Vartan's head, bobbing beside her knee in a pool of persimmon water.

"I'll kill you for this," Argentia promised, her cobalt eyes flaring. In that instant she was so enraged she didn't care if she died right there.

A wasted death, Carfax said in her mind. It was the ranger's ghost voice much more than the steel at her throat that stopped Argentia. She locked her temper down and surrendered.

Or appeared to.

While she stepped carefully from the tub, she was as focused and poised as a lioness about to pounce, waiting for the slightest mistake by her captor to allow her to turn the odds.

There was none.

She heard Shadow pounding against the bedchamber door. *Come on,* she prayed. But the door held. *Have to give him time....* She returned her attention to her enemy. Barefoot, Argentia still stood several inches taller than the booted woman. If she could disarm her, she should have the advantage in a hand-to-hand fight. "Who are you?" she demanded.

"Where did you get that?" the woman said, pointing to the dragon's tooth token dangling about Argentia's neck. "That is elf craft, and not for the likes of you."

"Don't even—"

The katana swept back but before Argentia could take advantage of the mistake she'd been waiting for, the woman struck her once with her free hand, her stiff fingers hammering the plexus of nerves below Argentia's breasts. It was an expert blow. Argentia was on her knees and gasping before she even knew what had happened. She barely felt the woman's hand behind her head, unclasping the mithryl chain, taking the token.

No....

Argentia surged, but the katana was back at her throat again faster than she could rise. She had never seen such speed. *The twins weren't that fast. Maybe not even Gideon-gil,* she thought, though the elf moved like this woman.

She heard the bedchamber door burst open. Shadow's dangerous growl filled the suite. "Here! Shadow!" Argentia shouted.

The woman darted her free hand into a pack. Pulled out a silver disc and dropped it onto the soaked floor.

Shadow hurtled into the bath chamber, his teeth bared for the kill.

The woman grabbed a handful of Argentia's sopping hair and stepped onto the disc.

All the world tumbled away.

24

"A superlative specimen, don't you think?"

The man's voice, wholly unfamiliar, drew Argentia out of the black. She felt cold stone beneath her bare flesh. *Where am I?* She knew they had walked the aether, though she had never seen a teleport gate like that disc. *We must have gone a hell of a long way for me to pass out....* She wanted desperately to open her eyes, but resisted, giving no sign that she was awake.

"Look at her," the voice continued. "The human form at peaks of beauty and conditioning—with no offense to you, my dear, who do not wholly qualify as human."

There was no response from whomever the man was addressing, but Argentia assumed it had to be the woman who had taken her.

"Yet you said she was easily captured?" the man continued.

"Child's play."

"Interesting. Perhaps her murder of Puma and Pantra was more luck than skill."

Argentia almost flinched at the mention of the cat-women. *So that's what this is about. But how could he know—unless the elf....*

It had to have been Gideon-gil. The assassin must have sold his knowledge of those final, fatal moments beneath Togril Vloth's Frost Palace. If so, he had sold a lie, for Tierciel Thorne, not Argentia, had killed Puma and Pantra.

But Thorne was dead, and there were no other witnesses besides Argentia and Gideon-gil. Argentia doubted whoever had taken her would believe her story over the elf's—especially since she'd certainly been trying to kill the twins.

"That is none of my concern," the woman said. "You hired me to deliver her. I have done my part. Now I will have my price."

"Not quite yet, I think," the man said.

"You would forget our bargain?" The woman's voice struck a warning note.

"Patience. First I will have proof she is sufficient for my purposes. If she is not, you have brought me nothing of value."

"Have a care—"

"Enough of this. I do not answer to you, and you were best not to forget that. Leave us. I will send for you when it is time to conclude our bargain."

"Don't tarry too long, wizard," the woman said.

Wizard? Not good.... Argentia heard no footfalls, but moments later a door slammed closed.

"Tsk. For an elf, she is often very abrupt," the wizard said. "But then, she is only half elven, so we must forgive her those more human shortcomings, don't you agree, my dear?"

Argentia remained still and silent.

"Come, come. Your shamming serves no purpose. I am sure that floor cannot be comfortable." At the wizard's words, the stones beneath Argentia grew suddenly colder: a biting frost that stung her skin like a burn. She sat up sharply, hissing.

"Much better. Now we can converse like civilized people."

The wizard was a tall man—even more so because the curled tips of his shoes rested on a disc that hovered a foot or so above the floor. Argentia had seen magical serving plates that floated through the air bearing food and drink in Togril Vloth's guildhouse, but never one that could carry the weight of a person.

The wizard's arms were folded beneath a large, star-shaped diamond that hung from a platinum chain around his neck. His robes and mantle were emerald and edged with golden glyphs. Atop his head, a brimless hat split into two hornlike peaks. His face was ruddy, with white hair falling past his shoulders, and two thin points of moustache drooping past his chin, flanking a white beard forked like twin stalactites. Above a wide, prominent nose, green eyes shone smugly.

"Who the hell are you?" Argentia demanded.

The wizard's lips twitched slightly at her harsh voice. "I am Mouradian."

"Sorry, doesn't mean a whole hell of a lot to me."

"I did not expect it would. But it will. That I prom—"

"Save it. I've heard it all before." Argentia rose, glaring like a hawk, unabashed by her nakedness and refusing to give the wizard the satisfaction of any display of modesty.

"Curb your insolent tongue or I will curb it for you," Mouradian said.

"Curb this." Argentia raised her middle finger at him.

"You were warned." Mouradian lifted the diamond star off his chest. It pulsed brilliantly. Pain ripped through Argentia: a wrenching hurt such as she had never known, as if her very body was being torn inside out. She tried to scream, but the pain stole breath and vision and she was back in the black before the light in the gemstone had even dimmed.

25

"Uhhh...."

Argentia woke to what felt like the worst hangover of her life. Her head was pounding, her stomach queasy. Every breath hurt. For a few moments these sensations were so debilitating that she forgot the events immediately preceding her unconsciousness. She remembered drinking and dancing with the Gryphons at the Salty Dog and—

Vartan....

That brought her back.

Groaning, she pushed up to her knees and opened her eyes. An unfurnished, windowless stone chamber came into focus.

Mouradian was there, still hovering on his disc. "Are you ready to speak more civilly?" Mouradian asked.

Argentia pinched her fingers to the bridge of her nose. Squeezed her eyes closed. Opened them again. "Are you ready to tell me what you want and where I am?"

"Admirable will," Mouradian said, stroking the forks of his beard. "Perhaps I was not wrong after all." He was silent for a moment, and then added. "You are on Elsmywr, the Emerald Island. *My* island. Dress, and I will show it to you."

"Do I have a choice?"

Mouradian's hand went to his star gem again, but he restrained himself. "Yes, Lady Dasani," he said coldly. "You may walk with me freely as my guest, or you may walk in fetters as my prisoner. But you will walk."

"Sorry, I missed the part where you owned me," Argentia said, smiling with all the warmth of a berg in the Sea of Sleet. Her temper was roused and she was reckless of her words, of her life.

Paid for it.

A branding iron materialized in Mouradian's hand, its tip glowing white-hot. "Let me remedy that."

Argentia tried to dive aside. Mouradian waved his free hand and said, "*M'anere!*" The magic of his command froze Argentia in mid-motion.

Mouradian thrust the iron against her thigh.

Argentia's head snapped back, cords standing in her neck as her scream nearly broke her voice. Unlike the bludgeon of the diamond's magic, this pain was a piercing intensity. She heard the blistering, smelled the sick, sweet, pork stench of her searing flesh. Tears poured unchecked from her eyes as Mouradian lifted the smoking iron away and released the paralysis, letting Argentia fall in a crumpled, shuddering heap.

"You are making this very difficult for yourself, my dear," the wizard said. "Yet I want very little. Merely that you give me your company for the afternoon and evening—"

Argentia raised her head. Tears tracked down her cheeks, mucous leaked from her nose, but her eyes burned with blue fire. "I will *never*—"

Mouradian laughed at her misinterpretation. "Assuredly not. Tempting as you are, that was never my intention. No, it will be enough that you walk the island and dine with me. I think you will find I have a rather unique opportunity to offer you."

The pain in Argentia's thigh was a thing alive and screaming for her attention, but she managed to keep focused on the wizard. "What—"

"Enough. Dress. I shall return in one hour."

"Dress in what? Your little bitch didn't give me a chance to pack my wardrobe."

Mouradian raised his hands. Argentia, hurt as she'd rarely been hurt before, couldn't help flinching. Hated herself for it.

But this magic was not meant for her. It sped in a rainbow shimmer around the chamber, scouring the walls, floor, ceiling. Everywhere its glimmer fell the room was transformed from a barren cell to a lavishly appointed suite.

The stone floor became worked wood, and Argentia now lay on an oval of deeply piled rug. A great bed dominated the wall behind her. To her left, pale light filtered through drawn curtains. Stone pottery held great tropical plants similar to some she'd seen in the jungle of Za.

"I trust you will find something to your liking," Mouradian said, gesturing at a huge oaken wardrobe standing beside an iron-framed mirror. "Please avail yourself of the bath, as well," he added. Behind him, a convex wall of glass rose from a tile curb, separating the bath from the rest of the chamber.

Argentia was not sure whether the wizard was creating all these furnishings or merely revealing them from behind some aethereal veil, but it was clear Mouradian was a powerful magus. *Maybe as powerful as Ralak, or even Relsthab....*

That was a frightening thought. It tempered Argentia's hostility. She could endure whatever pain and tortures Mouradian might devise better than he imagined, but to what end? Against such a foe as this, she would need every advantage she could get. *And I've got none as long as I'm trapped in here....*

Escaping this chamber became paramount to her. Right now she didn't see any way to do that save compliance.

"Fine. Now get out," she gritted, wincing as she started to rise. "You've had enough of a show."

"One hour," Mouradian said. He hovered over to the door. It opened at a wave of his hand and swung closed behind him.

Did not lock.

Argentia smiled through the pain. Perhaps there was another way after all.

26

One hour....

Already Argentia's time was running. She meant to be long gone when the wizard returned. *First things first....*

She limped to the glass enclosure. Her thigh and hip were throbbing, but she had a handle on the pain now. The opaque partition slid on a runner set in the tile curb, admitting her to the bath. A spout carved in the shape of a Brajenti elephant's head was mounted on the wall above a sapphire and a ruby. Ordinarily a shower gave Argentia great pleasure, but she doubted this one would.

She touched the ruby. Hot water jetted down from the elephant's trunk. Argentia turned her face to the spray, letting it soak her, washing the scum of partially congealed lather from her hair, the dried blood from her cheeks, forehead, and breasts. Pain flared as the water sluiced over her injured thigh. She ground her teeth together and endured it. Bent and rubbed vigorously at her legs, which were stained red from the knees down.

There was a collection of scented soaps in a recess in the tiled wall. Argentia ignored them. Instead, she hunkered beneath the water and let it pour upon her.

Thought of Vartan.

She had terrible luck with men. From her first lover, the blademaster Toskan, on almost to her thirtieth winter, she had known nothing but trouble in her relationships. Then had come Carfax, and he had been true until he breathed his last in her arms, killed by a demon during the hellish crusade to find the Wheels of Avis-fe.

Her husband's claim on her heart had lasted beyond death, and it would never leave her, but she was flesh and blood and vital, and could not hold a ghost. Though she mourned for many moons, eventually she hazarded another man. That relationship was doomed as well: Calif Skarn's treacherous life had ended on Argentia's blade.

Now Vartan, a passion of the moment, which was all of herself she could bear to risk any more, had been murdered while making love to her. She could still feel the press of his body against her, inside her, his hands on her breasts, his lips on her throat, the bump of his head against her leg as it bobbed in the bloody water, eyes forever dulled, mouth frozen open, no more to utter laughter or rallying cries in battle or groans of pleasure—

Stop it! Just stop, Gen. Vartan was gone. All she could do was let him go. Remember the good they'd shared, however brief.

No. I can avenge him, she thought. And a few moments later: *Then get out of this shower and go do it....*

She rose and shoved the glass partition open. Left the water running behind her, partly out of spite, partly out of hope that if the wizard had guards waiting in whatever room or corridor lay beyond this one, they might believe she was still in the shower, giving her at least a chance at surprising them when she came out.

Of course, it was just as likely the wizard was spying through a magical scrying device, in which case her ploy was useless and her attempt to walk to freedom would likely go no farther than the door.

Can't worry about that. Be damned if I won't try....

There were no towels hanging on the rail beside the shower; if they were elsewhere, Argentia didn't feel like searching. She dripped across the wood floor and the plush rug, ripped the spread off the bed, dried briskly with the quilted blanket, dropped it in a heap, and stood before the mirror. In addition to her usual pair of adornments—the silver-and-sapphire ring in her navel and the brightly colored dragonfly tattoo beside the shaven arch of her mons—now there was a third: the brand.

Argentia sucked air through her teeth at the sight of the hideous M burned high on the side of her thigh. It was just beneath a line of five scars on her hip; she had a matched set on the other side, all ten remnants of the cat-woman Pantra's desperate attempt to keep from falling with her sister and Tierciel Thorne to their deaths in an icy abyss.

Unlike those pale circles, Mouradian's mark was a livid red, the flesh around it swollen and inflamed. *Son of a bitch....* Argentia gingerly touched

70

the brand. Winced. There were no balms or lotions in the chamber to ease the pain, and nothing but her blade through the wizard's heart could ease the indignity of being treated like a piece of property, a beast of labor, a slave....

Come on, Gen. Wasting time....

She turned to the wardrobe. Within its wide space, which could have held a score of outfits, was only one set of clothes. *What the hell?*

She plucked up a thong the color of a robin's breast, cut in the slim style she favored. In fact, she owned a half-dozen just like it, though none in this shade. There was also a matching lace brassiere, a pair of leather pants in brushed gold, a corset-like garment in ruby leather with gold laces up its back that reminded her of a vest she'd bought in the Floating City of Khan, and a pair of boots that looked to be dead imitations of her own save for their color: like the corset, they appeared to have been steeped in blood.

At least there's nothing with sleeves.... She dressed quickly. Every item fit perfectly. *Why am I not surprised?* She tried not to think about the creepy similarities between her own clothes and these. The implication that she had been stalked and studied for some time without ever being aware of it was not a pleasant one.

She wondered instead what had befallen poor Shadow, and if the Gryphons believed she had killed Vartan and were hunting for her to take revenge. Was she wanted for murder by Harrowgate's Watch, as she'd been wanted by Thorne and his lieutenants in Argo during the cat-women's rampage? Was she a fugitive again?

Screw it. I'll deal with that when I get back....

Argentia ran her fingers through her hair. It lay wet and heavy on her back and was going to be a tangled, knotted mess, but there was no help for it. She took a final glance in the mirror. Her throat looked naked without the dragon's tooth. Anger roiled in her again. Like Carfax, the token was lost to her now. The ranger was forever beyond her reach, but she could still recover his token—and she meant to. *Half-elf bitch, or whatever you are. I owe you for Vartan* and *that....*

It was time to start settling some scores.

27

Argentia grabbed the mirror and toppled it as hard as she could. Her luck couldn't get any worse even if the silly legend was true.

Shoving the iron frame aside, she picked through the shards until she found one that had broken in a dagger-like shape. It wasn't much, but it could cut a throat well enough.

Makeshift weapon in hand, Argentia was walking to the door when she had another inspiration. Crossing to the curtains, she flung them open. Stared in stupid surprise as what she had assumed to be the light of day blinked out.

There were no windows in the wall, just stone. The light had been a trick of Mouradian's magic: an illusion to make it seem as if a view to the outside world was available. Argentia cursed. Now she didn't even know if she was above or below ground.

She would have to use the door after all.

Before she took hold of the knob she looked for glyphs etched in the doorframe. She saw none, which didn't mean they weren't magically concealed. *Nothing I can do about that....*

Cracking the door a fraction, she waited, listening.

There was only silence.

Argentia drew the door open just a bit. There was low light from an uncertain source in what appeared to be a bare stone corridor. Argentia edged the toe of one ruby boot across the threshold. Her whole body tensed in anticipation of an aethereal barrier that would hurl her back, forbidding her passage.

Nothing happened.

She eased out into the dimness. Looked around. The corridor was empty of guards and furnishings. The light came from crystal orbs fixed into the walls. Argentia reached back and closed the door behind her. Off to the right there was a doorway that opened into a stairwell. *Up or down?*

Argentia started down, trusting the instinct that told her that despite the dungeon-like quality of the corridor, she was still above ground. One flight, then two. On each landing there had been a doorway, but Argentia ignored them. Her plan was to take the stairs all the way to their end and see where that led her.

Then she heard the footsteps.

She was halfway down the third flight. The noise was coming from below. Argentia spun back the way she'd come and dashed out of the stairwell into another corridor. This one was better lit, with a richly detailed emerald green carpet running its length, several potted plants, paintings on the walls, and a guard posted not a dozen feet from her.

The guard was armored over the left half of his body. His right side was clothed in a pale green leather jerkin and trousers. His left hand held a small shield, and a short sword was belted at his waist. A helmet with a half visor covered his head and face down to his mouth.

He saw Argentia at the same instant she saw him, but the huntress recovered from her surprise faster. Racing forward—surely the last thing the guard expected—she reached him as he fumbled to draw his sword and jabbed the shard of glass into his throat, cutting short his cry of alarm. He fell with a crash, convulsing, his metal-clad arm thrashing as he gagged and choked his life away.

Argentia whirled around, praying the din had gone unnoticed and that the stair-climbers were not making for this floor. After a few moments where she was certain she was about to be caught, the corridor remained clear and she heard no noise from the stairs.

She bent over the guard, lamenting the fact that he wore no real uniform, just the piecemeal armor and leather clothes. Nothing she could effectively disguise herself with, but his weapon would be useful.

She took the sword. It was a heavy, clumsy instrument, as different from her katana as a butter spatula from a steak knife. She would make do.

When she tried to take the guard's shield, she got a surprise. The buckler was welded to the gauntlet and there seemed to be no way to remove the armor from the guard's arm. Curious despite her dire circumstances,

Argentia tried to lift off the guard's helmet, which was stamped with the same *M* she now wore on her thigh. It would not budge.

A mystery, but one that would have to wait for another time—if ever—to be solved. She'd lingered here too long already.

Argentia entered the stairwell again. She was three more flights down and crossing a landing when a pair of figures came through the doorway to her right. With no chance to run or hide, Argentia spun to fight.

The figures were not more guards, or even people at all.

They were chasecrows: sticks and straw and hay stuffed into servants' uniforms. Their heads might once have been pumpkins or some other gourd; now they were desiccated husks, faded to a sickly gray, with thickly stitched black X's for eyes and jagged lines for mouths. They looked like any of the thousands of chasecrows Argentia had seen guarding fields in her many travels—except that they were walking, their arms full of table linens and stacks of dishware.

"Back!" Argentia hissed. She swept her blade to the ready.

The chasecrows did not heed. In fact, they gave no sign whatever that they had heard her speak, or that they even saw her there.

Wordlessly, they passed by, their movements a series of jerks and shuffles as they continued their awkward passage down the steps, leaving dry, dusty bits and pieces of themselves behind.

Heart pounding, Argentia watched them go. *Where in the hell am I?* It was like she'd entered some madman's twisted version of reality, for surely no one of sound mind could envision servants such as these hideous things.

She started after the chasecrows, keeping a half-flight behind. Their pace was much slower than hers had been, but they would make a barrier between her and anyone coming up, and if anyone came from behind, she could barrel through the chasecrows easily enough—she hoped.

Luck was with her, however, and she never had to learn the answer to that question. Another three floors down, the chasecrows departed into a corridor. One last, long flight brought Argentia to the end of the stairs.

She emerged in a sort of hall: a large circular space with a ceiling some thirty feet above her head and hung with rows of iron chandeliers. At the opposite end of the hall were huge bronze doors, tarnished green by age and exposure. Whether they led out of this prison or deeper in, Argentia couldn't be sure. *But I'm going to find out....*

The sides of the hall were lined with alcoves. From some of these Argentia heard voices and saw the moving shadows of whatever people were in those rooms, but there was no one in the hall itself. She thought she could make it to the doors before anyone even realized she was there. *If I'm fast enough....*

She almost was.

As she sprinted out from the stairwell, going straight and hard for the doors, she was spotted by a guard who saw the blur of her passage as he looked up in frustration from the game of Lineage he'd been losing badly. He gave a startled cry and rose, knocking the table and scattering the deck of cards.

By the time he and the other guards got out of their alcoves, Argentia was already at the doors. *Please, please open!* She slapped her palms to the bronze. Pushed with all her might.

As imposing as the door appeared, it moved on well-oiled hinges, opening so smoothly that Argentia was almost sent sprawling. Sunlight flooded over her: brilliant, blinding. Argentia flung an arm across her eyes, staggering outside.

She spun and slammed the door closed. Thrust the sword through the hollows behind the handles: a makeshift door-bar. Wheeling around, she squinted against the glare of blazing afternoon, trying to get her bearings before the guards, who were cursing her and rattling the doors violently, finally shook the sword free or managed to sound a general alarm.

She stood on a stone platform at the base of an ivy-wreathed stone tower. There was a bridge before her, arcing over some great pit that might have been a quarry. On the far side of the bridge stood a collection of stone buildings. Beyond those was a vale ringed with verdant, woody hills. Forms moved about here and there—guards on patrol, she guessed—but none in were her vicinity.

She ran for the bridge.

28

Argentia was half way across the span when the alarum sounded.

Damn it! She spared a glance back. The sword had finally shaken free of the handles. She saw the pursuit from the tower: six armored men and a quartet of larger figures that she thought might be orcs. Then she was running on, the path narrow beneath her feet, a long fall into a pit full of stone convolutions awaiting her first misstep.

The alarum sounded again. Argentia lowered her head and sprinted. If she could just get across the span before the arrows started flying or guards showed up to block the far end of the bridge, she might have a chance.

But there were no arrows from the tower, and though there was a commotion from the buildings beyond the pit, she crossed the bridge without opposition. Another glance over her shoulder showed her that she was still being pursued, but had gained some distance.

The problem was where to go next.

Her immediate surroundings were barrack-like compounds, stone-and-thatch huts, and a fenced coop where colorful chickens roved. A short stone wall separated the strange village from fields of crops in full flourish. Beyond the fields, an expanse of emerald mead rolled to another, taller stone wall. On the far side of the wall, the tree-crowded hills blocked out whatever might lay past them.

Have to get to those hills.... Argentia had no idea how big the wizard's island might be, but the forested hills at least would afford her some cover, and perhaps even a place she could hide while she worked out a way off Elsmywr.

Several orcish guards emerged from the huts. They pointed, snorting in whatever passed for language among them. Argentia veered left, hustling around the far corner of a building that appeared to be a barn or granary. Momentarily out of sight from both the tower pursuit and the village guards, she stopped and took stock of her situation. It was risky to pause at all with her enemies closing in and the alarum sure to rouse Mouradian's attention—if it hadn't already—but if she continued running blind she was going to end up blundering into a corner and getting caught for sure.

She bent forward, panting, hands on her thighs. *Focus, Gen....* She looked around. There were fields ahead: tall shafts of golden wheat, mighty stalks of corn, and a great vegetable garden, all segregated by waist-high walls of mossy stone. Though it was deep in winter's chill across the rest of Teranor, it was summer-hot on Elsmywr, and the crops were thriving. She saw figures moving systematically among the rows of corn. The bright sun flashed off their scythes as they rose and descended, reaping.

To the left were more huts and a construction of wood and stone that looked like some half-formed siege tower. Several huge birds winged above it. Beyond that, nothing but open yard until the boundary wall.

To the right was a massive warehouse. She couldn't see past it, but maybe—

Running steps, just around the corner.

Argentia bolted for the cornfield. The first strafe of arrows cut the air around her, one slicing just above her shoulder. *Too close!* Argentia dodged left and right as she ran. A second volley chased her, but the shots all missed badly. She put on a final burst of speed. Hurtled the low wall, crashing into the tall corn stalks, which were much stronger than she'd imagined, and dealt her a painful thrashing as she fell down to the wet earth.

A third flight of arrows followed her, thwacking and snicking through the corn like deadly sleet. Argentia crawled hard to her left. Grinned when the next spray of missiles fell well behind her and to the right. Toskan had taught her that most people were right-handed and subconsciously favored that direction when attacking.

She slithered over mucky earth until she was deep in the corn, and then stopped. The plants rose up tall above and about her, hemming her in: a world of corn, forever and ever. Its smell, starchy and dank, was overwhelming. The plants were not silent: they rustled and whispered with a life of their own. Argentia felt a strange, almost malevolent sentience about the field, as if the corn would betray her if it could.

The pursuers smashed their way into the field, bludgeoning a path with their heavy weapons. Argentia could not see them, but heard them fanning out from the place where she'd entered.

Can't stay here.... Argentia gathered herself into a crouch, hesitated one last second, and ran blindly through the corn, arms crossed before her face to protect against the slapping leaves.

Guttural shouts, the language unintelligible but the meaning clear: she'd been spotted.

God damn it! Argentia veered several rows to the left. The guard was a shape trailing to her right, closing fast. Up ahead, a chasecrow was swinging its scythe, creating a reap path. Argentia ducked under the sweep of the tool and tackled the creature to the ground, feeling the crunch of dried twigs and straw beneath her.

She grabbed the scythe out of its stick-finger hands and scrambled to her feet. She'd never wielded a scythe in her life, and if she had a weakness with weapons, it was pole-arms. She hefted it anyway, feeling the awkward, forward-balanced weight of the thing, and whirled around, already swinging.

The guard only had time to throw his arms up in surprise before the scythe buried itself in his chest, piercing his leather armor and driving him down. He gave a porcine cry: a noise Argentia had only heard before from a spitted boar. Blood sprayed from his fleshy lips, spattering an ugly face dominated by a pig's snout and bristly chin. His fat body jerked once and went still.

Argentia released the scythe—it was too cumbersome to run with— and spun around.

The chasecrow struck at her with its stick-straw hands.

Even surprised as she was, Argentia was quick enough to dodge the assault by stepping backwards, but her boot caught the scythe's haft and she fell into the corn, breaking stalks and hitting the ground hard. The chasecrow loomed, moaning hideously as it reached for her. Argentia kicked out with both feet. Her boots crunched the chasecrow's chest and sent it flying across the reap path.

Argentia was up before the chasecrow hit the ground. She heard the guards closing in. Ran again, breaking through the last yards of corn and vaulting over the wall.

The drop caught her by surprise. She lost her balance as she landed on a grassy incline that descended steeply to the empty expanse of meadow. Stumbling a little, she righted herself and raced on.

The rich, green grass was knee-high. After the cornfield, the open space of the mead was glorious, the mild breeze flowing across it an invigoration. Argentia's stride lengthened. When she had put good distance between her and the field she dared to glance back.

There was no pursuit.

Far from relaxing, Argentia went harder still, flying over the springy ground. Only speed would save her now, and she was determined to make good on her flight.

The outer wall rose to block her way: thirty towering feet of rough-hewn stone. She threw herself at it, leaping as high as she could, reaching for handholds—

Passed clean through the stone.

Argentia fell to the ground, tumbling over in surprise. She sat up, shaking her head. The wall stood behind her, apparently solid. She reached out. Her hand vanished into the seeming stone. *Illusion! But why?*

Then the cold wind blew over her and she looked around and understood. The illusory wall marked the barrier of the wizard's climatic magic. Within its confines, the island was an idyll of perpetual summer. Without, the same winter that swept over the rest of Teranor also touched Elsmywr. The grass lay low and sere. The wooded hills, which had appeared so greenly alive, were barren climbs whose tall, skeletal trees were shaken of their leaves.

But they were still her safest path.

Argentia stood and started running again. The ground began to rise. Long shadows ran out from the trees to greet her.

She passed into the woods.

Heard the baying of the hounds.

29

"Oh for Aeton's sake—not dogs!" Argentia gasped.

She ducked into the first rows of trees. There was still no pursuit in sight. It might take the dogs some time to get her scent in the corn, but she had left a damning path across the meadow: trampled grass the most novice tracker could have followed without hounds to mark the way.

I can still make it....

Then quit wasting time....

Argentia caught a deep breath and started up the hillside. The woods were close about her and dim, as woods will grow towards the fall of day, full of gathered darkness and sunless tracts. Brambles and scrub brush, undaunted by the dead season, struck at her legs as if trying to trip her up. She went in a broken pattern, here and there doubling back, scuffing fallen leaves along her trail before heading up the hill again at a different point. If they were going to hunt her down, she was going to make them work for it.

Farther up the hill, the ground grew rocky. Boulders jutted amid the trees. Argentia scrambled over as many of these as she found in her path, hoping to further confuse her trail.

Up and up she went, picking her way as fast as she could, her unflagging determination supporting limbs heavy with exertion. Her breath came in cold gasps. Her sweat reeked of liquor. All the drinking at the Salty Dog, coupled with the fact that, excepting the period of unconsciousness that had followed her teleport, she'd not had true sleep in two days, had exhausted her more swiftly than might otherwise have been the case.

She persevered. Once she was free of the island, she promised herself she would sleep for three days straight before she even considered moving, but until she was away and safe, there would be no rest, and certainly no succumbing to weariness. *No, never....*

Argentia looked up suddenly. The woods had gone quiet.

Before she could dare to hope, the racket of the hounds lifted to her again, much nearer now than before.

Argentia mustered a last sprint, dodging and darting between trees. There was a break in the forest ahead, with the deep evening sky beyond, the sun setting in a smear of magenta clouds.

Made it!

The forest ended on a crest of thin grass and stone. Argentia ran to its edge. There she stopped, heedless of the pursuit, heedless of the wind coldly scouring her, heedless of all but the vista of her doom.

The hill ran down to a beachhead. Dark water rushed against bone-white sands. Beyond the breakline, a ring of jagged coral reefs and atolls poked like defensive battlements. Then there was only ocean as far as Argentia could see. No other islands. No hint of a mainland. *Nothing....*

Worse, there was no port, not even a fishing village with a single wooden pier, or any sign of a boat that she might commandeer or bargain her way onto to escape.

Despair dragged at Argentia's heart like a rusty anchor. She fought it. *Maybe on the other side of the island—*

Her desperate thought was interrupted by clapping.

30

Argentia spun around.

"Enjoying the view, my dear?" Mouradian asked, still clapping as he floated nearer on his disc. "I assure you, there is no way off Elsmywr save through my making."

Argentia dodged away from Mouradian, feinting toward the forest only to whirl and fling herself at the wizard, reaching for his throat.

Mouradian raised a glowing palm. The air before him solidified in a wall of aether. Argentia hit the glimmering barrier and crashed to the ground. "Why do you persist in this foolishness?" the wizard asked.

The pursuit burst from the trees. The orcish guards surrounded Argentia. All of them had blades leveled at her. Several held leashes to restrain the growling creatures that she had taken for dogs when she heard their barking. Now she saw they were men gone to all fours, their features hideously distorted blends of human and canine: long snouts and wet black noses, but men's brows and eyes and hair, like werewolves caught mid-transformation. They snarled and strained against their leashes, revealing mouths full of crooked black fangs.

Argentia scrambled to her feet. One of the porcine guards, surprised by the quick move, let its leash out. A dog-man lunged at Argentia. She kicked it in the face and it crumpled with a canine yelp. The guards raised their weapons.

"Enough!" Mouradian commanded. "I told you she was not to be harmed."

"Yar, Magus," the leader of the guards grunted. He was a massive creature, taller and broader than the largest orc Argentia had ever seen, with pale, bristling jowls, tusks overrunning his lips, and a meanness to his narrow, close-set eyes. He barked an order in the strange language that was not orcish but certainly no form of Tradespeak Argentia had ever heard. The ring of guards drew back a pace.

"What do you want?" Argentia demanded. She was wary of the orcs—or whatever they were—but her gaze kept straying back to the dog-men, all of whom wore pants and shirts of burlap and sat on their haunches. On their bare calves she saw the too-familiar M brand.

"No more or less than I told you before," Mouradian said. "I have a proposition for you. One that I am even more eager to make now that you performed so splendidly in the little test I arranged."

"What—"

"Bind her," the wizard commanded.

The guards pressed in. Argentia struggled wildly, but the guards were too strong and too many. Her arms were twisted behind her back and locked there with heavy manacles. She heard a length of chain fall to the ground behind her. "God damn you! Let me go!"

"Come, Lady Dasani." Mouradian laughed and gestured at the dog-men. "Much like my hounds, you are entirely too dangerous to trust without a leash. Now, let us to dinner."

31

Argentia's return to captivity was one of the most difficult walks of her life.

Worse than being a prisoner again was the harsh truth that she had never really been escaping. The wizard had intentionally left the door unlocked. He had been testing her, and she had played right into his little game.

She brooded most of the way down the hill, berating herself for being a fool, until finally Carfax's ghostly voice intruded. *Hush. You've been in worse waters...*

Argentia rallied to his voice again. She thought of fighting the twins in the dark in Vloth's Frost Palace, and the bridge beneath that pyramid, where she had hung over the abyss, tethered to life by only her whip and the strength of her grip. Of Hollowdale, waiting in a root cellar to be hanged by villagers gone mad. Of walking the plank of the pirate ship *Red Tide*. Of the vampyr's Bastion in Bracken Swamp and the delves of Darvandurm, where the Deep Spiders dwelt. Of the crypt of the Revenant King in the Wastes of Yth. Of boating past the Crashing Cliffs and down the rapids of the Drakbra. Of the dragon's den and the cave atop Mount Hoarde, where she had faced the demon.

She had survived all those things and countless more just as dangerous or worse. Sometimes her friends had been with her, others she had hazarded alone. Always she had survived. It was her nature.

Argentia raised her head and took stock of her situation, reminding herself that her original course had been cooperation until a chance to escape presented itself. That plan still rang true. The wizard clearly had no immediate intent to kill her. Was it possible he had no plans to harm her at all? *Didn't he mention some proposition?*

She was sure she would learn soon enough. In the interim, she would abide.

So resolved, Argentia turned her attention once more to the island and her captors, trying to glean any bit of information that she might turn against the wizard when the time was ripe.

They descended the hill and exited the forest, passing through the illusory wall into the temperate domain of the island wizard. Mouradian floated before the group as they crossed the meadow. The guards stomped along in a moving circle with Argentia as its center. The four dog-handlers and their charges marched off to one side.

The more Argentia studied the guards, the more certain she was that they were not orcs. *At least not true orcs....* There was too much of men in their forms. Their hands were human, not thick-fingered and clawed like an orc's, and their smooth pink flesh—the M was branded on their forearms, Argentia noted—was wholly unlike the greens and blacks of orc hides. Their faces were not precisely orcan, either, with porcine snouts and jaws and floppy ears.

Even more strange and troubling, however, were the creatures Mouradian had called his hounds. In all her travels, Argentia had never seen or heard of such things. She'd companied with a werefox for a time, and had even seen her transform into something half-woman, half-animal, but these creatures seemed fixed in some awful condition wherein their forms were mostly human, their behavior mostly canine. They went on all fours, heads low, hips high, in a clambering gait that looked agonizing just to watch.

Not even a world of werewolves, gryphons, and dragons could produce such abortive nightmares as these. *Then what are they?* Argentia's eyes narrowed suspiciously as they fell upon Mouradian.

They crossed back into the compound, circumventing the fields rather than retracing Argentia's path through the corn. Ahead were the simple huts and the incomplete wooden tower with those giant eagles Argentia had glimpsed during her escape circling above it.

A small form winged through the dusk towards them. It was a flying monkey. Monkeys were rare in Teranor, though Argentia had seen a few at gypsy carnivals and many more when she journeyed south to the Sudenlands, where the little animals were as ubiquitous as dogs and cats.

She'd never seen one like this, however, with ragged bat wings sprouting from its shoulders, a curling tail that was as hairless as a rat's, and patches of leathery scales marring its fur.

The monkey landed on Mouradian's shoulder. It gave Argentia an evil glance and a hiss when it felt the scrutiny of her gaze, and then began chittering and gesticulating wildly to the wizard.

"Very well," Mouradian said. He turned to Argentia. "We must detour for a moment, my dear. I am afraid there has been an accident."

32

Mouradian led the way to the wooden tower. As they drew closer, Argentia saw that the platforms were piled with gathered sticks, like great aeries. She wondered what their purpose was.

Ahead, a trio of flying monkeys flitted like giant gnats around a pair of tall men. The men were long-haired, naked save for loin cloths, slender of limb but powerfully built through the chest and torso, with great eagles' wings furled upon their backs.

My God! Argentia looked skyward again. In the last of the light she saw that what she had earlier mistaken for eagles were in fact more of these winged men, soaring and wheeling through the perfect dusk sky like the divae said to populate the highest reaches of Aelysium. Their forms were mostly shadow now, but that could not steal the majestic grace from their motions: a haunting beauty that sang of freedom from the bondage of earth.

A pair of porcine guards dragged a mangled form out from the shadows at the base of the tower. Argentia saw it was another of the bird people: a young woman. Like the men, she wore only a loin cloth. One of her wings was shattered, splinters of wood and sticks pierced her bare breasts and belly, and half her face was covered with blood.

"What happened here?" Mouradian asked. His tone was cold.

One of the birdmen stepped forward. "Magus, sister Ak'tali missed her landing." His voice was high and clear, his eyes somber. His skin was bronze, his face hawkish, and Argentia saw that what had appeared to be hair was really a crest of gorgeous brown-gold feathers that swept back from his brow and hung down his neck. His hands flexed and contracted in consternation; his fingers were tipped with long, curving claws, as were the toes of his feet. "She struck a nest."

Mouradian frowned. "The hatchlings?"

"Three were killed, Magus." The birdman bowed his head.

Mouradian stroked one of the long white tines of his moustache. "Pity," he said. "They are something of a work in progress, so some setbacks must be expected," he continued. He might have been speaking to Argentia, or merely musing aloud. "Though it is strange that the women have never flown so well as the men. Something in the pectoral construction, perhaps. Nonetheless, this one has paid for her folly."

Argentia, meanwhile, was still looking at Ak'tali. The birdwoman's eyes fluttered weakly. "She's alive!" Argentia exclaimed. Pushing through the guards before they could grab her, she knelt beside the broken creature. With her hands manacled behind her, there was nothing she could do to help, but she bent close to Ak'tali, smelling her feathery, moultish scent, leaning as close to her face as she could. "Hang on! You'll be all right," she urged. Looking up at Mouradian, she said, "You have to help her."

"Death were best," the magus said.

"No! You can heal her. I know you can. You made her," Argentia said, taking a stab she felt certain would hit true. The birdmen wore the M that she had realized was Mouradian's signature branded upon their chests. "Don't let her suffer."

"Why should I ease her pain? Why should I reward her for destroying my work? Three hatchlings. Have you any concept—" Mouradian waved his hand. "No, it will be death."

"Then you will go through me to kill her," Argentia said defiantly. She held her place before the birdwoman, gambling that, for whatever reason, the wizard needed her alive.

Mouradian studied her for a moment. "Very well," he said. "If you wish her to live, so be it. Once she is healed, amputate her wings," he instructed the guards. "Let her serve out her days with the sheep in the scullery, with ever only the memory of flight to sustain her."

At his sentence, Ak'tali opened her eyes—yellow orbs stained with pain—and uttered a feeble squawk of protest.

"Bastard!" Argentia snarled.

"I did not kill her, did I?" Mouradian said. On his shoulder, the flying monkey cackled. "Bring her," the magus said to the guards.

Argentia was dragged to her feet. She saw the other guards bear Ak'tali off, and briefly met the gazes of the two birdmen before she was herded across the compound. Was that silent gratitude or hatred in their hawkish eyes? She didn't know.

Twilight lay heavy upon the island. Magical light radiated from crystal clusters set along the footpaths to guide their passage. Ahead was the cavernous hole with the tower rising from its middle: an island upon an island. Four stone bridges crossed the great gap, intersecting at the tower's base. The tower itself was an ivy-wrapped stone column. Its top was crowned with turrets. It had no windows that Argentia could see. Escape would be by the doors, or not at all.

"My labyrinth," Mouradian said, tipping a hand towards the stone convolutions in the bottom of the pit as they crossed the span to the tower. "It is well your little escapade did not lead in that direction. No one who has dared enter that maze has ever reached its center alive."

If this impressed Argentia, she made no show of it. They continued in a silence that held until they had climbed the tower's many steps and arrived at her cell-chamber. Mouradian nodded at one of the guards, who unchained Argentia and shoved her unceremoniously inside. The blanket had been replaced on her bed. The shards of glass had been swept from the floor, but no new mirror stood in place of the toppled one. The water was not running in the shower.

"Dinner will be in one-half hour," the wizard said. "Please do something about that filthy outfit." A gesture of his hand and the door swung closed.

This time, it locked.

33

Argentia screamed.

It was a noise of primal frustration that ripped through the chamber as she fell to her knees on the thick rug. When its echo had died she screamed again, and then again, loosing all her anger at the wizard, at the half-elf, at herself upon the air.

She snapped to her feet, breathing hard, glaring about for something to destroy. She'd already wrecked the mirror, and the room contained no other objects. There was not even so much as a lamp. The light, vanished from the illusory windows with the fall of day, now came from a row of small crystals set along the ceiling's molding. Finally she seized a pillow from the bed and bashed it against the wall until its seams burst and the feather stuffing flew about her in a cloud.

Still angry, Argentia flung the dead pillow aside and paced hard about the chamber, trying to settle her thoughts. But the episode with Ak'tali had so incensed her that she didn't want to even pretend to cooperate with the wizard. Mouradian was clearly a madman, and whatever offer he was going to make to her was surely intended to end in her death. *He can't let me go. Not after what I've seen....*

Even so, Argentia had no intention of playing the wizard's little game. How she was going escape, however, remained a problem. Mouradian was one step ahead of her at every turn. What she'd seen of the island had shown her how isolated she was, but little else.

No, there was something....

It seemed to her that there had been an answer there somewhere: one useful thing the wizard had said that would allow her to turn all this in her favor. It tickled at the back of her mind, just out of her grasp. She let it go, trusting she would catch it when the time was right.

Meanwhile, she was doing herself no good at all stuck in this chamber. She had to be free of its confinement, even within the tower.

Though it was the last thing in the world she wanted to do, that meant going to dinner.

Argentia stripped and stepped into the shower again, smirking when she saw several towels hanging from the rail on the wall. The water was still blessedly hot. It washed away the filth of the cornfield, the clinging stench of the pig guards, and the sheen of her own sweat. Argentia grew calmer under the stinging spray. Her mind became clear, focused.

She washed vigorously with a lavender soap, until the steamy air behind the glass partition was flooded with its scent. She'd used her body to her advantage before. Deplorable as the idea was, if seducing the wizard gave her the chance to escape or kill him, she would do it. Based on Mouradian's reaction to her initial protestation, she didn't think it would come to that, but it never hurt to be prepared.

She cut the water. Toweled off. Stretched her arms up and rolled her head from side to side, relieving a crick in her neck.

This time, she found a gown in the wardrobe. With it was a pair of shiny black sandals that laced to mid-calf and another thong: gold this time, with a bright green dragonfly embroidered on the front. *For somebody who claimed he didn't want to lay me, he pays a hell of a lot of attention to my underwear,* Argentia thought as she stepped into the thong. *But maybe that's to my favor....*

The gown was not. Cut of a rich silk, with emerald-and-gold beadwork so fine it looked like the pebbled skin of a serpent, it was a sleeveless, backless sheath that hugged the curves of her hips and legs like a shadow, virtually pinning them together at the knees, where the beadwork ended and tiers of emerald taffeta and lace fell to the floor.

The fit was so exacting that Argentia had to take the dress off and tie on the sandals first. In the gown, she couldn't bend her legs enough to reach her feet. "Which was just the point," she muttered as she ran her fingers through her wet hair. The dress limited her motion severely. Running was impossible; she could barely walk. With no sleeves or gloves or accessories, there was no way she could conceal a weapon even if she could find one.

Once again, Mouradian had checked her. *But he'll slip,* she reassured herself. *He will. Even if it's just once—and I'll be ready....*

34

Precisely one-half hour after the door had locked, it opened again.

Mouradian had sent six guards for Argentia. The armored men were apparently custodians of the tower. She was struck by the similitude among them as they escorted her down to dinner. The piecemeal armor was the same, which was understandable, but their bodies were also alike in height and shape, right down to a twisting scar on each man's jaw.

Twins, she mused, thinking of Puma and Pantra. She wondered if the cat-women had an encircled M brand somewhere on their feline forms. If what she surmised was so, and the creatures on this island were the products of some hideous magical experimentation by Mouradian, had the twins also been created here? Was that why the wizard was seeking vengeance for them?

If that's really what he wants with me....

She had assumed upon hearing the wizard speak of her killing the twins that revenge was his intent, but now she bore his mark on her flesh, just like all the other things she'd encountered on the island. Was there some worse fate he had in mind for her than balancing the scales of the cat-women's lives with her own?

Guess I'll find out....

Nine flights down from Argentia's cell, they came to the dining chamber. A rectangular table that could seat twenty dominated the space. Argentia doubted there would ever be so many visitors to this forsaken place; the table was just another show of Mouradian's grandiosity. Three arrangements of Fantostian lilies in crystal vases sectioned the table, and pewter candelabras stood between each, giving the room a dim, suspiciously romantic light. Argentia wondered if she might use the candlesticks as weapons. *Maybe the candles, too....*

There were only two places set, both at the far end of the table. From the head seat, Mouradian rose to greet Argentia. "An Emerald Lady for the Emerald Island," he said. "Splendid, my dear."

"Whatever."

"Leave us," the wizard instructed. The guards departed. Mouradian motioned and the seat to his right slid out. "Join me, please."

Argentia came forward, exaggerating the difficulty the gown was giving her in walking, but not very much: she was well-fettered by the fashion. When she was seated, the chair moved her to the table.

Mouradian remained standing, studying Argentia. She returned his gaze coolly, though it burned in her to demand whether his mother had never taught him it was rude to stare. The bodice of her gown was heart-shaped with a subtle corset pushing her bust up, affording a generous view of the deep cleavage between the ripe mounds of her breasts. The wizard spared more than one glance there, but they were more the looks of an artist impressed with his craft than leers of desire. "Yes, splendid," he repeated. "But I do not fancy your hair so."

He raised a glowing hand. Argentia gasped as her tangled tresses lifted and piled atop her head. The damp of the shower vanished, and she was left with hair that she could tell even without touching was perfectly coiffed.

"There. Now you are exquisite," Mouradian assessed.

Argentia bit back a caustic remark. Mouradian had just fixed her hair; he might as easily use his magic to shear it off instead.

Satisfied, the wizard sat, and the meal began.

The service was on fine porcelain dishware the color of whipped curds and rimmed with emerald. The goblets were cut crystal, the utensils gleaming silver.

The servers were almost women.

Dressed as maids, they were plump, buxom lasses with curling hair like golden fleece, more silky and beautiful than any Argentia had ever seen. Their eyes were long-lashed, wide, brown, and kind, if touched with timorousness, but there the humanity of their faces ended. Where should have been noses and mouths were the sad, round snouts of sheep.

The ewes went dutifully about their tasks, bringing white wine, water, bread, and a salad of red and green lettuces, tomatoes, and mushrooms in a mustard dressing. Argentia's stomach growled. She'd not eaten since the Salty Dog, and she was famished. As much as she wanted to deny any debt to the wizard's hospitality, pragmatism overrode pride. She needed to eat, and she doubted she would have a better chance than this in the near future.

She lifted a fork. Attacked the salad. It was delicious—something she would find true without exception of every course that followed.

"I imagine that you must be wondering why I brought you here," Mouradian said at length.

"Puma and Pantra," Argentia said flatly.

"My twins, yes," the magus acknowledged. "I did so desire to meet their killer."

"You've met me. Now let me go."

"I think not. Not yet, at least," Mouradian said.

Argentia shrugged and watched eagerly as an ewe spooned a bowlful of pumpkin soup from a tureen. Mouradian continued talking. "As you no doubt have guessed from what you have seen of my little domain, I am a creator of things. The Great Maker—that's what they called me." His eyes narrowed, and Argentia had the feeling Mouradian was not reliving a particularly pleasant memory.

"The twins were perhaps my best work—though I shortly hope to surpass even their excellence—but they were not my first. I began more humbly than that. Ever have I understood what my more obtuse brethren refused to acknowledge: the power of the aether is the power to shape life, even to create life. They would not trespass upon such grounds, upon such 'hallowed and sacred mysteries,' as they called them. 'Playing at gods,' they said of my work. How right they were, for here upon Elsmywr, what is Mouradian, if not a very god!"

The wizard's eyes glowed. Argentia tensed to dodge whatever explosion of magic was about to come. But Mouradian calmed. "Forgive me. The folly of my brethren is a vexation with me still, though not one that shall trouble me much longer." He gave a brief shake of his head. "So, then. The beginning...."

The Island Wizard spoke.

Argentia ate, and listened, and found it very madness.

35

It began from small things. Inanimate things.

The art of wielding the aether to create great golems of stone or steel was lost to all save the dwarves, in whom the crafting magic ran deep, but breathing motion and function to common items was readily practiced among Teranor's magi. Argentia had seen such magic employed in Togril Vloth's guild and at Lord Blakney's manor, and she had battled gargoyles and animated suits of armor, so she was scarcely surprised that Mouradian's initial foray into perverting creation had been the chasecrows.

"In their function they are ideal," Mouradian said, pausing to fork a blackened piece of squash. They were on their third course: grilled chicken, liberally salted and herbed, in a wine sauce over rice and seared vegetables. Argentia had nearly cleaned her plate. "And that is precisely their shortcoming," the wizard continued. "They will perform any task unfailingly, but once directed, they cannot be diverted except by explicit command."

That, Argentia realized, explained why the chasecrows had ignored her on the stairs and why the one had attacked her in the cornfield. In taking its scythe, she had prevented it from completing the reaping.

"They tend to wear down physically, though their parts are easily replaced," Mouradian added. "These days I use them mostly as laborers and for menial work in my tower. I find my ewes much better at domestic tasks—but I move ahead of my tale."

After the chasecrows came the first of the bonding experiments, using magic to merge animate and inanimate material into a functional whole. The results were the tower guards. Their metal limbs were not encased in armor; they were steel prosthetics replacing amputated flesh and bone. The plate mail on their torsos and heads was fused to their flesh. Attempts to fully armor the guards had failed, their bodies unable to survive the shock of the synthesis, but Mouradian claimed the guards were nonetheless more formidable in battle because they were fearless of one half their bodies.

"I killed one with a piece of glass," Argentia said. She couldn't resist the jab.

Mouradian gave her a hard stare. "Yes, and proved only what I already knew."

"That you need better guards?" Argentia flashed an irreverent smile. Provoking the wizard might be dangerous, but it might also present her an opportunity to attack.

Mouradian only nodded. "Precisely. In a sense, that has been my entire project."

His success at merging man and metal prompted Mouradian to discover other ways to improve the human form. "Animal attributes readily suggested themselves. Men could be stronger, faster, more cunning."

"Puma and Pantra," Argentia reasoned, sipping on her wine while one of the ewes cleared away her empty plate.

"Not quite yet, my dear. It is comparatively easy to combine flesh with steel or wood or stone. But flesh to flesh is a more subtle art. I spent decades researching the process, creating new spells, refining old ones. When I began, it was from nature's template, by combining two animal forms."

Thus the flying monkeys were born.

It was not a perfect union. The virulence of the magic that had joined the monkeys with birds or bats had left them ragged things, but they had adapted to their new mobility with ease and served as overseers of the island.

"Then came the true tests: men and animals." Mouradian did not give Argentia the details of his experiments—how he came upon the power to hybridize species, or how his magic mirrors and other trinkets were sold to purchase the women who served to gestate these monstrosities—though he did speak of the rapid development of the offspring, which in the main reached maturity in three years, much more like animals than men, and of the difficult nature of his art.

"Half the offspring are stillborn. Of those that do deliver, only one in four will survive to maturity. It is a process in continual refinement," Mouradian said.

"It's madness," Argentia muttered over a spoonful of whipped chocolate.

"What was that?"

Argentia pointed the spoon at Mouradian. "You heard me. Madness."

Mouradian's pale green eyes narrowed dangerously. "Well. You shall view it as you see fit, of course. Bring the esp," he snapped at a nearby ewe. That got Argentia's attention. "Surprised, my dear?" Mouradian smiled a cool smile. "The elves are not the only ones to have mastered the secrets of that bean, I assure you. But to return to my account of my so-called madness..."

He spoke on as if Argentia's opinion mattered less to him than hearing the catalogue of his achievements. His first meld of man and beast had been the ewes. "Simple-minded serving wenches, easy enough to make and to control. It was when I moved to more aggressive species—pigs, for instance—that I began to encounter difficulties in temperament. The gatarines are intelligent enough, but they require constant discipline and militaristic drilling in their formative years to understand their place. They have great capacities for cruelty, to say nothing of their appetites."

Mouradian paused to let the ewes pour the esp. It sat dark and steaming in the porcelain cups, its scent of roasted pecans tantalizing to Argentia. Carfax had introduced her to the drink. A cousin of the more common caf, it was rarely to be had outside the even rarer company of elves. Esp had certain properties, perhaps magic, perhaps simply of the beans, that heightened reflexes and awareness for brief periods. *Couldn't hurt now....* Besides, she loved esp.

Mouradian had resumed speaking. After the gatarines came the hounds. "Good trackers but hardly the most functional of creatures, and prone to many illnesses."

The birdmen were his latest essay. "Flight is problematic, especially for the females, as you witnessed. They are slow to learn and there are very few of them. That is why the deaths of three hatchlings was such a blow today."

Argentia took a long swallow of esp and showed no sympathy whatever. Again, Mouradian seemed not to care. He merely continued his tale and came, at last, to the cat-women.

36

"Felines were the hardest project, one I was ultimately forced to abandon." Mouradian grimaced at this admission. "Many women did not survive the mating process. Those that did and carried to term...the tiger whelps are born more developed than most other species. They had a nasty tendency to eat their mothers at birth, after which they were ungovernable and had to be destroyed. Breedings with lions were all stillborn, as were those with cougars—save Puma and Pantra.

"It was, I suspect, something in the nature of their twinship that allowed the process to work. As you no doubt noted, they were rare in that their features were mostly human, while these others are almost all dominated by their animal components. I believe the sharing of the feline seed diluted it enough to make the births viable, but I am not certain and I have never been able to replicate the results.

"At all events, I took personal charge of Puma and Pantra. They were raised as my daughters, and were my prizes. Amazing creatures. You will never know how hard it was for me to part with them—or to learn of their deaths."

There was a decidedly threatening turn to the wizard's voice at the last phrase, but Argentia, who despite her outward stoicism had been listening to Mouradian's account with mounting horror, wasn't listening any longer.

Amazing creatures....

Amazing....

A maze....

Argentia came to her feet so suddenly she toppled the chair behind her. The ewes made startled noises, and even Mouradian looked at her with some surprise. "Going somewhere, my dear? A more pressing or interesting engagement, perhaps?" He rose as well. Two of the armored men appeared in the doorway at the far end of the chamber.

"Look—whatever you think, I didn't kill those two bitches," Argentia said. "I would have, but someone else beat me to it. He's dead now, and past your vengeance."

"Do not presume to know the reaches of my vengeance," Mouradian replied. His quick retort hid a dark thought. *If she did not kill the twins, perhaps I have wasted my efforts. Shrike did say she was easily taken...* He frowned. *Yet she was most intrepid in reaching the end of the island....*

"You've got the wrong girl," Argentia said. "So why don't you make this easy on all of us and just let me go?"

"I hardly think that's possible now, my dear."

"Then let's make a deal."

"You are in no position to offer me terms of dealing."

"Call it a challenge, then," Argentia said, plunging ahead. "Your little maze you're so proud of—I'll beat it."

Mouradian laughed. "I very much doubt that."

"When I do, you set me free. If I fail, I'll do whatever it is you took me to do. That's the deal."

The magus was silent, stroking his moustache as he considered. "You will not reach the door at the center of the maze alive."

"I will." Argentia's cobalt eyes blazed with unshakable confidence.

"Such spirit," Mouradian said. "So be it. You will have from tomorrow's dawn until full set of sun to reach the center. If you fail, you are subject to my will. If you fall, that renders moot all proceedings, of course. If you succeed, I shall release you, with the understanding that a spell shall be cast upon you to make you forgetful of your time here. I have many enemies and my work must remain secret."

Argentia nodded. "I reach the center and you return me to Harrowgate, alive and unharmed and unchanged—immediately," she added, not wanting to get trapped by failing to be specific enough in her terms."

"As you say."

"Then set a mage bond on it."

Mouradian's thin brows rose in surprise. "I should think my word sufficient bond," he said.

"I should think a magus of his word would have no difficulty sealing it with a bond," Argentia replied. A mage bond was a magical contract by which a wizard was bound to deliver a promised service. Argentia had some experience with them; Ralak's brother Relsthab had forged one with her promising her freedom from his service after she completed ten deeds of his choosing. The vow was made upon the aether itself, and a mage who broke faith lost his ability to touch the aether. Few such bonds were made, and fewer still broken.

"Very well, Lady Dasani," Mouradian said after a long moment of deliberation. He gestured and a parchment and quill appeared out of the aether. The paper settled on the table. The quill moved over it, inscribing the terms of the deal in emerald ink. "Satisfied, my dear?"

Argentia read the terms. All were as she'd outlined. She didn't like the part about having her memories razed, but she didn't see a way around that concession. *It'll be like waking up from a nightmare*, she told herself. She took the quill and signed her name.

Mouradian pointed his finger. The *M* appeared beneath Argentia's name. The parchment flared and vanished into the aether. "The bond is set. Tomorrow will decide your fate."

37

Dawn.

Argentia stood before the steps descending to the labyrinth. She wore the same red-and-gold outfit she'd first found in the wardrobe, either freshly cleaned after her crawl through the cornfield or replaced altogether (she rather thought this last more likely), with the additions of a waist-length red cape that hung over her left arm, a rakish black hat with a flat crown and a round brim filigreed with gold such as she had once seen the matatauros sport in their battles with the red bulls of Cyprytal, and most of her weapons. She had her whip, her daggers, and her katana back, but her handbow was missing.

Doesn't matter....

Armed, Argentia felt whole again. As she waited for Mouradian to open the great stone doors at the base of the steps, her heart quickened. Once again she was on the edge of the unknown. Another adventure, another challenge to meet and conquer.

"I will warn you one last time. No one has ever reached the door in the center of the labyrinth," Mouradian said. He hovered beside her on his disc as the first chill light crept into the day. "Are you certain this is the course you wish, my dear? I would hate to see your life wasted."

I'll bet you would.... "Just open the doors."

"So be it," the wizard said. *"Al-obreneth!"*

Argentia started down the steps as the labyrinth doors, mighty slabs of etched stone, swung open to admit her. She had no torch, but already the twilight of dawn colored the night. It would not be long before she could see clearly in the open-air maze.

"You have until nightfall to reach the center, Lady Dasani," Mouradian said. "Begin."

Argentia entered the labyrinth.

The moment she crossed the threshold, the doors slammed closed at her back with such force that she leaped ahead and spun around, half-drawing her blade before she realized what had happened. Letting out a ragged breath, she relaxed her grip on her katana.

She was edgy, and glad of it. This was the edginess of battle: warrior's nerves at a heightened sensitivity. There was no danger from the doors, but there was likely to be other danger in this place. Mouradian had allowed as much when he returned her weapons a few minutes earlier. "A fighting chance, my dear," he said with an arrogant laugh. "That is all."

Argentia ran her hands over the wall. There was no seam, no hint of the doors that had sealed closed behind her, merely smooth stone rising twenty feet above her. More of Mouradian's magic at work, its meaning all too clear.

She was in the labyrinth now. There would be no returning the way she had come.

But she had never meant to, and she pitied Mouradian if he believed that intimations of guardians within the maze or the prospect of being unable to get out again save by piercing the heart of this stone mystery would frighten her from her purpose.

Argentia gave her attention fully to the labyrinth. She was faced with an immediate choice: left, right, or straight ahead. She reached for the dragon's tooth token at her throat, again forgetting it was gone. Setting her teeth against a flash of anger, she considered the dilemma.

She was not unfamiliar with mazes. In Sormoria, she had led a party to recover the Crown of Re-Amon from a labyrinth beneath the Temple of Avis-fe. There she had governed her passage of the maze with the rule of sacred space, a bit of lore she'd picked up here or there directing that an honest pilgrim always moved to the left in holy places.

Mouradian's maze, however, was not a place of any sacredness, so it was doubtful the same trick would work. Argentia would have to rely on her own devices and instincts to outthink the maze's maker.

The most obvious choice was the path ahead, which moved her immediately away from the perimeter. A clever maze-maker would know that, so it was just as likely that path started toward no good end. But an even cleverer maze-maker would anticipate a clever traveler being aware of the first point, and so might place the true way and the obvious way together, knowing that the very obviousness of the course would cause most to shun it—

Oh, screw this.... Argentia shook her head, wiping away all such considerations. Went with instinct, ever her truest compass.

Went to the right.

38

It was a wicked maze.

The passages stretched on from turn to turn in a maddening uniformity carefully crafted to confound all sense of direction and progress. The floors were smooth stone broken at intervals only by wide, identically constructed drainage grates. The walls were likewise utterly devoid of telling markings. They were also enchanted, as Argentia had expected they would be. To test her theory, she carved a notch into the wall. By the time she'd sheathed her dagger again, the stone had resumed its gleaming, polished perfection, showing nothing of her cut.

That was fine. She had other means of keeping track of her way.

She went swiftly, choosing her route decisively, using the looming shape of the tower to guide her toward the center. It seemed ridiculously easy to navigate Mouradian's maze. By the time she'd been walking for an hour, making what she deemed was good progress towards her goal, she began to wonder if no one had reached the center because no one had ever tried before.

Then she walked around a corner and into the storm.

It rolled into the corridor, a broil of black shadow laying low above the walls of the maze. Argentia was soaked before she even realized what was happening. She looked up in astonishment at the deluge, then bent her head, pulled her hat lower, wrapped her dripping cape about her as best she could, and hurried on.

The downpour increased, the rain stinging, sloshing over her boots in sudden puddles. She could barely see. A dark shape opened on the left: a turn into another corridor where there was no rain. She almost ducked in, just to get out of the wet, even for a moment, but stopped. This was a wizard's maze. If she stepped into that corridor, there was no guarantee it would not seal behind her, and the passage she was in now felt like the right one. *Why else would it be defended with a thunderstorm?*

So she went on. A few minutes later, so badly soaked and beaten by the rain that she barely felt it any longer, she was rewarded by something that affirmed her instinct that she was heading correctly.

The rain became snow.

A howl of wind accompanied a plunge in temperature. Pelting rain changed to biting sleet, and the sleet to fat, slapping snowflakes.

Caught in the teeth of the blizzard, Argentia staggered from wall to wall, weaving against the buffets, snow-blind and gasping, shaking with cold. A white crust lay like a frozen shawl across her hunched shoulders. Already an inch of snow had fallen, and the storm showed no signs of abating.

She forged on. Slipped, falling to her hands and knees. Came up cursing, wiping her numb fingers futilely against her pants, trying to dry them. It was useless, so she huddled her arms together beneath her sodden cape and went on again through snow blowing so thick and hard it was like a fog.

Came to a junction. This time she went left.

The blizzard followed. Soon the snow in the corridor was piled in knee-high drifts. By then, Argentia was so disoriented she had scant idea of anything except lifting one leg after the other, stumbling forward. She had been caught in similar conditions in Nord and she had nearly died. Shadow had been her savior that dark night, but there was no Shadow here save her own: a poor figure that thrust ahead of her, shaking in the sunlight.

Sunlight?

As swiftly as the rain had become snow, the storm clouds broke apart to reveal brilliant daylight. Argentia stopped walking, let her arms fall to her sides, and raised her face to the light, blinking and dazzled, heedless of the snow that fell in sodden clumps from her head and shoulders, hardly daring to believe the storm had passed.

But it had.

The cold remained.

And grew worse.

The light took on that foil-sharp harshness achieved on only the most frigid of mornings. Its touch was devoid of all semblance of warmth. Argentia's breath escaped her madly chattering teeth in plumed gasps.

All the moisture in her clothing became ice, freezing her garments to her body, chilling her very bones. Her eyes were frozen open, her lashes icicles, her tears gelid rivers on her cheeks. She could not feel her ears, or her toes in her boots. She'd shoved her fingers into her mouth, but if they found any warmth between her blue lips, she did not know.

Dazed, she fought on, step by step, blackness hemming on the edges of her vision. Came to another junction.

Chose poorly.

She knew—though not for many minutes—because the cold was gone and not replaced by some worse thing. When the realization finally reached her frostbitten mind, she slumped against the wall. Slid down to the ground.

She understood now how people failed to reach the center of Mouradian's labyrinth. She understood it very well.

You must go back.... Carfax's voice in her mind.

No...

Despite her protest, Argentia was already moving, crawling back the way she had come. She did not rise to her feet until she had scraped and dragged her way for many yards. She was almost beaten, but there was something in her that would never yield, and it was this that brought her staggering back to the junction.

She felt the cold before she reached the intersection. It shivered through her like a blade. *I can't,* she thought. *I can't go back into that again. I'll die....*

But she had no choice, so she stepped bravely forward.

It was worse than she'd imagined. Worse even than her plunge into the arctic waters of the White Sea to capture the albatross egg that won the aid of the Tribe of the Walros against Togril Vloth. It stole her breath, but it could not steal her will. She made the correct turn this time, and struggled on, every step making her frozen garments creak and crack. Her pace slowed, her heart slowed.

The heat came upon her.

It struck like dragonfire, blasting her down, taking consciousness with it.

39

Wetness woke her.

Argentia sat up, startled by a cold trickle racing down her neck. She panicked for a moment, wondering how long she'd been unconscious, how much precious time she'd lost. She quickly realized it couldn't have been that long: the snow crusting her hat and the collar of her cape had only just begun melting.

Groaning, Argentia came to her knees. The labyrinth was infernally hot. The very air shimmered.

Beats the hell out of the cold....

Argentia rose and, after taking a moment to get her bearings, resumed walking. At first, the heat was a welcome relief. Her joints and limbs thawed, her flesh stinging as the cold left her. Her frozen garments became soaked again, but by now she was used to that discomfort.

Turn after turn she wound deeper into the labyrinth. Deeper into the heat. She began to steam. The air baked her. The maze had become a furnace without flame.

Like the rain and snow and cold, the heat was a familiar torment to Argentia. The Wastes of Yth had been like this. Just as in Nord, in the desert her deliverance had come from an animal: not a dog, but the ghost pegasi of the meja Sanla.

"No horses here," Argentia croaked. "Flying kind or otherwise." She uttered a horrible laugh. Her throat was parched, her lips cracked. Her eyes were sore and swollen, but she kept them fixed on the way ahead.

She peeled off her cape, dragging it behind her. Her pants had dried tight and stiff against her legs. She was no longer sweating. Perspiration evaporated even as it reached her skin, which was fever-hot and had taken on an ugly red cast, as if radiating heat from within to add to the deadly atmosphere.

Leaning on the wall for support, Argentia stumbled around another turn in the infernal maze. *Something....* She squinted painfully. The glazed air showed her images in duplicate and even triplicate—but there was still something there. A space of darkness on the ground. *A hole?*

She was dizzy. Was there one hole or four? Was there a hole at all?

Argentia swayed, tottering (she would never know how very close she came to tumbling into the hole, with half her left foot hanging out into space), and falling against the wall on her right.

The jarring impact gave her a moment's clarity, enough to see that it was just one hole and it did not reach across the passage. There was a narrow rim between it and the wall: not much, but enough. Keeping her back pressed to the stone, she shuffled, her feet never leaving the ground, scraping along, not daring to look down, fearful the hole would widen as she went.

Then she was past, and the heat was gone.

40

Bewildered, Argentia simply stood a few feet beyond the circular hole in the floor of the labyrinth. The temperature had returned to normal. Stranger still, her clothes were as dry and perfect as when she'd put them on in the darkness ere dawn, and her body showed no signs of the tortures she'd endured. No frost-frozen fingers, no heat-split lips or splotchy sunburn, no dehydration or exhaustion. It was as if the entire ordeal had never happened.

Illusion! Argentia remembered her chamber in the tower, which had at first appeared to be an empty cell. *I should have known. God damn it, I should have known!*

Cursing Mouradian for his abuses, Argentia marched forward. Her red boot heels clipped noisily on the smooth stone, marking stride after determined stride through the labyrinth.

Many intervolutions later, with the sun riding somewhat shy of noon, she came to the place she sought.

Deep in the shadows of the labyrinth there was a circular space surrounding the base of Mouradian's tower. Argentia gave a cry of triumph. *I did it! I beat you!*

She felt the deadness of walking for hours on end leave her legs as she rushed forward. The base of the tower was roughhewn and dark. She tracked around it, eyes gleaming in anticipation.

There was no door.

What the hell? "Mouradian! Wizard! I'm here!"

Her voice echoed into silence. No door appeared.

Wait. Maybe.... She laid her hands upon the wall. It was solid. Real.

Damn it.... For a moment she had hoped it was another illusion to deceive her into thinking she'd reached the center of the maze.

Argentia tore her hat off and slammed it down. Picked it up and flung it back the way she'd come. "You lying bastard—open the door!"

Silence still, and still no door.

With no clear idea of what to do next, Argentia stalked over to retrieve her hat. It had landed on one of the labyrinth's drainage grates. As she picked up the battered headgear, she stared at the many dark eyes of the drain.

"Son of a bitch," she muttered, looking back to the base of the tower where there was no door. *Because it's not really the center....* "That's it. That *must* be it!" Grinning, she jammed her hat on her head and dashed off.

M

Backtracking was a gift of Argentia's. She did not know how she had come by the skill, but her memory for retracing her steps was nearly perfect. It had saved her life many times in the past, and it served again on this day, returning her to this place that instinct told her was the secret to the labyrinth.

Crouching, she reached into the black mouth. Felt smooth, slick, polished stone, angled like a chute or slide. *Here goes nothing....*

Taking a deep breath—praying it wasn't her last—Argentia dropped into the hole.

41

The wind was screaming.

Was this Yth again? The Keening Canyon, from whence a wind of howls issued to sweep over the desert Wastes?

As Argentia flew along, she realized that there was indeed wind and screaming, but they were separate entities. The wind was the air flowing through the stone chute. The screaming came from her own lips as she slid down the slick, dark throat, hurtling on and on until at last she shot forth.

She skidded and rolled, aware suddenly of space around her, tumbling over before fetching to a stunning halt against what could only be a wall.

"Gah...." Argentia sat up, rubbing the back of her head and wincing. Despite her efforts to protect herself by keeping her arms tucked tight to her ears, she'd smacked her head a few times on the way down the chute.

Pressing a hand to the wall, Argentia stood up, relieved to find that her movements came without pain. She knew she'd been lucky: a ride like she'd had could have easily ended with broken legs or arms. *Or my neck....*

She patted herself down. All her weapons were there, but her hat was gone. It was a small loss, especially if she'd reasoned the riddle of Mouradian's maze rightly.

Argentia's guess was that the labyrinth had multiple levels, so that its true center was reckoned both horizontally and vertically. The drainage grates had clued her that there was at least one level below, and the hole—the single anomalous thing she'd encountered in her morning's walk through the mazeways—had seemed the likeliest way to access what waited beneath. *Clever, too,* she admitted. She'd avoided that hole as if falling in was the worst thing that could have happened to her.

As her eyes grew acclimated to the dismal environ, Argentia found the black was not quite pitch. Dim light filtered in broken bits from the ceiling up ahead, which meant there were passages here as well, not just oubliettes beneath the drainage grates.

There was no proof that this was the middle level, and not merely the second of some five or ten deeper iterations, yet Argentia though it was. The wizard's trick was good enough not to require further concealment, and if this wasn't the central level, why did the air here hang heavy with the stench of carrion?

This was a place of bones and death. Argentia was sure that when she found her way to its center, there would be a door waiting.

A door, and its guardian.

Keeping a hand to the wall, Argentia started toward the light from the drainage grate. One step. Two. Three. Four.

As she lifted her boot to place down the fifth step she stopped suddenly, perhaps feeling the subtle change—a slight updraft—in the environment or perhaps simply warned of unseen danger by her instincts. Either way, Argentia froze, and the fatal step that would have sent her plunging into a fathomless abyss stopped in midair.

She backed up a pace, knelt, and reached forward. Felt stone, and then nothing. *Aeton....* Argentia shuddered, thinking how very near she'd been to walking into Mouradian's trap. Crawling first left and then right, she marked that, unlike the hole on the level above, this pit stretched from wall to wall. There would be no edging around this time.

Have to jump it.... But could she? How far did it go?

If I just had my handbow.... She would have been able to see in the silver afterglare of her shot. She had wondered why Mouradian had returned all her weapons save that one. Perhaps precisely to keep her from gaining an advantage in the dark.

Not going to stop me... She drew one of her daggers and lobbed it out in front of her. Never heard it hit the ground.

Damn... She lobbed a second dagger, harder than the last time. This one clattered down on the far side of the gap. *Five feet at least. Figure six to be safe....*

It was doable.

She jumped straight up, reaching as high above her head as she could. Her outstretched fingers did not hit the ceiling. *All right. Good....*

Now came the hard part. Argentia went cautiously to the edge again, shuffling her boots ahead until her toes hung out into space. Then she went backwards, pacing off the distance until she reached the wall behind her. Nine steps. *But I'll be running....*

She returned to the edge. Put her back to the pit. Ran for the wall. Four strides, and on the fourth she would have to jump for all she was worth.

Argentia took a deep breath, gathering her will. Her muscles were twitchy with tension. *What if the ceiling is lower over the pit?* an insidious voice asked.

It's not.... She'd tossed the daggers high enough that they would have hit any kind of obstruction. *It's fine. I'll make it....*

What if—

She shut out the voice. She had to go now. If she thought about it much longer it would only make it worse. *Then go!* Her eyes were wide, hot. She sucked in a gasp of air. *Go go go!*

Argentia exploded forward, her long legs flying. The instant her right boot hit the stone for the fourth time she flung herself out as high and hard as she could, soaring into the black.

Falling.

Too short. Oh Bright La—

Argentia's foot hit stone. She pitched forward, scraping her knees, sprawling away from the invisible abyss. For a moment she lay still, then she raised her head and spread her arms and legs out. Felt solid ground as far as she could reach. A shaky laugh escaped her. She'd had some desperate escapes in her time, but for sheer nerve this might have surmounted them all.

While she waited for her lungs and heart to catch some reasonable pace, Argentia padded around with her hands until she found her dagger. No sense in giving up a weapon she might need later.

Ready to go on, she rose and drew her katana. The grate ahead gave a small space of light, but there would be other dark places, and possibly other traps as well. She'd been lucky enough to avoid this one. She wasn't about to test Fortune again.

42

Peering into his scrying font, Mouradian watched as Argentia, tapping her katana ahead of her like a blind old crone, set forth again to find the center of the labyrinth. "I believe she is going to make it after all," he said, turning to favor Shrike with a broad smile.

"She is lucky," the assassin said. She stood with her arms folded across her small breasts, a study in ebony save for her tanned face and a certain dragon's tooth token dangling about her neck. Mouradian had noted that token—and its aethereal strength—just as he had noted the handbow the half-elf now wore on her hip beside her array of daggers, but he made no comment. He had instructed Shrike to bring him Argentia Dasani. She had done so. What spoils she chose to take from her quarry were her business.

"True, but she is skilled as well. Brave. Inventive. Perseverant. How many have survived the upper level of the labyrinth, let alone figured the way below? And then to have avoided the pit."

"Luck," the assassin repeated flatly, her tone as dark as her glasses.

"You had best hope she is more than Fortune's favored child, my dear. If she fails this test, you will be without the answers you seek."

"We had a bargain, wizard!" Shrike flared.

"Yes, yes." Mouradian raised a placating hand. "You are a sad creature. What will you have left after you claim your great revenge?" He shook his head. "I pity you."

"I do not want your pity, wizard. I want the answers you owe me."

With a toss of her long, black ponytail, the assassin stalked from the chamber.

Smiling again, the Island Wizard returned his gaze to the image in the font.

43

Being watched....

Argentia didn't know where the eyes were coming from, but they were there. She could feel them upon her in the dark. The dark itself was another source for concern; the little light probing through the grates above her head had grown wan. She had been hours in the under-layer of the maze. In the world above, afternoon was slipping toward evening.

Her time was running out.

She kept on her way, going as quietly and swiftly as she could. Her blade still tapped out the pace before her, though there had been no more pits and no elemental tortures as she'd suffered above. Her boots occasionally splished through puddles or muck—there were fewer drains on this level—or scattered unseen things she knew from their rattle to be bones.

It was colder here below: the damp chill of a sewer or dungeon. The kind of air that always made Argentia feel as if her lungs were growing moldy with each breath.

Worst, however, was this feeling of being watched. Of being stalked by some unseen, unknown thing in the dark. Occasionally she would hear it, the tap-tap-tap of her katana broken by a snorting shuff of breath. Though there was surely distortion from the echo, Argentia got the sense that whatever was in these twisting corridors with her was very large.

M

Tap-tap-tap. Left.

Tap-tap-tap. Right.

Tap-tap-tap. Another right.

Dead end. Backtrack. Left.

Tap-tap-tap....

Shuff....

Tap-tap— Shuff....

Wait, wait. *Nothing*....

Tap-tap-tap. Left.

And so, through the labyrinth.

44

At first, Argentia could scarcely believe what she was seeing.

The maze had drubbed her with monotony. Though this did not weigh on her as viciously as it might on one unfamiliar with labyrinths and dungeons and other dark places of indeterminate end, it still dulled her faculties and wore her into a pattern of tapping and turning from one benighted corridor to the next.

Until now.

As Argentia rounded a bend, she saw a glimmering ahead. A faint radiance of bluish aether-light painted the air from around the next corner.

Had she come at last to the center of the labyrinth?

Her heart leaped up, sure that she had. This time, there would be a door and she would be free of Mouradian and his vile island.

The impulse to rush ahead was almost overwhelming. Argentia checked it. Caution had carried her this far. She would let it lead her on to the end.

She listened for the shuffling respiration. Heard nothing, but it was a bad silence, like the moment before the thunder breaks and the storm comes. *It's here. Waiting....*

Argentia crept forward. There was one last grate in the ceiling, then a space of blank darkness all the way to the corner up ahead, where the blue light tickled the undermaze shadows. Reminding herself again to be cautious, Argentia stepped past the spotted light from the ceiling grate, touching her way along with the katana as she moved through the darkness.

Suddenly she stopped. Darkness had crept into the blue light.

Shuff...

God damn it! The thing was between her and the source of that blue glow.

Between her and the door.

The shuffling increased. The stench of carrion was thick and rank. Heavy, ox-like clopping rang off the stones: low and slow at first, but then louder and faster as the thing approached the corner.

Caution abandoned, Argentia sprinted ahead, trying to make it around the corner before the labyrinth's guardian could trap her in this dark enclosure where her chances of defeating it would be bad at best.

She skidded into the blue light, closing her eyes at the last instant so she wouldn't be blinded after her time in the dim and dark. Opened them again a heartbeat later. Saw both the door—a blue-limned oval on the far side of a wide, circular arena—and its charging defender.

Then the bellowing thing was upon her.

Argentia flung herself to the side. She was fast enough to avoid the killing charge, but the beast's flailing hand caught her shoulder as she dove clear. Her arm went numb. Her katana went flying.

She rolled to her feet, dazed from the glancing blow. She didn't even want to imagine getting hit square-on.

The thing turned towards her, coming fully back into the chamber at the center of the labyrinth. Argentia was too far from her katana to recover it. She gave a brief thought to racing for the door, but the monster had a better angle, and she'd already seen its speed. It would trample her before she was halfway there.

Argentia backed away, staying along the curving wall. In the blue light, the monstrosity's flesh—the sickly, fishbelly white of grubs and larvae and other things not wont to see the light of day—took on a ghastly glow. Argentia couldn't believe the size of the thing.

Or that it once had been a man.

Now it was but another of Mouradian's creations: a hulking monstrosity legged like a bull, with the muscular torso of a man swelled to gigantic proportions, hunching beneath the weight of its massive, taurean head. A shaggy albino mane tapered almost to the base of its mighty back. Its arms bulged hugely, swollen with strength, and its red eyes glared hatefully above snorting, bovine nostrils pierced by a metal ring boasting the wizard's *M*. The dark shapes of ticks tangled in the fur of its snout.

Its mouth opened to show rows of jagged teeth, black as shards of burned pottery, as it bellowed a deafening challenge.

Argentia unfastened her cape, ignoring the pain in her arm. There would be time for pain later. "Come on! Yah! Come on!" She waved the cape, beckoning as she had seen the matatauros do. "Yah! Yah!"

The man-bull took the bait. Argentia watched the thundering approach, the very stones shaking beneath the charge, knowing she had to time this perfectly.

Now!

Argentia tossed the cape into the air. Spinning aside as the monster plowed past, she leaped onto the man-bull's broad back and looped her whip around its throat. The beast bucked and tossed, clawing at the choking cord. Argentia held fast, tightening her grip, pulling with all her strength.

The man-bull dipped forward, trying to spill her over its head. Argentia cinched her legs around its waist and yanked even harder. Roaring, the monster turned a circle, flailing at her as it staggered backwards.

Argentia looked over her shoulder in time to see the wall rushing up. *Oh shit....* She closed her eyes just before she was smashed between the stone and the man-bull. Her ribs snapped. Bright pain blasted the air from her lungs. She sagged, stunned, almost losing her grip.

No....

Growling defiance, Argentia clutched the whip tighter and scrambled up the man-bull's back, jamming her knees down between its huge shoulders. The precarious position gave her much-needed leverage. The whip was chafing her hands bloody but she hauled on the ever-tightening line, losing all sense of the chamber as the man-bull lurched about. Cords stood in Argentia's neck and arms. Her teeth were clenched against all the pain, her mind blank to anything but choking the monster down.

The man-bull snapped up to its full height, its head thrown back, arms raised, its entire body trembling with a last gasp of strength. Then it crashed to its knees and toppled on its face. Argentia stayed on its back, still hauling on the whip, lost in a killing haze as the beast thrashed and shuddered and stilled.

Finally, Argentia came back to herself. She stood over the fallen man-bull. It took an effort for her to open her torn, burning fingers and release the whip. Every part of her body ached. Her breathing came in ragged gasps. She coughed. Tasted blood. Touched her side gingerly, igniting a flare of pain from her broken ribs. *Not again. How many times now? Four? Five?*

Grim-faced against her many hurts, Argentia hobbled over and retrieved her katana. She returned to the defeated man-bull, which had regained consciousness and was struggling to rise.

I think not.... Argentia drove her katana home in its back, twisting the steel deep, piercing its heart. The man-bull collapsed, gave a final wheeze, and died.

Argentia nearly dropped beside the monster. Her vision was blurry and she could barely draw a full breath. She steadied herself and freed her katana. Too maimed and tired to bother putting her weapon away, she dragged it behind her as she limped across the arena. She had hurt her hip when she crashed into the wall—badly, it seemed, for the pain was increasing with each slow step. *Doesn't matter. Everything'll be better once I get through that door....*

Unaware that the sun had nearly set on the world above her, Argentia hobbled to the door. The oval of stone was inscribed with intricate runes. It had no handle, but when she touched it, it slid aside to reveal the blue light of an aethergate.

Bright Lady, thank you....

Argentia stepped through the doorway

45

and tumbled out of the mirror in a flash of azure.

It had hardly been a long teleport, but debilitated as Argentia was, it stole the last of her strength. She lay in a heap on the cold stone, certain she would never be able to rise again.

Until she heard the voice.

"You are most fortunate that I desire you alive, else I would flay the flesh from your bones to repay your damnable habit of killing my children," Mouradian said.

Argentia lifted her head, shaking off the dizzy haze. She saw the magus upon his hovering disc. He motioned to an unseen party. "Bring her."

At the wizard's command, two chasecrows shambled forward.

"What?" Argentia struggled to her knees, wavering for balance. Her cobalt eyes flared, sensing treachery. She managed a two-handed sweep of her blade that lopped the legs off the chasecrows, bringing them down. The strawmen thrashed like piles of kindling in a stormwind.

Argentia staggered to her feet. Leveled her blade at the wizard. "You gave your word," she growled. "Your mage bond."

"You mean this?" Mouradian gestured and the parchment bearing the bond appeared in his hand. He rubbed his fingers together and green fire sprang up, devouring the paper. "Little fool, that rubbish binds only magi of the Order. My arts are dark."

Snarling like a wounded lioness, Argentia sprang for the Island Wizard.

Mouradian lifted the star-shaped diamond from his chest. The stone flared with its blinding light. Once more Argentia felt as if she was being ripped inside out, twisted into a maelstrom of unspeakable anguish as the magic struck her down.

The diamond shone brighter still, and then dimmed. When it lay once more against the wizard's chest, it was weightier than before.

Interlude: The Great Maker

Power and vengeance.

These were the things that drove Mouradian of Elsmywr. The first had been his obsession since his earliest days. Its pursuit had propelled him far in the ranks of Teranor's magi, but the pinnacle from which he could have worked his will upon the crowndom was denied him.

They gave it to that fool Relsthab, and he conspired with the rest to exile me....

Thence, the spur of vengeance.

But the lust for power was still strong in Mouradian. He knew it would not be enough to wipe out Teranor's Order of Magi—though he would relish their every death—if he did not also gain for himself. Deprived of the mantle of Archamagus, he would have the throne instead. When his army had done its work, when all the magi who had stood against him were dead, their Ban upon him would be lifted and the Island Wizard would return to Teranor, appearing in glory to do what no other could and turn the dreadful tide.

The people—those that yet lived—would reward him with the throne. They would have to. Mouradian's intercession would sadly come too late to save the Crown.

For fifty years and more, since he had deceived the magi into believing him dead in a violent disaster, Mouradian had been at work crafting his invasion force.

For fifty years and more he had failed.

He had been near to success many times, but always there was some unforeseen check. The chasecrows were mindless and weak. The armored men were good fighters, but not good enough.

Then, in the blood of the hybrid monsters of Acrevast, Mouradian had discovered the secret to melding man and animal. He had harnessed it.

Again he was checked.

His best successes, the man-bull and the twins, had been accidents: creations unable to be replicated for reasons beyond even his ken. They had not been without their uses, however—especially Puma and Pantra, who in their striking similarity had provided the genesis of Mouradian's most recent work.

M

The topmost chamber of Mouradian's tower was home to the wizard's masterwork. Unique and fragile, it waited, suspended by chains above the center of the room and draped in black velvet. Argentia Dasani's body lay at the foot of this veiled construct.

Mouradian entered and surveyed the chamber. All was in readiness. "Now," he whispered. "Now, at last, it is time."

He passed a glowing hand over Argentia's body, healing all the damage it had sustained in the labyrinth. With a second gesture, he raised her body so it stood facing the black velvet drapery. Beneath that shroud was a mirror. A very special mirror.

The Mirror of Simulcra.

Mouradian had fashioned it with much toil and great expenditure of his powers. Yet in the beginning it, too, had been a failure.

He had sent one of his servants through the mirror and it had cast the man back a lifeless husk. Appalled, Mouradian consulted a minor demon whose essence he had bound to a bottle. The imp told him the Mirror of Simulcra would suffer no living thing to pass through it. "Separate the spirit and the body, but keep both quick. If dies the spirit, dies the body, and so true seen in a mirror," the diminutive fiend advised.

Mouradian knew of magic that could wrest the spirit from the body. It was part of the Forbidden lore of the shadowaether he had pursued in secret for many long winters. But to hold the spirit required a particular vessel: a diamond of precise cut and purity. There were perhaps three such stones known to exist in all Acrevast.

One of them was owned by Togril Vloth.

Thus it was that Puma and Pantra came to their new master, and the star diamond—now imbued with the fell magic of soul wresting—came to its place around the Island Wizard's neck.

Assured of success, Mouradian took the spirit from a gatarine and set the body before the mirror. This time, the image passed through the glass, only to emerge in mewling, bleeding, dying halves: the magic of the mirror had split the pig-man's dual essences, replicating each as single entities.

Enraged, Mouradian summoned the imp again, threatening destruction for its lies.

"No lies! No lies!" the imp screeched. "Master asked not of sending pig-men into crystal. Never will it serve, no never. The blood must be strained true, not of essence mingled from men and beasts."

So Mouradian saw his plans for creating his army of gatarines come crashing apart. But he was not so easily deterred. If it could not be pig-men, it would be men.

By then, however, there were no men left on Elsmywr save Mouradian himself and Kiel, the chief of his guards. The few other servants and soldiers he'd retained had been killed in accidents with the hybrid animals, or with the beast-men, or murdered by Kiel when they grew terrified of their master and tried to flee.

Kiel, fanatically devoted to the wizard, had already been the subject of the armor experiment. He volunteered for this service as well. Mouradian took his spirit with the Soul Wrester and set his body before the mirror.

This time he had success.

After a fashion.

It was not long, however, before Mouradian discovered that something—likely the armor he'd attached to Kiel's body—had interfered with the process. While Kiel's simulcra were physically perfect duplicates, their minds were stunted. Beyond a limited range of functions they were little better than the chasecrows. They would serve to guard his tower, but never to wage a war on Teranor.

To accomplish that, Mouradian knew, he needed a master fighter.

He needed Argentia Dasani.

Whatever her protests to the contrary, Mouradian knew Argentia had more than a hand in destroying his twins. Puma and Pantra had been in communication with the wizard before their deaths. They had told him much of Argentia—the first prey to ever escape them. Later, Togril Vloth recounted for him how the huntress had defeated the twins in battle.

Still seeking the perfect subject for his invasion force, Mouradian fixed on Argentia. Besides murdering his twins, the list of her exploits ran from slaying vampyrs to vanquishing demons, if one believed all the tales.

Now that he'd seen her for himself, Mouradian almost did.

Yes, she will be perfect....

"Haven't you finished yet?"

Mouradian turned to see Shrike standing in the doorway. "Patience, my dear. You are just in time."

"If it succeeds, I will have my answer. No more delays."

"Indeed."

The assassin set her hands on her slim hips and waited, watching as Mouradian stepped away from the mirror and intoned the words of the incantation. Light began to seep from behind the velvet draping: a lurid radiance that seemed to crawl with some unnatural vitality. It seared at Shrike's eyes, even through her ebony glasses.

Now, by Bhael-ur—let it work! Mouradian uttered the last of the spell. Swept his hand back. The black velvet cloth flew aside. Argentia's body was swallowed by a ruby glare.

Inexplicably, the dragon's tooth token at Shrike's throat glimmered fiercely. She caught her fist around it, cutting off that silver light.

The Mirror of Simulcra blazed. Beams of red light scattered out its infernal depths as if cast through a prism, striking six precisely set mirrors on the far wall. These sparked like flinted tinder, and then all the aethereal light went out in a final flash that made the assassin turn her head aside. When she looked back, the black velvet hung again upon the magic mirror. Rusty smoke drifted from beneath the covering.

Argentia's body stood where it had been, unchanged, unmoving.

Across the chamber, six of her reflections stepped forth from the mirrors and into life.

M

Five weeks later.

"You are ready," Mouradian said to the huntresses.

He had watched these six simulcra train and practice. He had duplicated Argentia's weapons for them, and they were masterful at their use. Neither the tower guards nor the gatarines had come close to challenging them at arms.

But Mouradian was aware of the deficiencies of those standards. A further test was in order. One that would truly show if his simulcra were the perfect replicas of Argentia Dasani they appeared to be.

To each of the six he spoke a final command. Then, stepping back, he motioned to the teleport discs set on the ground. "Go, and do not fail me."

With that, Mouradian sent his simulcra forth to strike the first blows of his great vengeance.

Part III

A Friend in Need

46

It was a perfect night for hunting.

A bright full moon lit the dark above the North Woods. The air was bitter, clear, and still, with no wind to carry Bertrant deSheaven's scent to his prey or to threaten the flight of his bolt.

He had heard the rumors—all the villagers of Ametryl had heard them—of the creature that wandered these woodlands between the banks of the Valdenthal and the shadows of the Gelidian Spur on the nights the moon was full. Many a trapper had seen it while setting his snares for mink and ermine and marmot: a glimpse of something sliding through the silver night, a sunbeam flash, there and gone. They said it was a fey thing and they made signs of protection when they spoke of it.

Bertrant had listened to this talk among the shouts and laughter and calls for another round in the taproom of the Potted Hydra. When the moon rose full again, the son of Beorant deSheaven, the great huntsman of these North Woods, decided to have a look for himself.

Have a look and kill the thing, whatever it was.

That should serve to quiet the whispers that he was a lazy lout who'd wedded the Mayor's daughter and was now living off his father-in-law's ample coffers, occasionally hunting stag and wild boar when the mood took him (and, of course, participating in the annual Great Hunt, which he usually won—he was, after all, Beorant's son, blessed with a true eye and a quick shot) but mostly only hunting up his next ale at the Hydra.

Tonight Bertrant meant to change all that. Tonight he would kill this Beast of the Wood, and his own reputation would shine brighter than his father's ever had. There would be no question of his prominence in the town, or his right to hold audience at the Hydra for any and all who wished to hear the tale of Bertrant the Slayer.

Provided the damned thing actually appeared.

Bertrant had stalked the woods on each of the previous two nights of the full moon, only to have the dawn send him back to his home frozen and dejected, having seen no hint of the mysterious creature. Tonight would be different. Tonight it would come. Bertrant was certain. Tonight it—

—was here.

Bertrant sucked in a cold breath as the bushes on the far side of a small glade opened and the golden fox passed into the clearing. Caught in the moonlight, its pelt shone like gilt metal in a dwarven forge. It was larger than any fox the hunter had ever seen, more the size of a sheep-herding collie. Its bib and paws and the tip of its tail were stark white. Its eyes, which seemed to fix on Bertrant for an instant across the distance, were luminous as suns. It barked once, a delicate, feminine sound, and then sat on its haunches, baying the moon.

Stay right there, pretty. Stay.... Bertrant slowly raised his crossbow, exhaling a plume of breath as he took dead aim—

"Shoot and it will be the last thing you do in this life."

The voice, deep and forbidding, rumbled from the pale giant who had stepped out of the shadows beside Bertrant. "Put the bow down," the figure commanded. Bertrant hesitated. "I said put it down!" A heavy boot stomped the weapon out of Bertrant's hands. He was jerked into the air, screaming as his bladder voided in a hot rush. "Don't kill me," he blubbered. "I'm the Mayor's son-in-law!"

The figure took a single stride and rammed Bertrant against a tree. "I don't care if you're the Crown's consort. Come near the golden fox again and you will die."

"All right, all right," Bertrant gasped. He was somewhat relieved that his captor, huge though he stood, was a man and not some ogre descended from the nearby mountains. "I meant no harm," he sputtered.

"You meant great harm!" The man shook Bertrant as a dog might a rabbit, drawing a terrified sob from the hunter. "Go, before I think better of my mercy!"

Bertrant was suddenly flying. He crashed down in some bushes, gathered himself up, pine needles and forest debris clinging to his cloak and clothing, and fled through the bracken into the dark.

The man watched him go. Shaking his head in disgust, he picked up the crossbow and smashed it apart against a tree.

The fox came trotting up, golden eyes gleaming, panting gently. "Come on," the man said. "Enough fun for one night. Let's go home."

47

Home was an abandoned stone hut hidden deep in the North Woods. Kodius and Kirin did not know how old it was, though it looked and felt very old indeed, or how long it had stood empty, but it was safe and secluded and it served their simple purposes well enough.

The barbarian and the werefox had been wandering Teranor together for the past three years. Kodius had left Nord twenty years earlier, fleeing the savagery of his homeland for a better life in Teranor. He had shaved the beard of his tribe and would never wear one again in tribute to his decision.

His intent had been to see all of Teranor, to immerse himself in new cultures and different societies, but he had only made it as far south as Telarban. There he had taken up with the brothers Steelfist, and he had companied with them until death claimed the dwarves during the hunt for the Wheels of Avis-fe.

It was during that quest that Kodius had met Kirin, who was then in the service of Ralak the Red. Though they had not fallen straightaway in love, they had ended that way—so much so that when their struggle against the talismans and the Prophecy was ended, Kirin forbore her own quest to rid herself of her affliction and wedded all her hopes to Kodius, who had embraced her dual nature without question.

Their meanderings had taken them from the Hills of Dusk to the Sea of Val. They stopped and stayed in towns and villages and cities they found along the way, enjoying the variety and pace of life in the different places. Kodius easily found work as a peacekeeper in taverns or hauling crates on docks or as an assistant to carpenters or masons or smiths. Kirin tended bar or worked in butcheries or poulterers or cooked in taverns.

They maintained only one rule: prior to the nights of the full moon they struck out into the wild again so Kirin could undergo her changes in safety.

Three months ago, they had come to the North Woods. It was mostly a coniferous forest, full of blue and gray and white firs and spruces, and even a few of the rare silverpines, cousins to the fabled silverleaves of the elven forests to the west. "It's like the best places in Nord," Kodius had marveled one day as they stood in the hollow outside the hut and decided that their wandering days had come to an end.

Kirin knew that her husband held few good memories of his frozen homeland beyond the Gelidian Spur. For him to speak of this wood in such terms said much of how deeply it had touched him. It had touched her as well, for she was attracted to any place of wild peace, and these tracts where bears and deer roamed free by clear streams rushing cold from the mountains struck a resonant chord in her soul. She knew they could have lived out the rest of their days together here in happiness.

But now—as ever—her curse had destroyed all that for them.

"We'll have to move on," Kirin said bitterly the morning after the incident with Bertrant deSheaven. "That rat will have all Ametryl scouring these woods for us by week's end."

There were often hunters and trappers in the North Woods, especially on the nights of the full moon. Though she had avoided any confrontation, Kirin knew she had not kept wholly out of sight. Rumor of her must have grown in the village and it had returned this moon to haunt her. Both nights prior to the last she'd sensed she was being stalked. When she told Kodius of it, he hatched the plan to bait the hunter and frighten him off.

"You should have just let me kill him and put an end to it!" she spat. Her golden eyes kindled. There was a part of Kirin, though she oft chose to forget it, which had wholly embraced the bestial aspect of her being. A part that loved the power and freedom that attended her fox form. That loved to run beneath the moon. To hunt. To kill.

Kodius set down his mug of caf. "If that would have changed anything, I would have done it myself. They would only come seeking his body, and revenge. Now they may come, or they may heed my warning."

"They'll come. They *always* come back. Come to kill the monster." Kirin let out a short laugh that was uncannily like a bark. "We were happy here, and I've ruined it! God *damn* it!" She swept her hand across the table, casting a basket of rolls to the floor.

"Kirin!"

She was trembling violently, though whether with anger or sorrow Kodius could not say. Kirin was temperamental at best, and her moods in the days preceding and following her transformations could be as tempestuous as the storms of autumn. What concerned Kodius now was that when Kirin was under duress she sometimes changed without the moon, becoming a creature half-woman, half-fox: a killing force of claws and teeth.

Though such a thing had not happened since the Battle of Hidden Vale, looking on her now he suddenly feared it might. He rose and took her in his arms, holding her tightly. "Kirin, stop. Everything's fine."

"I hate this!" she said, her voice muffled against his body. She was remembering all the awful times she'd been driven away: first by her horrified husband, who had actually led their village against her, then from other hamlets and villages in those early days before she had fully understood the nature of her curse, and now from this place, where she finally might have found a home. "I hate it all!"

Kodius sighed. He'd thought that after three years together they were past this. Apparently the problem had only been sleeping. Though many times in their wanderings they had not been far from villages when the full moon came, Kirin had run in the woods and fields unseen by men. Or, if she had been seen, they had moved on quickly enough that no trouble could come of it.

That's what changed, Kodius realized. They had settled here, and three moons straight the golden fox had run in the North Wood. *Why shouldn't she?* he wondered, a dull anger rising in him at the unfairness of it all.

He looked out the window. When they had found this place, that window had been an eroded hole in the stones. He had smoothed over the shape and fitted it with wood and glass and Kirin had purchased bright yellow curtains in Ametryl. It was just one of the many repairs they had been making, little by little turning back the work of time and the elements and making a ruin into a quaint cottage. There was a good deal more such work to be done, but they were proud of what they'd accomplished so far. It was simple, but it was true. It was theirs.

It was home.

He would not give it up so easily.

"If they come, they come," he said. "This place is ours. No one will drive us out. I swear it."

Kodius ran a hand over Kirin's short-cropped pinewood blonde hair. She tilted her face up to him. She was not pretty in any classical sense, but there was something striking and attractive about her nonetheless. Her features were sleek and narrow, small of nose and lips, foxlike. She'd been twenty-five on the night when she'd had her fateful encounter in the woods and time had stopped for her. She still look young—until one gazed into her eyes. In their golden pools, the many sufferings she'd endured in fourteen long years of seeking a cure to her cursed state showed like forty.

Now those eyes were lit with sudden hope. "Kodius! Do you mean it? We'll stay?"

"Nothing will move us, Kirin."

"Not even a summons from the Crown?" Ralak the Red asked as he materialized in a flash of aetherlight.

48

"Salutations," Ralak said, his ruby robes glimmering with motes of aether.

"By the gods!" Kodius exclaimed. "What are you doing here?"

"Am I not permitted to seek out my friends?"

"Spare me," Kirin said. "I know you too well. The Red Wizard doesn't pay social calls."

Ralak scratched his cheek, perhaps to hide a wry smile. He studied the barbarian and the werefox. Though they looked the most improbable pair, with Kodius standing close to seven feet tall and Kirin a wiry five-two, one only had to interact with them for a few moments to realize they belonged together as surely as two lovers ever had. Ralak was glad for them, especially for Kirin, whom he knew had battled long against herself, and likely battled still.

"As I said, the Crown requests your presence."

"The Crown? Why?" Kodius asked. He did not relish the fact that Ralak had found them here. He valued his freedom, and the idea of being kept under watch chafed at him. Of course, the Archamagus was powerful in the aether, and could well have sought them out on the moment, but Kodius doubted that was so. It was more like Ralak to know exactly where he would find people useful to him at all times.

"That is for her Majesty to say. Will you come or no? My time is short."

Kodius looked at Kirin. "What do you think?"

"Are we commanded?" the werefox asked.

Ralak clucked in disapproval. "Of course not. You are requested. As I can tell you have little interest in assisting an old friend, I will inform her Majesty you respectfully decline."

"What friend? What's happened?" Kodius asked.

Ralak turned away and waved a hand, opening a silver-blue portal in the air. "Farewell."

"Stop, damn you." Kirin cursed the Archamagus under her breath for baiting them. Waiting in their cottage wondering what the Crown had wanted would be a worse torture than waiting and wondering when the villagers of Ametryl would arrive with torches and gallows-ropes.

"Take us," she said.

49

"Da! Lunch, Da!"

Artelo Sterling looked up as his favorite sound in the world echoed through the barn. He was on his knees beside a wagon that was missing its rear wheels, and turned to catch Aura as she ran towards him. He swept her up, rubbing his blonde goatee against her face until she giggled with glee.

"Whiskers tickle!" Aura poked at Arelo's face, narrowly missing his eye.

Laughing, Artelo set his daughter down. "Okay. Away from the wagon, Aura," he said. The damaged vehicle was propped on a stack of stone blocks. Though Artelo had just been laying beneath it checking the axle for damage and was certain the support was secure, he took no chances with Aura's safety.

"Why, Da?" Aura asked.

"It could fall and hurt you. Go on."

Aura backed obediently away, looking with wide gray eyes—her mother's eyes; she also had Brittyn's golden hair—at the monstrous wagon.

"Did you want to set the wheels on first?" Pandaros Krite came out from the other side of the wagon. He was dark-haired and a bit taller than Artelo, but lacked his landlord's solid frame and strong build, though these past months working to ready the Sterling's small fields for the chill of winter had somewhat hardened hands and limbs that had spent the best of their youth laboring in books.

Artelo was busy making faces at Aura. Pandaros brushed hay fastidiously from his knees. He hated to be dirty. "Well?"

"Nah. We'll take care of them after lunch. Right, pumpkin?" He bent and picked his daughter up again—a slightly awkward movement because he was missing his left hand; a gilt steel cap covered in a leather harness sat over the stump of his wrist—and kissed her. She was wrapped in a wool cape and scarf and had a wool hat snugged down over her head. Artelo smiled. Although it was but a few seconds walk (or in Aura's case, run, for since she had discovered how to run it seemed she'd forgotten how to walk) from the cottage to the barn, her mother had bundled her up as if she were going to be out in the cold for hours.

"All right, if you're sure," Pandaros said. "I'll draw the water and be right in."

Artelo carried Aura across the yard. Their property was situated on a terrace halfway up a hillside. Below was the road to Thackery and beyond. Above was the crest of the hill, crowned with trees that, save a few sturdy pines, were all stripped of their leaves now. Ahead was the cottage, smoke curling from its stone chimney. The window shutters were cracked to expel some of the heat from the oven, and Artelo could hear Brittyn whistling in her pretty voice.

He struck the cottage door gently open with his hip, let Aura quietly down, and slipped into the small kitchen behind his wife, reaching for her.

"Ye try aught saucy and make me spill what I'm servin, sure 'twill go ill with ye, Artelo Sterling," Brittyn said, casting a coy eye over her shoulder as she spooned mashed potatoes onto a plate.

"Aeton hates cowards." Artelo slid his hand beneath Brittyn's fuzzy sweater to tickle her side.

"No—no!" She twisted towards him, the spoon flying from her hand. "No more!" she gasped between flinching fits of laughter. Artelo stopped tickling. He pressed his forehead into the loose, gilded ringlets of Brittyn's hair and rocked her in his arms until she calmed, her shuddery breaths relaxing. Her round, dimpled cheeks were as red as apples, her goose gray eyes wet with laughing tears. She slapped lightly at his arm. "Enough, now. Ye've had your fun."

"Not nearly enough," Artelo said, pressing his lips to Brittyn's neck.

"That sort of fun's for later. And after what ye just pulled, ye can count yourself lucky ye don't sleep in the barn with Pandaros tonight," she said.

"I am humbly sorry, m' Lady," Artelo said, bowing. "Shall I kneel and do my penance?" He ran his hand down the side of her skirt.

Brittyn leaned in, eyes bright, and kissed him. "'Twill be plenty of penance for ye, love" she promised. "Now where by Aeton did that spoon fall?"

"Poon," Aura said. She was sitting beside the table shoving fingerfuls of potatoes from the wooden spoon into her mouth.

"Naughty!" Brittyn exclaimed, gathering Aura up. "Ye know better, Aurora Sterling! You're not to be eatin things off the floor! Give that to your Ma."

Artelo leaned back against the table and laughed as Aura waved the spoon wildly, like a magus caught in some mad spell-casting frenzy. He reached and snared the spoon, setting it on the table. "Come here, both of you," he said, opening his arms and enfolding them in a warm embrace—

The outer room of the cottage blazed with aethereal light.

Brittyn screamed. Artelo released his wife and daughter and stepped between them and the light, a length of gleaming blade snapping from his wrist-cap. Aura started to cry.

"My apologies for disturbing this domestic bliss," said Ralak the Red.

50

Artelo's first thought after the shock of the Archamagus' sudden appearance had passed came unbidden and unchecked from the very depths of his heart: something had happened to Solsta.

It was not the Crown who was in dire need, however, and Artelo felt a guilty relief at learning that it was Argentia that Ralak had come to beg aid for.

"Ye can't do this!" Brittyn blurted, pointing at Ralak. Artelo tried to calm her, but she would not be stayed. "What gives ye the right to barge in here with yer fancy magic flashes and demand my husband come away with ye?"

"Peace," Ralak said calmly. "Artelo may do as he wishes. I am not here with the Crown's authority or her command, only as a friend of both your husband and Lady Dasani."

"How bad is it?" Artelo asked. The look of black betrayal Brittyn stabbed at him cut deeply, but he had to know.

"That I am here should tell you enough," Ralak said. His worst fear was that the danger went beyond Argentia's peril, and that some threat to all Teranor had been hatched, but of that he spoke nothing.

"Ye mean to go, don't ye," Brittyn said. Her eyes were pale fire.

"I—"

"Damn it, Artelo! Ye can't do this to me. Not again!"

Artelo looked helplessly from his wife to Ralak. Conflicted duties shadowed his face. While the Archamagus pitied the knight, he had little time to spend on such crises. "Stay or come, as you will, but decide now," he said. "I have others to gather."

"Then they'll have to help you," Artelo said, taking Brittyn's hand. He had left her once and it had nearly destroyed her. *I can't do that again....*

But there was pain in his voice and his eyes as he spoke, as if he was betraying himself as well as Argentia. *And what trouble must it be if Gen can't figure her way past it on her own?*

He forced the thought aside. "I can't. My duty lies here now, with my wife and my daughter. I'm sorry, Ralak. Truly."

"As am I," the Archamagus replied. He was not surprised—of all the aid he intended to gather to his purposes, he had been most doubtful of Artelo's—but it still rankled him. "Such selfishness does not become you, Sir Sterling."

"I'm not Sir Sterling anymore!" Artelo said sharply.

"It is not the armor that make the knight," Ralak said, shaking his head.

Before Artelo could even reply, Ralak vanished as he had come. This time, Aura clapped in childish delight at the scintillating burst of light.

51

Augustus Falkyn was just sitting down to an eagerly awaited dinner—his second of the day—when someone knocked at his door.

"Who calls at dinner?" he muttered. "Just a moment!" Still grumbling, the halfling pushed back from the table and stomped as fiercely as his hairy little feet could manage across his chambers. Augustus lived alone in a small apartment above a horticulturist's shop in Argo's Market Square: an arrangement that suited both parties well. The halfling was very fond of plants. The horticulturist, who dealt in exotic and expensive varieties of flora, was pleased to have a member of the Watch living on the premises to dissuade potential thieves. He had even agreed to let Augustus modify the chambers to better suit his size, though nothing had been done about the stairs, which often posed an annoying challenge to the magus on his way home, particularly if he was carrying parcels.

Just as Augustus reached the door, the knocking came again.

"I said a moment!"

"We don't have a moment," came the voice from without.

"Kest!" Augustus opened his door. "Come in. Why didn't you say it was you? What's the matter? I was just about to eat. Can I offer you something?" he asked hopefully.

Kest ducked through the door, which had been customized to five feet tall rather than the usual seven. Once across the threshold, he was able to straighten up. The ceilings were still of a standard height, but the furniture all was shrunken; it looked like a child's array of tables and seats, with the exception of one chair in the corner large enough to accommodate a human guest.

Kest did not sit. "Dinner's going stand cold, my friend."

"I knew you were going to say that," Augustus groaned.

"And I know you had a full meal already at the garrison, so stop whining."

"That was three hours ago." Augustus sighed, glancing longingly into his tidy kitchen and running a hand through his thick curls. "What's this about?"

"Gringoir sent me. Apparently we're wanted by a visitor of some import."

"Who? What visitor?"

"I don't know," Kest said. "I had to play errand boy because your oculyr's not working."

"It's working, it's just hooded! I'm off duty tonight. For that matter, shouldn't you be home with Lyrissa?"

Kest raised a placating hand. "Calm down. I was home, and I'd like to get back there sometime tonight, so if you don't mind?"

"Guess there's not much choice, is there?" Augustus said, waving his hands in disgust. "Let me get my pipe and cloak."

"Better that you get your wand and open an aethergate."

The halfling shook his head. "No dinner, no pipe, and now he wants me to conjure us across the city as well!"

"Yes, I weep for your suffering," Kest said.

Augustus looked up, a grin finally spreading on his cherubic features. "You should," he said. Drawing his wand from his belt, he summoned the aether.

52

"About time," Ethoven Vig huffed when Kest and Augustus entered the Court of the Magistrates. The round chamber was like an arena, with the Magistrates' chairs in a raised arc of judgment above a pit where the guilty stood to hear their sentences. All those seats were empty now; the three men waiting for Kest and Augustus were standing in the pit like common thieves.

Ethoven, the leader of Argo's Watch magi, had a pugnacious expression and a broad brow beneath a thatch of thick, unkempt white hair. He was short, bandy legged, and wide shouldered, with thick arms and big, knotty hands better suited to barroom brawls than to wand waving. Were it not for his robes he would have been more easily mistaken for a sailor or a dock laborer than a wizard.

Chief Magistrate Gringoir, lean and fit, his uniform crisp and spotless, looked as if he would be at ease taking tea with the Crown. His gray hair and moustache gave him a patriarchal air, almost grandfatherly until one looked into the blue eyes behind small spectacles. Those eyes were quick and shrewd and had seen much, both on Argo's streets as a young patrolman and later a Watch Captain, and most recently in this very court, where Gringoir's gavel presided over the fates of many.

Beside these two officials, Ralak the Red leaned on his silver staff.

"Archamagus!" Augustus exclaimed.

"Himself," Ralak said, inclining his head.

"Sir, what is this about?" Kest asked Gringoir.

"The Archamagus has come from the Crown to request your aid," Gringoir said.

"And he is not used to being kept waiting," Ethoven added.

"Tut. I know how much Magus Falkyn values his second dinner," Ralak said.

"I didn't eat one bite!" Augustus protested.

"I am sorry for that. I would not have disturbed either of you, but there is a mystery that requires solving," Ralak said. "Two mysteries, actually—one of which you are in part familiar with. That is, what has befallen Lady Dasani?"

Kest and Augustus exchanged confused glances. "Lady Dasani's dead, Archamagus," Kest said. "Her body was found in the park more than a month ago."

"Not so. A body that *appeared* to be Lady Dasani's was found in that park," Ralak said, raising a hand to stay Kest's protest. "You are not to be blamed for thinking her dead. The counterfeit is perfect. Yet rest assured, it was not Lady Dasani."

"Then who was it?" Augustus asked. He was relieved to hear Argentia still lived, but utterly confused by what the Archamagus was saying.

"Better to ask *what* was it," Ralak replied. "For it was a thing created from powerful shadowaether, and it bore the mark of its maker. *This* mark." Ralak reached a suddenly glowing hand into the aether and drew forth the silver disc with the M insignia. "Do you know it?"

Augustus gasped. "Mouradian of Elsmywr?"

Ralak nodded.

Kest asked, "Who's Mouradian?"

"A very dangerous magus who died fifty years ago," Ethoven said.

"I don't understand. How does a man dead for half a century fit into this? Isn't it much more likely that someone is using this Mouradian's mark to cause confusion?" Kest reasoned.

"No," Augustus said, shaking his head. His voice was quiet but sure.

"Why not?"

"A mage mark is unique to its maker. They can never be duplicated."

"Then—" Kest spread his hands in defeat. "Then I don't know."

"A mystery, as I said," Ralak agreed. "Yet I have not come here for answers. I have come to muster those I believe might help find those answers."

Kest and Augustus looked at Gringoir.

"Strange," the old magistrate said. "I do not remember you looking to me for permission the last time you ventured from your duties."

"Ah, we— Er…" Augustus stuttered.

Gringoir waved off the halfling with a smile. "All is well. Stay or go as you will."

"Her Majesty has not commanded your appearance," Ralak added. "None shall hold it amiss if you do not join us."

"I'll go," Augustus said.

"I will too," Kest said.

"Very good," Ralak said. "At dawn, present yourselves to the High Cleric at Wavegard. He will arrange your passage to Duralyn. You will be expected there."

"Thank you, Archamagus," Kest and Augustus chorused.

Ralak nodded. "Now, I must leave you. One last errand remains." He stamped the butt of his staff upon the stone floor of the Court and vanished in a mighty flare of silver light.

"Fortune follow you both," Gringoir said to Augustus and Kest. "Do honor to Argo and her Watch."

"We will do our best, Chief Magistrate," Kest said, saluting.

"I'll have to ask Rotellier to care for my plants," Augustus said as they left the Court.

"Didn't some of them die under his care while we were in Nord?"

"Thanks for reminding me. Three pard palms and an adder ivy from Sormoria—and he calls himself a horticulturist! But who else is there?"

"Magus Falkyn!" Ethoven was striding after them. "A warning." His stonemason's hand dropped on Augustus' shoulder and he drew the halfling roughly aside. "You knew the mark you saw. I knew the man. If Mouradian is behind this mischief, you must see to him. Better for us all he truly has been dead these many years. If he has not, he must find his way to death now. Look to it, Magus Falkyn. Look to it."

"I— I will," Augustus said, taken aback by Ethoven's sudden words. He fell in beside Kest again and walked on, troubled now by much more than who would care for his plants.

53

The Archamagus of Teranor was brought into the city of Shukosan in a ring of tridents.

The merfolk dwelling deep beneath the Sea of Val had almost no contact with the surface world, and they were glad of it. Three years earlier (as time was measured above; here below, there were only days and nights flowing endlessly as the tides) the order of their realm had been shaken when the last of the Wheels of Avis-fe had incarnated in their halls. A demon and company of adventurers from the world of sky and stone arrived in pursuit of the talisman. There was much treachery and death—including that of Sealeon, King of the Sea Elves—before the fiend had escaped with the Wheel, the adventurers with their lives.

In the aftermath, the merfolk rebuilt their society under the rule of Seakalon, son of Sealeon, and peace found the watery kingdom again. But the events were not forgotten, so when Ralak appeared in the depths of the ocean, he was met by outriders from the coral city and taken, as they supposed, prisoner.

For his part, Ralak was only too happy to have a guide to expedite his journey. The maelstrom called the Monster's Maw had been the marker for his teleportation, but beyond that he knew the way only by tale. He was using a magic potion to breathe the water—despite having crafted the potion himself, that first breath, drawing water in like air, had required a great deal of faith—and lighting his way through the dark fathoms with his glowing staff. Swimming in his robes was difficult, even with magic to aid him. When the cavalry of mermen arrived on their giant seahorses, he had been laboriously negotiating a kelp forest that seemed to have no end.

He accepted the rather hostile welcome with little concern. The mermen could not hold him against his will, whatever they believed. So escorted, the Archamagus came to the great canyon on the far side of the kelp forest, and at its bottom, Shukosan.

The city was beyond even the tales Ralak had heard from Argentia and the others who had come here seeking the Wheel. Great coral constructs rose from the depths of the trench. Their domes and towers glowed with phosphorescent algae that gave light to the shadowy water surrounding the palatial buildings of blue, pink, and purple.

Breathtaking, Ralak thought. *So this is what became of the renegade elves. No wonder they have never returned....*

Though he did not know the city, he knew its history from the legends that came down in children's tales. In ages eld, a group of elves had grown discontent with the world as they knew it and journeyed across the sea to discover distant lands. What they had found was the Monster's Maw, which sucked all their ships down—but not to death. Strong in magic, the elves had endured. Beneath the surface they began a new life.

Over time they had adapted to their environment. The Archamagus could still see the elven features of the mermen in their slender torsos, angular faces, pointed ears, and almond eyes, but from the waist down, where they should have had legs, were instead beautiful piscean tails.

The mermen led the Archamagus down into the canyon. The water grew colder. By the time they reached the mighty shell gates of Shukosan, Ralak had enacted a minor spell to protect himself against the elements. He wondered how the bare-chested mermen endured it.

They swam past brilliant seaweed gardens to the purple coral palace. There they passed through a second portal, this one conjured from the aether and shimmering with all the colors of Baltyr's Bow. Its magic gave ballast to Ralak's body. Though there was water all about him, he could walk upon the coral floor as he might on the land.

He was surprised to see that the doorway's dweomer had done the same for the mermen, who now boasted legs rather than tails. Their tridents, however, remained unchanged.

As they processed through the palace, Ralak marveled at the elegant simplicity of the construction. There were no doors. Arches and portals led from watery passage to watery passage. The phosphorescent algae, used much like the lightstones of the surface world, gave a peaceful greenish tint to the water. There were many round windows. Through these swam fish in brightly colored schools, the occasional sea-turtle, and even a few strange, dangerous-looking things that seemed to be combinations of turtles, lobsters, and scorpions.

There were merfolk also, men and women both. They cast curious eyes upon the Archamagus, but none approached.

At length, Ralak and his escort came to a third set of doors. Like the first doors, these were formed of nacreous shell and marked with gold crests depicting crossed tridents above a boat of many sails upon a whirlpool. Guards wearing green-and-black bandoliers opened the way.

Ralak found himself on the uppermost circle of an amphitheater of concentric rings. Algae glowed in stone braziers along the walls. A short flight of smooth-carved steps descended to a second tier where many mermen sat on stone benches ranging halfway around the chamber. The far side of the lower ring was an arboretum of multicolored seaweeds in coral pots, small tree-like shrubs, huge anemones, and sea lilies in pink and white.

A ripple went through the merfolk as the guards marched Ralak down the steps. "Another," they whispered. "Another of them has come." The Archamagus was scarcely concerned by this current of nervous suspicion. What he did not see in the chamber gave him hope his journey had not been in vain.

There were no guards save those accompanying him.

The company had fought a great battle here, he recalled, and had been severely outnumbered by mermen soldiers. Now the room was scarcely defended. Though the borders of the kingdom were patrolled as if Shukosan was at war, the rest of the city seemed at peace, which boded well for a diplomatic mission.

All conversation in the chamber ceased as the guards and Ralak reached the bottom of the steps. Ahead, a coral bridge, little more than a footpath, spanned the watery abyss of the center of the amphitheater to reach a great coral column that rose from unseen depths. Atop the column was an onyx chair carved from a gargantuan mussel. A crowned merman sat upon this throne. A trio of mermaids lounged on a carpet of thick emerald moss piled about the seat like cushions in a harem. Their skin was pale as marble, their flowing hair—purple on the one nearest the chair, green on the second, blue on the third—matched eyes as bright as gems. They were the most beautiful things in a realm of many beauties. Ralak could scarcely summon his wits enough to look from them to the throne.

"I am Seakalon, son of Sealeon, lord of Shukosan," said the crowned merman, breaking the sirens' spell. He was of a height and build with all the other mermen in the chamber, distinguished solely by the diadem upon his black hair. "Speak thy name."

"Ralak the Red, Archamagus and emissary of Solsta Ly'Ancoeur, Crown of Teranor."

"Thou art far from thy home," Seakalon said. The purple-haired siren glanced nervously at the King. He took her hand and gave it a comforting pat. "What business hast thou in our city, magus?"

"I am looking for Iz l'Aigle."

54

Iz braced himself for the impact.

He was hunched low over his seahorse, urging it through the coral strait. The tops of the crusty walls were lined with spectators, but Iz didn't hear their cheering as he hurled towards the pillars marking the finishing point of the race. He was ahead of his competitors, but the contest was not yet won.

Antentor, Iz's chief rival in all things in Shukosan, was closing fast, steering his seahorse with his knees and switching his lance between his hands as he bore down on Iz's mount. It was a tactic meant to disguise the moment and direction of his attack, but Antentor was arrogant and ultimately predictable. Iz already knew where the blow would come from.

And when.

They flew into the last length of the course. The other eight racers had been unseated earlier or were simply too far behind to catch up. Ahead, the strait bottlenecked so two seahorses could barely go abreast.

As the duo churned into this narrow mouth, Antentor struck.

The merman gave a final feint and thrust his lance at Iz. The tip of the coral spear was armed with a jellyfish whose sting would jolt Iz from his saddle and let Antentor coast to easy victory.

The strike came from Iz's left, where the patch sat over his missing eye. Antentor and most of the other mermen Iz had raced against presumed that patch was a weakness, a literal blind spot, but Iz was a veteran of many battles since the loss of his eye, and his reflexes were quick as a thief's. His crab-shell shield knocked Antentor's lance harmlessly aside, and he cut hard in front of the merman, forcing Antentor to back off or risk slamming into the rough wall.

The merman wasn't finished. He flung his lance at Iz's back, and this time it was Iz's turn to dodge hard, scraping against the coral, drawing gasps from the spectators above and giving Antentor the chance to draw abreast.

Their coral swords were out in the same instant. This was the most dangerous part of the contest. Iz had seen several merman badly injured or killed in these reckless duels.

The steeds bumped together, fighting to keep going forward. Iz parried blow after blow, but his defense was being beaten down. Antentor saw his advantage and swung a savage blow at Iz's head. It would have killed him had it struck, but the savvy man had already ducked, knifing his own blade between the seahorses.

Antentor recovered quickly from his miss. He reared to strike again.

Tumbled off his mount, saddle and all.

The seat's cinch had been neatly sheared by Iz's sword. Antentor could only hover in the water in helpless rage as Iz cruised past the finishing pillars with his arms upraised to the wildly applauding audience.

The other racers arrived and surrounded him, clasping his shoulders and congratulating him. "*Etanni, etanni,*" he said, thanking them as best he could in their own tongue, which over the past three years he was slowly coming to learn.

Antentor came last. "A subtle trick," he said in Tradespeak, doffing his crab-shell helm and giving Iz's forearm a quick, hard grasp. It was a polite gesture and acknowledgement of Iz's triumph, but there was only coldness in Antentor's steely eyes. "Next time thou shalt not have such Fortune."

"Fie, Antentor. Go and sulk elsewhere," came a dulcet call from above.

Iz's heart lifted and a smile spread across his face as he turned with the others to see Marina descending from the wall, her silver hair and tail shining in the azure water.

The siren draped her arms around Iz. "Well won," she said. Her voice was a whisper of silk against his ear.

Antentor gave them both a final, dark glance, and then swam off.

"Antentor will dare no harm to thee," Marina said, catching her husband's thoughts from his gaze, which followed the merman until he was out of sight. "Trust in me."

Iz nodded. He did trust her; it was Antentor he doubted. *And doesn't*

Marina always tell me elves don't reckon time as humans? He's waited three years. He may wait thirty.... Of course, in thirty years, Iz would likely be dead himself, but there was still Marina to think of, and—he hoped—their children.

He knew he would eventually have to deal with Antentor before he could truly be at peace here, but for the moment he would let it be.

The crowd was breaking up. There were no prizes won in these races save honor and the esteem of the merfolk—both of which Iz had been working hard to earn since his return to Shukosan. It was a long and difficult task to sway the sea elves. Sometimes Iz felt more like a novelty—some freak thing he might have seen in a cage at Carnival on his home island of Cyprytal—than a truly respected guest of the merfolk, but on a good day he believed that he was making progress.

The racing helped. Iz had learned early-on to ride the giant seahorses, which were at least as fast as their land-born cousins, but it was many months before his petition to enter the races was granted. When he finally did race, he discovered he had a knack for the competition. This was his fifth race, and he had won them all.

"Come on," he said.

"Wither?" Marina asked.

"Time for the victor to claim his spoils."

"La, and what spoils are these?"

Iz pulled her close and was about to kiss her when a commotion made him look up. Two royal guards were rushing towards them. They nodded deferentially to Marina as they drew near.

"What ist?" she asked.

"King Seakalon requires thee both."

55

"I can't friggin believe it," Iz said. "Ralak the Red!" They were seated on sponge couches in the quarters shared by Iz and Marina. "I mean...." He spread his hands. "How the hell did you find me?"

Ralak laughed. "Come now. When I sent you to Maneryl, did you not think I knew what you intended?" He gestured at Marina. Obedient to the magic of the palace, whose weighty water was more conducive to walking than swimming, the siren had transformed, returning to her elven shape. A skirt of some nacreous material fell between her legs, leaving their long lines bare to her waist, and a scalloped brassiere cupped her full breasts. Looking at her as she lounged upon the sponge chaise, Ralak wondered at the legend of the siren song, and if they truly needed to use their voices to capture unwary sailors.

"I should've known you'd figure it out," Iz said. Maneryl was the transmogrifist responsible for the magic that had altered Iz's lungs, making the water breathable to him on a permanent basis instead of with the aid of a potion such as Ralak was using.

"I am not surprised you returned," Ralak continued. "Only that you were accepted."

"The elves of Shukosan are not used to receiving strangers from a world they left behind," Marina agreed. There was no apology in her voice. "But in the case of my husband, let us say that I have some powers of persuasion that I used on his behalf."

Iz grinned. "What she means is that she told them if I wasn't allowed to stay, she and her sisters would sing this palace into rubble."

"'Tis not what I did!" Marina exclaimed, laughing and swatting at Iz. "Tell true."

"All right," Iz chuckled. "Marina's sister Tophiaz is King Seakalon's consort. She pleaded for me, and I think it helped that Seakalon remembered I was among those who tried to save his father from the demon."

"I thought you fled the palace under threat of death?" Ralak said.

"We did, but Marina...."

"I...made that well also." A shadow passed over Marina's face, like a cloud suddenly blocking the moon, as she recalled turning her song upon the soldiers of Shukosan to allow her love and his friends to escape.

"Tell me, how potent is your voice?" the Archamagus asked quietly.

"Strong," Marina murmured. "Yes, 'tis strong." She glanced at Iz. He nodded.

The siren transformed. Her argent tail lay across the couch where her legs had been. "Look there." She pointed to the far corner of the room, where a stone vase full of pink and purple coral branches sat upon a table. Keeping her hand extended as if to guide the line of her voice, Marina closed her eyes and struck a single piercing note.

The vase erupted as if sledged by a dwarven hammer. Shards and fragments blew out into the watery chamber. The coral fell to the floor, the bottoms of its stalks vaporized.

"Bright Lady," Ralak whispered.

"That was nothing," Iz said. "Trust me."

Ralak looked at Marina. She lowered her arm slowly and shuddered a little. When her silver eyes opened, the Archamagus saw a brief glimmer there that reminded him of the light in Kirin's eyes as the nights of the full moon neared; an awareness of a power within her that she both feared and loved.

A moment later that look had passed and Marina's legs again replaced her tail. "I will sweep that up," the siren said.

"Stay." Ralak raised his hands, summoning the aether. The remnants of the vase whirled up in a tight storm of bubbling water and vanished.

"That's a handy trick," Iz said.

"I have many of those. But you were telling me of your return."

Iz shrugged. "There's not much more to say. I have freedom to go where any Shukosanian goes, to join in any of their doings, but I'll probably be dead before I'm ever truly accepted here. And that's fine. As long as Marina's happy, that's all that matters."

"He is too modest," the siren said. "He hath become quite the celebrity of late, racing seahorses better than many of my kin."

"Ah, just luck," Iz said, but his one eye sparked, and Ralak knew the warrior still dwelt in the heart of the man despite the life of ease he had adopted here, fathoms below. He was glad to see it.

"Anyway, enough of this nonsense. Tell me all the news," Iz said. "How are Kodius and Kirin and Argentia?"

Ralak said, "That is why I have come."

56

In Duralyn of the Crown, those called by the Archamagus gathered.

After Ralak delivered Kodius and Kirin to Castle Aventar, the Norden and the werefox were provided a guest chamber and left to their own devices until evening, when they dined with Solsta. Their reunion was a fond one, though Solsta roundly chastised the pair for neglecting her in their travels.

"Pardon, Majesty. We were not near Duralyn until recently," Kodius said.

"And we did not wish to impose," Kirin added.

"It's no imposition!" Solsta exclaimed. "Right Mirk?"

The meerkat looked up from the end of the table, where he was fastidiously rolling a morsel of bread in a dish of soft yellow butter. "Mistress is right," he agreed.

"There, you see?" Solsta laughed.

"Our wandering is ended," Kodius said. Kirin squeezed his hand in happiness at this reaffirmation of his intent to remain in the North Wood. "We shall be near enough, and will do better not to be strangers."

"So easily?" the Crown teased. "No, I think you must be punished. You must tell me of all your adventures."

So they dined and traded tales. Afterwards, as they took tea in one of Aventar's sitting rooms, the Crown questioned Kodius and Kirin as to what roads they felt were safest to travel and which were most beset by bandits so she would know where to concentrate her efforts to make the routes between her cities safer.

Kodius's answer was interrupted by a knocking at the door. "Majesty," Ralak said, sweeping in.

Iz and Marina entered the chamber behind him.

"*Kodius?*" If Iz had been amazed to see Ralak, he was thunderstruck to see Kodius; the Archamagus had made no mention of gathering others when he bid them answer the Crown's call.

The Norden was just as stunned. "*Iz?*"

"Aeton's bolts! Well met!" Iz stepped forward, arms wide.

Kodius held off in shock, trying to reconcile this pale man with the olive-skinned Cyprytalyr who had been like a brother to him for more than a decade. The voice was the same, the neatly trimmed moustache and goatee were the same, the spiky black hair was the same, the eye patch was the same. He felt as if he was seeing a ghost. "Iz?" he repeated.

"Glad you haven't forgotten my name, jackass!"

Kodius roared a laugh, for this was the same old Iz indeed. He leaped up and hammered Iz with a bear-like embrace, hefting the smaller man off the ground. "Iz l'Aigle! God damn it's good to see you!"

"Hello, Iz," Kirin said when Kodius had deposited his friend back on his feet. She stood and leaned up and kissed him on the cheek. "Good to have you back."

"Good to be back." Then, realizing Marina was standing with the Archamagus, he held his hand out for her. She came forward, almost shyly. "You remember Marina?"

"You're not easily forgotten," Kodius said. "After all, we owe you our lives."

"I remember thee as well. Thee both," Marina said.

The werefox smiled, but her golden eyes were tinged with dark memories. She had been tortured during the company's imprisonment in Shukosan, and in the battle to gain the Wheel one of Marina's sisters had nearly killed her.

Give her a chance, she told herself. *Kodius is right. She saved us that day. You can't hold her to task for the crimes of her kin....*

Kirin surprised Marina—and herself—by coming and kissing her as she had kissed Iz. "Be welcome," she said, and meant it.

"Yes," Solsta said. "Be most welcome indeed."

They all turned towards the Crown, who had risen from her seat. Iz knelt, and Marina, after a slightly confused hesitation, did likewise. "Majesty," Iz said. "Forgive me. I meant no disrespect."

"None was taken. Please, get up and save such foolishness for some other place." They rose obediently. "Now tell me, who is this?"

"Majesty, this is my wife Marina, daughter of Malakhi of Shukosan. Marina, this is Solsta Ly'Ancoeur, Crown of Teranor."

"Again, welcome," Solsta said.

Marina looked surprised. Though she and her sisters were afforded places of high honor in Shukosan because of their special abilities, it was the males who ruled the city beneath the sea, just as their sylvan counterparts did on the surface. She recovered quickly, however, and made a formal curtsy, spreading the skirts of the flowing pink dress Ralak had provided for her in lieu of her native attire. "I am honored, Majesty of Teranor."

Solsta nodded. "Please, everyone, sit." She paused, looking them over as they dropped into the various cushioned seats and couches. She was touched with joy at having her friends around her again, even for this short period before she would ask them into danger.

"I am glad to see you all well," she said, settling back into her own chair beside the window. Moonlight shone through the glass. In it Solsta appeared both regal and beautiful to those who had not seen her in three years. *Older, too*, Iz thought. *But not so careworn as when I left. She's grown into her reign....*

Solsta felt his gaze and smiled. "Kodius and Kirin have told me of their travels," she said. "But you— I don't understand how you have come to dwell beneath the sea. When you went to retrieve the Wheel you went with Ralak's magic to aid you."

"Magic aided me again, Majesty," Iz said, and began the tale of his visit to Maneryl of Harrowgate and his return to Shukosan.

57

Long into the night Iz spoke, the others listening raptly and occasionally interrupting with a question. They had more tea and cakes, and a brief interlude in which Mirkholmes levitated various pastries off different plates, piling them until they stood taller than he did. The trick was accomplished to the delight of Marina, who was fascinated by the meerkat, and to the scowling disapproval of Ralak, from whose spellbooks the knowledge of that magic had been stolen. In the end, Iz came to the arrival of Ralak and the summons of the Crown to come to the aid of Argentia.

It had been Marina who decided their course. "Thy liege calls thee, thy friend is in need," the siren had said. "Thou art bound to answer, but thou shall not go alone."

"What do you mean?"

"For love of me thou hast embraced my world. Now I shall do the same for thee, if only for a little time."

"But—you can't. The air—"

"'Tis not the air that threats me. Remember, I am a siren, not merely a mermaid. I can breathe the air above the sea, but not forever. The span of a moon is granted to my sisters and me for which we may change the sea for land."

She did not speak of the risk associated with this: it was Writ that their moonlight glimpses of land when they surfaced to sing should lure sirens as their voices lured men, but that the siren who dared walk upon the land was doomed never to return to the sea of her own power.

All her life Marina had fought that draw. Curious though she was to know of the mysterious world that she, born in Shukosan, had never known, she loved the watery realm too much to satisfy that inquisitive urge. Now she would resist no longer—though the truth of the reason why she kept also secret.

She had scoffed at the threat of Antentor, but in her heart she feared he intended much harm to Iz. While she could face down the merman with her voice, she could not always be beside her husband. Were Iz to kill Antentor, even in self-defense, it would mean his execution.

Iz's success at the races had exacerbated the situation. Antentor would not long stand an outsider gaining popularity, especially at his expense. He was a subtle, dangerous foe. Marina was not sure how much longer she could shield Iz from harm.

In Ralak's arrival and request, the siren saw provident Fortune. They would leave Shukosan and its hidden dangers for a time. Whether they would ever return she knew not, but so much was her love for Iz—harbored in secret since that long-ago night when she had saved him from drowning off the coast of Cyprytal—that she had pitted herself against her people to aid him and his friends in their quest for the Wheel of Avis-fe. Now she would leave her people behind to be with him to whatever end Fortune rolled for her.

"A moon?" Iz asked. "What happens after a moon?"

"If we are then still bound to land, we must remain so forever," Marina said, concealing the fatalistic possibilities behind her beauty and the magic lilt of her voice. "With thee beside me, 'twould not be so terrible a fate."

"But I don't want you to lose the sea. You belong here. You belong with your people."

"I belong with thee," Marina said firmly. *For however much longer we are graced....*

"But… Are you sure about this?" Iz asked.

"'Tis my wish to see something of thy land and the many things I have known only from lore and tales."

Iz considered silently for a few moments, then nodded. "Alright. One month, no longer, Ralak. I'm not risking Marina's chance to return here. I'm sorry. I can't do that."

"Understood. Whatever help you can give will be greatly valued," the Archamagus replied. *And I do not think you need fear the time, old friend,* he thought. *If we have not saved Argentia in a moon, I doubt we will save her at all…*

58

They made the aetherwalk from Shukosan back to Ralak's tower in Aventar: a long journey of an instant that left Iz and Marina stricken on the floor.

For a moment Ralak feared that they were dead. Maneryl had told him about the magic he had worked on Iz, but in those first seconds it seemed that both the transmogrifist's assurance his spellcraft was reversible, as well as Marina's estimation of her ability to breath the air above the sea were both errant.

Finally they stirred, coughing and choking but recovering. Ralak provided fresh clothes to replace the minimalist garb of the merfolk and brought them down to the Crown and their reunion with Kodius and Kirin. That joyful meeting continued even after the Crown and Archamagus made their goodnights, leaving the two couples alone.

They were tired, but three years apart had them bursting with more tales and curiosity than had been satisfied. Conversation carried through the night and past dawn, from the sitting room down into the corridors of the castle and right on into the Throne Hall after the Sentinels came to escort them to their audience with the Crown.

They took seats at the table, still talking, paying little mind to the tall Nhapian in the Watch uniform and the robed halfling beside him. Iz lit a pipe Ralak had given him along with his new clothes. "Ah, my God, that's good," he said, drawing deep and blowing a smoke ring.

"Pretty!" Marina exclaimed. Smoking, like so many things in Castle Aventar, was novel to the siren. She was rapt at the architecture and decor and the food they had been served—tea, she thought, was wonderful—and her glimpses of the early light of day had nearly made her swoon with its beauty. She could scarcely wait to go outside, as Iz had promised they would as soon as their business with the Crown was ended.

Iz delighted in Marina's delight. He had not the slightest suspicion of how haunted a part of her was with the certainty that she would never see her home again. That sad foreboding she kept buried deep—and there were none in all Acrevast better at concealing their emotions than elves—giving herself over instead to the indulgence of a dream.

"Pardon me, sir. I don't think you should smoke in the Throne Hall," the Nhapian Watchman said.

Iz took another slow drag and exhaled the smoke in a plume. "You're probably right. But I haven't had a pipe in a long time, so I'm going to enjoy it until the Crown—the *Crown,* not some Argosian watchdog—tells me otherwise."

"Same old Iz," Kodius muttered, preparing to intervene.

There was no need.

The doors to the Throne Hall opened. Everyone at the table stopped and turned as the Crown approached, followed by Ralak, Amethyst Pyth, scampering Mirkholmes, and a blonde-bearded dwarf.

The two Argosians quickly rose from their seats and knelt. The four friends were following suit when Solsta waved a hand to stop them. "I told you last night, enough of that." Normally she would not have held such a gathering in the Throne Hall, but the gravity of the situation had dictated the choice. She did not want to have this conversation spoil her memories of a room she enjoyed. Even so, there was a limit to the amount of pompous circumstance she would tolerate from those close to her. "Rise, Captain Eregrin, Magus Falkyn. You are welcome again to Aventar."

"Magus?" Iz echoed. "Aren't you a little short for a wizard?"

"Oh? Then I suppose I am short for a Crown?" Solsta asked archly.

"No, no, ah, not at all, Majesty. It's just I've never—"

"Heard of a halfling magus, right?" Augustus said, tapping his hairy foot.

"Please, take no offense," Marina said, stepping between the two parties. "My husband's tongue oft runs ahead of his judgment and is lost." She smiled sweetly at Augustus and Kest. Without her true form, she could not wield the full power of her voice, but her dulcet tones were still strong and her beauty was undeniable. "Might we not all begin again as friends?"

"I think that would be a good idea," Solsta said.

Iz ground out his pipe and placed it on the table. "Iz l'Aigle," he said. Stepping forward, he extended his hand to the Watch Captain.

"Kest Eregrin." They clasped forearms. The others followed suit, with introductions made all around and a second batch of reunions.

"Griegvard Gynt!" Augustus exclaimed. "What brings you here?"

"If yer meanin t' Aventar, I'm th' ambassador from Stromness," the dwarf replied. "I live here. If yer meanin t' this meetin, same as th' rest o' ye. What that means beyond somethin bad happened t' Red I'm fer thinkin we'll all learn together."

"Indeed," Ralak said. He was anxious to get this council underway, but the reunions had taken on a life of their own, and idle talk went on in the chamber for several minutes.

Solsta joined in this, but felt strangely and sadly distant. As she listened to her friends, envy sliced at her heart to think how rich their lives were in ways that hers would never be. They had love and freedom to roam and wander as they pleased. She had neither.

No, nor will I, she reflected. An image of Ittorio flitted across her mind. The painter was still at work on her portrait, and though their banter remained flirtatious and she sometimes caught herself daydreaming about what his hair would feel like as she ran her fingers through it, nothing more had come of their time together. *Maybe it should...* She could not remedy her duty to the throne, which bound her life to her rule, but perhaps it was time to put an end to her self-imposed solitude.

First, however, there was a much more important task to address.

As if reading Solsta's thoughts, Ralak tapped his staff upon the stones. The gesture was small, but the echo filled the hall and silenced speech. "Be seated," he said. "Time is shorter than I would wish."

They sat. Solsta surveyed the gathering from her place at the head of the table. Kest and Augustus, who were not well enough acquainted with the Crown to know how she detested the throne atop the steps, were surprised that she joined them, but said nothing.

"My thanks for answering my call," Solsta said. "As you know, I have not asked you here for my own need. Argentia is in terrible trouble. We must help her."

"What trouble?" Kodius asked. He and Kirin had bandied guesses with

Iz and Marina, but knowing Argentia as they did, they realized it could be any type of trouble imaginable. Whatever it was, they'd concluded, it would be of the worst sort for her to need anyone's aid.

"Ralak can explain better than I," the Crown said.

The Archamagus cleared his throat, and the door to the Throne Hall opened again.

Solsta looked up to see who had entered. When she did, every thought of Ittorio flew from her head like leaves before a hurricane. She felt pale and flushed, cold and hot all over. Breathless at the sight of the figure in silver-shining armor.

Then she was on her feet, knocking her chair down in her haste. She bolted forward, heedless of the others, the circumstances, the propriety that should attend a Crown, her heart pounding his name even before it reached her lips:

"Artelo!"

59

Artelo had never imagined he would be back in this place.

More than three years had passed since last he stepped foot within the walls of Duralyn. Just the immensity of the Crown City was an adjustment for one whose world had become a hillside cottage and the occasional foray to the village of Thackery. Fortunately it was very early in the morning, and most of the city had not yet awakened. He was spared the bustle and congestion that would shortly dominate the city's concentric rings, and he moved toward the Royal Ring as if in a dream. His eyes were fixed on the spires of Aventar, their pinions flapping in the pewter dawn. How many times had he walked the battlements of the siege wall? How many times had he paced the interior courts while Solsta took the air of Aventar's magnificent gardens? How many times stood the watch outside her chambers, long into the night—

Enough! Remember why you are here....

M

"Where man?" Aura asked after Ralak had vanished from the Sterling's cottage.

"Gone," Brittyn said quickly. "And never ye mind him."

"Brit, I'm—" Artelo began.

"Best ye don't, Artelo Sterling," Brittyn said. He could see she was fighting tears. "Just let it be." She took Aura to the table and settled her in her seat. "Time for lunch, what's hot of it still to eat, at any rate."

"Brit, I meant what I said."

"I told ye, don't." Brittyn said, brushing past Artelo to the stove.

The door banged opened.

Brittyn jumped and gave a startled cry. Artelo snapped his head around as Pandaros burst in with the waterbucket. "Is everything all right?" he asked. "I saw a flash. I thought maybe something had caught fire." He looked at the bucket. "I mean, this was for lunch anyway, but…"

"Everything's fine," Artelo said. "We had a visitor, but he's gone now."

"A visitor?"

"You might have heard of him. Ralak the Red."

Pandaros' eyes widened. "The Archamagus? What— What did he want?"

"He was looking for someone."

"Oh? Who was he looking for?" Pandaros had paled but Artelo didn't notice. His gaze was far away.

Brittyn set the plates on the table; they clattered loudly in the silence behind Pandaros' question.

"Someone else," Artelo said with a grim smile.

They sat to eat. Only Aura seemed untroubled, demolishing her potatoes and carrots with innocent gusto.

Artelo spent the afternoon in the barn fixing the wagon. The shadow of Ralak's visit followed him like a curse.

60

"Brit?" Artelo called.

Evening had fallen. Pandaros had returned to the barn—by then he presumed that whatever had brought the Archamagus to the cottage had nothing to do with him and the medallion he had stolen from Promitius the Brown—and Artelo had just locked the sheep in their pen. Aura was sleeping in her tiny bed.

Brittyn was in their room, kneeling at the foot of their bed. At first he thought she was praying, though he'd never seen her do such a thing.

She turned and looked up. He saw that she was not praying but taking pieces of chainmail from an old trunk and stuffing the armor into a well-worn traveling pack. "What are you doing?" he asked.

"Packing ye." She was crying.

"But—" He took her hands, stopping her. "Brittyn? Why are—"

"Because I know ye, Artelo Sterling. I know if ye can help, then ye help. It's what ye do."

She looked at him and gave a little sigh. If Ralak's condemnation of selfishness had weighed on Artelo through the day, it had sat even heavier upon Brittyn, who knew her husband had stayed behind chiefly because of her own disapproval and anger. Finally, her guilt became too much to carry. As much as it frightened her, for his peace and her own, she had to let him go.

"I told you—"

"I know what ye said, and ye answered true enough. I'm glad that Aura and I are first in your heart." She sighed again, deeper this time, and wiped at her eyes. "But the wizard's right. Whether ye use a spade or a sword, ye are a knight through and through. I love ye for it, and with that love I send ye to help your friend."

Artelo was stunned. Three years ago, when he had abandoned Brittyn to ride to the aid of his friends in the Dragon Mountains, she had fought violently against his leaving, afraid he would be killed or—worse— reunited with the Crown.

He had gone despite Brittyn's protests, promising to return. He had kept that promise, choosing his wife over Solsta. In so doing, he had healed much of the jealous fear in Brittyn's heart, but until today there had been no test to prove it.

"Brit, I—"

"Shhh." She placed her fingers to his lips. "Ye must go, and ye know it. Go and come back to me, like ye did before."

"That was different," Artelo retorted. "I had a responsibility to see the Wheels destroyed. I have no idea what's happened to Argentia, but whatever it was, it wasn't my fault. My duty is only to you and Aura."

"And to your own self." Brittyn said. "Did ye not once tell me ye were no good to me if ye couldn't be true to yourself?"

Artelo nodded slowly.

"Then be true to yourself and go help your friend."

Artelo took Brittyn in his arms and pressed his forehead to hers. "Are you angry?" he asked. It was a lame question, but he meant it sincerely.

"I'm not happy, aye. Would the wizard had never come crowin at our door, and would ye weren't as ye are—but he did, and ye are, so it's best ye go, and with my blessing."

"Thank you," he said. He felt as if someone had lifted an anchor off his heart.

"Ye know how ye can thank me. Come back alive and whole."

"I will," he said. "I promise."

There was a long and awkward silence. "Will ye make Duralyn in time to catch the wizard?" Brittyn finally asked.

"Not by horse." It was three day's ride from the cottage to the Crown City, and Artelo doubted there was that time to spare. "I'll leave at dawn. Pandaros can bring me by the aether to the city, or as near as he can."

"Oh. Is that safe? He was just a 'prentice when his master died."

"I'll have to chance it. I think he's able enough. If he says the spell's beyond him, I'll take Snowfoot and get there as quickly as I can. What else can I do?"

Brittyn caught Artelo's collar in her hand, "If it's dawn that'll see ye off, I've thought of another way ye can thank me."

M

Dawn came too swiftly.

Brittyn, wrapped in a blanket, walked Artelo to the door. Pandaros, roused by Artelo in the twilight before sunrise, was waiting outside.

"I'll be fine," Artelo said. "Please don't worry."

"I worry when ye go to Thackery to bring milk and cheese, ye goose," Brittyn said. "It's me love for ye does so. But ye came back safe once, and ye will again. I'm trustin that."

Artelo kissed Brittyn, holding her tight and close, then bent over the still-sleeping Aura and kissed her. She woke, blinking. "Da's going away for a little while."

Aura nodded sleepily. "Kay, Da." She put her thumb back in her mouth. Artelo smoothed her hair and pressed his lips gently to her forehead again. *Keep her well and safe, Lady,* he prayed. *Keep them both well and safe until I return....*

"I'll be as swift as I can," he said.

"Swift's best, but alive and whole's all that matters. We'll be waiting for ye."

He nodded. "There are food and supplies enough in the root cellar. I'll send Pandaros straight back."

Brittyn started a little. Guilty thoughts of the lingering looks she sometimes caught Pandaros lavishing on her streaked across her mind like red meteors. She had never spoken of these things, not out of some intent to be unfaithful—she didn't even find Pandaros attractive—but because Pandaros eased Artelo's work and made it possible for him to spend more time with her and Aura. If the price of that was putting up with some leering, she would pay it.

I should say something, she thought, suddenly a bit nervous at the prospect of being left alone with Pandaros. *I will say something. If it continues, I'll tell Artelo when he gets back....*

"Brit? Are you all right?"

Artelo's voice drew her from her abstraction. "Fine. Just missing ye already."

"Miss you, too. But you were right: this is something I need to do. Argentia's like a sister to me. If we needed help she'd be here in a heartbeat. I have to try to help her."

"I know. Ye'd be brooding like some knot-headed ram else, and I'll not have it so. Not while it's in me power to change it." She kissed him lingeringly. "Go, love. Go safe and home safe."

61

So Artelo Sterling took his leave of wife and child.

Pandaros brought him by the aether to Duralyn. Not to Castle Aventar, for the apprentice had never been there, and even if he had the castle was proofed against magical access by all save the Archamagus. Instead they arrived at an inn called the Laughing Goat, where Pandaros had stayed one night during his flight from Promitius of Valon.

Not long thereafter, Artelo stood before the drawbridge of the castle. *Once I cross it, there's no going back*, he thought. But there had been no going back since Ralak had stepped out of the aether in his cottage, and he knew it.

Resolute, Artelo crossed the bridge and the courtyard beyond and mounted the steps to the doors of Aventar, where two Guardians met him. By chance, both knights had classed with Artelo in the Academy. They welcomed him and gave him immediate entrance.

The castle was the same as Artelo remembered it, right down to the lighting and the scents of stone and age. Even the sound of his boots as he walked was the same. It was as if he had traveled through the aether not only from the hillside cottage to the Crown City, but back in time.

He made for the Throne Hall, uncertain where the gathering Ralak had mentioned would be held. As it turned out, he'd guessed well. There were Sentinels at the doors, and Artelo knew the Crown's personal guard took over for the castle's Guardian knights whenever the Crown was in the Hall. They were older knights, but they recognized Artelo from his service and after an exchange of greetings they opened the doors.

Artelo stepped into the imposing hall and hesitated a beat, not certain he should believe what he was seeing. *It can't be....*

But his eyes saw true. There around a table were Kodius, Kirin, Iz, Amethyst Pyth, and some others whom he did not know. They were all staring at him in equal surprise. In that moment of recognition and realizing they were come for the same purpose, Artelo knew he had done well to heed Brittyn's words and follow his heart.

Then Solsta rose, tipping her chair in her haste, and ran towards him. All the world seemed to stop.

My God, she's even more beautiful, Artelo thought as she shouted his name, and he did not know what else to do but stand and wait and catch her as she flung her arms around him, grateful for the chainmail, so she would not feel how fast his heart was beating.

"Oh Artelo!" Solsta stepped back, looking up at him with those diamond-dark eyes that still were big and deep enough to drown in.

"Solsta. I— Majesty...." He knelt but she raised him swiftly up and started to reach to caress his cheek—then stopped herself suddenly, perhaps remembering there were others about, perhaps remembering that he was no longer hers to touch.

She dropped her hand and almost turned away, caught in the awkwardness of the moment, her face flushed, her pulse pounding like the waves of the sea in her neck and ears. The whole great throne hall seemed to have contracted to the space around Artelo.

Take hold, her father's voice warned. "I— I did not know you were sent for," she said. Her voice sounded breathy to her. She looked back to the table. Ralak, Kodius, Kirin, Iz, and Amethyst were already on their feet and coming forward, while Marina looked on with Kest, Augustus, and Griegvard, just as confused as they were. "Ralak?" Solsta arched her brow, waiting for an explanation. She used the moments to gather her wits fully back to her.

"I was not certain he would come," the Archamagus said.

"I'm here," Artelo said.

"Indeed," Ralak replied as the others crowded about Artelo to welcome him back. "And since you are here, and the last of those that were called, perhaps we might begin," he added when the din of greetings had died down.

"Yes," Solsta said, glad to have anything to tear her away from her whirling thoughts of Artelo. "Time is neither our ally nor Argentia's."

62

Here follows the tale of Mouradian of Elsmywr, as told to the company of the Crown by Ralak the Red.

M

Among the Order of the Magi, Mouradian was second in strength and governance of the aether only to Isulac of Orn, Archamagus of Teranor. In wisdom, however, the wizard of Elsmywr was but an apprentice. Heedless of the Forbidding of such pursuits, he delved in secret into the shadowaether.

"Many are the ways of the aether," Ralak explained. "But not all those ways should be walked. Some are simply too dangerous. Others are Forbidden. It was those paths Mouradian trod."

"What magic is Forbidden?" Kodius asked.

"Chiefly necromancy and demonic summoning, but there are others as well, more pertinent to this tale. We will come to them shortly," Ralak said.

As Mouradian's dark power grew, so too did the corruption of his mind. "For many decades he hid this from the Order," Ralak said. "Even so, there were signs: his impatience, and the things he made."

The Great Maker's title was well earned. Among his many inventions were aethergate mirrors, fonts of seeing, flying chariots, cloaks of invisibility, all manner of ensorcelled jewelry, levitating dishware, animated brooms and buckets for cleaning, horseshoes that made the animals run with the speed of fire, glasses that looked through objects, and myriad other trinkets whose catalogue, Ralak said, "would fill many tomes."

All these items Mouradian would sell in secret to the wealthy, without caring what purposes they might have been intended for. He used the profits to fund his profane arts.

Eventually the existence of the things Mouradian made in secret on his island came to the attention of the Order, for they were dangerous items in the hands of the untrained. Nobles entered magic mirrors expecting to walk the aether from one city to another and came forth mad, or blind, or not at all. Horses shod with Mouradian's shoes ran until their legs broke or their lungs burst. Even the more benign creations such as the animated buckets exhibited malicious behavior, spilling their contents on expensive rugs or flooding out larders.

"It was a thing the magi had long feared and guarded against by holding their craft as close as possible," Ralak said. "The Order resolved to curb Mouradian's power and make an example of him for any others who might be tempted to stray.

"Before they could take action, the demon came."

This demon was Ter-at, the same that for ages untold had sought the Wheels of Avis-fe. Its quest had taken it to Frostwood, home of the elves, and it had worked much mischief there before being discovered and cast forth. Not long afterwards, still searching for clues to the Wheels, it destroyed the village of Ranok, and Solsta's grandsire Techatemon Ly'Ancoeur had ordered its death.

Isulac Archamagus led a band of warriors and magi, including the paladin Sir Reisling with his holy sword Scourge, to hunt the demon. In that conflict the Archamagus and the paladin fell and Scourge was lost for a time.

The others, lacking the power to slay the demon, were forced instead to bind it with elven magic beneath a monastery on the Isle of Wikt. The story of its eventual escape and the culmination of its attempt to open the Shadow Gate upon the crest of Mount Hoarde is another tale: one known quite well to most of those gathered at that table, and in particular to Artelo, who had been there with Argentia in the last desperate moments on the mountaintop.

Ralak's concern now was with another thread of that tapestry: the aftermath of Isulac's death.

"By rights, Mouradian should have assumed the mantle of Archamagus, but the Order had already resolved that he be excommunicated. He was passed over in favor of my brother, Relsthab."

Mouradian came from Elsmywr to Duralyn for what he believed would be his investiture. When he learned otherwise, he flew into a rage and threatened to kill all the magi of the Order. "My brother's first act as Archamagus was to banish Mouradian back to his island," Ralak said. "A mighty battle followed in which some dozen magi, Relsthab and myself among them, fought Mouradian over land and air and even water, driving him back to his isle. Defeated, he sought to reap a final toll. 'I will rule you or be no more!' he cried, and broke his staff, bringing down doom upon Elsmywr."

Fire fell from the sky. The earth was sundered. The sea rose in thunder. Mouradian's tower—with him atop it—crumbled apart. "The whole island was swept under the Sea of Val. Destroyed," Ralak said.

"But if it was destroyed, and the wizard killed, then what—" Iz interrupted.

"Patience," Ralak said, lifting a hand. "I have told you what I witnessed. That does not make it truth." He paused. "The truth is that Mouradian did not die, nor do I now think Elsmywr was at all destroyed, though for fifty years and more I believed both."

"Then what happened? If he wasn't dead, what was he doing all this time?" Iz persisted.

"He was waiting. Waiting, and working. He has gone completely into darkness now," Ralak said. "Taken the Forbidden paths to evil knowledge."

"But what does this have to do with Argentia?" Artelo asked.

"Aye. What're ye meanin, wizard? Be speakin plain," Griegvard said.

"I will show you, instead, Master Dwarf."

Ralak waved a hand, opening a portal in the aether in which an image appeared: Argentia Dasani in perfect triplicate upon the dungeon table.

"Gen!" Artelo gasped. Iz dropped his unlit pipe onto the table. The others stared in horror.

"Yes—and no," Ralak said. "Each is Lady Dasani in form, but that is all."

"How in hell?" Kirin whispered.

"Simulcra," Augustus gasped. "Mouradian created simulcra."

"Indeed," Ralak replied, dismissing the disturbing image. He explained that using the aether to sustain and defend life was perfectly acceptable, but to create life with it was Forbidden. "Such magic is kept deeply secret, but it can be found. Mouradian did so and he has apparently mastered its use. Those are three of six simulcra of Argentia that I am aware of. The others were destroyed, but there may be more. Many more. And that is without addressing the possibility that he has also made simulcra of others unfortunate enough to have fallen into his clutches."

"Why is he doing this?" Marina asked quietly.

"I suspect he is attempting to make good on his threat to destroy the Order," Ralak answered. "All the attacks have been against magi. I see no reason that will change."

"Do you think he'll send more? That he can send more?" Kest asked.

Ralak nodded. "Until an end is made of this madness."

"What about Argentia?" Artelo asked. "Where is she?"

"A prisoner on Elsmywr, I should think," the Archamagus answered. "She lives—or so I hope. Mouradian needs her alive to make the simulcra."

"How can you know that if such magic is Forbidden?" Amethyst asked.

"Knowing a thing and using that knowledge are two quite different matters," Ralak said. His eyes glimmered, and for an instant he looked to Artelo every bit as mighty and imposing as his brother Relsthab had ever appeared in all the years the knight had served in Aventar.

"So she's a pris'ner. Let's bloody go get 'er free," Griegvard said.

"Not so easy," Kodius countered. "Prisoner I grant you, but how can we be certain she is on Elsmywr?"

"Good point," Iz said. "Just because the wizard survived doesn't mean he's still on that island. He might be keeping her prisoner anywhere."

"No," Ralak said. "The Order's Banishment forbids Mouradian to set foot upon any land where the Order holds sway. Had he attempted to do so, I would have known it. Rest assured, he is on Elsmywr, and there he must remain, for so long as the magi of the Order live, the Ban will hold him so bound."

"Then I'm guessin we're needin a bloody ship," Griegvard said.

"More than a ship, Master Dwarf," the Archamagus answered. "Much more."

Interlude: Two Torments

"It's not fair!"

Solsta's exclamation echoed in the marble confines of her bath chamber. All day this had been broiling in her: a confused cauldron of indignation. Now night had fallen and the object of her ire was far away.

Again. He's gone again....

"Stop it," she muttered, splashing water from a crystal sink up into her face. Those were just the sorts of thoughts that had been tormenting her for hours. She had survived the shock of Artelo's unexpected return, though it was fortunate she knew the history of Mouradian already, for all through Ralak's tale her mind had been swerved and her every thought seemed bent upon the knight, whom she had not seen since falling asleep in his arms on the eve of their return from the Battle of Hidden Vale. Before the dawn, Artelo was gone back to his wife, leaving behind only his heron-plumed helm and a note bidding Solsta farewell.

That had been the bitter end to a bitter campaign: one that had seen the Crown's forces triumphant over the demon horde but had reaped the death of her consort, Kelvin Eleborne, and the departure of Artelo, her first love and lover, from her life.

Until today....

The council had run on to noon. When the course was settled and the company outfitted, Solsta had gone with them to the Monastery of the Grey Tree. She had composed herself enough to speak with Artelo, inquiring about his child, managing not to wince at the thought that, in a world where Fortune had rolled differently, the joy lighting his features when he spoke of Aura would have been reserved for their own daughter.

"And you?" he asked. "Are you well, Solsta?"

At least he's stopped calling me Majesty.... "I am well," she lied.

At the monastery, she watched the company make the aetherwalk to Harrowgate, where a ship waited to bear them into danger. Returning to Aventar, she succeeded in meeting the majority of her afternoon's duties, but with only half a heart for them. She did not go to her portrait session in the evening. The thought of sitting before Ittorio now that she had seen Artelo again was too much for her.

She retired to her chambers instead, dismissing Herwedge for the night. Mirk, recognizing that his mistress was in one of her moods, kept well clear of her, fencing at his shadow until she had shut herself up in her bath.

Solsta sulked in her tub for an hour. When she emerged and stood dripping before the steamed-over mirror behind the pedestal sink, she was still angry with herself for behaving like some lovelorn girl. She'd believed she was finished with Artelo. How could just seeing him again scramble her emotions like some tornado tearing apart a village—especially when he was so clearly finished with her?

Are you so certain? a voice asked.

He had his chance. He chose her....

But in her heart, Solsta knew the truth was more complicated than that. If there was first-fault to be laid at anyone's feet, it was her own. *No. That's not fair either. It was Father who arranged my marriage....*

But you agreed....

I had no choice! It was duty....

And it was his duty to return to his wife....

Fine! I know that! "We settled that three years ago," she said to her reflection as it appeared in the gradually clearing mirror. She realized she was standing naked, her towel clenched in one fist. Slowly, she raised it up and began to dry herself.

By the time she was done, with one towel beehived atop her head and another wrapped about her body, she had rallied herself to the point where she believed she was going to be all right again, that everything with Artelo was in the past. "It was just the surprise of seeing him again. I'll be fine. I'm fine now," she whispered to herself.

Then she went out into her bedchamber and her eye fell on the crystal vase on the nighttable, where the heron feathers that had once plumed

Artelo's helm now stood guard over her sleep, and everything fell apart again.

"I hate you!" she screamed at a shepherdess she had never met. Collapsing onto her bed, she shook with sobs, horrified at her outburst against a girl who had done her no true wrong save claiming Artelo for her own. *And it was only because I sent him away....*

"Ah— God...." Solsta punched a pillow. Raising her stricken head, the towel now hanging askew, she shuddered out the words she'd not allowed herself to speak for three long years. Words whose truth had been brought from the vault of her heart in the moment Artelo stepped into the throne hall:

"Oh, Artelo— I love you so much...."

Burying her face against her arm, the Crown of Teranor wept bitter tears.

M

Argentia was going mad.

The huntress had no idea how long she'd been captive: time had no meaning here. She remembered the blaze of aether from the diamond at Mouradian's neck. The feeling of being torn apart. A flash of darkness. An explosion of light.

And then, this crystalline cell.

Argentia's mind reeled. She did not know if she was dead or alive. *What's happening to me!* She felt as if she was made of light. She held her hands before her face, watched them flicker like flame. Her body had lost its corporeality. She was a spirit. A silver-blue shade of herself.

She had experienced something akin to this when she battled the Revenant King, but that combat had lasted only minutes in the Wraith Realm and bare moments on Acrevast.

In the diamond prison of the Soul Wrester, the condition was eternal.

She would have screamed, but she could not summon her voice. She would have fainted, but there was no merciful unconsciousness in the Soul Wrester.

It was a Hell, and she was trapped in it.

Let me out! Argentia railed. No one answered. There was no Carfax-voice to comfort her. She was lost and alone and more frightened than she'd ever been in her life, She had to find a way free, a way to reunite this shade-form with the flesh-and-blood body she sensed still existed beyond this prison whose potent magic checked her as surely as the stone and mortar of a dungeon cell.

If she didn't, she might as well be dead.

But wish and will availed her nothing against the cursed cell. For time without telling, Argentia languished, and her spectral reflection mocked her, telling her it was useless to even dream of escape.

To Argentia, who prized her freedom above all, it was an unspeakable torture. No jailer to defeat. No lock to pick. No barred window she might fret open. Nothing but the smooth, bare, impervious crystal walls.

Twice those walls had flared with garish color, as if struck by ruby lightning. In those jagged afterflashes, it seemed Argentia could almost see the familiar silhouette of

(herself)

a woman, there and gone in an eye-blink.

The first of those flashes had not been long after her imprisonment, when time had not yet distorted like ripples across water. The second she could not place temporally, but it seemed so long ago that she was no longer certain if it was a memory or a hallucination.

She feared she was finally losing her mind. That the crystalline prison was wearing down her powers of resistance. Taking her into its madness.

Let me out! Let me out! she cried.

Wept tears of blue fire down her phantom cheeks.

Part IV

The Attack of the Simulcra

63

Mouradian was pleased.

This might have seemed strange, given the results of the six simulcra's attacks on the magi. Only Beltoran had died. Donparlion and Promitius had been wounded but survived. Ravagast, Maneryl, and Tonoto had not been harmed at all.

But the wizard of the Emerald Isle did not see failure in those outcomes. He saw progress.

At first, he had been furious when his scrying devices brought him images of his simulcra being destroyed. He quickly calmed. The beauty of the simulacra, he reminded himself, was that they were all expendable. As such, even in death they were useful. Those six failures had showed him the error of his designs and pointed the way to success.

Beltoran was dead, so it was clear the simulcra were capable of killing magi. Beyond that, Mouradian marked that in each case the simulcra had demonstrated some creativity when faced with problems, and all had at least gained access to their targets, in some instances breaching the formidable defenses of those wizards' estates.

Save for the remarkable Puma and Pantra, it was more than he could boast of any of his other creations.

So Mouradian was undaunted by the failure of the first six simulcra. He kept faith that his great war against the Order would come to its desired end.

And he made the second six.

M

The new simulcra had started their training immediately. Mouradian watched them almost constantly, with even more care than he had the first six. In the weeks that followed, it became clear that the simulcra were not truly perfect replicas of Argentia. Physically they were identical, but they lacked some ingenious spark that set her apart as a fighter.

They lacked her heart—and no magic mirror could ever duplicate it.

If that truth was beyond Mouradian, he still understood that to simply repeat the steps he'd taken to prepare the first six would only waste this next group. In light of the first failures, he changed the training of the second six to focus not so much on the combat skills they possessed innately, but on the techniques of hunting wizards.

Wielding his great powers of illusion, the Island Wizard created towers and manors and set them with magical defenses: gargoyles, glyphs, and traps. These were tricks also; he had no intention of harming his simulcra. Though he could make more of them, the Mirror would shatter if overtaxed, and it, unlike the things it created, was unique.

So Mouradian set the defenses to simply dispel the illusion if they were tripped, effectively ending the exercise. Over a fortnight, he watched as the six simulacra tried the different scenarios. Watched as they failed, and failed, and changed their tactics, and failed yet again, and changed, and failed, and changed, and finally succeeded, and succeeded, and succeeded.

Satisfied that there was no haven, not even Castle Aventar itself, that the new simulcra could not breach, Mouradian then made them come against him, again using illusory rather than true magic to make his attacks. Over the next weeks, the simulcra grew steadily better at assailing him, honing their speed and techniques to battle an enemy who wielded the aether, which was very different than a sword or spear.

They were nearly ready, but nearly was not ready enough. They would continue training until every last challenge had been met over and again. Until Mouradian was satisfied there was no defense any magus could put forth that their ever-growing capacities for adaptation and improvisation could not match.

There was no reason to rush. Even if his enemies had deduced the truth of the simulcra and Mouradian's feigned demise, he was safe upon his island. Elsmywr was unreachable without hazarding the aethereal Void, and no magus, not even Ralak the Red, had the power to dispel that.

Let them wait, and wonder, and fear. All to my advantage, Mouradian thought. He would wait as well. The Mirror of Simulcra would rest, gathering its power. The simulcra would train for their great task—in many ways the key task in the entire assault: one at which it was likely they would perish, but this time in success.

And then, the onslaught.... While the Crowndom reeled and the Order was in disarray, Mouradian would use the Mirror to its utmost, creating ranks of simulcra for the final conflict.

But all that was in the future. At present, he had these six and their incomplete training.

The wizard looked up to the sky, perhaps consulting invisible stars for their auspices, perhaps reading his own inner workings. "Another fortnight," Mouradian murmured.

In the interim, he had other business to attend.

64

Shrike had been a prisoner for six weeks.

The aetherdisc escape from her unexpected enemies in Telarban had returned her to Elsmywr. There, for perhaps the first time in her life, the assassin found herself possessed of a purpose not directly related to her vengeance upon Gideon-gil.

Her vengeance upon Mouradian.

That the Island Wizard might betray her had not been lost on Shrike; it was why she had stolen one of Mouradian's teleportation discs. When she rematerialized in the small chamber in Mouradian's tower, she had been swift to gather her senses. Her elven blood, easier acclimated to things magical, aided in her recovery after the arduous whirlwind of the aetherwalk. Her blades were out and ready almost the instant she emerged from the aether, before she was even certain if there were guards in wait.

There were none.

Shaking off the last effects of the teleport, the assassin went forth. The hallway and the landing of the stairwell were also unguarded. The problem was where to find the wizard.

Burning for the kill, Shrike let out a frustrated growl. Mouradian's chambers were above, as was the mirror room where he made his simulcra, but there was no guarantee he was not on one of the lower levels, or even that he was in the tower at all. He frequently passed long hours in his hideous laboratories, trying to perfect his elusive craft of making.

If Shrike went hunting for him, she would increase her odds of being discovered. It was not the armored men that concerned her, or even the swine, but things like those devilish flying monkeys, which might spy her long before she saw them.

She had come unknown into the tower. Surprise was with her so long as she did not waste it. *Then wait, and repay....*

Set in her purpose, the assassin made her way upstairs. Quick and silent as a cat's shadow, she came to Mouradian's chamber. She paused at the door, which stood open on the dimly lit space beyond. She could see shelves of books and part of a desk, but no sign of a bed or wardrobe, though those might have simply been out of her line of sight.

Shrike gave her attention to the doorway itself. There were no glyphs graven into the frame or lintel, but they would be there. Mouradian would never leave his rooms unprotected, even in his own tower.

The assassin ran her fingers over the stone. Felt the slightest tingling: her elven blood responding to the magic hidden in the doorway.

Smiling grimly to see her hunch that the runes were invisible had been on the mark, she took a small block from her pack. It was etched with arcane symbols that would deactivate the warding glyphs and allow her to enter the chambers. She was about to pass it over the doorway when suddenly she stopped. Once she was inside, she had no way to reactivate the glyphs. Mouradian would know something was amiss the instant he arrived just as surely as if she'd simply triggered the alarm.

Cursing under her breath, Shrike looked around. The hallway was narrow and not particularly well lit. There were no furnishings but there were shadows enough.

Shrike withdrew to the far end of the corridor, crouching low. In her black garb, she was nearly invisible in the gloom. When the wizard came, he would be facing her as he approached, but she had perfected the art of stillness. He would see nothing in the corner but gathered dark unless he came closer than his door.

If he did that, it would only speed him to his doom.

Shrike rehearsed the scene in her mind. She would wait until Mouradian turned to his door. As he disarmed the glyphs, she would attack, angling her approach along the wall behind him, reducing his chance to see her in the periphery of his vision. As for whatever magical perception he might possess, she would draw her thoughts deep within until the moment of her striking. The distance was a dozen feet: nothing at all to one of her speed.

Shrike closed her eyes behind her ebony glasses, bowing her head to minimize any chance of a reflection catching their surface, and slipped into that trance of partial waking the elves termed sleep, remaining acutely aware of all her surroundings without needing to use her eyes.

Waited.

65

Mouradian floated down the corridor on his silvery disc. He stopped before his door, raising a hand to dispel the glyphs.

In the shadows, the assassin's eyes opened. *Now....*

Shrike burst from her concealment, streaking towards the wizard, her dirks already out. There would be no exchange of words, only death.

She sprang the final distance, striking even as Mouradian sensed the danger and turned toward her, his hands blazing up aether. Her first slash found the wizard's throat an instant before her trailing hand speared the second dirk into his heart.

Both blades passed through Mouradian's flesh as through air.

Shrike knew she was undone even as the illusion vanished. The real Mouradian waited at the end of the corridor. He leveled his hand at her. Bursts of aether streaked from his fingers like flaming arrows.

Spinning and whirling, the assassin dashed unharmed through the fiery barrage. She had almost closed within range of her blade before the wizard planted the butt of his staff upon the stones. A wave of aethereal force knocked Shrike sprawling. Before she could rise, the glowing tip of Mouradian's staff touched her and paralytic magic held her fast to the floor.

The wizard gazed down upon her from his floating perch. "Foolish," he sneered. "Did you truly believe me so easily taken? Elsmywr is *my* island. I know all that transpires upon it." This was something of a lie: he had not known the assassin had stolen a teleport disc, but he had known the moment the aethergate opened upon her return. "You have provided me useful service, so I will afford you a courtesy I do not usually extend my enemies and ask you, what is the meaning of this treachery?"

"You know the reason," Shrike spat, struggling against the magical stasis. "You betrayed me and you will die for it!"

Mouradian tightened his grip on his staff. Vicious energy wracked Shrike until she lay almost unconscious. "I do not know what you are talking about," the wizard said. "But I know this: you will rue the day you turned against Mouradian, my dear. Rue it bitterly."

66

Shrike was brought to the tower's dungeon. There she was stripped of her clothes and weapons. Only the dragon's tooth token remained at her throat. The clumsy-fingered gatarines charged with imprisoning her had been unable to unclasp the chain, and the mithryl would not break no matter how they tugged.

A leather mask was placed over her head, covering her eyes. She woke in this darkness, which was not nearly as disorienting as it might have been. Shrike had spent most of her life in darkness—so much so that her eyes required tinted glasses to baffle the glare of daylight—and her other senses were more than able to compensate for the blinding hood.

It was a moment's work to discover that her hands were bound and that the shackle was attached to a hook dangling from a chain in the ceiling, forcing her arms to remain extended above her head. The balls of her feet and her toes barely touched the cold floor: just enough to bear her weight and prevent her from suffocating.

"Wizard!" Shrike shouted, not expecting him to answer, not even wanting him to. From the echo of her voice she divined something of the space of the cell. She filed the knowledge away. Listened for noises. There were none.

By the time Mouradian came for her, Shrike had assessed her situation. It was dire, but she still lived, and as long as she lived she would fight.

The thought that she might be raped held little fear for the assassin. Her mind had long ago transformed her body into a weapon. She had no concept of her own beauty, and had known neither love nor lover. Those feelings were foreign to her, as were passion and lust. She was a creature of ice, and in her frozen heart there was only the berg of revenge. Being raped would not kill her or break her, it would only build that vengeful impulse—now directed towards Mouradian as well as Gideon-gil—and make the wizard's death on her blades that much more gratifying.

But rape was not what Mouradian planned for Shrike.

He had other tortures in mind.

M

On the day Mouradian decided he would wait another fortnight before sending forth his second simulcra, the Island Wizard was no closer to breaking the assassin than he had been on the day he had taken her prisoner.

Though he had enjoyed many long hours abusing the half-elf, he remained perplexed by her seemingly motiveless malice. Shrike had sealed her lips, and no amount or variety of pain could make her speak.

Scream, yes, but speak, no.

Mouradian had employed many means in his attempt to extract the knowledge he craved. He could permit no such effrontery as Shrike had made, assaulting him and then holding herself silent when he demanded the reason behind her attack—a reason that, in truth, was inconsequential compared to the fact of the attack itself.

The wizard meant to know that reason nonetheless, if only to demonstrate his complete power over any who would dare make an enemy of him. He worked upon Shrike with every device at his disposal. Whips and blades and bludgeons mangled her body, bringing her to the brink of death, at which point the wizard would heal her with potions and spellcraft until she was as she had been before the torture began. He conjured fire ants to plague her. Drenched her with basilopard spittle, so the very flesh was eaten from her bones. Flayed her with a deluge of stone shards.

He could not break her.

Neither could he enter her mind and draw the secrets he wished from her. His intrusions there met with a snowstorm of rage so thick and strong that it was impervious to even his art.

For now.... As Mouradian descended from his observatory platform atop the tower, he assured himself that the assassin would eventually fold to his assaults. He admired her will and he was patient enough to enjoy this contest, which challenged his sadistic creativity. He was confident he would triumph. Shrike had endured for more than a month, but now that the wizard was satisfied with the progress of his simulcra, he was prepared to devote more than passing attention to the assassin. With his full focus bent to the task, she could not hope to stand. He would expose her weakness and put an end to her silence. *She will speak, and she will beg for mercy, and then she will die....*

But when Mouradian reached the dungeon, the assassin surprised him again.

She was already dead.

67

"Cast the body into the ocean," Mouradian said when the two chasecrows shambled into the dungeon.

The wizard was livid. The assassin had killed herself, likely by holding her legs off the ground until she asphyxiated, or perhaps by snapping her own neck as he had heard some of those Nhapian fanatics she had trained under were capable of doing. In death she had passed beyond even Mouradian's long reach. Such was his anger at this twist of Fortune that he would have thrown her corpse to the man-bull and watched it be devoured, but that child was dead as well, so he was denied even that spiteful pleasure.

With a final, disdainful glance at the assassin's slack form, Mouradian departed on his floating disc, leaving the chasecrows to their business. The two creatures unhooked Shrike's body from the chain, lifted it between them, and bore it towards the door, all with their customary silence.

Despite their animation, the chasecrows had no thoughts or emotions, so they registered neither shock nor surprise when the corpse in their arms suddenly writhed to life.

Shrike was fighting blind—the leather mask still covered half her face—but that was scarcely a disadvantage to one so accustomed to the night. Her deathlike trance had been a state induced by a combination of the elvish sleep inherited from her father and the discipline of the Nhapian monks that allowed the vital breaths and beats of her body to be so suppressed as to appear lifeless. The instant she arose from the trance she was fully aware of her position and fully in control of her body as she contorted and twisted, freeing herself from the chasecrows.

She landed in a crouch, perfectly balanced. Turning hard on one heel, she swept her other leg out, tripping the chasecrows down. She ripped at the laces behind her head with her bound hands, tearing away the mask. The world came back into focus.

The chasecrows were flailing, struggling to rise. The assassin leaped over them, darting to the chamber's corner, where all her belongings had been carelessly tossed by captors who did not expect their prisoner to leave their custody alive. Shrike snared Argentia's handbow from the pile of weapons and whirled around.

Silver shots slammed into the chasecrows. They collapsed, destroyed, their bodies aflame where the aethereal crescents had struck.

Shrike exhaled, glancing around. Her superb ears heard nothing, but that only meant no other guards were coming to investigate the commotion. It was no guarantee her path from the dungeon was clear.

One thing at a time.... The assassin returned to the corner. Now that the rush of combat had passed, she felt the dungeon's bitter cold. For six weeks she had shut that and everything else that she had suffered away in the adamant vaults of her mind. There those things would stay, locked down with all the other hurts she had suffered, until revenge emptied those oubliettes and made them unnecessary.

Shivering, she fished her lockpicks from her pack, unfastened the annoying shackles, and hurried to dress. There was still no noise beyond the crackling as the silvery flames ate away the remains of the chasecrows.

She pulled on her black thong and brassier, black leather pants, and thin black leather jacket. Stepped into her soft, supple boots. Strapped her belts across her slim hips. Last were her glasses, which had been cast carelessly aside but had not been broken. Like her weapons, they were made of Nhapian metal and glass and infused with the odd enchantments of the magi of those Eastern lands.

Shrike set the glasses over her gray eyes. Smiled chillingly. Once more prepared to do what she did best, the assassin left the cell of her torment behind and went to find the wizard.

68

Mouradian was in his laboratory.

The laboratory was divided into three spaces, each devoted to a different aspect of Mouradian's work. It was a den of horrors, though the Island Wizard did not perceive it as such.

The first section was a menagerie of sorts. Cages lined the walls, remarkable only for the chains that hung above thick pieces of torn and bloodstained bedding.

All manner of species resided in these prisons. Great mountain cats, thick-maned lions, and Nhapian tigers snarled at shaggy goats and grizzled wolves from the Hills of Dusk. A monstrous bull, black as an anvil save the mean red gems of its eyes, snorted at yapping dogs, capering apes, and huge lizards. The noises of all these creatures blended in a dissonant symphony as they paced their cages, stalking and clomping through straw and filth, barking and braying for a freedom that would never be theirs.

Once through this room, which at present was not fulfilling its true purpose, all semblance of normalcy vanished.

The second section of Mouradian's laboratory was like some nightmare nursery. The walls here were lined not with cages, but massive glass vats full of bubbling greenish fluid.

Suspended in these foul baths were Mouradian's women.

Bloat, pregnant hags, they hung listlessly, eyes blank, faces slack. Their pallid limbs were as swollen as their bellies, which pulsed and throbbed, full of unnatural life.

This was Mouradian's current crop of breeders. He had passed through many women in his long years of experimenting. When they first came to Elsmywr, sold to the wizard by one greedy flesh-trader or another, they had no idea what Fortune held in store for them. Mouradian wiped away their minds and gave them to the animals, chaining them upon the beds in the cages and letting the beasts, tricked into arousal by pheromonic perfumes extracted from the glands of females of each species, have their way with them.

Not all the women survived the intercourse. Those that did came to the vats.

Shrike, who had passed through the reeking menagerie with swift and fell intent, paused before these abominations. She had been to the laboratory once before, when she had been subjected to Mouradian's tour of his great works. Though hardly given to any emotion beyond anger, and certainly not possessed of any sororital humor, the assassin felt the same tug now that she had felt then: a revolted outrage upon gazing into the breeders' vacant eyes.

The wizard's voice sounded from the next room, cutting through Shrike's hesitation. All her thoughts again bent on revenge.

Shrike had come to the laboratory not long after her escape from the dungeon. Faced once again with the problem of determining where the wizard was, the assassin resolved it this time by going on the hunt. She captured the first tower guard she came across, demanding Mouradian's whereabouts. The guard knew nothing. Then he knew death.

It took the lives of two more of the metal-clad men and one of the ewes before Shrike learned that Mouradian had gone to his laboratory. She killed them all quickly, hiding the bodies as best she could but with no great effort. They would be found, but she planned on being done her business and far from this island before any harm could come of the discovery.

She escaped the tower by trailing a pair of chasecrows through a servant's door. There were no guards between her and the bridges. She made her way quickly over the labyrinth. A patrol of gatarine guards recognized her from her time on the island as Mouradian's guest, not as his escaped prisoner, so she came unmolested to the laboratory.

Now she crouched beside the doorway into the final chamber of Mouradian's mad workshop. Like the menagerie, this room was also lined with cages. The space in the middle held three massive steel tables. Two of these were cluttered with all manner of alchemical devices and spellbooks.

The third held the freakish white corpse of a thing that looked to be part man, part bull.

But that was not the strangest creature in the room.

This was the prison of the hybrids, from whose blood the critical ingredient of the fluid in the birthing vats was drawn. During her first visit, Shrike had been amazed to see the caged gryphon, the chimera, the gorgon (its potent eyes had been gouged out—there was no other way to safely keep such a thing); the harpies (muted for the same reason the gorgon had been blinded); the basilopard (its lethal venom sacs excised); and the centaur.

This time all she saw was the wizard.

He was across the chamber, speaking to the centaur. Narrowing her eyes behind her glasses, Shrike drew the hand crossbow and took careful aim. She'd expended six of the magical weapon's shots in the dungeon, but knew from the practice she'd taken with it that it could fire eighteen times before its magic needed recharging. A dozen shots remained at her disposal.

She would need only one.

"Sneer if you will, Chiryon!" Mouradian railed. "I tell you, it will succeed. Its blood is refined already—half human, half bull. It will make the ripening solution that much more potent."

"'Twill fail, as all thy attempts have failed," the centaur said wearily.

Shrike eased her finger back on the trigger, taking out the slack—

Changed her mind.

Holstering the crossbow, she drew a dirk. Silent as the Harvester's scythe, she closed the distance and slipped in behind the wizard.

"Thou seek'st beyond the province of men. Like thy creations, thou shalt come to ill." Chiryon's dark eyes gleamed as he spoke.

Mouradian read something of his danger in the sudden flash in the centaur's eyes—perhaps he even saw the reflection of the rising blade—and wheeled about. He was not swift enough to avoid the assassin's attack, but the dirk found his shoulder instead of the base of his neck. He toppled from his floating disc.

"Finish him!" Chiryon roared, vaulting to his hooves so swiftly the chains holding him strained. The gryphon screamed, flinging itself at its bars. The harpies took wing madly in their cage.

Shrike came for the kill.

But fast as the assassin was, Mouradian's powers were swift as thought. He conjured them to his defense even as he landed on the floor, sending a pulse of aether like a battering ram into the assassin. Shrike was slammed backwards. She struck the edge of the table and fell hard, dazed by the violent impact.

Mouradian's shock turned quickly to fury as he recognized his assailant. "You were better to have stayed dead," he hissed, lurching to his knees. Blood stained his emerald robes but he grimaced away the pain, thrusting his glowing hands forward like claws.

Jags of sparking aether crackled into Shrike before she could recover enough to dodge.

Screaming in agony, she tried to roll to her feet. Mouradian hit her with his magic again and again. Shrike's world blurred, the yowling of the hybrid monsters fading, the shape of the room spinning apart.

Failed, Shrike thought, knowing there would be no escaping death this time. She had made a single mistake—her first true mistake in all the many kills she'd executed—in not taking the shot from the doorway. It had been an awkward angle, but the chance had been there. She had let it pass, her cold, calculating mind overruled by the compulsion to drive the killing blow deep into Mouradian's flesh with her own hand, to stare into his eyes as they recognized his killer in the last instants of his life.

For that mistake, it would be Shrike who died instead. Mouradian would escape her. Gideon-gil would escape her. Both she and her parents would go unavenged. This was the empty end to an empty life.

Gritting a last bit of defiance, Shrike managed to close a hand over another dagger and pull it from its sheath on her belt.

The magic came.

The blackness came.

69

But, once again, Mouradian did not kill Shrike.

He checked the blast of unbridled aether that would have burst the assassin into screaming flames, sending instead a lesser bolt: enough to strike away consciousness, but not to kill.

He had thought of a better end for her.

A more useful end.

M

The mirror chamber.

In the alcove, the bodies of Kiel and Argentia stood in suspended animation, their spirits trapped in the star diamond hanging about Mouradian's neck. Shrike's body lay on the stones near the black-cloaked Mirror in the center of the chamber. The wizard hovered nearby on his floating disc. The shoulder and chest of his robes were darkened with the stain of his blood. Magic had healed the wound, which had been deep and nearly deadly. Shrike had missed her kill, but not by much.

Mouradian's eyes were closed. Though he appeared idle, in the fathoms of his wizard's trance his thoughts were whirling.

He wondered if he had erred. His mind was always on subduing the Crowndom, a sweeping objective that could only be achieved by ranks of warriors. Certainly Argentia was a superb fighter, but was she in fact the one he needed to dispose of the Order of the Magi? That task required a killer.

Did he not have before him a superlative one of those?

He had never considered Shrike as a tool for his end game. The assassin worked in darkness and shadow. It would be open warfare and battle that would strike the necessary terror into the people of Teranor to ensure that when Mouradian returned to their Crownless realm and put an end to the conflict he would be raised to the rule by the grateful adulation of the surviving masses.

So for certain it would be the redheaded ranks that marched upon the cities of Teranor. Should it also be those simulcra who executed the magi? Already there had been difficulties at that task. While he was confident the second six simulcra would improve on their predecessors' dismal results, was it possible that simulcra of the assassin might serve his purposes even better?

The deep ache in his shoulder told Mouradian this might well be so. Not only had the assassin successfully escaped his dungeon, she had come nearer to killing him than any foe he'd ever faced.

Should Argentia be the soldier, Shrike the executioner?

It was an intriguing possibility: one Mouradian decided he could not simply ignore.

On the floor, Shrike stirred.

Drawing a sharp breath, she sat up. It took an instant for her to focus on what she was seeing, for she was surprised to be seeing anything at all.

Then she recognized the black drapery and its implications.

"Ah, you are awake," Mouradian said, arising from his trance the instant he sensed the assassin had returned to consciousness. "Good. Now we may begin. I have once again extended myself to heal you, so please do not attempt anything foolish."

Shrike leaped to her feet.

Mouradian did not wait to see if she meant to fight or flee. He raised the diamond off his chest. Its light caught Shrike in mid-stride. The wizard watched as in that flash her spirit was torn free of her body and sucked into the gemstone like a shimmering streak of lightning retreating to the clouds.

The assassin's body dropped to the stones again: inanimate, but alive enough for Mouradian's intentions. He let the Soul Wrester, now glowing warmly as it assimilated another spirit, fall back to his chest. Levitating the assassin's body, he moved it before the covered Mirror. What he planned would result in one of two things. Either Shrike would be replicated and he would have a chance to test his theory, or she would meet the fate of the gatarines: her human and elven halves torn asunder to die in separate bleeding chunks on the far side of the Mirror, in which case Shrike would be no more use to him and he would kill her at his leisure.

Either outcome was entirely acceptable to Mouradian.

He began the incantation. Power flowed in the chamber as the shadowaether gathered. Mouradian gestured. The black shroud was swept aside.

The Mirror of Simulcra flashed its ruby light. Shrike's reflection shivered wildly within the convex confines of the Mirror's crystals.

The light went out.

"What!" Mouradian stared in shock at the darkened Mirror. The spell had failed. *How? Why?*

Fury rose in him. Before it could lead him to some rash action, Mouradian gestured violently for the shroud to cover the Mirror again and quickly left the chamber to find some answers.

M

The bottle imp materialized in a fume of sulfurous purple. It hovered on leathery wings above the mouth of the crystal vessel that was its prison, blinking its owlish eyes above the hawks' beak of its mouth. Its bat's ears twitched nervously as it wrung its thin, clawed hands together. "Ech, Magus?"

"The Mirror failed again," Mouradian said. "But not as before. This time it refused to even accept the image. Tell me why."

"What creature?" the imp asked. "Cannot know, cannot say."

"A half-elf."

"Ach! Elf! No, never, never elf! The elf blood is proofed against such magic. Broke did the Mirror? Shattered?"

"No. It darkened, but did not break."

"Very lucky that, by Bhael-ur. Try no elf, Magus."

Mouradian dismissed the imp and returned to the mirror chamber, his wrath tempered by the feeling that the imp was right: he had been very, very fortunate.

He swept Shrike's body up in a magical wind and deposited it in the alcove beside Argentia and Kiel. *Let her stay so and rot,* he thought. First the assassin had nearly killed him, and then she had nearly destroyed all his plans with an accident of her blood.

If the Mirror had shattered, Mouradian's hopes were ruined. He might still exact his vengeance on the magi, but he would never muster an army sufficient to conquer Teranor without the Mirror. To build another required materials nearly as difficult to come by as the Soul Wrester had been. Not impossible, but it would prove a great setback.

That he had avoided such a disaster he took for a sure sign all the stars were aligning to support his revenge. Still, that optimism was tainted with a hint of doubt: he would never know if the half-elf might have made a better weapon than the huntress.

There was no help for it. He was left with Argentia as the model for his simulcra, both soldiers and killers.

And so, a fortnight later, in accordance with his plan, Mouradian sent the second group of simulcra forth from Elsmywr to murder the Archamagus of Teranor.

70

In Duralyn of the Crown, six simultaneous flashes in the night heralded the opening of six aethergates.

To assault Castle Aventar by magical means was impossible. There were spells woven into the very stones that thwarted any attempt to access the grounds by walking the aether, to say nothing of the special modifications each Archamagus made to the defenses. Mouradian knew this, so he instead sent his simulcra into Duralyn with instructions on how to approach the castle.

The six arrived at various places in the city. The surge in the aether if they all appeared in the same place at the same time would have been large enough to attract attention, while six single aethergates opening at various points was not likely to arouse any suspicion at all.

The first of the simulcra came out of the aether onto the roof of the Tavern of the Laughing Goat. She slid along the incline, used her boots to arrest her momentum, and lay fighting off the dizziness and nausea of the long teleport. The noises of the night around her—human traffic on the streets below, voices raised in laughter and conversation, the clatter of hooves on cobbled ways—were all foreign to her experience on the isle of Elsmywr, but not frightening. They were oddly familiar, though she could not say why.

A few minutes later, she rose and moved carefully up the roof to get her bearings. At the apex she paused beside a smoking chimney and took in the spectacle of night over Duralyn. The air was colder than it had ever been in the controlled climate of the wizard's island. She hugged her cloak tighter about her bare arms. The night wind blew her red hair out behind her, carrying more sounds and scents she found strangely not strange.

The city was all shadow and light: dark hulks of buildings broken by the glowing eyes of windows. Above, the moon was bright in a black sky diamond-dusted with stars. Below, a few people were passing by, and she saw other pedestrians on the adjacent streets.

She looked toward the center of Duralyn, where Mouradian had told her the castle stood. Aventar's spires rose mightily above the city, but it was what the simulcrus saw beyond them that truly held her.

There, distant in the cold moonlight, loomed the black crags of the Skystones.

The mountains stole the simulcrus' breath. There had been hills on Elsmywr, though she never had occasion to climb them or see the vast ocean that lay beyond Mouradian's vale, but the mountains dwarfed everything she'd imagined. Their titanic shapes thrust towards the very heavens. It seemed the stars themselves might with little effort settle on those peaks.

The simulcrus felt something move inside of her as she stared at those mountains: some deep and tidal urge to try those heights herself, to taste the air upon those peaks—air that must be even colder and purer than the air of this crowded city—and from that vantage look to see forever.

Kill Ralak Archamagus....

The command cut through the panorama and the dream of mountaintops, silencing the pulse of adventure that had quickened the simulcrus' heart. She worked her way down the far side of the roof, caught her legs around a drainpipe, and slid silently into the alley behind the tavern.

The moment her boots touched the ground, she was off and running.

M

The second simulcrus was also in an alley. She materialized amid a heap of refuse and stumbled for balance before falling to her knees. Her hand pressed into something slimy. She raised it, catching a whiff of putrescence.

"'Ere! What're ya bout?" a form beside her in the dark groaned. "Lemme be."

The simulcrus jerked back in surprise. There was man in the garbage. He was struggling up now, fumbling for her in the dark. He reeked of things

(liquor, vomit)

she could not quite place, though it seemed once she'd known these smells.

The man's hand fastened on her cloak, pulling her down. "This're Gabin's place. Go find ya own bed," he threatened, raising a knife. The little light in the alley glinted off the steel blade.

Kill Ralak Archamagus....

At the sound of the command in her mind, the simulcrus came to full focus. Her palm shot forward, crunching into Gabin's face, breaking his nose and sending him sprawling. His wheedling scream turned into a choked noise of pain. The simulcrus ignored him, making for the mouth of the alley and the avenue beyond, which would lead her to the castle.

M

The third simulcrus stepped out of the aether into a park.

She knelt and shivered in a dark copse of skeletal trees. Listened to the restless nocturnal creatures scurrying about their nightly rounds.

The park was deserted. When she had recovered from the teleport she made her solitary way along the well-tended paths and out the wrought-iron gates into the streets of the city.

She was in a residential district, the houses mostly dark. Beyond them, the shape of the castle rose tall in the moonlight. That was where the Archamagus was. It was where she was commanded to go as well.

M

In similar fashion, the fourth, fifth, and sixth simulcra came into the Crown City.

From disparate locations, they converged on Castle Aventar. Direct assault was impossible. Guardian knights patrolled the wall of the Royal Ring, the courtyard surrounding the castle, and the siege wall on the far side of the moat. The great doors atop the steps beyond the drawbridge were guarded and held fast with magic.

The simulcra would come upon their quarry by another way.

71

The third simulcrus was the first of the six to arrive at the Monastery of the Grey Tree. She scaled the property's wall. Went from shadow to shadow across the grounds, passing clusters of trees and shrubs and large isolated boulders.

Came to the well.

Before his exile, Mouradian had spied out many secrets about Castle Aventar. As the apparent successor to the title of Archamagus, he believed this was his right.

Among these was the secret of the escape tunnel that ran from the castle to the Grey Tree's well.

The simulcrus descended a stone ladder to the bottom of the well, which in actuality held no water and served no purpose other than window dressing for the escape route. She use a moonstone to guide her down a tunnel to a locked door. An application of basilopard spittle took care of the lock. Beyond the door, steps led up to a short passage and a second door. This one was not locked. It opened into an empty wardrobe in an unoccupied chamber of the castle.

Drawing her blade, the simulcrus left the chamber and went to kill Ralak the Red.

72

Solsta stood by her window and looked out into the night.

She was clad in her armor: a shining chain corset and pleated steel skirts over silvery platemail for her arms and legs, all enchanted to be no heavier than garments of wool. Her rapier was belted at her hip. She had not placed her helm, winged with eagle feathers, on her head, but it was ready should she have need.

She did not think she would.

She was alone in her chambers. There were eight Sentinels, not the usual two, outside her doors. Once again she had been relegated to waiting.

She hated it.

That others could put their lives at risk while she was forced to remain locked away and safe had never sat well with Solsta. Yet rebel against it as she might, she could not change the fact that she was the Crown. Among those sworn to protect her, her wellbeing overruled all other concerns.

Especially since I've no child... That thought, plucked at random from the angry whirl of her mind, brought an image of Artelo and another pang of regret for what could not be. It also crystallized the import of her protection. When her parents and Ralak's brother had been slain in a fiery assassination, the workings of the Crowndom had carried on with little difficulty. Ralak had taken Relsthab's mantle and Solsta had come into the inheritance of the throne.

Now things were different. If Ralak died, the Order of the Magi would elect a new Archamagus from their ranks, just as before. If Solsta died, there would be no such smooth transition. The nobles of the Peerage would have to nominate a new family to take the throne. With their penchant for greed, bickering, and self-promotion, achieving a consensus could take months or even years. The Archamagus would steward the realm for that period, but the true danger was not in the time that might elapse with no enthroned Crown. Rather, it was that the Peerage might choose poorly and leave Teranor in the hands of an evil or negligent ruler. It had happened before.

Ultimately, it was up to Solsta to remedy this by providing an heir to the throne, perpetuating the rule of Ly'Ancoeur that stretched back unbroken for nine generations. It was an obligation Solsta was not sure she could meet. She wanted to; wanted a son or daughter who might learn from her example and grow up to build upon the good things she was trying to do in her own reign.

But a child needed a father.

Solsta had been forced to wed against her wishes once already. Would she be forced to do so again simply to ensure the future of her line? Could she face that?

The first time, she had kept her match with Kelvin Eleborne to honor her father's word and to secure the help he'd sought from the Peerage against the Trade Alliance. Now, with no such compulsions, could she live a lie of her own making, even for the good of the Crowndom?

I've given so much already, she thought bleakly, looking to the table beside her bed, where she'd set her diadem next to the vase of heron feathers. The weight of that jewel-encrusted band seemed to pull at her, drawing her toward the inevitable answer.

Frustrated, Solsta started to pace. Her only fortune in this whole wretched matter should have been that her youth gave her the gift of time. Then came a night like this, when her home was under assault. Though she was likely not the target of these attacks, she still might be in danger. It made her to wonder if she truly did have as much time as she wanted to believe.

Running a hand through the white Mark in her hair, Solsta tried to force such thoughts from her mind. In the end she would do as she must, as she'd always done, and would live with her choice. But her emotional turmoil after Artelo's return had not subsided very much in the fortnight since the company's departure, and she hoped with all her heart that her future might be something other than what she feared it would be.

Oh for the love of Aeton—stop this mooning, Solsta Ly'Ancoeur! Shaking her head, she picked up a book. She would not let despair keep hold of her. She had overcome the loss of Artelo once (or so that willful part of her insisted) and she would do it again. As for tonight, she would read and await word that the intruders had been taken.

Still, as she opened the gilt-edged book she felt very much alone. She wished that Mirk was with her, but he was out with the others in the castle.

Hunting.

73

The simulcrus came to the tower of the Archamagus. The wooden door leading to the tower was unremarkable; she knew it because Mouradian had described it and its location with respect to the secret passage before sending the six on their way.

The simulcrus glanced about. The hallway was empty. She pulled on the handle of the door. It was locked.

As she took the vial of basilopard spittle from her belt-pouch again, an eye opened in the wood of the door and fixed her with its accusatory glare.

The simulcrus took an astonished step backwards.

From around corners at opposite ends of the hallway rushed two groups of knights, a voluptuous woman, a man in livery, and a wolfish dog with a meerkat riding on its back.

"Halt!" one of the knights shouted.

The dog growled angrily. "Not the Lady," the meerkat cheeped.

A bolt of lightning leaped from the eye's pupil and struck the simulcrus dead.

M

Ralak had anticipated that the attacks on the Order's magi were but a taste of some greater terror Mouradian meant to unleash. Knowing full well the terms of the Island Wizard's banishment, he sent word to the Order to be on the alert for a certain redheaded huntress. He did not notify the Watch. If Argentia should somehow escape, or should the rescuers succeed, he did not want her treated as a criminal once she was home again. Besides which, the Order had many more ways of spying out their quarry than even Teranor's most effective Watchmen.

Neither did the Archamagus neglect his own defense, adding several new protective spells to Castle Aventar. Ironically, however, it was an old glyph that turned the trick on the intruders.

Three years earlier, during the Gathering of the Wheels of Avis-fe, a mad guildmaster named Frollo Chillmark had discovered the secret tunnel between the monastery and Castle Aventar. He took for a hostage Amethyst Pyth, whom he had followed through the tunnel in the first place, and stole the Wheel from the castle's vaults.

Eventually, Pyth was rescued, Chillmark dealt with, and the danger of the Wheels conquered, but Ralak did not forget that the safety of the castle had been threatened by that one gap in its defenses. He had set glyphs in the tunnel, and it was these that alerted him to the imminent danger before the first of the simulcra ever set foot within Aventar.

Of course, he had been expecting one, not five. As he materialized in a flash next to the charred, smoking corpse of the simulcrus, the remaining four intruders were foremost in his mind.

"Now for the others," he said. "Swiftly, before they can cause too much havoc." He closed his eyes, seeking through the aether. All the Guardians and Sentinels on duty had been ordered to stand their posts. The castle domestics were confined to their chambers. Anything moving in Aventar could only be the simulcra.

Ralak's eyes opened, glimmering with power. "This way."

The knights, Amethyst, Shadow, Mirkholmes, and Ikabod followed Ralak down the corridor to intercept the next simulcrus. The butler had suffered much in not being able to join the quest to save Argentia, especially since she had risked life and limb to recover him from the clutches of Togril Vloth. He was too old for such exploits, he knew, and would likely be more of a liability to Argentia's rescuers than any true help.

Tonight, however, when Ralak and the others came to get Shadow to make certain that what appeared to be Argentia was not in fact her, he had taken up an old but reliable crossbow and silently joined them. He might do little good besieging an island, but he could still help defend the castle.

Now, coming last in the chase, he paused and glanced at the smoldering wreck outside Ralak's door. He knew it was not Argentia...and yet in a sense it was. The horror of seeing her red hair go up in redder flames, of smelling the stinking, burnt-pork char of roasting flesh coming from a form identical to Argentia's was enough to stagger him.

Steady, old man… Ikabod hurried after the others, wondering if he had not made a mistake in coming. The crossbow trembled in his grip. He accounted himself a good mark with the weapon, but he did not think he could turn it upon one of these simulcra, even to save his own life.

M

Two of the simulcra had arrived at the tunnel at the same time and came into the castle together. They were making their way down an empty corridor when a door slammed open and a group led by the Archamagus charged towards them.

One of the simulcra, Mouradian's command ringing in her head, stood to fight. The other fled from what she recognized as impossible odds.

"After her!" Ralak cried as the Sentinels engaged the remaining simulcrus. In a short, frenzied battle she killed three of the knights before they finally cut her down.

Shadow chased the fleeing simulcrus, his deep barks echoing in the long hallway. As the distance closed, Mirk hit the simulcrus with aetheral darts. She stumbled. Shadow was on her in a storm of teeth.

It was over by the time the others arrived.

74

The fourth simulcrus discovered the charred remnants of her sister near the tower door. That spoke clearly of danger, and instinct told her that the Archamagus would no longer be found in this tower.

She searched the empty halls of Aventar. As with the other simulcra, it was the defenders of the castle who found her first.

She flung a dagger at the Archamagus. He batted the blade aside with his glimmering staff. The simulcrus fled, but chose poorly, turning into a passage with no exit.

Brought to bay, she fought well, killing two Sentinels and wounding three more before they put an end to her—and her death did give the last of the simulcra that had invaded the castle a chance to accomplish Mouradian's task.

M

The fifth simulcrus had followed the sounds of running boots and the clash of combat. She came upon an old man, a woman, and the Archamagus, all with their backs to her as they watched the fray.

As she swept her katana back to strike the Archamagus from behind, the light of the corridor's lamps glanced off her sword. This flicker-glow reflected off Amethyst's many bracelets, glaring up into her eyes, making her turn.

"Look out!" Amethyst cried, shoving Ralak aside and flinging her armlet at the simulcrus. The enchanted jewelry uncoiled in the air, a golden serpent striking out to sink its fangs into the simulcrus' cheek.

Screaming, the simulcrus staggered into the wall, losing her sword as she fell to her knees, half-blinded by the agony of the venom pulsing in her head.

Ralak loomed above her, his red robed form blurred to triplicate by her tear-flooded vision. "Wait! Wait!" she cried.

Ralak hesitated.

The simulcrus pulled a dagger from her belt. Lunged at the Archamagus. A crossbow bolt slammed her down into death.

Ikabod lowered his weapon. "Unnatural thing," he said. The voice of the simulcrus—a tone nothing at all like Argentia's—had crystallized the truth of these duplicates for him in a way their appearance never could.

"My thanks," the Archamagus said. He closed his eyes for a moment. Nothing stirred in the aether.

The attack on Castle Aventar was ended.

M

As for the sixth simulcrus, who had been the first of them to arrive in Duralyn, she had gone from the roof of the Laughing Goat to the streets of the Crown City, but the image of the mountains in the moonlight would not leave her mind. Though at first she moved to obey Mouradian's command, she soon wandered from her course, wending through Duralyn like a lost child.

Even before the last of her sisters had fallen, she had gone unnoticed over the wall of the city and vanished into the wilds of the night, in whose darkness she passes from the concerns of these tales....

75

"Are you prepared?" Ralak asked Amethyst Pyth.

Outside Castle Aventar, the first pale twilight before the coming of winter day shaded the sky pewter. Within the castle, things had returned to normal. In the wake of the attack of the simulacra, the patrols of Guardians resumed their rounds. The wounded were tended. The five slain Sentinels were prepared for burial. At Solsta's command, Mouradian's five simulcra were taken to the dungeon and burned along with the other three. "I will not have that filth in my home a moment longer," she said, and would brook no argument, even from the Archamagus.

Ralak, who was under no illusion that the threat of the Island Wizard had ended with their victory tonight, would have preferred to examine the simulcra for clues as to their making, hoping to discover hidden vulnerabilities. He acquiesced to Solsta, however, for he had no leisure for such examinations, and even less for arguments.

He had no leisure at all.

A journey of the utmost import was calling him on his way. Before the sun rose, Aventar would be far behind him.

Far behind us, he amended. "Mistress Pyth, are you prepared?" he repeated.

"Yes," Amethyst replied, making a final adjustment to her emerald green cloak. "As prepared as I can be, I guess." She was a strong woman who did what she needed to do, but she had ever undertaken adventures—especially ones into the wilds—reluctantly or under the direst of circumstances.

Unfortunately, these were such circumstances.

"Only two can attempt the parlay," the Archamagus said. "That is the Eld law. In this matter it still stands."

"I know, but—"

"There is no *but*, Mistress Pyth," Ralak said. "Our chances of success are slim at best, yet I know of no other way we might help our friends. A woman's voice will make our plea stronger."

"I was under the impression that you were making this suit alone, Archamagus," Solsta said from the doorway. She was still dressed in her armor and carried her helm under her arm. She had taken it earlier, when she went to the servants' wing to personally inform the staff that all was well.

Ralak was not certain how long Solsta had been standing in the doorway of the chamber, but he suspected it was too long. "I reconsidered, Majesty," he said.

"Then I suggest you reconsider your choice of companion as well. I will go with you."

"No, Majesty," the Archamagus said. "It is—"

"It is not a matter for discussion," Solsta snapped. "I will go." Ralak started to speak again, but the Crown interrupted him with an imperious wave of her hand. "You say a woman's voice lends our case strength. How much more strength then comes from the woman who is also the Crown? These are my friends whose lives are at stake as much as they are yours. I will not sit idly and wonder if I might have done more to help them."

"Majesty, are you sure?" Amethyst said. "I can go."

Solsta smiled at her. "I know you would do this if I asked, and you would serve well. But it is a duty I must see to myself."

"Majesty," Ralak said. "This is a needless risk. Mistress Pyth will go."

"I will go," Solsta replied.

The Archamagus could sense the Crown would not be moved. It reminded him of when she had announced that she would ride at the head of the army against the demons. What an outcry there had been against her that day—yet she had gone then, and she would go now. There was no real way Ralak could stop her. He might cast a spell setting her to sleep, but he would have to answer for that action when he returned and he did not want her trust in him to be spoiled. *Besides, she speaks true. Hers is the voice that would ring strongest....*

"As you wish, Majesty," Ralak said. "If we are to do this, the time is now." He held the Staff of Dimrythain before him. "Take hold, and do not let go."

Solsta donned her helm and seized the staff. Its silver wood, etched deep with arcane runes of power, was warm in her hands, like a thing alive.

"Go safe and safe return," Amethyst said.

"There is none better than Ralak to keep me safe," Solsta said. *Except Artelo...* She put the thought straight from her mind. "We'll be back before you can miss us. Tell Mirk good-bye for me." After the battle, the meerkat had ridden Shadow triumphantly back to Solsta's chambers and gone promptly to sleep.

"I will," Amythest said.

"I am ready, Ralak," Solsta said.

"All hinges upon this," the Archamagus murmured. "If we fail, I have sent them to their deaths."

"We will not fail," Solsta said.

I pray you are right, Ralak thought, and opened the aethergate.

Interlude: The Bargain

They were in darkness.

The aetherwalk took the Crown and the Archamagus far to the west, where night yet lingered on the land. They came out of the teleport in a crater that once had been a mountaintop. Solsta knelt, trying to recover herself after the grueling travel. She felt as if every fiber of her being had been shredded apart, blown across the leagues, and then hastily reassembled—which essentially was what had happened.

While he waited for the Crown to recover, Ralak made a light and surveyed their surroundings. He had never stood in this place, but he had seen it once from the vale below. That memory had allowed him to align the aether to bring them forth here; not perfectly—they had actually fallen several feet to the ground (Solsta was so dazed that Ralak doubted she even realized this, though she might feel it in her bruises later on)—but the risky spellcasting proved worth the chance.

Not ten paces from where they had materialized was a fissure.

The gash in the stone was a ragged space wide enough to march several horses abreast. The air about it was foul with sulfurous fumes. Ralak frowned, but there was no choice. This was their path.

"This way, Majesty," he said. Helping the Crown to her feet, he led her into the earth.

M

"Ralak?"

"Yes, Majesty?"

Solsta's hand tightened on Ralak's arm. Their voices were very small in the black. Even the glimmering light at the tip of Ralak's staff did little to comfort them. It pushed back the immediate shadows so they could discover that there was nothing beyond them but shadows, shadows everywhere.

"What is that noise?"

He heard it now: a deep rumbling, rolling toward them from some unknown distance ahead in the dark. A cataract. A tidal wave.

A roar.

"WELL, THIEVES! YOU DO SCANT CREDIT TO YOUR PROFESSION TO COME SO OPENLY INTO THE DRAGON'S DEN!"

Ralak and Solsta cringed beneath the buffeting voice, which blasted over them like a thunderstorm on a summer's afternoon. *Aeton alive!* Ralak thought. *Why didn't I announce us? Had that been fire, we would both be dead!*

But he knew why he had not spoken. They had been making their descent for only a matter of minutes—the fissure had joined a tunnel winding downward through the mountain—and were nowhere near the depths where the dragon laired. *Yet it knew....*

It was a humbling reminder of how vastly superior the great creature was to all other things on Acrevast. "Speak to it," Ralak whispered. "Swiftly."

"YES, SWIFTLY," came the thunder from the deep. "AND CEASE HISSING AS IF WE WERE DEAF. BAD ENOUGH YOU ARE THIEVES, YOU ARE RUDE THIEVES AS WELL."

"Pardon us, Mighty One. We are not thieves at all, but the Crown of Teranor and her Archamagus come hither to seek succor in our hour of need," Solsta said.

There was a storm of inhalation from the hidden dragon. "INDEED? WAS IT NOT COMPACTED THAT WE WOULD BE LEFT IN PEACE? WHY WOULD YOU BE OATHBREAKERS?"

"Not lightly do we bear that mantle," Solsta said, continuing in the formal speech of the parlay. "We have made so bold only because we have nowhere else to turn. Thy dread strength alone can aid us. Will thee not hear us, at the least?"

"FLATTERING," the dragon murmured. There was a long pause.

Ralak and Solsta waited for their answer, fearing it would be an unequivocal rejection, in which case they were lost before they had even begun.

"VERY WELL," the dragon said. There was a glimmering of silver in the darkness before them. It formed a shape like a doorway. "COME INTO MY PARLOR."

M

An instant's aetherwalk later, Solsta was standing beside Ralak in the dragon's den.

They were on the edge of a pit that vanished into darkness. The stone beneath their feet was charred, as if it had endured a fire of titanic force. All around the pit, piled high as hills, was an incalculable treasure trove. Great heaps of gold, platinum, and silver: an avalanche of coins far in excess of the greediest imaginings. There were gems also: veins of diamonds, emeralds, rubies, and sapphires threaded amid the metallic mountains like rainbow streams pouring down from the heights.

Mingled with this wealth were weapons and armor, all in mithryl shining bright and bold and mighty with age and power, and other artifacts and baubles: chests gaping to reveal stores of pearls or stacks of onyx; bejeweled cups and crystal plates, the least of which Solsta suspected would fetch enough coin to refurnish the banquet hall in Aventar; ancient leather tomes; statues in gleaming bronze, the craft of which had passed from memory save perhaps in the dwarf holts.

But it was not the pit or the trove that held Solsta's gaze.

It was the dragon.

It lay amid the hoard, a monstrosity of red-gold scales. Solsta could see only its head and the coil of its neck, thick as a murkwood tree. The rest of the beast was lost to the shadows in the depths of the cavern, for the lair was lit only by the lurid light of the dragon's huge, reptilian eyes. Those lamps were fixed firmly on the Crown and Archamagus. Solsta felt so exposed that she shivered despite the stifling, infernal heat of the lair.

They had first met this wyrm, Dracovadarbon, after the Battle of Hidden Vale. In the intimate proximity of this second meeting, Solsta achieved a new understanding of the awesomeness of the titanic creature that not even seeing it route the demon hordes could rival. Upon the field it had been revealed in its destructive glory. Now all that power was reined in, like some elemental forge that had been banked and waited merely the cue of the smith to conflagrate. That very quality of absolute power held in check made the dragon all the more impressive.

All the more terrifying.

As if sensing the effect it was having, the dragon slowly raised its immense head. Melted gold from its rich bed dripped down a visage crusted with ridges of scales, crowned with horns long and thick enough to impale many men. Its jaws, bristling with a forest of fangs, unhinged in a tremendous yawn, revealing a tongue as thick and limber as the gargantuan serpents rumored to dwell in the jungle deeps of Za, and a maw into which Solsta and Ralak could have marched with room to spare.

The head settled back onto its gilded pillow. "FORGIVE ME. I WAS DOZING ERE YOUR ARRIVAL." That may well have been true, but Solsta still had the distinct feeling that the yawn—like the display of its preternaturally acute hearing—had been a designed to establish the degree of superiority among the players upon the cavern's stage. "WELCOME, CROWN AND MAGUS."

Solsta and Ralak bowed low. "Most dread Majesty of wyrms," Solsta said, somehow finding her voice to continue the palaver. She turned her words fully to the High Speech, in which it was proper and respectful—not to mention very wise—to address a dragon. "We are honored and grateful thou hast received us in our need."

"RECEIVED—NO MORE THAN THAT," Dracovadarbon said. "A DRAGON'S EAR IS NOT FREELY GIVEN. WE MUST HAVE SOMETHING OF YOU IN EXCHANGE FOR AUDITING YOUR REQUEST."

"What can we offer that thy Omnipotence hast not already acquired?" Solsta asked. Looking at the hoard, it seemed there was nothing they might add to increase its value.

"THERE IS A THING THAT YOU CAN BRING US," Dracovadarbon replied. Vast though its holdings were, the dragon's memory for treasure was infallible. It knew without hesitation what item it was lacking. "IT BELONGED TO THE LAST OF YOUR KIND TO VENTURE HERE. LADY DASANI, YOU CALL HER. *SISTER*

OF FIRE IS OUR MORE FITTING NAME. THE ELF TOKEN SHE WORE ABOUT HER NECK. WE WOULD HAVE IT."

Ralak and Solsta exchanged glances. "Alas," the Crown said. "That we cannot give, Dread One."

The dragon snorted. "WE HAVE MADE OUR PLEASURE KNOWN. WOULD YOU DARE DENY IT?"

"We must," Solsta said. "Lady Dasani is lost to us. 'Tis on her behalf that we have sought thy aid." She paused and then added, "Yet even were this not so, that token is not ours, but Argentia's to give, and she refused it to thee once before."

Solsta knew she was treading dangerously here. Still, she would not make a promise to the dragon she was not certain she could keep—especially when the matter was further complicated by the fact that, even in the doubtful event that Argentia was rescued and agreed to pay the dragon's ransom, the huntress was no longer in possession of the token in question.

"SO SHE DID," the dragon mused, more to itself than its guests. Its blazing eyes narrowed. "YOU SAY OUR SISTER IS LOST?"

Solsta nodded. "A prisoner in a place beyond our means to find her."

The dragon snorted again, plumes of acrid smoke steaming from its nostrils. "WE FIND THIS NEWS DISPLEASING."

"Then help us to remedy it," Solsta replied, throwing her hope on this unexpected turn.

"YOU VENTURE BEYOND THE TERMS OF THIS PALAVER." The dragon fell into silent consideration that seemed much longer to Solsta than it was. "IF NOT THE ELF TOKEN, THEN THE SWORD THAT SLEW THE DEMON IN THE CAVE ABOVE."

There was no more cave above—the entire crest of Mount Hoarde had been obliterated in the destruction of the Wheels of Avis-fe, which presumably had also left the pit in the floor of Dracovadarbon's cave—but Solsta and Ralak knew well enough of what the dragon was speaking.

"Scourge," Solsta said.

"A NOBLE NAME FOR ITS KIND." Dracovadarbon said. "WE WOULD HAVE IT FOR A TOOTHPICK." The dragon's scaly lips wrinkled back in a grotesque caricature of a grin.

"How swiftly can we return with it?" Solsta asked Ralak. The sword was in the vaults of Castle Aventar.

"Afternoon at the earliest. Even I must have some respite between these castings."

Solsta turned to the dragon. "Thou shalt have of us the sword Scourge, and in exchange shall hear our plea of aid for Argentia. If this is fairly spoken, then we shall take our leave, that we may return again with all speed."

"MOST FAIRLY SPOKEN, CROWN OF TERANOR, BUT WE WILL NONETHELESS SET ANOTHER CONDITION FOR OUR BARGAIN."

"What condition, King of Dragons?"

"SEND YOUR MAGUS TO RETRIEVE THE SWORD WHILE YOU REMAIN IN OUR COMPANY FOR THE SPAN OF THIS DAY."

"No! Majesty, do not agree!" Ralak blurted. He did not know what mischief the dragon was about, but he could not allow Solsta to stay here alone. *I never should have let her come at all....*

A dangerous gleam sparked in the dragon's eyes. "WE WERE NOT ADDRESSING YOU, MAGUS."

"Why dost thou wish me to remain, Lord of Destruction?" Solsta asked. In part she was trying to defuse the potential conflict between Ralak and the dragon, but in part she was morbidly curious.

"BECAUSE WE WISH IT," the dragon said. "SAVE A FEW WELL-CRAFTED BAUBLES, THE COMPANY OF A BEAUTEOUS DAMSEL IS PERHAPS THE SOLE REDEEMING VALUE OF YOUR SPECIES. BAUBLES WE HAVE MANY. CONVERSATION WE HOLD MORE DEAR."

"Then I shall stay, as is thy wish." Solsta said. The thought of remaining alone for a day in this place with this creature was awful, but she would endure it if it meant securing the aid of the dragon, without which their venture was surely lost.

"Majesty, no!" Ralak protested. Solsta waved him to silence.

"EXCELLENT," Dracovadarbon said. If a dragon could purr in satisfaction, it had just done so.

"Swear to me you will not harm her!" Ralak said, stepping forward. His staff glowed with a fierce light.

Faster than sight could follow, the dragon's forelimb slammed down on the far side of the pit, shaking the very earth and sending Ralak and Solsta tumbling off their feet. "DEMAND US NAUGHT, MAGUS!" Dracovadarbon warned, pointing a single talon reproachfully at the wizard. "IF WE INTEND HARM, HARM WILL BE DONE, AND THAT SPLINTER YOU CARRY WILL MEAN NOTHING IN YOUR DEFENSE." The dragon shook its great head in obvious disgust. "HOW SWIFTLY EVEN THE MOST LEARNED OF YOU HUMANS FORGET. UNLESS WE ARE MUCH MISTAKEN, YOU ARE NOT VIRGINAL, ARE YOU, CROWN OF TERANOR?"

Solsta was taken aback by the question. "No," she said, thinking of Artelo again. "I'm not."

"YOU SEE, MAGUS, SHE IS PERFECTLY SAFE."

From your appetite, maybe.... But dragons were powerful in many ways, Ralak knew. Though honorable if they could be induced to give their word, they were full of serpentine tricks and old, subtle cunning that they frequently turned to ill for no cause save their own amusement. Chief among these less obvious weapons was their voice. In the tales of eld, men were said to have gone mad just conversing with a dragon, or even merely from lingering too long in one's proximity.

Now Solsta was expected to survive a day in isolation with the greatest of all dragonkind. She was strong, but was she strong enough? Ralak prayed so, for she was set in her course, and the dragon in its terms.

Unthinkable as it was, he would have to leave her.

"Keep thy word, dragon. No harm."

"GO YOUR WAY, LITTLE MAGUS," Dracovadarbon replied with a dismissive flick of its talon. "RETURN WITH THE SWORD SCOURGE AT THE APPOINTED HOUR."

"Must it be a day?" Ralak asked, trying one last desperate play. "Lady Dasani and our other friends are in danger. The distance to reach them is great already, and grows with each hour."

"WE DO NOT RECKON DISTANCE AS YOU DO, MAGUS. WE WILL ARRIVE IN TIME TO GIVE OUR AID—IF YOU WIN IT TO YOUR CAUSE. THAT CANNOT HAPPEN UNTIL WE HAVE THE SWORD. WHILE YOU LINGER, IT IS YOU WHO INCREASE YOUR FRIENDS' RISK."

"Go on," Solsta said. She took a deep breath, marshaling her courage. *I survived the vampyr. I can survive this....* "Go quickly."

"One day," Ralak promised. "No moment longer."

"AND NO INSTANT LESS," Dracovadarbon reminded.

Nodding grimly, Ralak vanished in a flash of aetherlight.

Solsta was alone with the dragon.

Part V

The Siege of Elsmywr

76

Artelo watched the gull flying ahead of the *Reef Reaver*.

Though the knight knew it was only coincidence, it appeared as if the seabird was leading them on. Sooner or later it would veer away, drawn by some vagary of the air currents or some distraction on the rolling sea, but for the moment it seemed to be pointing the *Reef Reaver* towards the mysterious island of Elsmywr.

M

The company's aetherwalk had taken them from the Monastery of the Grey Tree in Duralyn to Coastlight Cathedral in Harrowgate. There they were met by Colla, High Cleric of the port city. When they had recovered from the teleport, Colla escorted them to the docks, where they discovered the *Reef Reaver* waiting for them.

Kest and Augustus had last seen the black-sailed, black-hulled schooner escaping Argo's harbor, taking Argentia Dasani out of their clutches after they had tried to arrest her on suspicion that she was involved in the death of their companion, Vendimar Stelglim. Iz, Kodius, and Kirin had all shipped on the vessel on the journey to find the sea elves of Shukosan. They were stunned to learn that the *Reaver* was no longer a pirate ship, but a pirate hunter in the service of the Crown, and that she no longer belonged to Skarangella Skarn, but to Argentia.

"Skarn's Sultan of Sormoria now. Took the rule after his father's death," said Dorn, the First Mate who was acting captain of the vessel. "He gifted the *Reaver* to Lady Dasani for her helping him secure the throne."

"I think there's a story here," Iz said.

Kodius laughed. "Does that surprise you?"

"Nope." Iz grinned. They knew Argentia too well to be surprised that she'd filled the three years since they'd parted with adventures.

"Good tale, too," Dorn confirmed. "But I'm not the one to tell it. I was stuck on the *Reaver* guarding a bunch of prisoners we captured before Skarn got called home."

"I can't believe that rogue's the Sultan of Sormoria," Iz muttered.

"Then there is hope for you yet," Marina said lightly, setting them all to laughing. The siren had enjoyed her brief foray onto land, but a change had come over her almost as soon as they set foot on the ship. It was as if being in such proximity to the sea returned her to a more natural state of ease and comfort.

Iz was glad for it. He knew that—whatever her protestations to the contrary—Marina had come to the surface mostly for him, and he had feared his world, so different in so many ways from hers, would drive her mad. That he had taken the same risk in going to Shukosan had never crossed his mind.

In truth, the people, the congestion, and the noise of Duralyn, where they had walked for a brief hour before departing the city, and even the docks of Harrowgate, with their constant bustle of loading and unloading, had been nerve-wracking for Marina. But she had persevered, letting her wonder overawe her fears. Now she was surprised with a joy she'd never dreamed of experiencing: a trip upon the waves in one of the ships that she had hitherto only glimpsed gliding by when she and her sisters surfaced to sing.

M

The journey was good for the company.

They knew grim battle would be waiting for them when they arrived at Elsmywr. To dwell on it overmuch along the way only stole the pleasure from days that might be their last. Thus, while Argentia's plight and their own danger were never far from their minds, they tried not to fixate on them.

Over the passing weeks a camaraderie grew among the eight. Iz, Kest, and Augustus overcame their frosty beginning. The former thief reminded the Watchmen of Tiboren Gyre, their companion who had fallen in the collapse of the Frost Palace. This was a touch of melancholy for them, but it also helped them deal with Iz's perpetually running tongue. Kest's esteem for his new companion also grew when Iz took him down to the last shot in a marksmanship match that ended with them shooting from the prow of the ship to a target fixed on the aft rail.

"You shoot well," Kest said, extending his hand after the contest was decided.

Iz clasped his forearm. "So do you, for somebody with two eyes. Besides, you were lucky."

Kest shook his head in exasperation. "How was I lucky?"

"Yes, this I've got to hear," Augustus said.

"I got smoke in my eye on that last shot." Iz had been smoking fiendishly for the whole voyage, knowing that once he returned to Shukosan there would again come an end to his pipes.

When he looked at Marina, he considered it a small price.

77

The voyage was a time of continued reunion as well. This was true of Kest, Augustus, and Griegvard, but even more so of Iz and Kodius. Three years apart had not dampened their almost fraternal bond. They traded tales of what those years had brought, and reminisced over their time companying with the Brothers Steelfist.

"Pound ye!" Kodius barked in a surprisingly good imitation of a dwarf. They were sitting in the stern of the ship with Kirin, drinking rum from a cask provided by Dorn and watching the sun fall away, turning the *Reaver's* wake into a trail of fire across the Sea of Val. "That's what Beem always used to say. 'Bloody pound ye!' Remember?"

"How could I forget?" Iz laughed. "That and 'Reavers never quit' were the only two things he knew how to say."

"Askairit," Kodius said. "I'm not askairit."

Iz nearly choked on his drink. "Yeah, that, too," he agreed when he'd stopped sputtering.

"You shouldn't make fun of him," Kirin chided, though she was smirking. The werefox had never known Beem, only his brother Walkyr, but Kodius had regaled her with countless tales of the bald dwarf's manias.

"True," Iz said. "He could never take a joke when he was alive. Probably still can't as a ghost."

That set them all to laughing again, but when they calmed, they raised a clear and sober toast to the dead dwarves, who for all their faults and vices had been brave and true when the moments of their stands came.

As Iz reached for the cask to pour new measures, a great cry went up from the starboard rail. They were startled to see that most of the crew gathered there and leaning over the side.

"What the hell?" Iz muttered, rising. Kodius and Kirin were right behind him as he hurried over to see what was amiss.

What he saw was a school of purple dolphins leaping and playing alongside the *Reef Reaver*—and among them, her silver tail flashing like a spill of coins in the fading sun, Marina.

The siren kept easy pace with the dolphins. She was a sight splendid and magical: breathtaking in beauty and grace. The sailors pointed and gasped and shouted in amazement to see a legend come to life. Iz had a terrifying moment where he was certain one of the crew would draw a crossbow or hurl a lance down in a fit of superstitious terror to kill a thing he believed a harbinger of doom.

His fear proved groundless. Some of the men were frightened at first, but even these came to realize that there was no evil in Marina as they watched her frolic with the dolphins. The majority simply looked on in awe, searing the image into their memories so they could recount the tale to their children and their children's children—or at least to the table at the first tavern they found when they made shore.

Finally, Marina bid the dolphins farewell and swam closer to the black hull of the *Reef Reaver*. A rope was lowered to her. A half-dozen men hauled her glistening and dripping out of the water. Liquid pearls slid down her tail, which shimmered and changed as she rose, transforming back into her amazingly long and lovely legs as she was drawn back aboard to the cheers of the gallery.

"Show off," Iz said, holding his cloak out to wrap his naked wife. Kirin had gathered up the gown the siren had abandoned just before diving into the water.

For a moment, Marina looked distant and distracted, as if her mind were still racing along with the dolphins. Then she glanced around, her eyes growing wide to see all the people crowding about her. She flushed deeply, perhaps at the accolade of the sailors, perhaps realizing that, though elves were careless about exposing their bodies, humans were not, and she had just put on quite a display for the crew.

"I am sorry," she said, lowering her gaze shyly. "Have I done amiss? I meant no harm."

Iz felt her begin to tremble. "No harm." He grinned, hoping that would reassure her, but he did not like the frightened tone in her voice.

The best thing he could do now was to get her away from everyone before they began to badger her with questions, even innocent ones, and made her more uncomfortable.

He swept Marina up in his arms. Kodius, anticipating Iz's action as only those who have fought together for many years can, was already clearing a path through the sailors.

"I am sorry," Marina repeated, clinging to Iz as he followed Kodius. "I could not resist their music."

"All's well," Iz promised, pressing a kiss into the salty tangle of Marina's silver hair. Then he took his wife below to their cabin, where they made a sweeter music all their own.

78

The days passed.

Of all the company only Artelo did not come to fully embrace the spirit of the group. Even Kirin found an unexpected new friend. It was not Marina; though they remained cordial, Kirin could never quite succeed in warming completely to the siren, despite the fact that the sea-elf was in many ways as much of an outsider as the werefox. Rather it was the other estranged member of the group, Augustus Falkyn.

That friendship began, however, with Griegvard Gynt.

On their first night aboard the *Reef Reaver*, the dwarf had approached Kirin and told her he remembered her from Stromness. "Bravest damn thing I e'er seen, ye fightin Barlow Burrowgelp t' save yer man's life," Griegvard said. "Course, ye ain't th' slip o' girl yer appearin, but what o' that? Proud t' ship wit ye."

Kirin was speechless. Still, Griegvard did not seem to be mocking her. *Maybe not, but he'll think you're mad for certain if you don't say something....* She forced her way past her skittish instincts. "Thank you. Would you be proud to drink with me, too?"

Griegvard's wild blonde beard parted in a wide grin. "Aye, now yer talkin like a lass after me own heart!"

They marched over to a tun lashed to the rail. The dwarf dug a couple of mugs out of a crate and poured them both healthy measures. "Success o' th' voyage," he said. They clashed cups and drank.

"Bah!" Griegvard spat. "Watery swill! Need a dwarf t' show 'em what real brew tastes like. Blackstone stout—that's th' stuff'll put hair on yer chin!"

Kirin, who thought the grog was quite potent and who needed only the moon to put hair on her chin, swallowed hard. "If you say so," she managed, wiping her watering eyes.

"Room for one more?" Augustus asked, plopping down on a nearby barrel and lighting a long-stemmed pipe. Kirin knew from her travels with Ralak that magi favored that style of pipe, but the halfling looked ridiculous with it. *For that matter....*

"I don't mean to pry," she said as Griegvard poured Augustus a measure, topped off Kirin's, and filled a fresh cup for himself. "Back at the castle my friend said he'd never heard of a halfling wizard. Neither have I, though I companied with the Archamagus and have known many magi. How did you come by your craft?"

Augustus drew on his pipe and then blew a complex arrangement of interlocking smoke rings into the air. He hated this question, but Kirin had seemed sincere in her curiosity, so he told her of his strange (for a halfling) love of learning and his ability to touch the aether—discovered when he conjured rain to douse a fire. "Except I couldn't control the magic yet. I ended up causing a flood!"

Not so amusing was his abandoning of his hillside village, where his interests first branded him an oddity, then an outcast. Kirin, who had faced a similar circumstance, found her heart moved by his tale.

Forced from his home, Augustus had gone to Argo, where he convinced Ethoven to take a rather great risk by accepting him as an assistant. Under Ethoven's tutelage, Augustus grew in learning and ability. He passed his Trials, was accepted into Argo's Watch, and assigned to the company of Tierciel Thorne, in whose command he and Kest Eregrin had crossed certain cat-women, chasing them and Thorne and Argentia across half of Acrevast.

"That's another tale, and not for tonight. Now you," he prompted.

"Now me what?" Kirin asked.

"Your tale. It's not every day one gets to ship with a changeling."

Kirin's golden eyes narrowed.

"Griegvard told me," Augustus said. "And speak only if you wish—I meant no offense," he added quickly, seeing the lethal glare the werefox flashed at the dwarf. Griegvard slugged down another mug of the grog he professed to disdain, wiped his mouth on his sleeve, and stared impassively back.

Kirin calmed. She had accepted what she was, but she had never gotten past her hatred of the creature that had made her this way. Those memories, even many years after that fateful night, were bile. Yet the halfling had answered her question, which was no doubt just as painful for him. *Does he not deserve the same?*

The werefox ran a hand through her platinum hair. "It was a long time ago," she began.

M

That exchange of histories marked the werefox and the halfling as friends. For Artelo there was no such bonding. No forging of new friendships, no true reconnection with those of the past. He listened to the tales of Kodius and Kirin, Iz and Marina. He heard Kest, Augustus, and Griegvard narrate what they knew of the events that culminated in the destruction of Togril Vloth's Frost Palace. On his own behalf, however, he had little to contribute beyond a glowing report of his daughter.

"Unless you want the tricks to crop rotation, sheep-shearing, or mending wagon wheels, you've heard the best of my three years," he said. His tone was genial and his dealings with the company and the crew unfailingly polite. Certainly Kest, Augustus, and Griegvard found naught amiss with him. They did think his reluctance to speak of his time as a knight strange, but recognized him as a private person and let it be at that.

Those who knew him better marked how much time he spent in solitude, gazing lornfully out over the horizon. It worried them.

Iz was the first to breast the issue, drawing Kodius and Kirin into a speculative conversation, but it was Marina who settled the matter.

"Let him be," the siren said. "'Tis plain he is suffering in love."

"Yeah," Iz agreed. "But with who?"

79

The gull was gone.

It must have veered off, for Artelo could no longer see it ahead of them. There was empty blue sky and sea on to a distant horizon, but no bird. He wished he could turn his thoughts aside so easily.

The knight felt as if he was being torn apart. How could just one look at Solsta have resurrected emotions he'd left dead and buried three years ago?

Maybe because they were never really dead....

Artelo tried to shut that voice out, but it would not relent. He was tormented with the image of Solsta running toward him, crying out his name, the Mark in her hair brighter than he'd remembered, the sound of her voice sweeter, the brown of her eyes more liquid and deep. Three winters had taken the last of the girl out of her; she was fully a woman now, more beautiful and regal than ever before.

Stop! Just stop! You're a fool to even think on such things. You're a wedded man—start acting like it! Whatever you had with Solsta is in the past, Artelo told himself. *It's over. Done. Dead....*

But was it?

A month ago, he would have answered 'Yes,' unequivocally and without hesitation. Now that he'd seen Solsta again, could he truly say he was so sure? If he was, then why was he standing in the prow, apart from all his friends, waging this internal battle day after day?

All right. Fine. But even if I do have feelings for her, nothing can come of them....

Except—here was the hell of it—he was fairly sure that wasn't true. He'd seen the look in Solsta's eyes. It had been like a banner unfurling from the ramparts of Aventar to assure him that if he was still harboring feelings, he was not the only one.

Feelings? That pestering voice returned, its tone almost mocking now. *Can't you at least be honest with yourself? That was love. She loves you— maybe even more than when she was yours....*

It was this, much more than merely seeing Solsta again, which had sent Artelo into a spin like a falcon winged by a stone. Not that he believed Solsta loved him more than Brittyn did, or more truly than Brittyn, but that Solsta had always been much more reserved in her displays of affection. To see the blazon of her heart so nakedly—

No. That's not it....

Near to the mark, perhaps, but not the center. While Solsta's position and the secrecy of their love had dictated their very formal and proper behavior in public, in their private, stolen moments she'd been fiercely ardent.

The truth was that she'd finally been Solsta the woman when she should have been Solsta the Crown. Her feelings had so overwhelmed her that nothing, not even the strictures of her public persona, could stop them from bursting forth in her eyes and her voice.

And she ran. She ran *to me....*

It was all the proof he would ever need that the woman who had once exiled him in order to abide in an arranged marriage and act in the interests of the crowndom instead of her heart would never do so again. Love had conquered Solsta completely.

Artelo slammed his wrist-cap against his palm. "This isn't fair!"

What's fair? There is no fair, there's only Fortune. When She turns on you, you can roll with Her or be crushed under. You couldn't help all those things that tore you and Solsta apart, but you rolled with Fortune. Now you have Brittyn, and if—

"If I didn't leave her three years ago, how the hell could I now? Leave her, leave Aura.... No," Artelo finished aloud.

He knew it wasn't all as simple as that. For one thing, Artelo had been suffering from a magical amnesia when he met Brittyn. He'd had no memory even of who he was, never mind his love for Solsta. *But that doesn't change what happened between Brittyn and me. That doesn't change my duty as a husband, as a father....*

This was the same argument he'd held up at his last parting with Solsta. It was true then. It remained true now. He did love Brittyn, and he had bound his troth and his life to her.

"I won't betray you, Brit," he whispered. But the image that rose in his mind was of eyes as dark and bright as starry midnight, and they held him. "Stop, please. Let me go. You have to let me go."

His hand vised around a line until the cable, hard with winters of salty weather, chafed against his palm. *I should never have come back....*

You're a knight through and through....

He heard Brittyn's voice now, and knew she was right. He had chosen true in going to Aventar, whatever heartache it cost him.

With a great effort, he forced his thoughts of Solsta aside. He had other things to worry him. They all did.

Chief among them was the Void.

With that cue Artelo's mind, momentarily free of the fetters of secret longing, returned to the gathering of the company in Castle Aventar, and the dwarf Griegvard Gynt saying they would need a ship to rescue Argentia....

80

"Much more than that," Ralak said. "But before we continue this palaver, let me put you to the question. Your friend is in need. The Crown will not command your aid. Let any who wish to depart do so now, freely and without shame, for much will be risked against Mouradian and all who set forth may not return."

Instinctively, Solsta looked to Artelo first. He smiled at her. "Again I offer my sword to your service, Majesty," he said without hesitation. "I will go."

Kodius glanced at Kirin. She took his hand. "We're with you," she said.

"As are we," Kest answered for himself and Augustus.

"Aye," Griegvard said.

Iz nodded as well. "We wouldn't have come otherwise. But I still don't know about this island. I sailed the Sea of Val for years and I never heard of Elsmywr."

"Of course not," Ralak said. "For all intents it was destroyed a decade before your birth."

"You just said you thought it wasn't," Kirin objected.

"And so I still say."

"An island's either there or it's not," Iz said.

"Wrong." Ralak replied. "Elsmywr is there—and it is not. What I and the other magi saw that day was the illusion of its destruction. The island exists, but no man will find it, no ship sail upon it, no magic discover so much as a trace of it."

"You don't mean—" Augustus began.

"I do, Magus Falkyn. Elsmywr has been concealed in the Void."

"What's this Void nonsense?" Amethyst asked.

"Another of the Forbidden paths is that of the Void," Ralak said. "A field of shadowaether is created around an object, one so powerful in its illusion that what it covers it hides from existence and detection by senses and magic alike. So a ship might smash upon the stones of Elsmywr without ever knowing what wracked it, though I think few have, for the island is thankfully removed from the major trade routes across the Sea of Val."

"Mouradian is powerful with the shadowaether if he could create a Void for his entire isle," Augustus said. *No wonder Ethoven warned me that he was too dangerous to suffer to live....*

"Yes. Too powerful. That is why he must be stopped," Ralak said.

Solsta shook her head. "Stopping Mouradian is not this company's goal. They are going to rescue Argentia. If the wizard falls in the conflict, well and good. If he lives, he will be dealt with later."

"Agreed, Majesty," Ralak said. "I apologize if I seemed to suggest otherwise."

Before they could get to Argentia or contend in any fashion with the wizard of Elsmywr, the company would have to deal with the Void and the ring of jagged coral concealed in the waters around the island.

A reef with but one opening to the sea.

Kest said it reminded him of the mouth in the seawall surrounding Argo Harbor: a narrow strait too dangerous for ships to pass in darkness. "The only difference is that ships sail in and out in perfect safety during the day."

"A luxury you will not have," the Archamagus noted.

"Can't you just teleport them in?" Amethyst asked.

"No." Ralak explained that the Void was a dark variant of some of the magic used to protect Castle Aventar. It could not be breached by any spell, only passed through physically. To do that ran the risk of the reef.

"Not to fear," Ralak said. "I do not intend for such to be your end." In his typically cryptic fashion—Artelo wondered if this was a trait Ralak had learned from his brother Relsthab, or one shared by all magi—the Archamagus declined to share his secret knowledge. "It is three weeks' journey to Elsmywr," he said. "Trust in me. I will provide the way past the Void. You must only be ready when the time is upon you."

M

It was with Ralak's parting words rattling through his troubled mind that Artelo set his gaze back on the point ahead, where the bird had vanished. There had been something strange about its disappearance. Something too abrupt, as if the gull had been swallowed by the sky.

And where is it? the knight wondered, looking around. *Why don't I see—*

A sense of danger, bred by his training and rusty with disuse, rose like hackles. *Oh Aeton—*

Artelo spun away from the rail, praying he still had time to save the ship.

81

"Ware! Ware!"

Aboard the *Reef Reaver*, company and crew rallied to Artelo's wild cry. Kodius and Kirin were among the first to reach him. "What is it?" the Norden shouted. Artelo raced right past him, making for the helm, where Dorn was at the wheel.

"Turn aside! Aside!" the knight shouted, waving his arms. The wind tore his words away.

"What?" Dorn could see there was trouble of some sort, but he had no idea what Artelo was trying to say. "Be calm," he ordered when the knight rushed up to him. The barbarian and werefox were close behind. Iz and Marina and the others were approaching from the stern. Many of the crew had paused in confusion to watch the scene. They had heard Artelo's shouts, but they could see no danger.

"Turn her!" Artelo shouted. "If you don't turn her, we're all going to die! We're upon the Void!"

"What are you talking about?" Iz grabbed Artelo by the shoulder. "The Void? We're still a day away from where the island's supposed to be."

"We're not! We must have caught a good wind or something. I don't know what happened but if we don't turn this ship right now, we'll be arguing about it from the bottom of the sea!"

"What you're saying's impossible," Iz said. He had consulted the charts just that morning and had expected one more day of clear sailing before they would face the danger of the invisible reefs.

"No, no it's not. The bird," Artelo said. "Didn't any of you see the bird?"

"What bird?" Dorn asked.

"A gull. It was out in front of us and then it just vanished."

"Maybe it—"

"No." Artelo shook his head. "It didn't change its course. It vanished. Believe me. Turn the ship."

"Cap'n?" Delmian, the ship's Second Mate, stepped up. He was a tall, rugged man with a bristle of gray beard and a look of weathered leather to his face. "Beggin your pardon, but he's right, Cap'n," he said. "'Bout that bird. Seen it too. Damn strange thing, but true."

"Turn her," Artelo begged.

Dorn was already spinning the wheel. "Man the mainmast! Starboard—hard as she goes!" He didn't know if Artelo was right or not, but Delmian's word had convinced him that there was something strange at work here, and he was not about to risk the ship. He would turn the *Reaver*, drop anchor, and they could send a boat ahead to investigate.

But it was too late for that.

The *Reef Reaver* did turn her prow to starboard in a full-sailed lurch that spilled many of the crew to the deck, but her momentum continued on her original course, which now pulled her black hull side-on towards doom.

"What the hell?" Iz rushed over to the rail. He could see the current running hard beneath them, dragging them along. It flowed like a fast stream, cutting through the normal undulations of the ocean in a way he'd never seen. *Magic....*

Iz raced back to where Dorn was still fighting with the wheel. "It's no good," Dorn gasped. The captain's broad face was flushed with anger and exertion as he tried to force the ship out of the drag.

"We're caught in some current," Iz said. "It's not natural. Can't be. No normal current could tow a ship like this against full sails."

"It's magic, all right," Augustus said, reaching out to touch the aether. He could feel the spell in the water, and it was strong. "But what—"

"Where does it stop? Can you tell?" Kodius asked.

"Why—"

"Because that's where the Void is, right?" Kest said, catching the Norden's thinking.

"I—" Augustus closed his eyes again, focusing his concentration on the streaming water. He could see the magic, glittering like spilled emeralds, bubbling and rushing perpendicular to the *Reef Reaver*—and suddenly stopping as if it struck a wall. "Oh my. There, yes. I can see the stream, then it just vanishes."

"How far?" Iz asked.

"I don't know. I've no gift for dead reckoning. That's Kest's thing. But not far. Less than a mile by the look of it." Augustus ran a hand through his curly hair. "What do we do?"

There was stunned silence. They didn't know how long they had been caught in the magical current—long enough to bring them to the end of their journey a day early—but its purpose was clear enough: to draw ships that trespassed too near Elsmywr to their destruction on its reefs.

"Ralak said he'd take care of the Void," Kodius said. He couldn't believe the Archamagus had failed, but he had. *I don't think he knew about this current, either....*

"Bah! What we get fer bein fools enough t' trust a wizard," Griegvard spat. *Stupid way t' die, too. Killed by some damn rocks....*

"There must be *something* we can do," Artelo said. He could not stop thinking of how the gull had simply vanished. Was it still flying in the invisible skies beyond the Void, or was there some magic that waited to smash it out of that air, just as the reef waited for them?

"Drop anchors!" Dorn's order was obeyed, but the ship barely slowed at all. "Trityn be damned!" Dorn turned to Augustus. "You can see what's pulling us?" The halfling nodded. "How far now?"

Augustus peered into the aether again. Saw the emerald stream breaking upon that hideous blankness that spread across the water like the Harvester's cloak. "At this rate? Minutes, maybe less."

"Can't you stop the ship?" Kirin asked Augustus.

"No. Mouradian's shadowaether's too strong. Even if it wasn't, I'm not sure I could stop a ship this big anyway."

"Cap'n? The men." Delmian pointed to the crew. They were still at their positions, but a palpable nervousness hung over them like a threatening storm cloud. Chaos would not be far behind.

Dorn knotted his big hands around the wheel. He could feel the force of the drag through the wood. It hadn't been noticeable when they were keeping course with the current, but now that they had turned against it, it wrenched on the *Reef Reaver* as if it meant to ply the very wood from her hull. *And it might. We may never even reach the reef. Break apart before we crash....*

Either way, it meant death, and there was nothing any of them could do to stop it.

"Tell the men to hold their posts," he said. "Stand them to whatever end, you hear? We'll get out of this."

"Aye, Cap'n!"

The company watched Delmian rush down and begin issuing orders and encouragement. The gesture had worth only in its bravery.

Kirin clung to Kodius' arm. The barbarian wanted to speak some comforting words for her, but he couldn't find his voice. He had faced death before—they all had—but this was different: like the moments after the Sundering of the Shadow Gate, watching as the fiends poured thousands strong through that gash between planes, rolling down into Hidden Vale, where the Host of the Crown would meet them.

No, it's worse. At least we could see the demons.... This was a disembodied terror. Though the day was bright around them, Kodius felt like he was lost in some unknown dark, where the anticipation of some invisible dread stole breath and courage and strength.

He folded Kirin tightly into his arms. Kept his eyes fixed ahead in a gesture of defiance. He would not see what killed him, but he would face it all the same. And he would hold Kirin to the end. Only death itself would rip her from his grasp.

"Going in good company, at least," Iz quipped.

Kodius had to smile. "The best," he said.

They all echoed the sentiment. Perhaps instinctively, they had separated into two groups: Kest, Augustus, and Griegvard in one and Kodius, Kirin, Iz, Marina, and Artelo in the other. They reached to clasp forearms one final time with whoever was nearest.

Artelo nodded to Kirin, but his thoughts were on Solsta, Brittyn, and most on Aura, whom he would never see grow to womanhood. Tears ran down his cheeks, hot even in the headwind. *I'm so, so sorry....*

Kest was sharing similar regrets about Lyrissa and the children they would never have together. *How much longer?* he wondered bitterly. Finally he could stand it no longer. Snapping an arrow to his bow, he launched a shot out ahead of them. It cut across the sky, arcing down towards the ocean. Before it struck the waves, it was sucked from sight: there one instant, then simply gone.

"Three hundred yards," Kest said, his voice strangely devoid of emotion.

Three hundred yards... Artelo cracked his knuckles. If Kest's read was accurate—and there was no reason to doubt the archer's knowledge of his range—they had reached the last seconds of their lives.

He waited. They all waited, company and crew, as the *Reef Reaver* was hauled unwillingly toward her destruction.

Two hundred and fifty yards...

Two hundred...

One hundred and fifty...

Augustus closed his eyes. He saw the beautiful and deadly green aethereal tide shrinking and shrinking—

Marina screamed.

82

When Iz felt Marina convulse he thought her elven eyes had somehow pierced the Void and seen the reef that could not now be more than a hundred yards ahead. But she was pressed front-to-front against him, facing over his shoulder.

Facing behind them.

As Iz turned, there was a hurricane noise and darkness fell upon the *Reef Reaver*, blotting out the midday sun.

The shadow of the dragon.

Panic seized the ship as the monster passed overhead. No one was immune from it. Even the bravest of the crew ran for cover or simply fell and cowered. Marina screamed again. Kest let his bow fall from numb hands. Augustus stared as if petrified. *A dragon....* He had known of their existence, of course, and heard the rumors of their role in the Battle of Hidden Vale, but this was beyond anything he might have imagined. Even those of the company who had seen the dragons route the demon horde were stunned with shock and awe.

In a single downbeat of its mighty wings, the dragon outdistanced the *Reef Reaver*, shaking the ship in its passing. Golden fire exploded from its gaping jaws.

Fire against which nothing—not even the Void—could stand.

The sky ahead of the *Reef Reaver* began to shimmer like a desert mirage as Mouradian's magic broke beneath the onslaught of the dragonfire. Where moments before there had appeared to be nothing but ocean now was revealed an island of dead hills, a placid bay, and—not fifty yards ahead of the *Reef Reaver*—a ring of jagged coral.

Aeton's bolts! We're going to hit! Artelo realized. The current still had them, and there was no way to avoid the foam-sprayed reef.

"Brace! Brace!" Dorn cried.

"Too late!" Iz shouted.

Then the reef was gone.

The dragon turned its fire upon the coral, immolating the barricade in the ship's path, boiling the water and the melting the reef down to the sandy bottom.

The *Reef Reaver* plunged into a world of steam. The scalding fume reeked like charred rock and left many men choking and burned before the ship came forth from the cloud into dazzling daylight.

The dragon was waiting.

It hovered, smoke trailing from its monstrous jaws, as the *Reef Reaver*, free at last from the current, was brought to a halt by her dragging anchors. On deck, the company and those of the crew that had not fled below tried to wrest their minds back from amazement: that they were alive, that the ship was intact, that there was a dragon lingering off the starboard bow, its slow, tremendous wing beats churning the sea below.

It was a magnificent monster, with red-gold scales overlapping like crusty plate armor all along its body, which was easily the length of the *Reef Reaver* and more. Its sinuous neck dipped, bringing its head to the level of the deck. "WE BELIEVE THANKS ARE CUSTOMARY AMONG YOUR KIND WHEN LIVES ARE SAVED."

It waited. No voice rose from the *Reef Reaver*. "SPEECHLESS?"

They were—even Iz. Finally Artelo found his courage. "Our thanks," he said, stepping forward. He had seen the dragons rain fire upon Hidden Vale, but by the time he descended from the crest of Mount Hoarde into the valley they had long vanished back into their lairs. Faced with one now, he wondered how Argentia and Walkyr had stood and bargained with this creature to secure its aid against the demons.

The wind from the dragon's wings was a buffet of brimstone, the flame in its eyes enough to sear a mind to madness, and the smoke trickling black from its mouth had an odor unlike anything the knight had known: a scent that might have broiled up from the earth at the making of the world. But chiefly what Artelo felt as he made his way to the rail to address the flying leviathan was the dragon's titanic strength: an elemental force undimmed by the long ages that sat upon its horned crest. A power that could not be stopped or stayed by anything on Acrevast.

"Our thanks," he repeated. Then, because he truly could not think of what to say next, he knelt by the rail and bowed his head.

The dragon seemed satisfied. "A DUTIFUL COURTESY, KNIGHT."

"Majestic Wyrm," came a small voice from the ship. "Thanks indeed we give, for thou hast saved many lives. Say why hast thou come, and if we may be so bold as to entreat thy further succor," Augustus said. He had remembered the dragon lore and made his address in the High Speech.

"YOU SMELL OF AETHER, BUT NEVER HAVE WE SEEN SO SMALL A MAGUS," the dragon mused. "YOUR QUESTION IS FAIRLY PUT. WE HAVE COME FOR THE LADY DASANI."

The company glanced each to the other. One shock was rolling in on the heels of the next. This was Ralak's answer to the dilemma of the Void. That alone would have been enough, but if the Archamagus had somehow bought the dragon's help in their attempt to rescue Argentia....

We can't fail! Iz pumped a fist in the air. "What the hell are we waiting for? Let's go get her!"

"INDEED!" Dracovadarbon boomed, mounting to the sky again.

Dorn watched the spectacle of the dragon rising, shook his head as if to make certain he did not dream, and then started barking orders. The anchors ran up. The black sails ran down.

The *Reef Reaver* gathered speed again, riding in the wake of the dragon toward the white beaches and rocky coves of the isle of Elsmywr.

83

Mouradian surveyed his army.

The Island Wizard's hand had been forced by the disaster at Castle Aventar. Night and day he worked, the Mirror of Simulcra burning and blazing, straining the limits of its considerable magic to produce a force ten-thousand strong.

He would need them all.

Even now, the thought of the catastrophic failure of the attempt to murder Ralak the Red made Mouradian scowl beneath the twin points of his hat. That the Archamagus had somehow caught wind of the attack and been prepared for them was the only explanation Mouradian could accept. He did not know how it had happened, and that was not truly important, so long as it was what had happened. If it was not, if his simulcra had succeeded in breaching the castle and five of the six (he did not know what had happened to the last one, and this, too, vexed him) had been killed by Ralak when every advantage should have been theirs...if they were not, in fact, the master fighters and killers Mouradian needed them to be, but merely physically superb shells....

He could not think on that. Would not think on that. That was madness.

Instead, Mouradian had accepted the harsh, unpalatable truth that Ralak had outflanked him and focused all his energies on the next phase of his war. He believed he still held several advantages. The Order could not be certain, even now, that he was their foe: not when they believed him dead. Even if they were certain, they could not come to Elsmywr, for no magic could penetrate the Void, and the riptide that drew any vessel unfortunate enough to come too near the island irrevocably toward watery death on the reef would sink even the Crown's armada. Most importantly, they could not in so little time be prepared for the onslaught Mouradian meant to unleash.

Setting Argentia's body before the Mirror of Simulcra, Mouradian spoke the replication spell again and again, until the Mirror smoked and he was exhausted with the strain. Six at a time them were taken from the tower, armed, and set in the fields to await their orders. All the things of Elsmywr gave the simulcra wide berth. The bird-men did not swoop above them, the gatarines made no attempt to abuse them. Even the flying monkeys did not molest the red-haired figures that stood upon those fields in their unmoving lines, still and terrible as statues given breath.

Mouradian cast, the Mirror reflected, and the ranks grew.

Until now.

Mouradian had stopped partly from a sense that the Mirror was taxed and needed rest, partly from his own exhaustion, but mostly because he was satisfied that his forces were sufficient to begin his war.

Ten thousand simulcra to crush them and break them, Mouradian thought as he looked down upon the assembled army. He would launch his assault upon several key cities at once, forcing the defenders to spread their forces thin. He would conquer by sheer attrition, for as long as the Mirror stood it would make and make and make....

Once the occupations were completed, Mouradian would begin the systematic elimination of the Order. Other enemies could be taken prisoner, but every magi who had a hand in Mouradian's banishment would be killed.

When that purge was concluded, the Ban dispelled, and the Crown dispatched, Mouradian would free Teranor from the scourge of the simulcra and begin his reign.

The wizard returned his thoughts to the present. He had yet to impose his instruction upon the minds of the simulcra, commanding them to hunt and kill. Their physical prowess was innate, but it needed direction. Once that was done, there would remain only the conjuring of the aethergates. Mouradian had considered crafting individual discs for his soldiers, but such an effort would have required more strength than he had at his disposal.

Never had the wizard been so tired. The wound the assassin had given him still ached in his shoulder, and the strain of creating so many simulcra had taken a heavy toll. Could she see him, Argentia scarcely would have recognized the man who had captured her. Gone was the ageless, hale bloom of health. His moustache and beard had lost their luster and his robes lay loosely upon his frame. Only his eyes were unchanged: pale green stones glittering with deep intellect and will. Their focus was turned inward now, as Mouradian gathered his reserves to cast his next spells.

And then—

Thunder? Mouradian looked up in confusion. His magic controlled the climate of Elsmywr. It did not rain on the island unless he bid it do so, and even then he called no thunder. Storms frequently swept across the Sea of Val, of course, but they were deflected by the Void. The noise he had just heard—a tremendous rending that had seemed to shake the sky—had sounded much too near.

The wizard's eyes widened in disbelief. All around the island he could see the shimmer in the air, as if he was looking on heat rising up from the baked floor of a desert.

But this was not heat Mouradian saw. It was the Void.

As he stared, shocked beyond any response, the magic that had held his island in its invisible shell shattered with a noise like the very crack of doom.

Mouradian staggered as if he had been physically struck. "Impossible," he gasped. "No. Impossible. Nothing could—"

There in the distance the wizard saw the one thing that very much could.

Soaring above the sea, its monstrous wings propelling it with awful speed, was a dragon. Upon the water behind it, a black ship coursed at full sail.

Rage contorted Mouradian's haggard features. "Meddling wyrm!" he spat. In all his many winters he never would have imagined that he would be undone by dragonfire. "You shall pay dearly for this!"

Raising his staff above his head, the wizard channeled all his strength into a single strike. A wind surged up, flapping his emerald robes, sending his hat flying away. "*Eloin-han!*" Mouradian cried.

A bolt of black-and-green lightning cracked the blue sky.

Struck the dragon down.

84

Dracovadarbon fell.

Mouradian's shadow lightning knocked the dragon backwards in mid-flight, flipping it head over tail. Smoke poured from its blasted chest as its limp body plummeted toward the sea.

On the *Reef Reaver*, Argentia's rescuers stood stunned. The attack had come almost too quickly for them to realize what had happened. One instant the mighty wyrm was soaring on ahead, leading them in a charge that could not fail to overwhelm their enemy. The next it was falling like a meteor.

THOOM!

It pulverized the sea. Water exploded. A mushroom cloud of steam erupted from the roil where the dragon had been engulfed, rising hundreds of feet, spreading to blot the sky.

The *Reef Reaver* was flung and tossed by a sudden storm of waves. It was as if the sea had been stricken by the blow and thrashed in agony. The black ship rocked and rolled, plunging into troughs, rising over crests, but she held her course for the island.

"What do we do?" Kirin shouted as the company clung to lines to steady themselves on the heaving deck. Moments ago, their hopes of success had been boundless. Now they were desolated. If the wizard could fell a dragon, what chance did their little band have?

"We must go on!" Artelo shouted over the roaring water. They had passed into a veil of fog that was almost like rain. The island appeared smeary at the far end of his vision, but it wasn't what he could see that worried Artelo, it was what the wizard could see. They were easy targets for lightning or fire or whatever other aethereal strikes Mouradian could devise.

Artelo wasn't about to wait to find out. Not only were they in danger, Argentia was as well, for who knew what the wizard might resort to now that his enemies were nigh. The best way to keep the ship and the huntress safe was to give Mouradian other targets to deal with. "We've got to get to shore—fast."

"How're ye suggestin we do that?" Griegvard asked. His feet remained steady on the rocking deck while the others lurched and clung for balance.

"Through the aether," Kest said, picking up on what Artelo had in mind. He looked at Augustus. "Take us as far as you can."

"That won't be far with this many," the halfling replied. But he drew his wand nonetheless.

"Keep the ship in the mists," Artelo said to Dorn. "That should give you some cover."

"And keep her moving," Iz, a veteran of many sea battles before his discharge from the Cyprytalyr militia, added. "You'll be safe," he said to Marina, hoping to reassure her, though in truth he was certain of no such thing.

"What dost thou mean?"

"You'll be safe here on the ship."

The siren shook her silver head. "I am coming."

"No. It's too dangerous. There's going to be battle, and you're no fighter. Not in these conditions."

"I care not. I am coming. I have not followed thee from Shukosan to abandon thee to danger now. I do not fear it."

"Marina—"

"La. And if 'twere I who went into battle against the enemies of my home, wouldst thou remain behind and watch me go? Thou wouldst not, and thou knowest so. Do not demand such a sacrifice of me."

Iz had no answer for that, so he just nodded. *Aeton, keep her safe,* he prayed to a god who had never before seemed so useful to him.

"Ready." Augustus said. His wand was glimmering.

"Soon as we're near enough for boats, I'll have a party out after you," Dorn said. From the look in his eye, there was little doubt who would be leading the reinforcements. "Fortune follow you."

Before any of the company could answer, they were enveloped in a flash of silver-blue light from the halfling's wand, and gone.

85

Atop the tower, Mouradian had crumpled to the stone roof. He dragged himself to his feet and stumbled to the parapet. The only sign of the dragon was a steaming churn where the monster had sunk from sight, but the ship was still afloat and sailing over heaving waves.

Another bolt of magic would have done for it, but Mouradian had spent his strength felling the dragon. As he watched, willing himself to recover, he saw an easily recognizable flash from the ship. An instant later, a second flash appeared atop one of the hills of Elsmywr. *They are coming....*

Gripping the stone of the parapet, the stricken wizard leaned forward. He was for the moment bereft of his magic, but he had other defenses.

"Kill the intruders!" he cried. "Kill them all!"

The command echoed into silence. For a moment, all was still in the vast yards and fields on the far side of the tower's moat.

Then Mouradian's army began to move.

86

In Argentia's diamond prison, a very strange thing had happened.

The crystal walls and space of her confinement had gone abjectly black, as if all the power had drained out of them. It was a shadow that lasted only a moment, but that was more than enough to get Argentia's attention.

If it was possible for a spirit to be exhausted, Argentia was. If it was possible for a spirit to be tortured, Argentia was. If it was possible for a spirit to be despairing, Argentia was.

All because of the red light.

The ruby flashes had become the bane of Argentia's existence, throwing their blinding glare almost constantly upon her, wrenching at her, leaving her reeling, as if the garish light was pulling her apart in a manner similar to an aetherwalk.

Over and again this would happen, until Argentia felt too sick and dizzy to stand—though of course she could not collapse or pass from consciousness, nor could she even close her eyes. The Soul Wrester's magic held her in a kind of stasis, forcing her to endure the relentless strobing.

Endure she did, but even Argentia had her breaking point. The hellish light was inexorably driving her from sanity. She was able to anticipate the flashes by a brief thrumming—like a chanting—that echoed in the crystal walls just prior to the light. She had grown to dread that prelude almost as much as the blast of brilliance that followed. The light itself reminded her of the Blood Moon of Yth and the fell things that had crawled from death to life beneath that spill of sanguineous illumination. This light, too, was magic, she sensed.

And evil.

Even before the darkness fell upon the crystal, however, there had been no ruby light for some time. There had always been pauses in the red storms, but those had been barely enough for Argentia to recover herself before then next bludgeoning flash. This one had been long enough that Argentia marked it. Wondered at it.

Then came the black.

It was frighteningly complete, although short in duration, and it aroused a welter of confusion in Argentia. She could not know that her confinement was tied to Mouradian's power, which had set the spells of soul-reaving upon the diamond, or that when the wizard's strength waned the crystal grew gloomy. Even so, when the shadow came she sensed that something had happened in the world beyond her prison.

For the first time in she knew not how long, Argentia's hope kindled.

87

"Whoa! Whoa! Don't—" Kodius lunged and grabbed a handful of Griegvard Gynt's blonde beard, steadying the dwarf, who had been about to step back a pace as they materialized out of the aether.

There was no ground behind him.

Augustus' teleport had almost been strong enough. The halfling had targeted a spot he'd seen on a hilltop in front of a tangled, dead forest. But eight was more than he had ever taken through the aether before. Though the distance was not that far, he had come up short of his mark, landing them near the edge of the rocky hilltop.

Very near the edge.

"Get yer damn hand out o' me beard," Griegvard grunted, which Kodius knew was the dwarf's gruff way of thanking him. The Norden looked around. They were upon a windy bluff. There was a desolate wood ahead.

"Come on," Artelo said, drawing his sword and setting off at a run. The others followed, weapons ready, uncertain when the danger would come, but certain that it would come. Iz cast a glance behind. The steam over the bay was dissipating. He could see the *Reef Reaver* tracking closer to shallow water. So far, there had been no other strikes like the bolt that had felled the dragon. Iz wasn't sure if he should take comfort in that, or be very afraid. He looked to Marina, who had hitched up the skirts of her gown and was running fleetly beside him. She managed a quick smile, beautifully brave. *Keep her safe*, Iz prayed again. *Just keep her safe....*

They entered the winter-withered trees. The cold wind rattled through the skeletal branches like the laughter of the dead. "What an awful place," Augustus muttered, drawing his cloak closer about his robes. Griegvard, stomping beside him, grumbled something unintelligible and kept casting wary glances at the trees and thorny scrub brush. Like all dwarves, he was mistrustful of trees, preferring the solid dependability of rock and stone. This forest had a particularly unwholesome feel to it. Even the daylight slanting through the twisted canopy looked pale.

The company hurried, eager to be free of the grim confines. They had just begun their descent on the far side of the hill when Marina tripped. Though not used to such exertions, the siren had run easily enough over the barren plateau, but in the woods there were roots and half-hidden rocks to snare her. One of these caught her slippered foot and sent her sprawling.

"Wait!" Iz shouted.

"I am not hurt," Marina said, already picking herself up and trying not to wince at the abrasions on her smooth palms. Her face was flushed with embarrassment. "Just clum—"

Her words turned into a scream as the thing swooped down upon her head.

The siren fell backwards, clutching and swiping at what appeared to be a giant bat. The company had an instant to take in the attack before the air was swarming with the things.

Kodius ducked as one of the creatures strafed past his face, swatting at him with small claws. *Not bats!* The wings were bat-like, but they were set upon the bodies of monkeys. Monkeys were not native to Teranor, and certainly not to frigid Nord—the few Kodius had seen had been at gypsy carnivals—but these creatures did not appear even native to Acrevast. Patches of their fur were missing, replaced by reptilian scales. Their tails were better suited to rats, and their limbs were gangly, with lumps and knots protruding at strange angles.

Whatever they were, the flying monkeys were certainly enemies. Agile and vicious, they attacked again and again, darting in and dodging out, tormenting the company with their chittering screeches and filthy, raking claws.

Iz grabbed the one torturing Marina, flung it to the ground and stomped it savagely under his boot, relishing the crunch as its fragile bones broke. As he reached for his wife, something wet and foul struck his stubbled cheek. He touched it instinctively, wiping away a smear of feces. "You friggin—"

The culprit was perched on a branch nearby. It chattered malicious laughter and hurled another handful of feces at Iz. This one splatted off his chest, but Iz didn't even feel it. He had gone into the red-washed world of battle. He seemed not to even aim his handbow, merely to point the weapon and pull the trigger. The bolt snapped out, a steel flash in the dim wood.

Crucified the monkey to the tree trunk.

Iz pulled Marina up, his anger burning hotter still when he saw the shallow cuts on her forehead and cheek, some dangerously near her eyes—

"Look out!" Kodius shouted.

Iz ducked Marina back down, narrowly avoiding a pair of monkeys sailing in from the side.

Kodius wiped both the attackers away with one swipe of his morning star.

"Thanks," Iz said.

"Some things never change," Kodius grunted, knocking a third monkey out of the air.

"Usually it was me saving you, jackass." Iz did a fast reload on his handbow. Shot another monkey down.

"Three years underwater and he's completely lost touch with reality," Kodius said, shaking his head. "Sad, sad, sad."

Marina looked at both men as if they were crazy.

"Will ye bloody come on?" Griegvard waved them forward.

Fighting on the run, the company was about half way down the wooded hill, the monkeys harassing them all the way, when Kirin was bitten.

88

The attack came from behind, the monkey landing hard on Kirin's shoulder. Before she could twist and force it away, its ugly little head darted forward and its toothy jaws snapped closed on her ear.

Kirin screamed in agony as blood slid hot down her neck. Her golden eyes rolled up in their sockets. Her last clear and horrified thought was: *Did it bite off my ear?*

Then she changed.

Her body bucked. Her hair began to grow from its short brush to a thick golden mane. Her face contorted, nose and mouth pressing forward into a vulpine snout, teeth sharpened into fangs. Her shirt and pants split as tufts of fur burst from her torso and limbs. Her fingers became claws, and when her golden eyes rolled back down, there was nothing human in them.

There was only the fox.

Growling, Kirin snatched the monkey off her shoulder. She shook the squealing, screeching thing violently, then returned its bite with one of her own. Blood sprayed her face like a crimson mask. She spat the monkey out, threw her head back, and howled.

The noise shivered the wood to silence. The company stared at the changeling. "Kirin!" Kodius shouted, seeing his wife caught once more in that strange half-transformed state: not human, not fox, but the violent hybrid that the Norden feared. He reached for her, hoping to calm her before the bestial part of her took full hold.

Kirin sprang easily past him, leaping high to snare another flying monkey out of the air, shredding the little beast. She caught two more with her next leap, taking one in mid-flight with a snap of her jaws. The rest chittered in terror at this unexpected harrier and fled away into the trees.

"Kirin!" Kodius cried again. The werefox turned and regarded him with those luminous eyes, then snarled and raced off. "No! Wait!" Kodius rushed after her, afraid of what her recklessness would lead her to. The others followed. None of them had been badly hurt but they were struggling to rationalize this first taste of Elsmywr's defenses.

"What were those things?" Iz gasped as they pelted down the hill. "They weren't really monkeys."

"No," Artelo said, thinking of the scaly patches and strange tails, to say nothing of the wings. "I don't know *what* they were."

"Mouradian's madness," Augustus said. "And not the last of it we'll meet."

"Let 'em come!" Griegvard said, slapping his axe and churning on.

89

Some hard-run minutes later, with Kirin still leading, the company burst free of the dead wood. They found themselves in a vale ringed by hills much like the one they had descended. Yellow, dry grass limped away before them, straggling to a halt at the base of an imposing wall: thirty feet of rough gray stone that rose to block their way. Beyond the wall, the top of a tower probed the sky.

Kirin stopped. She was crouched low, as if ready to spring. Her glowing eyes were fixed on the wall on the far side of the vale. Her ears were flattened against her sleek, fox-like head. She was panting out low growls. Kodius stood behind her, but did not touch her. The others gathered near.

"How much rope do we have?" Artelo asked.

"None," Griegvard said. "Packs're on th' boat."

Artelo started to retort, but stopped himself. He couldn't blame anyone for their lack of preparedness. They had been taken unawares, arriving a day ahead of when they'd expected, and then there had been the Void, the dragon, the wizard's attack. *We're lucky we've got our weapons....*

"Never mind the rope," Augustus said. "I'll get us over that wall."

"Good to have a wizard around," Artelo said, clapping the halfling on the shoulder.

"Just make sure you can get us out again once we're in," Kest said.

"Don't worry, I—"

The simulcra burst like a flood tide through the illusory wall.

Though they had seen the three in Aventar and knew in principle what Mouradian had been about on his island, none of the company was prepared for the sight of the army of the simulcra. Watching the approaching force was like seeing Argentia in a prism, her image broken and reflected endlessly over.

Oh, Gen.... Artelo's stomach turned in revulsion at this violation of his friend. His arm felt weak. He wondered if he could strike these things, even to defend himself.

I'd better, he thought. There was no mercy in the dull blue eyes of the simulcra.

Then Artelo realized it didn't matter if he could strike or not. They could make no stand against such numbers. Hundreds of simulcra were rushing across the sere land, katanas lifted in the winter light, red hair streaming, and more passed through the wall with every second: an endless vomit of huntresses.

"Ah, this might be a problem," Iz said. He had replaced his pipe with a splinter of wood: a custom from his days in Cyprytal's navy that had always brought him luck in battle. *Hope it still works....*

"But not yours!" exclaimed a voice behind him.

90

Ralak the Red emerged from a silver burst of aether.

"Leave them to us," the Archamagus said as the astonished company wheeled about. Even as he spoke, there came flash after flash of brilliant light, filling the space between the wood and the fallow field like dawn blazing up from the cusp of the world: aethergates opening in fiery succession as the magi of Teranor emerged to answer the threat of Mouradian.

Old and young, clad in robes and cloaks of every color of the Order, bearing staffs and wands and spellbooks, they had come to Ralak's call. Sixteen magi had fought in the Battle of Hidden Vale, the rest having remained behind to defend the various cities. That was the largest gathering of wizards any of the company had ever seen—yet here were four times that at least.

"Ethoven!" Augustus exclaimed, catching sight of his mentor.

The head of Argo's Watch Wizards nodded. "Without doubt."

Then there was no more time for astonishment, for the simulcra were almost upon them. "How many of these things are there?" Iz shouted. What had been hundreds now looked to be many more than a thousand, and there appeared to be no ebb to the army. Simulcrus after simulcrus rushed through the phantom wall like red ants streaming towards a victim staked outside their hill.

"Not enough." Ralak smiled with impossible confidence. "But they are not your concern. We will deal with Mouradian's abominations. Find Argentia. Get her out."

"How?" Artelo said. "We'll never fight past that many! Not even with your aid!"

"Do not be so certain of that, Sir Sterling," the Archamagus said. His dark eyes glimmered. "Yet why should you fight them at all, when you can simply go over them?"

Ralak nodded to Ethoven and Promitius, a wizard in dun robes with gold arcana scrawled along the hems. The two magi stepped forward. Their hands began to glow, and the company felt themselves rising off the ground.

"Bloody Hell!" Griegvard exclaimed, clutching his helm to his head. Moments later they were hovering some forty feet in the air, wrapped in aethereal light.

"Go!" Ralak commanded. As if a great wind had risen at their backs, the company was propelled forward, flying above the sea of simulcra and towards the wall.

Save for Augustus, who had used such levitation before, it took several moments for the company to adjust to the sensations of flying. Iz and Marina were reminded of swimming in Shukosan. To Griegvard and Kest it was like racing along in an ore cart on the iron rails of Stromness. For Kodius, Kirin, and Artelo, there was simply nothing they had experienced to match this.

The ground rushed by. The wall loomed closer. What held the company's attention most, however, were the blazes of light from below as the battle was joined between the magi and the simulcra.

Red lightning and blue fire bolted from staffs and wands and outstretched hands. Simulcra were struck dead by the dozens, blasted burning to the ground. Still the tide came on. The simulcra knew no fear, only the command of Mouradian. The archers among them fired a volley of arrows. These were repelled by sparking shields of aether from other magi, but afforded the simulcra time to spread their numbers wide like water diverting around rocks, forcing the magi into a defensive circle with Ralak, Ethoven, and Promitius at its center.

M

Atop his tower, Mouradian watched the simulcra advance. His initial command had called for only the forward ranks—several hundred—to crush whatever enemies were coming down the hill. It turned out to be only a party of eight. *What fools, to send so few against me*, Mouradian gloated, anticipating a rout of moments. Before that battle had even begun, however, the Island Wizard suffered the shock of seeing aethergates open at the edge of the wood as the magi—not such fools after all—made themselves known.

Mouradian recovered quickly. Where others might have seen disaster, he saw sudden opportunity. How much easier would his conquest of Teranor be if he could strike down dozens of magi at a shot here upon his very island? "More!" he commanded his waiting simulcra. "More! Kill the magi!"

In moments, the ranks of simulcra were moving after the vanguard. Mouradian would send all ten thousand if necessary, but he would have the victory.

As the simulcra flooded the fields, a small group of the attackers lifted into the air and begin flying toward the wall. The simulcra, intent on the magi, did not take note of them.

Mouradian did.

Though still sorely tired, a measure of the Island Wizard's powers had returned to him. *Enough to deal with this rabble....* He raised his staff. Stopped.

There was a better use for his magic.

M

"Break their ranks!" Maneryl of Harrowgate cried, thrusting his hands at a cluster of red-haired attackers. The transmogrifist's greatest gifts lay in his ability to change the nature of matter, as he had done when he'd given Iz the ability to breathe both air and water. He summoned his power now to shift the ground beneath the simulcra to oozing mud that swallowed them hungrily down.

All around the circle, the magi used their spellcraft to similar advantage, preventing the simulcra from closing to strike at them with their weapons. Still, there seemed to be no end to the red tide. Climbing and leaping over the corpses of their sisters, Mouradian's army came inexorably on.

"They cannot hold without us much longer!" Promitius shouted. He,

Ethoven, and Ralak were still focusing their efforts on sailing the company past the wall.

"They will hold," Ralak said. Even if the simulcra broke their circle, the magi could put swift distance between them and their enemies by escaping through the aether. The true hope for victory lay with the company. The Archamagus meant to give them every chance he could.

He saw them pass over the wall—

Green-black lightning from Mouradian's tower struck the circle of magi, blasting four wizards from life and hurling others to the ground.

The torrent of simulcra engulfed the survivors.

91

The company had passed over the wall. It was like entering another world. Summer heat struck like a warm slap. The grass below was a vital emerald. The crop fields were ripe. Beyond them stood the buildings of the wizard's compound and the tall tower. To their left, rushing through the illusory wall, were the simulcra. *So many!* Artelo could see no end to their forces.

Suddenly shadow-lightning crackled overhead. Artelo heard an explosion from behind them. The magic sailing the company along failed.

For a heart-stopping instant they plunged earthward. But after the sudden lurch, the magic caught them again and they began a gliding descent.

Ralak's voice sounded in Artelo's mind. *We can send you no farther. The rest is upon your blades to win or lose. Fortune follow you!*

With that, the magic left them. They dropped the last few feet to the springy grass, stirring up a cloud of insects and scattering small birds, which flew off chirping in alarm. The scents and sounds of high summer were all around them. When they glanced back at the hilltop visible above the wall, the trees they saw there bloomed with vigorous life. *Illusion,* Artelo shook his head. *How powerful is this wizard?*

He thought they would learn that answer all too soon.

"Hurry!" Artelo was not sure how he had become the unspoken leader of the group—Kest and Augustus seemed to defer to his rank as a knight, and the others to something intangible: Solsta's absolute faith in him, perhaps. Whatever the cause, the mantle had fallen to him. Artelo welcomed it much as he welcomed the feel of steel in his hand and upon his body. Battle made him alive in a way nothing else could imitate. While he would never seek it out willfully, he had been away from it for three years and had discovered a part of him actually missed it.

He was already running ahead as he urged the company on. Kirin loped after him. The others started to run as well.

The simulcra spotted them. A branch broke off from the trunk of the army: two score coming to tend to this new enemy, obedient to Mouradian's command to kill all intruders.

"Run on!" Kest cried. The simulcra had the angle; there was no hope of winning a race to the cornfield ahead. He stopped and unshouldered his bow. Augustus stopped with him. "Hurry!" Kest waved at Artelo. "We'll slow them down."

Artelo started to argue but recognized that Kest was right. "Go! Go!" he shouted at Iz and the others. "Griegvard! Come on!"

"Bah! They can't be bloody slowin 'em all." The dwarf heaved his broad axe to the ready and charged the simulcra.

"What are you doing?" Augustus cried as the dwarf ran past him.

Griegvard turned his head and grinned ferociously. "Time fer some cuttin!"

First came the shooting.

Kest bent his bow, the arrow nocked beside his chin. Took aim. Hesitated.

It was like preparing to kill Argentia.

He let his vision widen to take in the spectacle of all the simulcra running at them. Their numbers dispelled the illusion that he was in fact aiming at Argentia. He remembered his horror at seeing the first of these creatures in Argo, struck down in the park by an arrow almost identical to the one he was about to shoot, not understanding then that it was not the Argentia, but a counterfeit. Remembered showing the body to Ikabod, and the stricken furrows of loss on the butler's old face.

Kest's bow sang. An instant later, Augustus' wand sparked. Arrows and aethereal bolts pierced the ranks of the simulcra, killing a half-dozen.

Griegvard rushed upon the rest.

"Drim damn yer false red heads!" he roared, hurtling into the simulcra like a boulder crashing down a mountain. Steel rang loudly in the summer air, punctuated by the dwarf's bellowing. Kest and Augustus saw three of the simulacra fall to Griegvard's mighty axe.

A dozen of their sisters buried the dwarf in a pile of limbs and blades.

"Griegvard!" Augustus shouted. He started to run forward, but skidded up short as the remaining simulcra, still better than a score strong, bypassed the scrum, coming for him and Kest and the rest of the company, who had just cleared a short wall and vanished into the corn.

Augustus struck two of the simulcra down with quick blasts from his wand. Kest, firing faster than he ever had before, dropped another four before he ran out of time to shoot.

The simulcra were upon them, blades gleaming, death in their dull blue eyes.

Kest stumbled back, shouldering his bow and going for his sword in the same desperate motion.

"Here!" Augustus grabbed Kest.

Teleported.

The simulcra slashed open the air where the Watchmen had been an instant earlier. They paused in confusion, trying to understand how this quarry had escaped them.

A flash of silver erupted from the cornfield, followed by bursts of motion that shook the tall green plants.

Twenty-one simulcra saw and rushed after the company.

92

The corn held dangers all its own.

Kest and Augustus stepped from the bright aether to join the others just as they entered the field. "Where's the dwarf?" Iz asked.

Kest shook his head.

"We won't let his sacrifice be in vain," Artelo said. Sorrow for the loss of Griegvard would come later. Now there was work to be done.

Kodius took the point, using his great size and matchless strength to force a path through the corn. The stalks were tough and resilient. They beat and snapped vengefully back at him. The barbarian was soon covered in clinging, itching corn leaves and sweating with his exertions.

In the dense rows, visibility was almost nonexistent. The company couldn't see beyond Kodius, and their crashing passage masked the noises of the pursuit coming behind and the enemies lurking ahead.

Kirin was a step behind and a little off to the side of Kodius. When the scythe swept out from an adjacent row, she reacted with animal swiftness, throwing herself into the corn, snapping stalks and ears. The weapon whistled over her head.

Stabbed Artelo in the chest.

The knight gave a cry and fell backwards. His assailant staggered into sight, still clinging to its weapon. It was a hideous mockery of a human formed of bundled sticks and dried hay, its clothing tatters of coarse, patchwork cloth, its stitched X-eyes malevolent slashes. The gash of its mouth emitted a groan as it hunched forward, trying to free its scythe.

Chasecrow! Iz's mind was still trying to assimilate a thing he knew from his childhood days on the l'Aigle farm in Cyprytal with this shambling horror even as he shoved Marina behind him and lashed out with his cutlass, sending the chasecrow's head flying off.

The chasecrow stayed on its feet, still jerking at the scythe. Iz severed its arm with his second strike and hacked open its chest with his third. A blast of green sawdust spewed from that wound. The chasecrow toppled forward and was still.

"Get this goddamned thing off me!" Artelo shouted from beneath the chasecrow. Kest and Iz quickly shoved the thing to one side. The knight lay on his back, the scythe jutting from his breastplate. Marina gasped in despair.

"I'm not hurt. Not hurt," Artelo said, more to himself than the others. He grabbed the scythe and tried to dislodge it. "Ah, damn—"

"Let me." Kodius wrenched the scythe free. The barbarian started to cast the tool aside, then thought better of it. It was for reaping, after all. He could put it to good use.

"Are there any more of those things?" Artelo groaned as Iz and Kest pulled him to his feet.

"Yes," Augustus answered from above them. He had levitated himself above the corn to get a better look at where they were. He saw other scythes bobbing above the green and gold sea of corn. "And trouble at our backs," he added as he lowered himself to the ground again.

"Can you run?" Iz asked Artelo.

The knight pressed a hand to his chest. It hurt, but no blood was seeping out of the split in his armor. The tip had not penetrated the chainmail corset he wore beneath that shining steel. "I'm fine."

"Then we'd better run. This is no place to make a stand."

"There's a break not far to the right. A row's been harvested," said the halfling.

Kodius led the way again, clearing the corn much more easily with great sweeps of the scythe. In moments they were free of the plants, standing in a wide, chaff-littered lane. They could see the far end of the field a few hundred yards ahead, and the buildings of the compound and the tower waiting beyond.

Much closer were the noises of their enemies closing in around them.

Two chasecrows emerged from the corn into the reap row ahead of them. Their ragged look and jerking steps were almost comical as they came forward, but there was nothing amusing about their rusty scythes.

The company was better prepared this time, however. Kodius proved as adept at hacking down chasecrows as corn. He split one clean in two with a mighty swipe. Turned toward the other only to see it was already staggering back, its woody form ablaze. It carried the fire into the corn, where the flames quickly began to spread.

"Maybe that wasn't such a good idea," Augustus muttered, lowering his wand.

"You think?" Iz shook his head, flipped his splinter to the other side of his mouth, grabbed Marina's hand, and ran.

The others were fast to follow. Kirin raced out ahead, springing on another chasecrow, tearing it apart. There was no relish for the werefox in killing such things—no sweet blood to spray over her teeth and tongue—but the rage was strong with her in this half-transformed state, and the chasecrows were enemies, so she would kill them anyway.

Minutes later, the company climbed over the short stone wall segregating the field from the yards of the compound. "Now what?" Kest asked, swatting a corn leaf from his hair and looking around. "Where do we go?"

"I don't know, but we can't stay here," Augustus said.

Behind them, the corn was a crackling bonfire that had claimed two of the simulcra by sheer luck.

Nineteen of the relentless things were still giving chase.

The company saw the practice yards to the left, full of rank upon rank of simulcra. They were relieved to discover the force was finite. As they'd watched the simulcra charge, Iz and Kodius had both thought of the demon horde that had flooded Hidden Vale, pouring through the Shadow Gate in a numberless tide. They had feared Mouradian had accomplished a similar feat with his dark magic.

Small blessing. There are still thousands of them.... Kodius had little hope that even the magi could stand against so many.

He turned his gaze ahead. The scattered buildings reminded him of Nord, where nothing was built for beauty. There were stone-and-thatch huts, a brick barn or storehouse of some sort, low rectangular buildings that looked like barracks, and others of less identifiable natures, but all were utilitarian in design.

Beyond the buildings were the two towers. The distant one was built of wood and looked more like a gigantic scaffold than any true building. The nearer was a tall thrust of ivy-wreathed stone protected by a pit spanned by three bridges.

"There!" Artelo shouted, pointing as a figure rose above the parapets, staff in hand, emerald robes blowing in a violent wind. It could only be Mouradian.

"Can you reach him?" Augustus asked.

Kest plucked an arrow from his depleted quiver. *It's a long way, but—*

All around the yard, doors banged open and the baying of hounds filled the air.

93

Orcish creatures piled out of the huts where they had kept hidden in wait for the company. Partially armored men burst from the barracks and other buildings. Strange, hunched men ran with them, growling and barking like dogs. The simulcra were closing from the corn, cutting off any chance of escape.

"This way!" Artelo charged ahead, heedless of the danger. The others were hard on his heels, Iz half-dragging the stumbling Marina. They met the gatarines in a savage clash. The pig-men of Elsmywr, though cruel and violent things, were unused to being challenged. The sudden attack surprised them. Before they knew what was happening, company had stormed through their ranks.

Artelo's blade rose and fell with quick and often deadly strokes as he led the way to the nearest building. Heedless of what might wait on the other side—it could not conceivably be any worse than the situation they were in—he yanked the door open and rushed into darkness. Iz, Marina, Kest, and Augustus piled in behind him. Kodius and Kirin, bringing up the rear, were run down by the freakish dog-men.

Kirin sensed the attackers at the last moment. She spun and sprang, meeting the first of Mouradian's hounds in mid-charge. Teeth snapped and tore on both sides, but the werefox had claws and ripped the dog-man open even as it bit her shoulder bloody.

Kodius heaved a hound off his back before it could catch hold. A blast of his morning star pulverized it as it leaped for him again.

"Kodius!" Artelo shouted from the doorway. There was a goatish stench in the room behind him, but that was the least of his worries right now. The gatarines, the guards, and the simulcra were converging on the barbarian and werefox. The knight started back to help them but Kodius waved him off.

"Kirin! Come on!" Kodius yanked the werefox from her kill. Felt fire in his arm as she clawed him, a murderous light in the golden eyes of her changeling face. "Go!" Kodius shoved her hard towards the doorway. Sprinted in after her.

"Down!" Kest shouted.

As Kodius dove to the ground, Kest fired two arrows out the doorway, drilling a pair of simulcra backwards into death.

Artelo flung the door shut. *There'd better be a lock....*

There was.

Artelo threw the bolt an instant before a gaterine slammed against the door, shuddering its thick wood. It was a strong barrier, but it would not hold forever.

It doesn't have to. Just long enough for me to figure a way out...

He was about to call for a light, but Augustus had already set his wand's tip glowing. The company huddled in the little illumination. They were blood spattered, wounded, weary, beset by foes they did not understand, and surrounded by a menagerie of agitated beasts: great cats, dogs, swine, eagles, sheep, and other animals, all caged in filth. Beyond the touch of the halfling's light, darkness swam back in.

"Where are we?" Kest asked, bewildered.

"Safe, I think," Artelo said, though he had not yet lowered his sword. "At least for the moment." Outside, things were growling and snorting and raving in some unknown but threatening tongue, thwarted but far from relenting. Bodies crashed like battering rams against the door. In their cages, the animals paced and made restless noises.

"Just what the hell are those things out there?" Iz said. He had torn his shirt and was wrapping a binding around Marina's hip, which had been slashed by a gatarine's knife. The siren winced, but did not complain.

"I've never seen such monsters," Kodius said. His left arm was bleeding down the bicep where Kirin had torn him.

"You would not if you traveled every realm in Acrevast," Augustus said. "They are more of Mouradian's fiend-works." Looking at the imprisoned animals, the way the Island Wizard had warped the good uses of the aether into these perversions became revoltingly clear to the halfling. It was an abuse of power so outrageous that Augustus had no doubt why Ethoven and Ralak had ordered Mouradian to be killed—or that they were correct in their sentencing.

"Break it down!" shouted one of the simulcra outside the shelter. Like Ikabod in the castle, Artelo was relieved to hear its voice bore no resemblance to Argentia's.

Something slammed against the doors. Wood splintered.

Kirin snarled, lunging forward. It was all Kodius could do to restrain her. The things they'd fought out there might not have seemed different from the werefox—like Kirin, they were part human, part beast—but there was something essentially wrong with them. Kirin was cursed, but her fox form and even this berserk changeling shape were still part of a naturally ordained order. The children of Mouradian's insanity were twisted things that had never been meant for life. Kodius might come to pity them later; now he just saw them as an obstacle to rescuing Argentia and getting off this nightmare island before any more of their company was killed or wounded.

"Whatever they are," the barbarian said. "We need to get past them and to that tower. There weren't—"

"Strangers! Come quickly!" called a voice from the dark.

94

"Quickly!" the baritone voice repeated.

The company turned in surprise. Behind them, the door shook with another splintering blow. How many more it could sustain they did not know.

Artelo started into the darkness hiding the voice. "Are you mad?" Iz grabbed his arm. "That could be anyone back there. A room full of guards, the wizard—"

"We have to face the wizard eventually," Artelo replied. But that wasn't why he was going. The simple truth was that there was something in the voice that he trusted. He didn't know why, but he did. "Bring the light," he said to Augustus.

The others followed the halfling and the knight, leaving the strange menagerie, entering the second chamber of Mouradian's laboratory. The light from Augustus' wand glanced off great glass enclosures that looked filled with greenish water. There were other shapes in that water, but the company passed by without looking closely at the horrors surrounding them. Perhaps that was best.

They came into the last chamber just as the wood of the door to the laboratory cracked. Augustus made his light brighter, revealing the metal worktables, the alchemical apparatus, the massive albino corpse of a man with a bull's head, and the creatures in the cages.

"Thundering Sturm!" Kodius exclaimed, looking on the gryphon, the blinded medusa, the basilopard, the harpies, and the centaur that had called to them.

The man-horse was shackled to the floor with thick chains. His lower body was a deep chestnut color, but lacked the luster must have owned in winters past, before captivity and torment had worn upon it. His bronze-skinned torso was muscular still, with shaggy hair on its arms and chest that matched the shade of his hide and the thick, curling locks of its head and beard. His face was stern and almost equine in its cast: broad of brow and long of nose, with huge, deep, dark eyes.

"I am called Chiryon," the centaur said. "If you are foes of the magus, give us freedom and we shall give you aid."

Artelo didn't know why or how long these creatures had been prisoners, only that they stood to turn the tide of this battle greatly in their favor if they fought beside them. *Or....* "We will free you, but you have to help us get into the tower. The wizard must be stopped."

"I will do so with pleasure," the centaur said.

"Iz, the locks?"

The thief already had his picks out.

"Never mind those, this is faster." Augustus sent a bolt from his wand, bursting the key plate on the cage door.

Iz entered the centaur's cell and went to work on the centaur's chains. "My thanks," the man-horse said, rising to his mighty height and thrusting forth from the cage that had been his sad world for many long winters. The company stared at him, awed by his majestic beauty and power. "Now the others."

"Are you sure it's safe?" Augustus asked. These were some of the most feared and deadly creatures known on Acrevast.

"Their hatred of the wizard runs deep," Chiryon assured them just as a crash sounded from the outer room. The door had finally broken. The guards and dog-men and gatarines were charging silhouettes in the sunlight that flooded the shadows of the laboratory.

"We'll have to chance it!" Artelo exclaimed. "Free them!"

The halfling's wand sparked again and again, bursting locks.

"Stay back!" Chiryon warned the company as the first of Mouradian's guards rushed in.

They were promptly torn limb from limb by the chimera.

Roaring, hissing, and bleating from its three heads, the monster folded its wings, forcing itself through the door and into the next wave of attackers. The lean, swift gryphon followed, screeching in fury. The basilopard, a spotted feline with a lizard's head that even deprived of its deadly acidic spittle could deliver fearsome bites, was right behind.

With the harpies winging past to attack from above, the long-imprisoned monsters vented years of torment on the gatarines and armored guards. The company stood back and listened to the savage slaughter as the laboratory was turned into a killing floor. Glass shattered. Equipment crashed. Foul fluid flooded the room. The screams of the dying were overwhelmed by the roars of the monsters as they tore through the island's defenders and headed for the broken doors to a world of sun and air they had not seen in decades.

"Follow them!" Artelo cried.

95

From the top of his tower, Mouradian watched with gleeful satisfaction as the simulcra put the Order's wizards to rout.

His forces had taken massive casualties. Aethereal fire and lightning had scorched hundreds. Sudden rifts in the earth had swallowed scores. Even in melee combat the magi had proved capable of killing the simulcra almost as easily as a reaper harvesting wheat.

All in vain.

As Mouradian had foreseen, his numbers were simply too many. Bolstered by the green-black bolts Mouradian summoned from the darkened skies, the simulcra finally broke the ranks of the magi. With every wizard that watered Elsmywr with his or her blood, Mouradian was one step closer to ending the Ban that had checked him for half a century.

He saw the flashes of aethergates as some of the surviving magi, too wounded to continue battling, took themselves to safety. Their force was a shrinking island in a sea of simulcra. Victory was—

What?

Sudden chaos in the periphery of his vision drew Mouradian's gaze closer to his tower. He had seen his trap sprung, the gatarines and guards and simulcra converging on the fools attempting to assault his tower, and paid them no more mind. The destruction of the magi was of much greater import.

Now he saw a disaster.

His forces were under attack not by the invaders, but by the monsters he had kept captive. He watched as the gryphon snatched a gatarine into the sky, rending it with beak and claws and dropping its mauled body through the thatched roof of a hut. Moments later, three terrified ovine women came bursting out of the hut's door, only to be swept into the chimera's fatally indiscriminate embrace.

The basilopard sprang upon a dog-man. A quartet of harpies harried a simulcra to the ground. The medusa grabbed a bow and quiver from a fallen simulcrus. Arrows sped death into guards and gatarines; the monster's uncanny accuracy was clearly unaffected by her lack of eyes.

The chimera, done its quick work on the defenseless ewes, charged into a squad of guardsmen, scattering them. The leader of the gatarines—a huge hulk nearly seven feet tall—bellowed and tried to organize some defense, but with little success.

Mouradian shook his head in disbelief. This could not be. *It will not be....* With a swift gesture, the Island Wizard called for reinforcements of his own.

96

The company rushed out of the laboratory just as a rank of simulcra diverted from the field toward the yard. Unlike the token group that had assailed them earlier, this force was a more than a hundred strong. Even with the monsters' aid Artelo did not think they could hold against so many.

Maybe not, but this time we can outrun them.... "To the tower, quickly!" Artelo shouted.

"Wait, wait!" Iz said. "Take her, please," he bid Chiryon, thinking Marina would be safest upon the centaur.

"Very well."

"Get on his back, like a seahorse," Iz said to Marina.

"Not without thee!" the siren demanded.

"Just go!" Artelo urged.

"All right, all right. We'll lead," Iz said.

Chiryon dipped low to accept his riders, straightened smoothly and surged forward. His first steps were tentative, almost awkward—it had been years since he had run—but like most magical creatures, centaurs were not grossly subject to the passage of time. There was strength in Chiryon still. In moments he hit a smooth stride, then a gallop, racing toward the bridge.

M

Mouradian watched the simulcra stream into the yard and the intruders flee these suddenly overwhelming odds—except they were not fleeing.

The cursed and hated Chiryon was leading them over the bridge to the tower.

"Fool!" Mouradian shouted. "You have long deserved death. Now it is delivered!"

Pointing his staff, the Island Wizard called the lightning.

M

Chiryon was galloping at full speed when the green-black bolt of shadowaether sundered the stone span before him. "Hold fast!" he cried. Iz grabbed Marina tightly around her waist and jammed his legs as hard as he could against the centaur's heaving sides.

Then they were airborne.

Chiryon's leap carried them above the blasted, crumbling stone. The smoke-filled air was charged from the lightning stroke; Iz could feel it in his teeth and behind his eye: a sudden buzzing pain as they soared over the gash and came down on the far side. Chiryon's hooves skidded on the landing. For one terrifying instant Iz was sure they were going to be spilled off the side to their deaths in the stony depths below.

Then the centaur righted himself and charged the tower doors.

M

The company had just reached the bridge when the lightning shook the stone. "Look out!" Kest cried uselessly.

They saw the centaur leap at the last instant, clearing what was now a gaping space in the stone and coming down safely on the far side.

"Too far to cross," Kodius said. The lightning had torn a hole in the bridge at least a dozen feet long. Kirin might be able to clear it, but for the rest of them there was no way across unless they used another bridge. There was little chance they could reach one of those with the wizard waiting above to pick them off. *Iz, old friend, I think it's up to you now....*

Artelo had come to the same conclusion.

He watched the centaur barrel towards the doors of the tower, rear back, and slam the portal with his hooves. The doors buckled but held. *We have to give them more time....*

The knight looked back to the yard. The monsters they had freed were attacking anything that moved. The gatarines, guards, hounds, and few simulcra from the original pursuit were in disarray, but they were not the foes that concerned Artelo. It was the other rank, the hundred simulcra that Mouradian had diverted, that would be their doom.

There was no hope against such odds, yet there was nothing for it but to fight.

Bright Lady, be with us....

Artelo circled his sword above his head. The sun lanced off the blade, turning it to brilliant gold. "At them! At them now!"

M

Above it all, Mouradian watched the intruders turn from the bridge and rush back toward certain death upon the swords of the oncoming force of simulcra. He smiled. This was almost ended.

A boom reverberated from the base of the tower as the centaur blasted the tarnished brass doors open. Mouradian was not concerned. He would deal with Chiryon and his riders if the defenders he'd left within the tower did not do the work for him.

The Island Wizard raised his head, confident in his victory once more.

And was greeted by the impossible.

"No," Mouradian gasped, stumbling backwards. "No—it cannot be!"

97

"Ready the boats," Dorn ordered.

He had steered the *Reef Reaver* as far into the shallows as he could to give the landing craft the shortest distance to the island. He had seen strange bolts of magic from the threatening skies above the hilltops and heard the echoing din of combat, but how the day stood on Elsmywr he knew not.

Dorn meant to learn that answer.

"Drop anchor," he ordered. "All hands—"

"Cap'n!" Delmian grabbed Dorn's brawny shoulder.

"What is— By the gods!" Dorn exclaimed as he turned to look where Delmian was pointing.

To starboard of the *Reef Reaver*, the sea frothed and spewed like a giant cauldron set to a mad boil.

"Cap'n, what—"

A column of fire shot from sea to sky.

The *Reef Reaver* was rocked by sudden, titanic waves that sent even the most tried sailors stumbling. "Merciful Trityn!" Delmian shouted.

The fire continued to scream upward, driven by an incredible strength. The stricken sea steamed and roiled and thundered in the eruption of the dragon rising.

It came forth like some prehistoric ern bursting from the waters at the dawn of the world. The heavy strokes of its mighty wings shed a deluge from its gargantuan form as it rose and rose, mounting to the very sky that it had scorched with its furious flames.

Aloft once more, Dracovadarbon loosed a mighty roar that drowned the triumphant cheers of the *Reef Reaver's* crew and echoed over Elsmywr with the promise of dire vengeance.

"WIZARD!"

98

Ralak smote another simulcrus with his staff. He and forty-three magi still stood against the odds. The others were slain or had retreated. The Archamagus was faced with the grim reality that he and the rest would soon be forced to make the same choice. They could not hold against such numbers for much longer. The magic that empowered their weapons and shielded them from harm was fading, even his. Once it was gone, the simulcra, whose dead lay thick upon the fallow fields but who seemed nonetheless to have no end to their ranks, would overrun them.

If the magi stood, it was to the death. If they fled, they did so knowing that they might never have such a chance to defeat Mouradian again.

Ralak wished he knew how the company fared. If Mouradian was killed, the magi could make their escape, for without Mouradian to govern them, the simulcra were an empty threat. But the Archamagus could not spare even a fraction of his power to seek the answers beyond the wall of Mouradian's compound.

A sword flashed at him. He blocked it with his staff, sending up blue sparks. A second simulcra darted in from the side. Ralak parried her attack as well. A third dove at his knees, trying to wrap her arms about his legs. He drove the glowing butt of his staff through her back like a hot knife through butter. Thrust a palm at the first simulcrus, hammering her down with a blast of aether.

He was not swift enough to block the second simulcrus again. Her katana lashed crosswise, inside the guard of his staff—

Rang off another katana.

Tonoto of Exetus forced the simulcrus aside and finished her with a deft combination. He bore many wounds, but managed a wide grin at

Ralak. "I always told you the sword was of use," he said. "You should have studied its art."

"Why, when I can do this?" Ralak freed his staff and whirled it above his head, spraying daggers of aether that felled a half-dozen simulcra.

But it was false bravado, and both magi knew it. Still, they fought on, their defensive circle shrinking and shrinking: forty-four to forty to thirty-eight, with thousands still arrayed against them.

Then the dragon came.

They heard its roaring challenge moments before it swept over the crests of the hills, the winds of its passage tearing trees from the ground, shaking all that stood in its wake. For an instant it seemed the dragon, bent solely on the destruction of Mouradian, would simply blast past, but its encompassing vision saw the cluster of magi and their plight.

Never slowing in its flight, it swung its head around and loosed its flames upon the simulcra. The fire rolled through their ranks, incinerating them by the score, leaving only smears of ash on the earth of Elsmywr. The hard-pressed magi lifted their glowing hands and staffs in salute.

Dracovadarbon snorted acknowledgement. Dipping lower, it sent fire into the deeper ranks of the simulcra, punching flaming holes in the army and knocking them to the ground by the hundreds with the turbulence of its flight. It might have destroyed the whole field, as it and its kin had done to the demons in the Hidden Vale, but it had been hurt by Mouradian's lightning as it had not been hurt in aeons, if ever, and it meant to pay back that injury over all else.

With a final swipe of its tail—a thunderbolt that lashed all in its path from life—the dragon winged past the wall and on towards its enemy.

99

The company followed Artelo into the fray.

Kodius and Kirin flanked the knight to the left, Kest and Augustus to the right. As they plunged into the guards and gatarines they were quickly separated. Kest, who was a much better marksman than swordsman, went down fighting two of the armored guards. He was pierced once and then again. Hit the ground before he knew he'd fallen. The guards raised their swords above him.

The last thing Kest saw as the darkness came was a flying shape, all claws and fangs.

"Kest!" Augustus screamed. His little voice was lost in the battle-clamor, but his wand spoke loudly, firing bolts of aether to stun his enemies, clearing a path to Kest and Kirin, who crouched atop the torn, lifeless guards, her balefully glowing eyes already seeking her next kill.

Up ahead, Kodius roared to Sturm for strength and lay waste to a trio of guardsmen with one-handed blows of his morning star. He bashed a dog-man aside. Stumbled over the medusa's corpse; her statuesque torso had been hacked bloody, her throat viciously gashed. The chimera and gryphon still scourged the simulcra, but Kodius could not spot the harpies or the basilopard.

Pain exploded in his already wounded arm: a clubbing blow from a gatarine he'd not seen rushing him from the side. Kodius whirled, swinging through the hurt, blasting his morning star across the porcine thing's chest, ripping it open, trying to keep pace with Artelo, who was driving through the ranks of their foes like a spear.

The knight was caught in the full fury of battle, heedless of all but the next enemy and the next and the next, clashing with them and cutting them down—until he met the leader of the gatarines.

The towering beast was easily the size of an ogre. It was also much faster than it's ponderous appearance suggested, striking with a giant cleaver that Artelo barely got his sword up to parry. They crossed weapons so hard the knight felt the blow all the way to his feet. He feared his blade had shattered, but it held and the two combatants staggered past each other, spinning for the second strikes.

Artelo went low, gashing the gatarine's leg. It would have been a crippling blow had he finished it, but the cleaver crashed upon his shoulder just as his blade bit. The impact drove Artelo to his knees. He lost his sword. Stars burst behind his eyes. He couldn't feel his arm at all.

Head ringing, he punched out instinctively. His capped wrist hit the gatarine's ample gut, which sagged beneath its armored coat.

Snick!

Six inches of steel stabbed into the gatarine's pink belly.

The gatarine squealed and bent double, clutching the spurting wound. Artelo surged to his feet. Drove an uppercut with his wrist-blade into the gatarine's goiter. Ichor sprayed. The gatarine toppled like an avalanche of flesh.

Artelo went to a knee beside it, fighting waves of pain as the gatarine gasped and gurgled and died. He saw the shapes of simulcra approaching. *Sword...* He reached for the blade, but trying to grab and lift it sent a bolt of agony up his arm. The gatarine's cleaver was still stuck in his armor. His shoulder felt shattered.

With only his wrist-blade to defend him, Artelo rose to face the onslaught of the simulcra.

Saw them wiped away by dragonfire.

100

Mouradian stared aghast as the dragon rose from the depths of the sea. He watched it strafe the field where the magi fought, then the yard where the few fools and escaped monsters battled against his guards and simulcra, and he was still frozen with shock when its flaming eyes lit on him.

The Island Wizard paled beneath that hate-filled gaze. He had struck the dragon down with all the shadowaether at his disposal. It had not died. It did not even appear hurt as it soared high over the island, closing on the tower like doom incarnate.

The great jaws gaped. The fire came.

Mouradian escaped an instant before the roof and balcony conflagrated, teleporting down into the chamber of mirrors. Moving with frantic speed, he conjured a silver disc and flung it down, opening an aethergate to a place of safety. All was lost here. He would flee to fight another day, but first the Mirror of Simulcra had to be saved. The rest—his laboratory, his creations, even Argentia Dasani—he could do without. They were all replaceable. The Mirror was not. He had to move it into the aether, where it could be held until he needed it again.

He had just lifted his hands to cast that spell when the dragon's tail caved in part of the roof, bringing burning stone down in a fiery hail. At the rear of the chamber, the receiving mirrors that had cast forth an entire army of simulcra toppled and shattered. Fresh flames blazed up in the chamber, but Mouradian hardly saw them.

One of the chains suspending the Mirror from the ceiling had snapped.

"No!" the wizard cried. He dropped his staff and leaped forward, shoving Argentia's body aside as he reached for the wildly swinging Mirror.

A growl louder than every lion on the Veldt of Makhara roaring in concert sounded from above.

Dracovadarbon swung tight pass around the tower and reared up to unleash one last blast of its deadly breath and make an end of the wizard. Before it could, a storm of stings engulfed its head: arrows from the simulcra below, a group of whom had turned to those weapons to finally bring down the chimera and gryphon and now set them against the dragon.

The arrows struck Dracovadarbon's mouth and nostrils. One particularly lucky shot almost took the dragon in the eye, but was flicked aside by the monster's blink. Such attacks could not kill the dragon, or even really harm it, but they further infuriated the wyrm, who forgot for a moment the vulnerable wizard and swooped down upon the yard. "INSECTS!" it thundered. Its maw filled with molten death.

Reprieved, Mouradian caught and steadied the Mirror upon its single supporting chain. The heat in the chamber as the voracious dragonfire spread over the stones was awful, but the wizard forced himself to focus through the blazing air and rising smoke. He began to conjure again—

Whirled at a clatter of hooves from behind him.

101

Chiryon bore Iz and Marina through the tower at a gallop. None of Mouradian's guards could so much as slow the mighty centaur. Those that tried were simply trampled under hoof. Only once had Iz needed to draw his handbow, shooting down a guard who set up behind a potted palm and tried to snipe them with a crossbow.

Up the winding stairs they went, floor after floor, Marina clinging to Chiryon's muscular back, her silver hair streaming in Iz's face. The centaur seemed to know instinctively where the wizard would be found, for he never faltered as he mounted towards the top of the tower. Iz and Marina could only hang on and pray he was right.

They burst into the chamber of mirrors. It was a ruin. Its ceiling was partially torn away, its rear wall gone entirely. Fire and rubble were everywhere.

"Death!" the centaur cried. The flames had not yet reached the doorway, so there was no barrier between him and Mouradian. He reared back so suddenly he threw his riders, and charged forward, his great hooves flashing at the wizard.

But he underestimated Mouradian.

Swift as a snake, the Island Wizard gestured for his fallen staff. The black stick leaped from the stone and speared into Chiryon's side.

The centaur's slashing hooves missed their mark as Chiryon staggered. His hind legs buckled, spilling him heavily to the floor.

"Death, yes," Mouradian sneered. "But not mine!" Extending his hands, Mouradian sent jags of shadowaether into Chiryon. The centaur's head snapped back, his eyes erupting from their sockets, blood spraying from his lips as his whole body spasmed, seized, sagged, and was still.

Mouradian turned his gaze to the centaur's riders. They lay in a heap, the man stunned, not moving, the woman twisting over, struggling to rise. The wizard glanced behind him. No sign of the dragon. He would dispatch these other two with one strike, send the Mirror to the aether, and be gone.

Stepping forward, Mouradian raised his glowing hands.

M

At the end, in those final instants, Marina did not see the furious fire or palling smoke: things hideous and foreign and terrifying to her. She had no real time for thought or regret, only for one last act and the understanding of why her heart had been so insistent on following Iz to the surface and this island: *So he may go safely on with his life….*

She was changing even then, the skirts of her gown ripping as her legs shimmered and shifted into her silvery tail. She pushed up off the hot stone floor, mindless of the blistering flesh on her palms, lifting her torso and drawing a breath of hot, stinking air.

As the wizard raised his glowing hands to strike, Marina loosed that breath with all her power, all her love.

Her voice pierced the air like a silver sword. There was a small, glass-breaking sound, and then a larger shattering as the Mirror of Simulcra surrendered to the siren's song and blasted apart, spraying the air with a thousand glittering crystal shards.

The shadowaether vanished from Mouradian's hands. He died looking down in astonishment at the hole in his chest where Marina's killing note had stabbed clean through him.

102

Outside the burning tower, the magi and the company were still fighting. They battled through exhaustion. Battled through wounds. Battled to the last. The dragon gave them hope of eventual victory, though they doubted many of them would see it.

Even so, they held true—the magi in their dwindling circle, the company around the body of Kest Eregrin—and made their stands.

It was in these last moments, when every stroke landed in desperate and stubborn defiance of death, that the unstoppable tide of simulcra suddenly fell to the earth like puppets with their strings snipped as the Mirror that had tied them to life shattered in the tower room high above.

Artelo stared in blank disbelief. He raised his good arm to the heavens and lifted his blood-spattered face in a great cry of relief and victory that was echoed by the survivors on both fields.

They did not know how, but they knew the day was won.

M

Iz, stunned from the fall from the centaur's back, clutched his ears against Marina's keening: a sound so high and tight it was felt more than truly heard. He saw the wizard topple over into death, but it took him a moment to realize what had happened. Then the noise stopped and he shoved up, the wizard and the fire and Argentia all forgotten as he saw his wife, her tail slapping the stones in agony as she suffocated.

"Marina!"

She rallied to Iz's cry, her mouth moving in choking efforts to breath. She had done what she must, knowing that to transform on land was irreversible and that the siren shape that had empowered her voice could never survive out of water. She felt darkness coming, and peace: a coldness away from all this heat and lurid light.

Iz was still shouting. She could not hear him, but reached over a long distance to touch his face one last time....

"Marina!" Iz clutched his stricken wife, insensible of the gathering smoke, of the fire closing in. She had saved him—likely saved them all—but the cost was too great. *Oh Marina, no....* He pressed his mouth to hers, trying vainly to force air into lungs that in this form could never accept it without water upon her skin. And there was water—a whole ocean—but too far away.

He had to try. Jerking to his feet, Iz lifted Marina, who was much heavier now with her tail, and staggered for the door.

103

Light and noise.

These things filled Argentia's diamond cell. The light was not blood-garnet this time, but the white-gold of winter dawn. The noise a piercing note, shatteringly high. Argentia had an instant to wonder—

—then she was sucked forward into that vortex of illumination, streaming along like a leaf in the tide. *It's happening!* she thought gloriously.

The light engulfed her. Swallowed her.

Spat her out into a world of smoke and fire.

Argentia's eyes snapped open.

She started like a sleeper waking after too long trapped in the clutches of a night-terror. Breath quickened her body: a protracted gasp of smoky air that was noisome with char, baking with acrid heat. She jerked upward to find that the true night-terror was just beginning.

Oh my God! Fire was all around her, closing in fast. She rolled instinctively, not feeling the pain of hundreds of slivery cuts as she crunched over shattered glass. Her mind was jumbled: she was free of the prison, but where was the wizard? What had happened in this chamber? Was the fire an accident? How had she been freed?

She shut the questions out. There would be time for them later. Now she just had to survive.

Scrambling to her feet, Argentia sucked in a reflexive breath. Choked on it. Coughing violently, she wiped at eyes blurred by tears and smoke. Looked for an exit. Saw the shape of the man bent over a strange-looking body. Heard him shout something that might have been a name.

Iz? Then, with more certainty, though she had no idea how her old companion had come to be on the wizard's island: *It is* him....

She tried to cry out to him. Choked again on the smoke.

M

In the alcove, Shrike found her feet. Still reeling in the wake of her sudden freedom from the crystal prison she'd believed would be her eternal torment, she gathered up the scene in the infernal chamber. She saw with mingled satisfaction and disappointment that Mouradian was dead, though not by her blades. *Burn, you bastard*, she thought—

A strong hand seized her ponytail and slammed her into the wall. Dazed, she slumped to her knees before a hulking apparition of flesh and metal. The steel hand clamped on her throat, lifting her into the air as Kiel, his shade released from the Soul Reaver along with Argentia's and Shrike's, returned to his body and the sole purpose of his existence: defending Mouradian's island.

He knew nothing of the disaster that awaited him beyond the spreading flames, only that this woman was alive in a chamber full of destruction. His soldier's instinct said she was an enemy. He would subdue her and let the wizard decide her fate.

Or so he thought. Then Shrike jammed Argentia's handbow under his chin and pulled the trigger four times in rapid succession.

Kiel's helmet was made of steel reinforced by Mouradian's magic. It held its shape as the handbow's first two aethereal crescents macerated everything from Kiel's jaw to the crown of his skull, but bulged at the third blast and exploded apart with the fourth, sending a geyser of blood, brain, flesh, and bone into the smoke-dark air.

Kiel collapsed, pulling Shrike down with him. His hand had remained locked on her throat even in death. She tore free and rose, gasping and gagging in the inferno.

The fire was almost in the alcove. Most of the chamber beyond was burning. *Have to get out....*

Shrike saw a glimmer of silver on the floor beside the dead wizard. Ran for it.

M

Argentia gasped, trying vainly to breathe so she could call for Iz again. As she sidestepped a lash of fire, her tear-struck eyes saw four winged forms dive out of the skies, two making for Iz, two coming for her.

Yes! "Here!" she wheezed, reaching for them—

They veered away with wild, terrified speed.

Argentia stared after them, stunned by the sudden reversal. *What*—

The stones trembled beneath her. She heard a hurricane noise.

Saw the dragon.

It filled the smoky sky above the ruins of the tower chamber, coming to finish its reckoning with the Island Wizard.

Aeton—no! Desperate, Argentia turned a circle in the thickening smoke and searing heat, seeking a way to flee, a place to hide. As she did, the black-clad form of the assassin vaulted out of the alcove, sprinting towards Mouradian's body.

Towards the silver disc on the stone beside the corpse.

Argentia saw her one chance. She sprang forward, but the winds of the dragon's approach played havoc with the fire in the tower chamber, fanning it up in great hedges, cutting off her path.

The shadow-shape of the assassin darted past on the far side of the flames, lunging for the disc.

No choice....

Argentia plunged through the dragonfire. Dove in flames at the assassin.

104

As the company's cries of victory lifted over the fallen simulcra, they were buffeted by a staggering gale.

Dracovadarbon hurtled low overhead. The dragon's tail whipped into Mouradian's laboratory, exploding the building as surely as a missile from a catapult. With mighty thrusts of its gargantuan wings, the dragon rose higher into the air. At first the company did not know what it meant to do. Only when it had circled wide, swinging out over the ocean and turning back toward the burning tower did they realize.

"No!" Artelo cried. "They're still in there! Stop!" He ran toward the ruined bridge, waving his good arm. "Stop!"

"Iz! Marina!" Kodius raced after Artelo. "No! No!" Kirin chased him, barking wildly. Augustus, kneeling beside Kest, tried to summon up some last spell that might serve their need, but he was exhausted, and the aether would not come to his call.

The dragon could not be stopped.

It started its charge, the fire already forming in its gaping mouth. It knew the wizard was dead, but its fury was unslaked. It meant to wreck every vestige of Mouradian's power, wiping all signs of the wizard from the face of Acrevast in recompense for the injury it had suffered.

As the company watched in helpless horror, the dragon roared flame upon the broken top of Mouradian's tower: an unrelenting torrent that burned through floor after floor until the entire edifice, bathed in fire, gave a great groan and collapsed.

Dracovadarbon uttered a final, triumphant bellow and flew off into the clouds and smoke.

M

So ended the siege of Elsmywr.

Mouradian's tower had crumbled almost to its base. The wreckage continued to burn and melt away beneath the intense and lingering heat of the dragon's fire: a monumental pyre for the company's three lost friends.

No one said a word. There was only mute disbelief.

Gone, Kodius thought. *I can't believe he's gone. Iz....* Somehow it seemed to the Norden that his brave and cocksure friend lived a step beyond the Harvester's reach. Death would have come for Iz eventually, but Kodius had always envisioned it would be when Iz was old and enfeebled, resting at ease in a bed after a long life and a dotage recounting numberless adventures to his children's children—not a sudden, senseless end like this, cut down in the prime of life and love.

And Argentia....

If it was difficult for Kodius to fathom that Iz was gone, it was impossible to believe the huntress had fallen as well. Even more than Iz—more than any of them—Argentia had embodied life, with a thirst for adventure and experience that would never be quenched.

Yet it had been.

No, not quenched. Burned.... Kodius lifted his bitter gaze toward the smoke-choked skies, but of the dragon that had wrought this disaster there was no sign. *It's so wrong,* he thought angrily. He understood that the dragon's target had been the wizard, and that it could not have possibly known their friends were in that tower, but the attack had been wholly indiscriminate: an act of elemental wrath without thought to—

A hand gently touched his hip. He turned. "Kirin," he whispered.

The battle done, the enemies killed, the rage had left Kirin and she had regained her human shape. She was covered with blood and gore—her hands and arms and face were painted in the stuff—and her clothes were torn almost to ruin, but she was alive and what wounds she'd taken were already healing with the strength of her cursed nature.

Kodius pulled her close, wincing at the pain in his wounded arm. "You're hurt," Kirin said, alarm in her golden eyes.

"'It's nothing," Kodius said, shrugging. That injury and the dozens of other gashes he'd suffered didn't seem to matter now. He would see the fall of night and the rise of the next day. Iz and Argentia would not.

Kirin sensed his mounting anguish. Pressed her head to his side. "I'm so sorry."

"All this death," Kodius muttered. "All for naught."

"Perhaps not," Artelo replied quietly. There was a strange light in his eyes that made Kodius, who had been certain the knight would say Mouradian's death was worth the cost of such a sacrifice, stop the angry retort already rising in him.

"Iz and Marina are lost," Artelo continued. "Maybe Argentia's not."

"What do you mean?"

"We don't know if she was even in that tower," Artelo said. "The wizard was there, and Iz and Marina went in, but was Argentia in there? We assumed she was, but we don't know. Not for sure."

"Then we'll search," Kirin said, rallying to Artelo's revelation. "All these buildings, and if we have to we'll wait until the fires die and...." She trailed off. Searching those ruins for evidence of the death of their friends was not something she would easily face any more than would Kodius or Artelo. *But we will try if we must. If there's hope....*

Kodius nodded. Nothing could mitigate the loss of Iz and Marina but the possibility that Argentia yet lived meant some true good might come of all this madness.

Together, the trio turned from the specter of destruction to begin their search. Before they could do more than survey the yard, where bonfires still burned with the stench of roasting pork from the dragon's strafing run, and several buildings and huts had been flattened by the monster's wrathful passage, they heard Augustus shouting.

105

"He's alive," the halfling said excitedly when the others reached him. "Kest's alive! I think I stopped the bleeding in time." He pointed to the bandages, torn from his own robes, which had been hastily tied to Kest's chest. "He'll need a cleric, but he's alive. We have to get him help."

"The ship," Artelo said, looking down at the bloodied and unconscious Watch Captain. He scarcely knew the man, really, but that one less life had been tolled on this island made him glad nonetheless. "The *Reef Reaver's* surgeon can help him. Can you aetherwalk?"

Augustus shook his head. "Not yet. I'm still too weak. But there must be something we can do. Maybe Ralak or Ethoven...." He stopped. Where were the magi? What had happened in the other battle beyond the wall?

"We'll carry him," Kodius said. Stooping, the Norden lifted Kest into his arms.

"What about Argentia?" Kirin asked. "Some of us should stay and—" She turned sharply, her nostrils flaring. *Sheep?*

Three maids were peering from the doorway of one of the nearby huts. They flinched as the company looked towards them, backing away into the building again.

"Please, wait," Artelo called. "We mean no harm. Come out."

The women reappeared, this time emerging from the hut but stopping well shy of the company. They were dressed like servants and had pleasing figures and long, silky blonde hair that looked spun from sunlight. Even at this distance, however, Artelo could see there was something off in the shape of their faces, which had softly rounded snouts instead of human noses.

They stood very close to one another, and though their fearful, glossy eyes were busy taking in the scene of slaughter all around them, they seemed more to be waiting for Artelo to speak—to command them—again. "Who are you?" he asked.

The ewes looked to each other, as if trying to decide how to answer. It was perhaps the first question that had ever been put to them. "The wizard's sculleries," one of the ewes finally said. She had a soft, submissive voice.

"You can come closer," Artelo said. "It's safe now."

The ewes obeyed, coming near enough that conversation was possible without shouting. Even so, they shied from Kirin, as if recognizing the predator in her, just as she had recognized prey in them.

"How many are you?" Artelo asked.

"Ten," another of the ewes answered. "But some of our sisters were in the tower and some ran away and we do not know where they are."

"We were gathering eggs from the chickens," the third added, pointing a plump hand towards the hut. "We heard the noises. We were afraid."

"Listen to me," Artelo said. "There was a woman on the island. A woman with red hair. Did you see her?"

The ewes exchanged that confused and frightened look again. Artelo, impatient for answers, wanted to shake them. "Did you?"

"We did."

"Where?" Kodius asked. The ewes jumped at his deep voice.

"There," one of the ewes said.

"There," the second added.

They were pointing to the corpses of the simulcra.

Artelo closed his eyes, fighting against frustration. It was impossible. There had been thousands of red-haired women on Elsmywr. How could he explain the difference between the simulcra and Argentia? "Never mind," he said, shaking his head.

"No, wait. Did you see where they came from?" Augustus asked the ewes. "Did they come from the tower?"

Say no, Artelo willed, catching the implications of the halfling's question. The simulcra had originated from Argentia. It stood to reason they must have been marched out from where Mouradian had been making them. *Please Bright Lady, let them say no....*

"Yes. The tower," one of the ewes said.

"Still doesn't mean she was in there today," Kodius said, trying to hold to the fleeting hope that Artelo had given them. "Was there no place but the tower where a prisoner might be kept?"

"What is a prisoner?"

"A prisoner is…"

"A guest," Kirin said, improvising in what she hoped would be a way these strange women could understand when words failed Kodius. "A guest of the wizard?"

The ewes conferred again with the same excruciating slowness. "We do not understand," one said.

"Forget it," Artelo said. "We're wasting time." He started to walk away, then stopped and turned back. "You are free. The wizard is no longer your master," he said to the ewes. "Go." They looked at him as if uncertain what he meant. "Go," he repeated, more harshly than he intended.

Curtsying hurriedly, the fearful-eyed ewes retreated, stepping daintily around the litter of corpses and returning to the coop.

"What will happen to them?" Kodius wondered, shifting the burden of Kest in his arms.

"I don't know," Artelo said. *And I don't really care…* The last of the ewes passed through a slant of sunlight from the clearing skies before entering the coop. Her flashing golden hair reminded the knight acutely of Brittyn. He was filled with a deep and complete need to be gone from this hateful place. To be back at his cottage with his wife and daughter.

He turned his gaze a last time to the fatal, fiery rubble across the broken bridge. They had come to stop this very thing, yet Fortune had rolled against them. Their best had not been enough.

"Come on." Artelo led the company away from the death and destruction, refusing to linger on good-bye when there was a life they could yet save.

Argentia would have wanted it that way.

106

With Mouradian's death, the power of his illusion faded. All the island was now withered and winter sere. The company trudged along over a tract of land that not long ago had held an army, feeling their wounds now, and the exhaustion that followed battle.

Kest was still unconscious. The cloth of his binding was soaked with blood, but not dripping. There was some color in his cheeks. His breathing was shallow but steady. Kodius, who had experience tending many such hurts, thought it was possible that the grim looking wounds had pierced flesh and muscle but no vital organs.

Still, tarrying could only hurt the Kest's chances, so Kodius forced strength from some unknown reserve into his legs and arms and increased his pace.

They crested a rise. Stopped in astonishment.

"Took ye bloody long enough," said Griegvard Gynt.

The dwarf was seated atop a heap of simulcra. His armor and helm were dented and scarred from myriad blows they had turned aside, but he had given better than he received and made his tally for the battle at fifteen.

"Griegvard!" Augustus exclaimed joyfully.

The dwarf grinned through bloodied lips. "Bah! Takes more'n a bunch o' silly lasses t' do fer me!" He hopped down. Surveyed the company. "That's all o' ye?" he asked gruffly.

"All," Artelo said.

"What about Red?"

The knight shook his head.

"In th' fire?" the dwarf asked.

Artelo nodded.

"Seen it from here. Gave me a bloody bad feelin." Griegvard spat on the ground. "Curse these stones," he muttered. "Didn't think that one had it in her t' die."

None of them had. Though the sky overhead was the blue of a bright afternoon, the company went on under a caul of sorrow.

M

Ralak was waiting for them by the water.

The magi who had survived—better than a third of their number had passed through death's door into the aether—had departed, but the Archamagus had lingered to see matters on Elsmywr through to their end. He would not leave until he knew what other costs had been paid to gain the day's victory.

He feared they would be high.

Standing with the Archamagus were the sailors from the *Reef Reaver*, come too late to give any aid, and four strange beings the like of which none of them—company, crew, and Ralak himself—had ever seen before. More of Mouradian's creations, these were bronze-skinned, bare-chested men in loincloths with the wings of eagles folded upon their muscular backs.

As the company approached, Ralak turned from his conversation with this odd quartet. "Hail and well met," he said.

Kodius, his strength finally spent, let Kest slip down to the soft sand. "He needs aid. Quickly," he said.

"Much the same could be said for all of you," the Archamagus observed. Privately, he was relieved. More of the company had returned alive than he would have believed possible. *Yet the tally is great. Too great....*

"Take him to the *Reaver*," Dorn ordered some of his men. "Have Wanpo tend him. Tell him there'll be more wounded coming."

As several sailors lifted him, Kest groaned. His eyes fluttered open. "Hurts," he whispered.

"You'll be fine," Augustus said, hurrying over and clasping his friend's hand. "We'll get you well and back to Lyrissa, I promise."

Kest managed to nod, then slipped into unconsciousness again.

The halfling watched the sailors bear Kest to one of the boats and row him out to the *Reef Reaver*. "Where are the other magi?" he asked Ralak. The slaughter they had passed in the field before the hills had been incalculable: thousands and thousands of simulcra littered the battleground, which was scorched and cracked and in places still burning. They had seen no magi corpses, but that was not surprising. When wizards fell their bodies were made one with the aether that had empowered them in life. "They all can't be dead."

"Hardly," Ralak replied, placing a comforting hand on Augustus' shoulder. "And Ethoven was not among those who did fall." The halfling nodded in relief; though all the deaths saddened him, he was still pleased that his mentor had survived.

"Even so," Ralak added. "A high cost has been paid for our victory today."

"Higher than you know," Artelo said bleakly. He looked down and toed the sand with his boot. "Argentia's dead. We failed utterly. Iz, Marina, Argentia—all gone, and for naught!"

"Hardly," Ralak repeated. The Archamagus was surprised that the knight, of all the company, would say such a thing. "The threat of Mouradian is ended. Many lives were lost today, but many more were saved. Sometimes that greater good is worth the price. It was so at Hidden Vale," he reminded them. "It is so today. If Acrevast is a worse place without Lady Dasani, it is a better one without Mouradian of Elsmywr."

"Is he dead?" Kodius demanded, his temper flaring. The greater good Ralak spoke of was easier to accept when it did not cut its sacrifices so close to the heart. He had sworn he would not suffer such a dismissal of his friends' deaths. Kirin placed a restraining hand on his arm. He hardly felt her touch. "Do we even know that? He fooled you fifty years ago."

"He is dead," Ralak said.

"How can you be sure?"

"Because I told him—and I saw Mouradian die, you jackass!"

Kodius, who was glowering down at the Archamagus, turned in shock at that impossible voice.

Iz and Marina were wading out of the shallows.

107

Iz was still fully dressed, his clothes soaked to his body. Marina wore only her husband's cloak, the sodden covering wrapped tightly about her. "Marina killed him," Iz continued as they reached the others, who were gape-mouthed in astonishment.

"Never mind that!" Kodius crushed his friends to him in a mighty embrace.

"Thought ye were dead," Griegvard said bluntly.

"We all did," Kirin added, hugging Marina with surprising but unadulterated fondness. "When we saw the tower fall..."

"We weren't in it," Iz said.

"But how?" Artelo asked, clasping forearms with the drenched thief. "What happened?"

"They did." Iz pointed to the four birdmen.

He told them of their winged saviors swooping down to bear them from danger moments before the dragon destroyed the structure completely.

Of glancing back, praying that the other two birdmen had similarly saved Argentia.

Of shouting: "She must reach water!" to the birdman carrying Marina.

Of Elsmywr streaming beneath them, every instant of the flight an eternity, until the other birdman dipped to the water and dropped Marina beyond the waves, where her limp form sank immediately out of sight.

Of shouting: "Put me down!" to the birdman, who obliged, sweeping over the crewmen from the *Reef Reaver*, who had just dragged their boats to shore, and the robed figure of the Archamagus to deposit Iz on the sand.

Of racing into the water without pausing to hail the wizard or even thank the birdman as he splashed toward the place where Marina had vanished.

Of seeing Marina's gown floating up ahead, and screaming her name.

But of his joy as she burst from the sea before him like Cytha leaping from the foam off the coast of Cyprytal in the mythlore of his homeland, droplets spraying from her silver hair and pale torso as she flung her arms about him and kissed him ardently, he said nothing,

He had no words for it.

The siren had been nearly dead when the birdman got her to the water. The sea had restored breath and life to her mer-form, but it had been a near thing. Despite her show of ebullience, the siren was still very weak. Being in the water helped her, so they had remained there while Iz told Ralak all that had transpired in those last moments in the tower and the *Reef Reaver's* crew stared in amazement at the birdmen who had saved the thief and his wife.

His tale complete, Iz turned to the birdmen. "You have my debt and thanks forever," he said, bowing low. "But what were you doing there? Why did you come?"

"The wizard was a cruel master," the birdman called Ik'tari answered. "Wings he gave us, but a boundary was placed in the sky. The brothers and sisters of the aerie had no freedom to fly as we longed to fly. We are glad to see him gone."

"But that is not why we came," added the other, named Ak'kara. "The woman of your kind with hair like flame risked herself to help sister Ak'tali in her need. We sought to repay her kindness by saving her. Alas, ere brothers Ok'taka and Ik'kali could reach her, the fire-lizard came."

All the birdmen—particularly Ok'taka and Ik'kali, who had fled the sudden wrath of the dragon—bowed their heads in sorrow. "We are most sorry," Ok'taka murmured.

"Sorry? You're *sorry?*" Artelo snapped. "That's it? She died because of your cowardice and—"

"Easy, easy," Iz said, catching the knight's arm. "We *all* failed Argentia. If not for them, Marina and I would be dead, too, remember?" he added.

"I—" Artelo looked away. He blew out a long breath. "You're right." He faced the birdmen again. "I apologize. It's just...hard to accept."

The birdmen nodded. It was uncertain whether they understood what

Artelo was trying to say, but they seemed to. They were amazing creatures: beautiful and strong enough to transcend the foulness of their maker.

"What will you do now that the wizard is gone?" Kodius asked. "You are free."

Ak'kara shook his head, rustling the gorgeous, feathery hair that flowed past his shoulders. "This is our home." He pointed back over the hills, where several shapes that appeared at this distance to be large birds were circling above the dwindling plume of smoke from the razed tower. "We know no other."

"Then you shall keep it," Ralak said. "The magi will return and cleanse this place of all remnants of Mouradian's work. Elsmywr shall belong to Ik'tari, Ak'kara, and your brothers and sisters."

"There are other survivors," Kodius said. "Women they seemed, though not wholly. Their faces were like..."

"Sheep," Kirin supplied. A vulpine gleam lit her golden eyes.

"We know them," Ik'tari said. "They tended sister Ak'tali after her accident. They are welcome. They will help the island to flourish again."

"Then it is settled," Ralak said.

"Look!" Augustus interrupted, pointing down the beach.

108

Pain.

It rolled over Argentia in waves. Acrid smoke poured off her as she lay gasping on cold, rough stone.

What had happened in the tower in the moments following her freedom from the Soul Wrester had all been instinct and reaction. She remembered diving through the fire, tackling the assassin around the waist, hanging on as the half-elf pitched forward onto the silver disc, the flash of the aethergate, and—

The fire....

Argentia thrashed reflexively, unaware for an instant that the flames were already extinguished. The aetherwalk had saved her life, snuffing out the fire by making her incorporeal.

Even so, the damage was horrific.

Argentia knelt and then came unsteadily to her feet. Every movement brought sharp new agony. She hurt everywhere, especially her face. *Burned. How bad?* Her hands and arms told part of the tale. *Oh God—bad....*

Something slinking on the periphery of Argentia's vision snapped her attention from the beginning of a brutal self-discovery.

"Don't move," Argentia ordered. Her voice was a croak, but it must have carried, for the assassin stopped.

Shrike had seen Argentia but had paid her no mind. She was hurt herself, her hips and thighs seared by dragonfire when the huntress had tackled her into the aethergate, and cared only to figure out where she was—some sort of coastal cave, judging by the nearby sound of the sea—get away from this island, and resume her quest to destroy Gideon-gil.

Then she heard Argentia's command to stop. She did, turning to face the huntress. A cruel smile crept over her lips. She wondered what the lovely Lady Dasani would think if she saw herself in the mirror behind her.

"The wizard betrayed both of us," Shrike said. "Let it end at that. There is no reason we cannot walk away from here and never cross paths again."

Argentia shook her head. "No."

"Disappointing. I've no reason to kill you," Shrike said, her fingers creeping toward the handbow on her hip.

"I've a reason to kill you," Argentia said, her cobalt eyes cold as she remembered Vartan's head bobbing in the tub. She was wounded and weaponless and had no idea how she was going to win this fight, but she'd be damned if she wouldn't try.

"Pity," Shrike said. "Good-bye."

Argentia saw her handbow rise in a silver blur. She dove aside, expecting to be blown open by an aethereal crescent.

The shot never came.

As Shrike stared in surprise at the fire-mangled weapon, Argentia scooped up a handful of pebbles and flung them into the assassin's face. They bounced off her glasses and stung her cheeks and mouth, more startling than damaging, but they served their purpose.

A lioness springing upon a jackal, Argentia hurled herself at Shrike and wrestled her to the ground. She landed an elbow to the assassin's jaw, knocking her strange glasses from her head. Shrike squirmed like an eel, but Argentia would not be denied. She pinned Shrike on her back. Hit her in the hard in the face.

Shrike fought to stay conscious through the explosion as her nose broke. She jabbed a knee into Argentia's back. Used the split-second reprieve to draw the knife concealed in her boot.

As Argentia's fist rose again, Shrike struck.

The knife pierced Argentia's charred corset, plunging deep into her side. The world tilted in a blinding flash of agony. Argentia threw a hand down for balance. Felt something steely between her fingers and the stone. Snatched it and lunged, stabbing at the assassin.

Shrike gave an abortive cry, stiffening as if lanced by some aethereal current.

Darkness, sudden and complete, claimed her.

Argentia collapsed atop the assassin. For long moments she just lay there. When her shuddery breathing steadied some and it seemed she was going to live at least a little longer, she forced herself to her knees. Winced in pain. The assassin's little knife still jutted from her bleeding side. Had the blade been any longer, she would have been finished.

She heard Skarangella Skarn's voice, an echo out of the far away Keening Canyon, telling her she had the luck of the damned. "You might be right," she whispered. Not only had she survived a potentially lethal blow, her own desperate strike had proved fatal to the assassin. A trickle of blood ran down Shrike's cheek from her punctured eye, where the stem of her glasses had pierced into her brain.

For Vartan, bitch... A flash of silver caught Argentia's attention. She reached down and drew the dragon's tooth token up from Shrike's chest. *And this is mine....*

Unclasping the chain was hard work for her blackened, blistered fingers. Argentia persevered, focusing all her will on the task until she had refastened the chain about her neck. When the token settled into its familiar place above her breasts, she felt as if a missing piece of her had been restored. But the skin that the dragon's tooth lay atop was black as burnt steak, and Argentia was terribly afraid.

Every part of her body hurt; the knife wound in her side was the least of it. She had never known such pain. She could see that she had been burned and that she needed aid, but her mind was awhirl with questions that sought to pull her attention everywhere but her body. What had happened in the tower? How had she escaped the crystal prison? Was Mouradian dead? Where was she now? Where had the dragon come from? Why had it come? Was that really Iz she'd seen in those fleeting instants before...

Enough, Gen. Figure it out later....

She rose on weak legs. Turned around. Saw the teleport disc lying on the stones.

And the mirror.

A full-length oval in a claw-footed iron frame, it was a thing of powerful magic, intended to convey Mouradian to safety in the event that he was forced to flee Elsmywr.

The only place it conveyed Argentia was into madness.

She stared at a reflection that was not her own. The figure in the mirror was a ruin, its clothes burned to tatters, its body a mass of oozing sores and cracked, charred flesh. Its long, red hair had been scorched to a jagged tuft. And its face....

Oh my God—no....

Raising an arm to ward off the ghastly specter, Argentia staggered out of the cave.

109

"What is that?" Kirin asked as she followed the halfling's pointing finger.

"A simulcrus," Augustus answered. A last one of Mouradian's creatures that had somehow made it through the battle and had the misfortune to wander down to the beach, only to find enemies there as well.

"Doesn't look so good," Iz said, noting the figure's meandering, drunken steps. "Wonder how it survived."

"It didn't," Griegvard replied, slapping his axe against his palm.

M

Argentia did not know where she was going, or why. She was badly wounded and deep in shock, desperately trying to rationalize what she'd done to survive.

Her path wove along the beach, often stumbling into the edge of the water. She did not feel the wetness against the remnants of her boots or the salty wind cutting her blasted skin. Did not hear the surf. Did not see the black ship anchored in the bay, or the figures approaching on the beach.

"Halt or die!"

The voice was familiar to her: the voice of a friend. Argentia stopped walking. Raised her head. *Artelo? Iz? Griegvard?* She did not know how they had come to be here, but here they were. All her friends, coming toward her.

With weapons drawn to strike.

What? Why—

All too late she realized the simple and appalling truth. Her friends did not recognize her. They saw the same monstrous form she had seen in Mouradian's mirror, and they thought it an enemy.

"No! Don't! Wait!" Argentia flung her hands up as the company came on, heedless of her shouts and—

110

"CEASE!"

Dracovadarbon swooped from the sky. Its tail slammed down between the company and Argentia. The shockwave flung them all from their feet, ringing their ears with its percussive force.

The dragon settled upon the beach, its wings stirring turbulent waves along the shore, sweeping grit into the air. "WOULD YOU FOOLS KILL THE VERY ONE YOU CAME TO SAVE?" it rumbled.

"What are you talking about?" Artelo demanded, scrambling to his feet. He was too desolated by the events of the last hours to care for the politics of politeness, even with a dragon. "Argentia's *dead*."

"WHAT IS THIS YOU SAY?"

"You heard me. She's dead. You killed her when you burned down that tower."

"YOU ERR, KNIGHT," the dragon warned. Smoke rose from its nostrils. "SEE BETTER WHAT IS BEFORE YOU."

Across the barrier of the dragon's tail, Artelo saw the figure rise. The form was burned almost beyond recognition. Could it be that the dragon was right? That this was truly Argentia and not one of Mouradian's many imitations?

Then a shine of silver caught his eye: the sun glaring off the dragon's tooth token hanging at the figure's throat. It was something that had existed on none of the simulcra they had seen fall.

"HAIL, SISTER OF FIRE," the dragon proclaimed.

"Aeton's bolts," Ralak whispered.

"Argentia?" Artelo asked. She looked at him, and he realized that the eyes of the simulcra had also been different: blue in shade, but lacking in some vital spark. These eyes, however, were totally and completely Argentia's. He would have known that cobalt gaze anywhere. *It's her—but my God, what happened to her?* "Gen?"

She nodded slowly, as if uncertain herself.

"Oh, Gen...."

Argentia saw the appalled amazement on Artelo's face. It was mirrored in the looks of all the company, and brought the full realization of her ruin slamming into her.

She collapsed on the sand.

111

"Place her in the Captain's quarters," Ralak instructed Dorn. He had used his magic to stabilize Argentia but he had never seen such burns on one who lived, and the dagger in her side was dangerously close to her heart. "She needs all the medicine you have. Spare no speed. I will join you shortly."

"Cap'n...." Dorn touched his forehead in salute to the stricken huntress. Then he and his men took her swiftly out to the waiting *Reaver*, giving a wide berth to the dragon, which was a truly terrifying spectacle in such proximity.

Satisfied that Argentia was no longer in danger from her misguided friends, Dracovadarbon dipped its head to the company, holding them all in its lambent gaze. "WE WILL SPARE REPARATION FOR YOUR RUDENESS, KNIGHT," the dragon said. "YET BE WARNED: DO NOT TRY THE PATIENCE OF A DRAGON TWICE."

Artelo accepted this rebuke silently. He did not regret his anger, but if the dragon had played a role, even inadvertently, in Argentia's fate, it had also played one in saving her from their own attack. *Maybe it can do more....* "Can Argentia be healed?"

"Yes, there must be something," Augustus added. "Some magic—"

"SHE HAS TASTED OF DRAGONFIRE. THERE IS NO POWER KNOWN TO MEN OR MAGI THAT CAN RESTORE WHAT OUR FLAME UNDOES."

The company looked at each other, sickened by this doom.

"WOULD YOU TAKE OUR COUNSEL ON THIS MATTER?" the dragon said. Without waiting for an answer, it continued: "LET HER

BE. SHE IS STRONGER THAN YOU WEEN. SHE WILL FIND HER WAY."

Then Dracovadarbon spread its wings and lifted into the sky. It rose with lazy power, fanning the sand and sea into squalls, then turned out over the water, propelling itself with stronger strokes now, mounting higher into the blue until it passed beyond the reach of sight but never, for those who stood the beach of Elsmywr that day, of memory.

112

When the dragon had vanished in the distance, the company rejoined the rest of the landing party from the *Reaver*. "We take our leave," Ralak said to the four birdmen who still waited by the lowering boats. "For your aid, you have our thanks and the promise of Ralak the Red that the magi will return to help you rebuild this island to something worthy of its name."

The birdmen bowed to the Archamagus and the company. "We will expect you," Ik'tari said. Then he and his brothers took to the sky to bring the joyful news of their emancipation and inheritance to the rest of the aerie.

"Time for us to go, too," Iz said. The others looked at him in surprise. A pipe, which somehow had survived the soaking he had taken in the ocean, was smoking in his mouth. He was certain it would be his last for a very long time.

"What do you mean?" Kirin asked. "You'll make the voyage back, won't you? Ralak can return you to Shukosan."

Iz shook his head. "Marina's too weak. If we stay, she'll be slower to recover. She needs the water—and I need her." He put his arm around his wife, who looked chagrinned and very weary but managed a grateful smile as she rested her wet, silver head upon his shoulder.

"What about Argentia?" Artelo asked. "How can you just leave her like this?"

"Nothing we can do for her anyway," the ultimately pragmatic Iz replied with a shrug. He took his pipe from his mouth and studied it for a moment. Blew a ring of smoke. "Dragon said as much. She'll either come through this on her own, or she won't. Me holding her hand won't change anything."

Artelo shook his head. He couldn't give up so easily. There had to be something they could do to help Argentia.

"A great debt is owed you," Ralak said to Marina. "The Crown does not forget such services as your voice provided. If ever the elves of Shukosan have need, call on Teranor and we shall answer." Marina looked greatly embarrassed and more uncomfortable than she had since first meeting the company. "I only tried to help. I am sorry I could not do more for thy friend.

"All will be well," Ralak said. He was not at all certain he believed that, but this was the time for parting, not laments.

The company exchanged embraces. "Well met," Iz said, coming last to Kodius.

The barbarian nodded. "Well met, indeed, my friend. If you and Marina ever return to Teranor, there will be a cottage in the North Woods waiting to take you in," Kodius said. He'd never really thought Iz was back for good, but a selfish part of him had hoped that Iz would remember what he'd left behind and choose to stay. Yet he could not fault him for following his heart, so he embraced his decision instead.

As those bound for the *Reef Reaver* took to their boats, Iz stripped his shirt and boots, left his pack on the shore, and followed Marina into the surf. They paced the boats out to the black ship and waited until all were aboard. Then they dove beneath the surface. Moments later, Marina's tail broke through, waving a silver farewell and drawing a cheer from the company and crew.

And so the friends were parted—until the next time Fortune would call them together....

113

The Crown of Teranor waited on the docks of Harrowgate.

Three weeks had passed since the *Reef Reaver* set out from Elsmywr. Now, at last, her black sails materialized on the horizon.

Solsta had come to the port city that morning to greet the ship bearing her dearest friends back to her. She watched the vessel make its approach with mingled relief and trepidation.

Ralak had left the *Reef Reaver* early in her voyage home. Returning to Aventar, he reported to Solsta all that had transpired on Elsmywr.

The Crown was glad of the victory for her imperiled realm and horrified by what she understood of Argentia's fate. Yet that was not the cause of her nervousness as she waited with her retinue for the *Reef Reaver* to pull into port. Artelo was on that ship. She would have to face him again, and face him with the full knowledge of what she felt in her heart.

Solsta shivered at the thought and wrapped her ermine cloak tighter about her.

"Are you cold, Majesty?" Ralak asked. Beside the Archamagus, Amethyst was heavily bundled against the chill of the late winter wind blowing off the Sea of Val. Ikabod was present also. Shadow sat patiently next to the butler, with Mirk huddled against his side, the meerkat using the dog's bushy tail for protection against the dismal, overcast weather.

"No," Solsta said. Thunder rumbled in the distance. She turned her gaze back out to sea.

M

By the time the ship berthed, the noise and bustle of Harrowgate's docks had grown quiet beneath a persistent fall of icy rain. Ralak had offered to conjure a magical shield against the weather, and Amethyst had tried to convince Solsta to return to the carriage that had taken them from Coastlight to the docks. Solsta would not hear of it. Her companions sensed she was in one of her moods, so they wisely let her wait in the storm.

The gangplank of the *Reef Reaver* clapped down. Squinting beneath her dripping hood, Solsta saw Artelo leading the company ashore.

The knight stepped onto the dock and paused for a moment. He enjoyed sailing, but it was still good to have his boots back on solid ground.

He looked at the group waiting for them. *Solsta....*

Swallowing hard, he steeled himself and went towards them, raising a hand and smiling a greeting through the rain. For a moment it seemed all would be well. Then Solsta lowered her hood and Artelo found he could not hold her gaze. Tension flickered between them like lightning in the clouds above.

"Majesty," Artelo managed, bending forward in as much of a bow as he knew Solsta would permit.

"Thank God you're safe," Solsta said. She seemed about to come to him, but held herself in reserve. Artelo nodded, unable to find words. "All of you," Solsta added, lifting her voice and sparing them further awkwardness as the rest of the company made their way off the *Reef Reaver.* "Welcome home."

One by one they came before the Crown: Kodius, Kirin Vulpya, Griegvard Gynt, Augustus Falkyn, and Kest Eregrin.

The Watch Captain was walking under his own power, albeit with steps slow and tentative on the slick ground. He was still in tremendous pain, but he could handle that. Pain meant he was still alive and returning to Lyrissa.

"I am glad you are well," Solsta said to him. Ralak had told her of Kest's wounds, for at that time the Archamagus had not been at all certain Kest would live to make port.

"Thank you, Majesty," Kest said, bowing stiffly.

"Where is—" Solsta stopped.

A barefoot figure whose head was shrouded in black cloth in the manner of the women of Makhara stood on the gangplank. The scarves hid most of her face and the ragged remnants of her hair, but her forearms and hands were visible, and they were burned black as peppers left too long over the fire.

Argentia.... Though Ralak had warned her, Solsta was still stunned. But Shadow, recognizing his mistress much as the dragon had, gave an elated bark and rushed forward, barreling up the gangplank and leaping into Argentia, nearly knocking her into the water. She staggered, wrapping her arms around the great dog and falling to one knee. "Shadow," she whispered. "Oh, Shadow...." She'd never thought to see the faithful wolf-dog again. She buried her shrouded face against his wet, silver-black fur and hugged him tightly.

Slowly, Argentia rose, stroked Shadow's head, and led him down to the dock. She was cold and wet, but did not feel either against the numbness that had been born within her.

Like Kest, Argentia had boarded the *Reef Reaver* unconscious and wounded. Over the course of the voyage, the Watch Captain had recovered.

Argentia had not.

Wanpo's medicines and Ralak and Augustus' magic worked in tandem to heal what they could: the knife wound, broken ribs, smoke-scorched lungs, scores of cuts from broken glass. But to the damage inflicted by the dragonfire they could give no aid.

When Argentia at last awoke, she refused to leave her chamber. No entreaty by Artelo, Kodius, Griegvard, or any of the company could move her. She took what food was brought to her, but she refused to see or speak to anyone for any reason.

Until, one day, she called for Ralak.

114

The Archamagus entered an almost dark cabin. "Sit," Argentia said. She was seated in the room's only chair, which stood beside a shattered mirror. Ralak moved to the edge of the bed.

Argentia looked at him. Her face was black as a goblin's, its flesh corrugated by fire. Her equally blackened hands, clenched in fists upon her knees, made a stark contrast to her pale linen pants and loose shirt: things borrowed from crewmembers in sizes large enough not to cling to her ruined skin.

"What happened?" she asked. Her voice was tight. Cold.

"What do you mean, Argentia?" Ralak replied. He had told her when she woke that they had done all they could for her. The damage from the dragon would remain with her until the end of her days.

Argentia shook her head: a sharp, angry gesture. "What did Mouradian want with me? Something happened, Ralak. To me. I was trapped in that crystal prison, but that wasn't all. I want to know what happened and I want to know *why.*"

Ralak hesitated.

"You know, don't you?" It was not a really question.

"I know," Ralak said.

"Tell me." Argentia demanded.

"No good can come from this knowledge."

"God damn it, Ralak! Tell me what you know!"

So be it.... Ralak nodded. "I will show you, instead. But remember, it was your choice to see this."

The Archamagus waved his hand, opening a window in the aether that looked back upon Elsmywr and the fields of the dead simulcra.

Argentia gasped. The image was inassimilable. "That's—They're...me." She turned again to Ralak, who dismissed the awful picture. "But how?"

Sighing, the Archamagus told her of the Forbidden magic of simulation, the history of Mouradian, his use of Argentia's form to attack Teranor's magi, and the mustering of the forces to save the huntress and overthrow the Island Wizard.

Argentia digested all of this in silence. Finally she asked, "Are they all dead? Those things?"

"All," Ralak confirmed.

"Go," Argentia said. "Get out."

"Argentia, we are your friends. Do not shut us from you. Let us help."

She pointed at the door.

Shaking his head, Ralak departed. The door closed and locked behind him.

M

Argentia remained within her cabin for the entirety of the voyage, haunted both by what she'd suffered and by what she'd seen: an army drawn in her image. Ranks by the hundreds, the thousands, filling the yards of Elsmywr. Simulcra raped from the template of her body by the perverse magic of the Mirror.

I can't think on this. I'll go mad....

She squeezed her eyes closed, the movement scrunching the charred flesh of her cheeks. The images remained: ten thousand corpses strewn upon a field. Corpses in her likeness. Corpses that were rising. Reaching for her with her hands. Condemning her with her eyes. Corpses that kindled even as they closed upon her.

Moaning, Argentia retreated from the ghosts of the simulcra as far into the vaults of her mind as she could.

They followed her all the way to Harrowgate.

115

Now here were her friends: those who had risked much to rescue her and those who had waited and worried for her fate. They called to her, but their voices made a cacophonous echo. Who was she now? She knew her name, but did not know herself. Not in this burned, ruined shape.

"Please, stop," she said. Her mouth was dry. She swallowed hard, wincing when her lips, withered and split as a hag's, pressed together. She felt very small and weak. "I know you came for me. To help me. Thank you. Someday I'll repay—"

She could bear no more. Could not face her friends now. Could not face anyone now. She needed more time to come to terms with what had befallen her.

Feared she never would.

"I'm sorry," she whispered, choking on her words.

"Argentia." Solsta stepped forward, reaching for her. "It's all right."

"No it's not! Nothing's all right. Nothing will ever *be* all right! Nothing! Better you'd left me to die!"

With a sob of despair, she turned and ran.

Shadow barked sharply.

"Lady Dasani!" Ikabod started after her.

"Stop!" Solsta cried—but to the butler, not the huntress. She had been near enough to see the anguish in Argentia's eyes and knew there was nothing they could do to help her now. She turned to the company. "Let her go," she commanded.

Ikabod was going forward anyway. Artelo stepped in front of him. "Stay," the knight said. "You cannot help her."

"You mean to just abandon her, then?" Ikabod demanded.

His rebuke met with silence.

The voyage home had been no easy thing for the company. None of them could begin to fathom what Argentia must be suffering. It was only after their repeated attempts to draw her forth and let her lean upon their friendship were rebuffed, that all of them—even Artelo—were forced to face the harsh truth that Iz had been correct in his assessment back on Elsmywr.

Argentia alone could decide her fate now.

With heavy hearts, the company stood and watched the huntress pelt down the docks of Harrowgate: a fleeing phantom melting into the sleet-gray air.

Fading.

Gone.

Epilogue

Duralyn.

Kest and Augustus had made their farewells at Coastlight and took the aethergate from the cathedral back to Argo to resume their duties in the city's Watch. The others took the gate to the Crown City, emerging from the monastery of the Grey Tree into a chill afternoon. Though spring was nigh by the calendar, the cold had lingered across the realm. What had been icy rain when the *Reef Reaver* docked in Harrowgate had fallen as snow in Duralyn. It lay over the streets and rooftops, blanketing the city in frosty white beauty that the company could not wholly appreciate.

The cloud of Argentia's flight lingered over all of them. Ikabod suffered it most acutely. It had been difficult for the butler to leave Harrowgate at all. He felt he was betraying Argentia, and that he should remain in the port to be available at need. Solsta had convinced him otherwise. "We've no idea she will stay in Harrowgate. You know her better than anyone. If she is determined to run, she will run."

Ikabod could not dispute that. The last time Argentia had run, she had been fifteen years returning. Still, that had been different. Argentia had been running towards something, even if only she understood what it might be. Now she was running from something. She was wounded and afraid and Ikabod's heart broke to see her suffer so. "Are we not her friends, Majesty?" he asked. "Her family? How can we turn our backs on her and leave her like this?"

"Bah! Was she turned her back on us," Griegvard said. "But ye mark me, she'll turn round again. We'll be waitin' when she does. That's what friends do."

"Sometimes that is all they *can* do," Solsta added.

Ikabod nodded reluctantly. At Solsta's insistence, he agreed to split his time between Castle Aventar and the Dasani estate, holding to the hope that eventually Argentia would come to one or the other of those places.

For the rest, the return to Duralyn marked only the beginning of another road.

Kodius and Kirin took their leave after pledging again that they would not be strangers to the Crown. Griegvard went also, companying with the barbarian and werefox until they turned off for the North Woods, then making his own way west to Stromness and his king and kin.

"Will you see me to my door, or will you, too, run away at my gates?" Solsta asked Artelo. Her tone was light—perhaps too light. Something in it made Artelo wary, but he assented.

At the base of the castle's steps they lingered for a few minutes, waiting for a horse to be brought for Artelo. Amethyst, sensing that Solsta had not asked Artelo to come this far simply to give him a steed and a farewell, ushered the others away. "I'm freezing! Come on, inside," she ordered, marching Shadow, Mirk, Ralak, and Ikabod up the steps and into Castle Aventar.

The Crown and her knight were alone.

That same awkward silence that had found them on the dock rose again. They stood there, each about to speak, then stopping, perhaps not knowing what to say, perhaps afraid to say it. It was as if, all at once, the hourglass had turned on its head and poured back the sand of years to the awful days prior to that fateful afternoon in the Royal Gardens, when the pair, both struggling with their growing feelings for each other, had taken a path behind a tall hedge of silver-firs and Solsta had tripped (or seemed to—Artelo was never certain she had not feigned that accident, and Solsta only laughed when he questioned her) and Artelo had caught her and then she was in his arms and they were kissing....

Now it was only the plumes of their breath that mingled wordlessly in the cold air. Just when the silence became unbearable, when it seemed that one or the other must speak or both their hearts would burst, there was a clatter of hooves on stone.

Solsta gasped. Artelo dropped a hand to the hilt of his sword and turned, seeking the danger that had startled her.

It was only a page leading a horse across the courtyard. "Old habits," Artelo said, relaxing his grip on his sword and chuckling nervously. Solsta said nothing. It was too hard for each of them to look at the other, so they both watched the page approach with such intensity that it was all the poor boy could do to make his bows and retreat to the stables.

"Well," Artelo said when the page had departed. "This is your door, Majesty, as promised. Thank you for the horse. I will see it returned. But now, with your leave, I must go." His voice had begun with the same feigned lightness Solsta had used outside the gates, but by the end it had dropped to almost a whisper.

"Stay a moment," Solsta begged, catching Artelo's arm as he turned to mount up.

"Solsta," Artelo began. He could sense where this was going, and it was not good. It was his fault; he should never have agreed to come back to the castle. *Best to stop it before—*

Solsta pressed her gloved fingers to Artelo's lips, silencing him. Her eyes, so liquid and dark, threatened to drown him like nightfall upon day. "My father taught me plain speech is best, so I will speak plain," she said. Somehow her words were steady. She appeared composed, but she was trembling inside. "Artelo—"

But she couldn't say it. The love she felt for him—and sensed he felt for her—had no room for shepherdesses or children or vows of wedlock. It cared nothing for station or duty or honor. If she struck this spark, it would burn like dragonfire and leave nothing in its wake but ashes and anguish.

She could not allow that.

She managed a smile. "Go safe," she said.

Wheeling quickly to hide her tears, Solsta hurried up the steps. The golden doors of Castle Aventar closed resoundingly in her wake.

For a long minute Artelo stood and stared at those doors. The Guardians who kept them stared back, impassive.

Finally, knowing there was no recourse else—not if he meant to be true—the knight turned away, mounted his steed, and rode into the winter afternoon.

M

Three days later.

Artelo rounded the last bend in the road before his hillside cottage. He had ridden hard, but if his body was weary, his mind was rested. The time alone, with the emptiness of snow-clad days and the solitude of snow-clad nights had given the knight the space he needed to come to terms what had happened—or, more aptly, what had not happened—in front of Castle Aventar.

He knew what Solsta would have said, and he was grateful that she had somehow turned away before they came to that precipice. *If she hadn't....*

Best not to think about that.

In a cottage, on the *Reef Reaver*, with leagues of land or sea between them, it was easy to choose the duty and love he bore his family over the flame that still burned in him for Solsta. But there before the steps of Aventar, when he needed only to reach out his hand to draw her in, it was not so certain a choice.

That was a hard admission for Artelo. It shamed him, but he consoled himself with the fact that he had held true in the end to the dictates of duty. He could have called to Solsta on the steps, or chased her into the castle, but he had let her go.

Part of his heart might always belong to Solsta, but it was a part that lived in the past. The rest of it, the rest of him, was bound to the life he had made in the present. *Here. Home....*

He looked up at the cottage, quaint and simple but still perfect and all he needed. He had been too long away. He did not regret going after Argentia, but now that he had returned no summons, no appeal would move him from this place. If Iz could go back to his undersea home with Marina and be confident his friends would carry on in his absence, Artelo could do the same.

And I will....

He hitched his steed to the post beside the well. He would bring her to the barn later. Tomorrow Pandaros could ride her back to Duralyn. Right now, the only thing Artelo wanted was to hear Aura's gleeful laughter as he lifted her up and spun her about.

Instead, he heard silence.

No birds. No sheep. No Brittyn whistling in the cottage. Nothing. *Something's wrong....*

Sudden fear made Artelo's mouth run dry. *Calm down!* a voice in his mind said. *There's nothing wrong....*

He did not quite believe that voice, however, and he hurried up the hill, slipping twice on the snow-covered slope, catching himself with his hand, not feeling the bite of cold against his fingers or the jarring wince in his shoulder, still sore from the nearly crippling blow dealt him by the giant gatarine, desperately hoping to catch a glimpse of Brittyn in the window that would show him he was a fool to worry.

He reached the terrace. An odd snow creature—three great, lumpish balls stacked atop each other with a single stone for an eye in the topmost—greeted him. Brittyn and Aura must have built it. The creature made Artelo smile for a moment. Then he looked past it, to the cottage.

The door was hanging open on twisted hinges.

"Brittyn! Aura!" Artelo drew his blade and rushed in.

No one answered, but the scene screamed at him: shattered furniture, smashed pottery, and on the wooden floor Brittyn so prided herself on keeping clean, so much blood.

Oh no. Please no.... Artelo felt sick. He stumbled in a circle, staggered into the bedchamber.

That room was also empty.

Artelo fell to his knees beside the bed, clutching the blanket in his hand. What had happened? Whose blood was that? Where were Brittyn and Aura and—

Pandaros! Had the wizard saved them? If they'd been attacked by goblins from the Gelidian Spur, which was not so distant as Artelo would have wished, had Pandaros managed to get Brittyn and Aura away to safety?

Jerking to his feet, Artelo sprinted from the cottage. As he crossed the threshold, he saw a thing he'd missed when he'd rushed in: a splash of red upon the snow.

The bloody footprints dragged a trail across the white ground. Someone had survived in the cottage and made for the barn.

The knight ran, oblivious to the jumble of other tracks that crossed the snow-covered yard toward the woods. He burst into the shadowy space of the barn, shouting for Brittyn and Pandaros.

Froze in horror.

Brittyn was there, her back to him as she struggled to lift a saddle onto their horse. She was uncloaked and barefoot. Blood ran from beneath her torn skirt and down her calf in a scarlet ribbon.

She did not turn at Artelo's call or as he rushed towards her. Only when he grabbed her shoulder did she react, screaming and wrenching about, tearing away from him, bumping against the horse, which whinnied and shied as far as its tether would allow.

The saddle crunched down on Brittyn's foot hard enough to break bones. She didn't flinch, didn't even feel it. Her world was already boundless pain.

Artelo could only stare at her. On Brittyn's blood-streaked face was a look of abject terror. Her gray eyes were haunted and mad. Her blonde hair was clotted with gore. Below her breasts, the tatters of her white blouse were soaked crimson.

"Artelo!" she gasped. Hope brightened her gaze for an instant. She reached for him. Her legs buckled.

He caught her.

"Brittyn! Brittyn!"

To be continued...

Printed in the United States
By Bookmasters